HE'S TRYING TO CUT MY LINE!
HE'LL KILL ME!

Desperately Kinsman grabbed the line that connected him to his Manta spacecraft and snapped it hard. He tumbled wildly, but saw the wave created by his snap race down the line. The intruding Russian cosmonaut found the section of line he was holding suddenly buck violently out of his hand; the electron torch he had used spun away from him and winked off.

Both men moved at once—the cosmonaut jetted away from the Manta, looking for the torch; Kinsman hurled himself toward the ship's hatch, planting his boots on the hull and grasping the open hatch in both hands.

He could be safe and inside in an instant, but . . .

That sonofabitch tried to kill me.

Kinsman coiled catlike on the edge of the hatch and sprang at his enemy. . . .

Kinsman

Ben Bova

A DELL BOOK

Published by
Dell Publishing Co., Inc.
1 Dag Hammarskjold Plaza
New York, New York 10017

Portions of this novel first appeared, some in substantially different form, in the following publications: *Again, Dangerous Visions*, edited by Harlan Ellison; *20–20 Visions*, edited by Jerry Pournelle; *Analog, Science Fiction/Science Fact;* and *The Magazine of Fantasy & Science Fiction.*

Dell ® TM 681510, Dell Publishing Co., Inc.

ISBN: 0-440-14527-9

Reprinted by arrangement with The Dial Press

Printed in the United States of America

First Dell printing—June 1981

To Mark Chartrand, despite his puns

Kinsman

AGE 21

From the rear seat of the TF-15 jet, the mountains of Utah looked like barren wrinkles of grayish brown, an old threadbare bedcover that had been tossed carelessly across the floor.

"How do you like it up here?" the pilot asked.

Chet Kinsman heard his voice as a disembodied crackle in his helmet earphones. The shrill whine of the turbojet engines, the rush of unbreathably thin air just inches away on the other side of the plastiglass canopy, was nothing more than background music, muted, unimportant.

"Love it!" he answered to the bulbous white helmet in the seat in front of him.

The cockpit was narrow and cramped. Kinsman could barely move in his seat without bumping his own helmet into the plastiglass canopy that covered them both. The straps of his safety harness cut into his shoulders; he had tugged them on too tightly. The oxygen he breathed had a cold, metallic tang to it.

But he felt free.

"How high can we go?" he asked into his lip mike.

A pause. "Oh, she'll do a hundred thousand feet if you want to push her. Thirty thou's good enough for now, though."

Kinsman grinned to himself. "A lot better than hang gliders."

"Hey, I like hang gliding," the pilot said.

"Sure. But it doesn't compare to this. . . . This is *power*."

"Right enough."

Power. And freedom. Six miles above the tired, wrinkled

old Earth. Six miles away from everything and everybody. It couldn't last long enough to suit him.

Ahead lay San Francisco and his mother's funeral. Ahead lay death and his father's implacable anger.

Life at the Air Force Academy was rigid, cold. A first-year man was expected to obey everyone's orders, not to make friends. No matter if you're older than the other first-year cadets. A rich boy, huh? Spent two years in a fancy prep school, huh? Well snap to, mister! Let me see four chins, moneybags, four of 'em!

Yet that was better than going home.

His father had refused to stop off at the Academy when he took his ailing wife from their estate in Pennsylvania to her sister's home in San Francisco. Kinsman had avoided taking leave to visit his mother. There was time for that later, after his father had gone back East to return to running his banks.

And then, suddenly, swiftly, she was dead. And his father was still there.

Instead of taking a commercial airliner, Kinsman begged a ride with a westward-heading Air Force captain.

If t'were done, he told himself, *t'were best done quickly.*

Now he was flying. And happy.

Suddenly the plane's nose dropped and Kinsman's stomach disappeared somewhere over his right shoulder. The pilot rolled the plane, wing tips making full circles in the empty air, as they dove toward the desert—which now looked as flat and as hard and gray as steel. Kinsman swallowed hard and felt his pulse racing in every part of his body.

"Try a low-level run. Get a real sensation of speed," the pilot said.

Kinsman nodded, then realized he couldn't be seen. "Okay. Great."

In less than a minute they were skimming across the empty desert, engines howling, going so fast that Kinsman could not see individual rocks or bushes, only a blur of brown-gray whizzing just below them. The roar of the engines filled his helmet and the whole plane was shaking, bucking, as if eager to get back up into the thinner, clearer air where it had been designed to fly.

He thought he saw some buildings in the blur of hills off to his left.

"Whoops! Highway!"

The control yoke between Kinsman's knees yanked back toward his crotch. The plane stood on its tail, afterburners screaming, and a microsecond's flicker of a huge tractor-trailer rig zipped past the corner of his eye. He felt the weight of death pressing against his chest, flattening him into the contoured seat, turning it into an invalid's couch. He couldn't lift his arms from his lap or even cry out. It was enough to try to gasp out a breath.

They leveled off at last and Kinsman sucked in a great sighing gulp of oxygen.

"Damned sun glare does that sometimes," the pilot was saying, sounding half annoyed and half apologetic. "Damned desert looks clear but there's a truck moseying along the highway, hidden in the glare."

"That was a helluva ride," Kinsman said at last.

The pilot chuckled. "I'll bet there's one damned rattled truck driver down there. He's probably on his little CB reporting a flying saucer attack."

They headed westward again, toward the setting sun. The pilot let Kinsman take the controls for a while, as they climbed to cross the approaching Sierras. The rugged mountain crests were capped with snow, bluish and cold. Like the wall of the Rockies that loomed over the Academy, Kinsman thought.

"You got a nice steady touch, kid. Make a good pilot."

"Thanks. I used to fly my father's plane. Even the business jet, once."

"Got your license?"

"Not yet. I figure I'll qualify at the Academy."

The pilot said nothing.

"I'm going in for astronaut training as soon as I can qualify," Kinsman went on.

"Astronaut, huh? Well . . . I'd rather fly a plane. Damned astronauts are like robots. Everything's done by remote control for those rocket jockeys."

"Not everything," Kinsman protested.

He could sense the pilot shaking his head in disagreement. "Hell, I'll bet they even have machines to do their screwing for them."

It was an old house, atop Russian Hill. Unpretentious, Victorian, big enough to contain a hockey rink on its ground floor. The view of the Bay was spectacular; the people who lived in this part of San Francisco had the quiet power to see that none of the new office towers and high-rise hotels cluttered up their vistas.

Neal McGrath opened the door for Kinsman. His normal scowl changed into a half-bitter smile.

"Hello, Chet."

"Neal. I didn't expect to see you here."

"He needed somebody to take charge of things for him. This has hit him pretty hard."

McGrath often reminded Kinsman of a Varangian Guard, a tall, broadshouldered, redhaired Viking who hovered by his Emperor's side to protect him from assassins. His ice-blue eyes looked much older than his years. He was barely twenty months older than Kinsman, but his suspicious scowl and low, throaty voice gave him an air of inner experience, of wariness, that strangely made people trust and rely on him.

Kinsman had known him since McGrath had been the ten-year-old who helped the gardener mow their lawn. Now McGrath was a key aide to his father, and was being groomed for one of the family's seats in the House of Representatives. He would be a senator one day, they all knew.

Stepping from the bright sunshine into the darkened foyer of the old house, Kinsman asked:

"Where is she?"

"In there." McGrath gestured toward a set of double oak doors that rose to the ceiling.

Kinsman let his lone flightbag drop to the marble floor. "Is my father . . ."

"He's upstairs, taking a nap. The doctor's trying to keep him as quiet as possible."

McGrath bent to pick up Kinsman's bag. "There's a room for you upstairs—how long will you be staying?"

"When's the funeral?"

"Tomorrow."

"I'm leaving right afterward."

"A lot of the family is flying in from the East. They'll expect to see you after the funeral."

Kinsman shook his head. "I can't stay."

"If it's a matter of fixing things with the Academy I can call . . ."

"No. Please, Neal."

McGrath shrugged and started toward the broad, stern dark-wood staircase, his footsteps echoing on the cool marble floor.

Kinsman went to the double doors. A mirror hung on the hallway wall just beside the doors, and he saw himself in it. His mother would not have recognized him. The blue uniform made him look slimmer than ever, and taller, despite the fact that he had never quite reached the six-foot height he had coveted as a child. His face was leaner, dark hair cropped closer than it had ever been, blue eyes weary from lack of sleep. His long jaw was stubbly; his mother would have insisted that he go upstairs and shave.

He slid the doors slightly apart and stepped into a room that probably had been a library at one time, or a parlor, the kind where women of an earlier generation served tea.

Now it was too dark to see the walls clearly. The high windows were muffled in dark draperies. The only light in the large room was on the casket. Kinsman's mother lay there, embedded in white satin, her eyes closed peacefully, her hands folded over a plain sky-blue dress.

He didn't recognize her at first. The cancer had taken

away so much of her flesh that only a taut covering of skin stretched across the bony understructure of her face. All the fullness of her mouth and brow were gone. She was a gaunt skeleton of the woman he had known.

And her skin looked waxy, unreal. Kinsman stared down at her for a long time, thinking, *She's so tiny. I never realized she was so small.*

He knelt at the little wooden prayer rail in front of the casket, but found that he had nothing to say. He felt absolutely numb inside: no grief, no guilt, nothing. Empty. But in his mind he heard her voice from years earlier:

Chester, you get down from that tree before you hurt yourself!

Yes, Mommy.

You could have a fine career as a concert pianist, Chester, if you'd only practice instead of this ridiculous mania for flying.

Aw, Ma.

I do wish you'd be more respectful to your father. He's proud of what he's accomplished and he wants you to share in it.

I'll try, Mother. I'll try.

If I sign this, Chester . . . if I let you join the Air Force, it will upset your father terribly.

I've got to get away from him, Mother. It's the only way. I'll put in for astronaut training. It'll all work out all right, you'll see. He'll be proud of me someday.

"You finally got here."

Kinsman turned his head and saw the tall, austere figure of his father framed in the doorway.

He got to his feet slowly. "I came as quickly as I could."

"Not quickly enough," his father said, sliding the doors shut behind him.

Kinsman pulled in a deep breath. They had fought many battles in front of his mother. He had been a fool to think that today would be much different.

"It . . . she went so fast," he said.

His father walked slowly toward him. "At the end, yes.

The doctors said it was a mercy. But she suffered for months. She wanted to see you. You could have eased her pain."

He realized suddenly that his father was old and probably in pain himself. The man's hair was dead white now, not a trace of its former color. His eyes had lost their fire.

"I talked with her on the phone," Kinsman said, knowing it sounded weak, defensive. "Almost every night . . ."

"You should have been *here*, where you belong."

"The Air Force thought differently."

"The Air Force! That conglomeration of feeble-minded, professional killers."

"That's not true and you know it."

"I could have had any one of four United States senators bail you out of your precious Academy! But no, you were too busy to come ease your mother's last days on Earth."

"None of us knew she was that close to the end."

"She was in pain!" The old man's voice was rising, filling the nearly empty room with its hard, angry echoes.

"I couldn't come," Kinsman insisted.

"Why not?"

"Because I didn't want to see you!" he blurted.

If it surprised his father, the old man didn't show it. He merely nodded. "You mean you couldn't *face* me."

"Call it what you want to."

"Sneaking around behind my back. Forcing your mother to sign the papers so you could join the Air Force. The only son of the most prominent Quaker family in Pennsylvania—joining the Air Force! Learning how to become a killer!"

"I'm not going to kill anyone," Kinsman answered. "I'm in line for astronaut duty . . ."

"You'll do what they tell you to do. You surrendered your soul when you put on that uniform. If they tell you to kill, you'll kill. You'll bomb cities and strafe helpless human beings. You'll drop napalm on babies and you'll do it when they tell you to."

"I'm not going to be involved in that!"

"My only child, a warrior. A killer. No wonder your mother died. You killed her."

Kinsman could feel waves of fire sweeping through his body. Against the pain, he said, "That's a rotten thing to tell me . . ."

"It's true. You killed her. She'd still be alive if it weren't for you."

The pain flaming through him was too much. Fists clenched against his sides, Kinsman brushed past his father and strode out of the room, out of the house, out into the bright hot sunshine and clear blue sky that he neither felt nor saw.

By the time he realized it was getting dark, he found himself in Berkeley. He had walked for hours and then, without even thinking about it, stepped into one of the sleek BART trains that whooshed through a tunnel under the Bay.

He was sitting in a bar. The sign on the window said it was a coffee shop, but the only coffee you could get had Irish whiskey in it. Kinsman hunched over a cold beer and looked into the mirror behind the bar at the girl with the guitar singing:

Jack of diamonds, queen of spades,
Fingers tremble and the memory fades,
And it's a foolish man who tries to bluff the dealer . . .

Through the coffee shop's big front window, Kinsman could see the evening shadows settling over the Berkeley streets. Students, loungers, street people, eased along the sidewalks, most of them in shabby denims or faded khaki fatigues. Kinsman felt out of place in his crisp sky-blue uniform.

As he watched the night deepen over the clapboard buildings and the lights on the Bay Bridge stretch a twinkling arch across the water, he realized that he had spent most of his life alone. He had no home. The Academy was cold and friendless. There was no place on Earth that he could call his own. And deep inside he knew that his soul was as austere and rigid as his father's. *I'll look like him one day*, Kinsman knew. *If I live long enough.*

You can't win,
And you can't break even,
You can't get out of the game . . .

She has a lovely voice, he thought. *Like a silver bell. Like water in the desert.*

It was a haunting voice. And her face, framed by long, midnight-black hair, had a fine-boned, dark-eyed ascetic look to it. She sat on a high stool, under a lone spotlight, bluejeaned legs crossed and guitar resting on one knee.

He sat there silently urging himself to go over and introduce himself, offer her a drink, tell her how much he enjoyed her singing. But as he worked up his nerve, a dozen kids his own age burst into the place. The singer, just finished her set, smiled and called to them. They bustled around her.

Kinsman turned his attention to his warming beer. By the time he finished it, the students had pushed a few tables together and were noisily ordering everything from Sacred Cows to Seven-Up. The singer had disappeared. It was full night outside now.

"You alone?"

He looked up, startled, and it was her.

"Uh . . . yeah." Clumsily he pushed the barstool back and got to his feet.

"Why don't you come over and join us?" She gestured toward the crowd of students.

"Sure. Great. Love to."

She was tall enough to be almost eye level with Kinsman, and as slim and supple as a young willow. She wore a black long-sleeved pullover atop the faded denims.

"Hey, everybody, this is . . ." She turned to him with an expectant little smile. All the others stopped their chatter and looked up at him.

"Kinsman," he said. "Chet Kinsman."

Two chairs appeared out of the crowd and Kinsman sat down between the singer and a chubby blonde girl who was intently, but unsteadily, rolling a joint for herself.

Kinsman felt out of place. They were all staring wordlessly at him, except for the rapt blonde. *Wrong uniform*, he told himself. He might as well have been wearing a badge that said NARC.

"My name's Diane," the singer said to him, as the bar's only waitress placed a fresh beer in front of him. "That's Shirl, John, Carl, Eddie, Dolores . . ." She made a circuit of the table and Kinsman forgot their names as soon as he heard them. Except for Diane's.

They were still eying him suspiciously.

"You with the National Guard?"

"No," Kinsman said. "Air Force Academy."

"Going to be a flyboy?"

"A flying pig," said the blonde on his left.

Kinsman stared at her. "I'm going in for astronaut training."

"An orbiting pig," she muttered.

"That's a stupid thing to say."

"She's upset," Diane told him. "We're all a little on edge today."

"Why?"

"The demonstration got called off," said one of the fellows. "The fuckin' mayor reneged on us."

"What demonstration?" Kinsman asked.

"You don't know?" It was an accusation.

"No. Should I?"

"You mean you really don't know what day tomorrow is?" a bespectacled youth asked from across the table.

"Tomorrow?" Kinsman felt bewildered.

"Kent State."

"It's the anniversary."

"They gunned down a dozen students."

"The National Fuckin' Guard."

"Killed them!"

"But that was years ago," Kinsman said.

They all glared at him as if they were blaming him for it.

"We're gonna show those friggin' bastards," said an intense, waspish little guy sitting a few chairs down from Kinsman. *Eddie?* He tried to remember. The guy was frail looking, but his face was set in a smoldering, angry cast, tight-lipped. The big glasses he wore made his eyes look huge and fierce.

"Right on," said the group's one black member. "They can't cancel our parade."

"Not after they gave their word it was okay."

"We'll tear the fuckin' campus apart tomorrow!"

"How's that going to help things?" Kinsman heard his own voice asking.

"How's it gonna *help*?"

"I mean," Kinsman went on, wanting to bounce some of their hostility back at them, "what are you trying to accomplish? You tear up the campus, big deal. What good does that do?"

"You don't make any sense," Eddie snapped.

"Neither do you."

"But you don't understand," Diane said. "We've got to do *something*. We can't just let them withdraw permission to hold our parade without making some kind of response."

"I'd appeal to the Governor. Or one of my senators. Go where the clout is."

They laughed at that. All but Eddie, who looked angrier still.

"You don't understand anything at all about how the political process works, do you?" Eddie asked.

Now I've got you! "Well," Kinsman responded slowly, "an uncle of mine is a U.S. Senator. My grandfather was Governor of the Commonwealth of Pennsylvania. Several other family members are in public service. I've been involved in political campaigning since I was old enough to hold a poster."

Silence. As if a leper had entered their midst.

"Jesus Christ," said one of the kids at last. "He's *really* Establishment."

Diane said, "Your kind of politics doesn't work for us. The Establishment won't listen to us."

"We've gotta fight for our rights!"

"Demonstrate."

"Fight fire with fire."

"Action!"

"Bullshit," Kinsman snapped. "All you're going to do is give the cops an excuse to mash your heads in—or worse. Violence is always counterproductive."

The night, and the argument, wore on. They swore at each other, drank, smoked, talked until they started to get hoarse. Kinsman found himself enjoying it all immensely. Diane had to get up to sing for the customers every hour, but each time she finished she came back and sat beside him.

And still the battle raged. The bar finally closed and Kinsman got up slowly on legs turned rubbery. But he went with them along a dark Berkeley street to someone's one-room pad, up four creaking flights of outside stairs, yammering all the way, arguing with them all, one against ten. And Diane stayed beside him.

Eventually they started drifting away, leaving the apartment. Kinsman found himself sitting on the bare wooden floor, halfway between the stained kitchen sink and the new-looking water bed, telling them:

"Look, I don't like it any more than you do. But violence is *their* game. You can't win that way. Tear up the whole damned campus and they'll tear down the whole damned city just to get even with you."

"So what's the answer?" Diane asked.

Kinsman gave an elaborate shrug. "Well . . . you could always do what the Quakers do. Shame them. Just go out tomorrow in a group and stand in the most prominent spot on campus. All of you . . . all the people who were going to march in the parade. Just stand silently for a few hours."

"That's dumb," somebody said.

"It's smart," Kinsman retorted. "Non-violent, conscience-stirring. Always attracts the news photographers. An old Quaker trick."

A burly-shouldered kid with a big beefy face and tiny squinting eyes crouched on the floor beside Kinsman.

"That's a chickenshit thing to do."

"But it works."

"You know your trouble, Flyboy? You're chickenshit."

Kinsman shrugged at him and looked around the floor for the can of beer he had been working on.

"You hear me? You're all talk. But you're scared to fight for your rights."

Kinsman looked up and saw that Diane, the blonde smoker, and two of the guys were the only ones left in the room. Plus the muscleman beside him.

"I'll fight for my rights," Kinsman said, very carefully because his tongue wasn't always obeying his brain. "And I'll fight for yours, too. But not in any stupid-ass way."

"You callin' me stupid?" The guy got to his feet.

A weightlifter, Kinsman guessed. *And he's going to show off his muscles on me.*

"I don't know you well enough to call you anything," Kinsman said.

"Well I'm callin' you a chicken. A gutless mother-fuckin' coward."

Slowly Kinsman got to his feet. It helped to have the wall behind him to lean against.

"I take that, sir, to be a challenge to my honor," he said, letting himself sound drunk. It took very little effort.

"Goddam right it's a challenge. You must be some goddam pig—secret police or something."

"That's why I'm wearing this inconspicuous uniform."

"To throw us off guard."

"Don't be an oaf."

"I'm gonna break your head, wise-ass."

Kinsman raised an unsteady finger. "Now hold on. You challenged me, right? So I get the choice of weapons. That's the way it works in the good ol' *code duello*."

"Choice of weapons?" The big guy looked confused.

"You challenged me to a duel, didn't you? You have impeached my honor. I have the right to choose the weapons."

The guy made a fist the size of a football. "This is all the weapon I need."

"But that's not the weapon I choose," Kinsman countered. "I believe that I'll choose sabers. I won a few medals back East with my saber fencing. Now where can we find a pair of sabers at this hour of the morning . . . ?"

The guy grabbed Kinsman's shirt. "I'm gonna knock that fuckin' grin off your face."

"You probably will. But not before I kick both your kneecaps off. You'll never see the inside of a gym again, muscleboy."

"That's enough, both of you," Diane snapped. She stepped between the two of them. The big guy let go of Kinsman.

"You'd better get back to your own place, Ray," she said, her voice flat and hard. "You're not going to break up my pad and get me thrown out on the street."

Ray pointed a thick, blunt finger at Kinsman. "He's a narc. Or something. Don't trust him."

"Go home, Ray. It's late."

"I'll get you, blue-suit," Ray said. "I'll get you."

Kinsman said, "When you find the sabers, let me know."

"Shut up!" Diane hissed at him. But she was grinning.

She half-pushed the lumbering Ray out the door. The others left right behind him and suddenly Kinsman was alone with Diane.

"I guess I ought to go too," Kinsman said, his insides shaking now that the danger had passed. Or was it at the thought of going back home?

"Where?" Diane asked.

"Back in the city . . . Russian Hill."

"God, you *are* Establishment."

"Born with a silver spoon in my ear. To the manner born. Rich or poor, it pays to have money. Let 'em eat cake. Or was it coke?"

"You're very drunk."

"How can you tell?"

"Well, for one thing, your feet are standing still but the rest of you is swaying like a tree in a hurricane."

"I am drunk with your beauty . . . and a ton and a half of beer."

Diane laughed. "I can believe the second one."

Looking around for a phone, Kinsman asked, "How do you get a cab around here?"

"You don't. Not at this hour. No trains, either."

"I'm stuck here?"

She nodded.

"A fate worse than death." Kinsman saw that the room's furnishings consisted of a bookshelf crammed with sheet music, the water bed, a formica-topped table and two battered wooden chairs that didn't match, the water bed, a pile of books in one corner of the floor, a few colorful pillows strewn around here and there, the water bed, two guitars, and the water bed.

"We can share the bed," Diane said.

He felt his face turning red. "Are your intentions honorable?"

She grinned at him. "The condition you're in, we'll both be safe enough."

"Don't be too sure."

But he fell asleep as soon as he sank into the soft warmth of the bed. His last thought was an inward chuckle that he didn't have to spend the night under the same roof as his father.

It was sometime during the misty, dreaming light of earliest dawn that he half awoke and felt her body cupped against his. Still half in sleep, they moved together, slowly, gently, unhurried, alone in the pearl-gray fog, feeling without the necessity to think, murmuring without the need for words, caressing, making love.

Kinsman lay on his back, smiling peacefully at the cracked ceiling.

Diane stroked the flat of his abdomen, saying drowsily, "Go to sleep. Get some rest and then we can do it again."

It was hours later by the time Kinsman had showered in the cracked tub and gotten back into his wrinkled, sweat-scented uniform. He was looking into the still-steamy bathroom mirror, wondering what to do about his stubbly chin, when Diane called through the half-open door:

"Tea or coffee?"

"Coffee."

Kinsman came out of the tiny bathroom and saw that she had set up toast and a jar of Smuckers grape jelly on the table by the window. The teakettle was on the two-burner stove, and a pair of chipped mugs and a jar of instant coffee stood alongside.

They sat facing each other, washing down the crunchy toast with the hot, bitter coffee. Diane watched the people moving along the street below them. Kinsman stared at the clean bright sky.

"How long can you stay?" she asked.

"I've got a funeral to attend . . . in about an hour. Then I leave tonight."

"Oh."

"Got to report back to the Academy tomorrow morning."

"You have to."

He nodded.

"But you're free this afternoon?"

"After the burial. Yes."

"Come down to the campus with me," Diane said, brightening. "I'm going to try your idea . . . get them to stand just like Quakers. You can help us."

"Me?"

"Sure! It was your idea, wasn't it?"

"Yeah, but . . ."

She reached across the table and took his free hand in both of hers. "Chet . . . please. Not for me. Do it for yourself. I don't want to think of you being sent out somewhere to fight and kill people. Or be killed yourself. Don't let them turn you into a killer."

"But I'm going into astronaut training."

"You don't believe they'll actually give you what you want, do you? They'll use you for cannon fodder, just like all the others. The Mideast, Africa, South America . . . they'll put you in a war plane and order you to kill people."

He shook his head. "You don't understand . . ."

"No, *you* don't understand," she said earnestly. Kinsman saw the intensity in her eyes, the devotion. *Is she really worried that much about me?* he wondered. And then a really staggering thought hit him. *Is he? Is my father . . .*

"Come with us, Chet," she was pleading. "Stand with us against the Power Structure. Just for one hour."

"In my uniform? Your friends would trash me."

"No they won't. It'd make a terrific impact for somebody in uniform to show up with us. We've been trying to get some of the Vietnam veterans to show themselves in uniform."

"I can't," Kinsman said. "I've got to go to the funeral, and then hitch a ride back to the Academy."

"That's more important than freedom? More important than justice?"

He had no answer.

"Chet . . . please. For me. If you don't want to do it for yourself, or for the people, then do it for me. Please."

He looked away from her and glanced around the shabby, unkempt room. At the stained, cracked sink. The faded wallpaper. The unframed posters Scotch-taped to the walls. The water bed, with its roiled sheet trailing onto the floor.

He thought of the Academy. The cold gray mountains and ranks of uniforms marching mechanically across the frozen parade ground. The starkly functional classrooms, the remorselessly efficient architecture devoid of all individual expression.

And he thought of his father: cold, implacable—was it pride and anger that moved him, or was it fear?

Then he turned back, looked past the woman across the table from him, and saw the sky once again. A pale ghost of a Moon was grinning lopsidedly at him.

"I can't go with you," he said quietly, finally. "Somebody's got to make sure that the Nation's defended while you're out there demonstrating for your rights."

For a moment Diane said nothing. Then, "You're trying to make a joke out of something that's deadly serious."

"I'm being serious," he said. "You'll have plenty of demonstrators out there. Somebody's got to protect you while you're exercising your freedoms."

"It's our own government that we need protection from!"

"You've got it. You just have to exercise it a little more carefully. I'd rather be flying. There aren't so many of us up there."

Diane shook her head. "You're hopeless."

He shrugged.

"I was going to let you stay here . . . if you wanted to quit the Air Force."

"Quit?"

"If you needed a place to hide . . . or if you just wanted to stay here, with me."

He started to answer, but his mouth was suddenly dry. He swallowed, then in a voice that almost cracked, "Listen, Diane. I wasn't even a teenager when the first men set foot on the Moon. That's where I've wanted to be ever since that moment. There are new worlds to see, and I want to see them."

"But that's turning your back on this world!"

"Damned right." He pushed his chair away from the table and got to his feet. "There's not much in this world worth caring about. Not for me."

At the door, he turned back toward her. She was at the table still. "Sorry I disappointed you. And, well, thanks . . . for everything."

She got up, walked swiftly across the tiny room to him, and kissed him lightly on the lips.

"It was my pleasure, General."

He grinned. "Hell, I'm not even a lieutenant yet."

"You'll be a general someday."

"I don't think so."

"You could have been a hero today."

"I'm not very heroic."

"Yes you are." She smiled at him. "You just don't know it yet."

Unshaven, in his shabby uniform, Kinsman stood at his father's side through the funeral, rode silently in the cortege's limousine to the cemetery, and watched a crowd of strangers file past the casket, one by one, placing on it single flowers that his mother had loathed all through her life.

As they rode back toward Russian Hill in the velvet-lined, casketlike limousine, Kinsman turned to his starkly silent father.

"I know I've disappointed you," he said in a low swift voice, "and I also know that you wouldn't be so angry with me if you didn't love me, and weren't worried about me."

His father stared straight ahead, unmoving.

"Well . . . I love you too, Dad."

The old man's eyes blinked. Without moving a millimeter toward his son, he whispered, "You are a disgrace. Staying up all night and then showing up looking like a Bowery derelict. The sooner you leave the better!"

Kinsman leaned back in the limousine's seat. *Thanks, Dad*, he said to himself. *You've always made it so easy for me.*

* * *

Neal McGrath drove him down 101, toward the Navy's Moffett Field, weaving the Triumph through knots of traffic and past hulking, huffing diesel tractor-trailers.

"You're sure you can pick up a flight back toward Boulder?" McGrath asked.

"Sure," Kinsman yelled, over the highway noise. "The guy I rode out with told me he's going back late this afternoon."

McGrath shook his head as he carefully flicked the turn signal and pulled around a station wagon filled with kids.

"The family's going to be very disappointed that you didn't stay for dinner."

"My Dad's not. He threw me out."

McGrath gave a snort. "You know he didn't mean that."

"Sure."

"Where the hell were you all night, anyway? You look like you got rolled in an alley."

"Just about." Kinsman told him about Diane and her campus activists as the Triumph zoomed down the highway.

"Jeez, what an easy lay. Was she any good?"

"No complaints."

The airport turnoff was approaching. McGrath slid into the right-hand lane.

"Neal . . . I don't even know her last name."

"So what?"

"So look her up for me, will you? Maybe the family can give her a little help . . . with her singing career."

"I'm a married man, kid." McGrath grinned.

Frowning, Kinsman said, "You don't have to put yourself in a compromising position. But she's a good singer. Maybe somebody in the family can get her more attention, better bookings . . ."

"Going to reform her, eh? Turn her into an Establishment lackey."

"Yeah. Why not?" Kinsman looked at McGrath. He was smirking. *You just don't understand, Neal.*

* * *

Later that afternoon, forty thousand feet over the Sacramento Valley, with the sun at their backs, Kinsman felt the cares and fears of the Earth below easing out of his tense body.

"How'd you enjoy Frisco?" the pilot asked.

"I didn't see much of it," Kinsman said into his lip microphone.

"Didn't stay very long."

"Neither did you."

The pilot's voice in his earphones broke into a chuckle. "Long enough, pal. Overnight is plenty long enough, for some people."

Kinsman nodded to himself.

They climbed higher. Kinsman watched the westering sun throw long shadows across the rugged Sierra peaks.

"Sir?" he asked, after a long, thoughtful silence. "Do you honestly think that astronaut training would turn a man into a robot?"

He could see the shoulders of the pilot's flight suit and the featureless white curve of his helmet. There was nothing human about it.

"Listen, son, *all* military training is aimed at turning you into a robot. That's what it's all about."

"But . . ."

"Just don't let 'em get away with it," the pilot said, his voice almost passionate. "Hold onto yourself. The main thing is to get up here, away from 'em . . . get flying. Up here they can't really touch us. Up here we're free."

"They're pretty strict at the Academy," Kinsman said. "They like things done their way."

"Tell me about it. I'm a West Point man, myself. But you can still hold onto your own soul, boy. You have to do things their way on the outside, but you be your own man inside. Isn't easy, but it can be done."

Nodding to himself, Kinsman looked up and through

the plane's clear plastiglass canopy. He caught sight of the Moon, just clearing the horizon far ahead of them. It looked bright and close in the darkening sky.

I can do it, he said to himself. *I can do it.*

AGE 25

He was flying west again, with the sun at his back. Two years of "peacekeeping" in the volatile Middle East, where he flew a fighter plane, had gone by without firing a shot. And it had taken almost another two years before he had finally been assigned to astronaut training.

But now Kinsman was relaxed and happy as he held the controls of the supersonic twin-engined jet. Months of training in the elaborate mock-up of the Space Shuttle were behind him. He was heading for the real thing: spaceflight duty.

He was sitting in the right-hand seat of the jet's compact cockpit. The plane's ostensible pilot, Major Joseph Tenny, seemed half asleep in the command pilot's seat.

Far below them was the empty brown desert of New Mexico. They had left the Johnson Space Center, near Houston, at sunrise and would land at Vandenberg Air Force Base in southern California in time for breakfast.

The plane was as beautiful and responsive as a woman. *More responsive than most*, Kinsman thought. The slightest touch on the crescent-shaped control yoke made the plane swoop or bank with a grace and power that sent a shudder of delight through him.

"Sweet little thing, ain't she?" Tenny murmured.

Kinsman glanced at the Major. Chunky, short-limbed, barrel-chested, Tenny looked completely out of place in a zippered flight suit and visored gleaming plastic helmet.

His dark-eyed, swarthy face peeped out of the helmet like some ape who had gotten into the outfit by mistake.

But he grasped the controls in his thick-fingered hands and said, "Here . . . lemme show ya something, kid."

Kinsman reluctantly let go of the controls and watched Tenny push the yoke forward sharply. The plane's nose dropped and suddenly Kinsman was staring at the mottled gray-brown of the desert rushing up toward him.

"Shouldn't we get an okay from ground control before we . . ."

Tenny shot him a disgusted glance. "By the time those clowns make up their minds we could be having Mai Tais in Waikiki."

The altimeter needle wound down. The engines' whine was lost in the shrill of tortured air whistling angrily over the plastic canopy a few centimeters from Kinsman's head. The plane dove, screaming. The desert filled Kinsman's vision.

And then they zoomed upward. The untouched yoke in front of Kinsman pulled smoothly back toward his crotch as his pressure suit hissed and clamped a pneumatic hold on his guts and legs, to keep the blood from draining out of his head, to keep him awake and alive while the plane nosed upward, smooth as an arrow, hurtling almost like a rocket, up, up, straight up into the even emptier blue desert of the sky.

Kinsman wanted to let loose a wild cowboy's yell. Instead he said only, "Wow!"

Tenny said nothing, but the gleam in his devilishly dark eyes told Kinsman there was something more to come. The afterburners were screaming now as the plane climbed higher, cleaving through the thinning air.

Then Tenny nosed it over again.

Suddenly Kinsman's arms were floating up off his lap. His stomach seemed to be dropping away. He was falling, falling—but still strapped to his seat.

"Free fall, kid. Zero effective gravity. How's it feel?"

Kinsman gulped twice. Despite everything his inner ear

and stomach were telling him, he realized that he was not falling, but floating. *Free! Like a bird, like an angel! Free of gravity.*

"Great!" he heard himself shout. "It's terrific!"

The plane was nosing down again, and Kinsman could feel weight returning to his limbs. His heart was pounding. He could feel its throbbing in his ears.

Tenny eased the controls back and they were on a level course again, precisely at the altitude where they had started.

"Get used to it, kid. You're gonna be in zero gee a lot —if you make it in the astronaut corps." He took his hands off the yoke. "Take it. Take us into Vandenberg."

Still trembling a little, Kinsman grasped the half-wheel lightly, tenderly. Its touch calmed his hands.

"They useta give trainees weeks of zero-gee flying," Tenny was telling him. "Take 'em up in big transports and fly the same kind of arc I just put us through. Get a few seconds of effective free fall at the top of the arc."

"Why haven't they done that for us?" Kinsman asked. "Instead of spending all our time in the Shuttle simulator, we could have . . ."

"Too expensive," Tenny said. "Instead of twenty, thirty flights per trainee, now they can load you up in a real Shuttle, go up into orbit, and spend a coupla days in zero gee. That way they find out who can handle it and who can't—fast."

"Well, I can handle it," Kinsman said.

"We'll see."

"I did all right just now, didn't I? It was fun!"

Tenny grinned at him. "Look, kid. You can fly jets. You can fly the Shuttle simulator just fine. Next to Frank Colt, you got the highest grades of the whole damned bunch. But that doesn't mean you can fly the real thing. You've been doing great in training so far, but you haven't been up against the real thing yet."

"I'll do all right."

"Sure you will. But you're gonna have to impress the

new boss, not me. Colonel Murdock's the commanding officer. We'll both hafta make him happy."

"What's he like?" Kinsman asked.

"Desk jockey from what I hear. I've never served under him before."

"I don't see why they didn't keep you in charge. You've been running our training program so far."

"And two other majors have been running the same programs for two other squads of trainees. So we get a light colonel to sit on top of all of us. That's the Air Force, kid: solid brass, all the way up the shaft."

Kinsman laughed.

But Tenny was serious. "Something else, too. None of you guys have gotten close to Frank Colt . . . I don't like that."

"The black Napoleon? He's not easy to get close to."

"Maybe he needs a friend," Tenny said.

Kinsman thought of Frank Colt, the one night that the guys in their squad had gone out to play pool together. The intensity on his black face as he turned a friendly game into a gut-burning competition. How Colt had found the weakness in each and every one of the other men and finessed, angered, cajoled, or kidded each one of them into defeat.

"He's a loner," Kinsman said. "He's not looking for a friend."

"He's a black loner in an otherwise white outfit."

"That's got nothing to do with it."

"The hell it doesn't."

Kinsman started to reply, then hesitated. There were a dozen arguments he could make, three dozen examples he could show of how Colt had deliberately rebuffed attempts at camaraderie. But one vision in Kinsman's mind kept his tongue silent: he pictured the squad's only black officer eating alone, day after day, night after night; he never tried to join the others at their tables, and no one ever sat down at his.

* * *

Kinsman almost laughed when he first saw Colonel Murdock.

Twenty-four astronaut trainees, all first lieutenants, twenty men, four women, all of them white except one, were sitting nervously in a small briefing room at Vandenberg Air Force Base. The air conditioning wasn't working right, and the room was dank with the smell of anxiety. It was like a classroom, with bare, government-green walls and stained, faded acoustical tiles across the ceiling. The chairs had writing arms on them. There was a podium up front with a microphone goosenecking up, and chalkboards and a rolled-up projection screen behind it.

"Ten-HUT!"

All two dozen lieutenants snapped to attention as Colonel Robert Murdock came into the room, trailed by his three majors.

He looks like Porky Pig, Kinsman said to himself.

Murdock was short, round, balding, with bland features and soft, pudgy little hands. He was actually a shade taller than Major Tenny, who stood at the podium behind the Colonel. But where Tenny looked like a compact football linebacker or maybe even a petty Mafioso don, Murdock reminded Kinsman of an algebra teacher he had suffered under for a year at William Penn Charter School, back in Germantown.

Colonel Murdock scanned his two dozen charges, trying to look strong and commanding. But his bald head was glistening with nervous perspiration, and his voice was a trifle too high to be awe-inspiring as he said, "Be seated, gentlemen. And ladies."

Kinsman thought back to his algebra teacher. The man had made life a terror for the whole class during the first few weeks of the semester, telling them how tough he was and how difficult it would be for any of them to pass his course. Then they discovered that behind the man's threats and demands there was nothing: he was an empty shell. He could be maneuvered easily. But once he discovered he had been manipulated by a clever student, he was merciless.

Kinsman fought hard to stay awake during the Colonel's welcoming speech. *All the usual buzzwords.* Teamwork, orientation, challenge, the honor of the Air Force, pride, duty, the Nation's first line of defense . . . they droned sleepily in his ears.

"Two final points," Colonel Murdock said. The lieutenants stirred in their chairs at the anticipation of release.

"First—we are operating under severe budgetary and equipment restrictions. NASA gets plenty of bucks and plenty of publicity. We get very little. The rest of the Air Force gets what it wants out of Congress, pretty much. We don't. We are locked in battle to prove to Congress, to the people of the Nation, and—yes—even to the Pentagon itself, that the Air Force has a valid role to play in manned spaceflight missions.

"It's up to you to prove to the Nation that manned operations in space shouldn't be left to the civilians of NASA. When Congress someday approves the change of our service's name from just plain Air Force to Aerospace Force, which it should be, it's going to be your work and your success that gets them to do it."

Kinsman suppressed a grin. *Never studied rhetoric, that's for sure.*

"Second point," Murdock went on. "Everything you do from now on will be by the buddy system. You're going to fly the Shuttle as two-man teams. You're going to train as two-man teams. You're going to eat, sleep, and think as two-man teams."

Kinsman shot a glance at Jill Meyers, the only woman in his eight-officer squad. The expression on her snub-nosed, freckled face was marvelous: self-control struggling against a feminist desire to throw a pie in the Colonel's face.

". . . and we're going to be ruthless with you," Murdock was saying. "You will be judged as teams, not as individuals. If a team fu . . . eh . . . fouls up, then it's *out!* Period. You'll be reassigned out of the astronaut corps. Doesn't matter who fouled up, which individual is to blame. Both members of the team will be out on their asses. Is that clear?"

A general mumble of assent rose from two dozen throats. "Sir?" Jill Meyers was on her feet. "May I ask a question?"

"Go right ahead, Lieutenant." Murdock smiled toothily at her, as if realizing for the first time that there were women under his command.

"How will these teaming assignments be made, sir? Will we have any choice in the matter, or will it all be done by the Personnel Officer?"

Murdock blinked, as if he had never considered the problem before. "Well . . . I don't think . . . that is . . ."

He stopped and pursed his lips for a moment, then turned away from the podium to confer with the three majors standing behind him. Instinctively, he held a chubby hand over the microphone. Jill remained standing, a diminutive little sister in Air Force blues.

Finally the Colonel returned to the microphone. "I don't see why you can't express your personal preferences as to teammates, and then we'll have them checked through Personnel's computer to make sure the match-ups are compatible."

"Thank you, sir," Lieutenant Meyers said. She sat down.

"In fact," Colonel Murdock went on, "I don't see why we shouldn't get a preliminary expression of preferences right now. Each of you, write down the names of three officers you'd like to team with, in order of your preference."

Tenny and the two other majors looked surprised. The briefing room dissolved into a chattering, muttering, pocket-searching scramble for papers and pens or pencils.

Kinsman found his ballpoint pen in his jacket pocket with no trouble, but had to borrow a sheet of tablet paper from the man sitting next to him. Then he found himself staring at the blank paper resting on the arm of the chair.

Who the hell do I want to team up with?

The magnitude of the question seemed to hit everyone at once; the room suddenly became deadly quiet.

Kinsman glanced at the tall redheaded woman sitting in the front row. He hadn't met her yet, but she had damned good legs and a pleasant smile. *But what if she can't take zero gravity or she's a lousy pilot or something else goes wrong? Then I'm out in the cold.*

Jill Meyers was a smoothly competent pilot, Kinsman knew from the weeks they had worked the Shuttle simulator in Texas. *But so is Smitty, and D'Angelo . . . and Colt.*

Colt was the best man of their eight-officer squad in the simulator. If what Tenny had told him was correct, he was the best of the whole two dozen trainees. The idea of teaming with a woman had its charm, although Kinsman was far more interested in the redhead than in Jill. Yet . . .

He looked down at the blank sheet of paper and wrote three names on it:

Franklin Colt
Franklin Colt
Franklin Colt

That evening Major Tenny threw a party.

He hadn't really intended to, but right after dinner at the Officers' Club, most of his squad members congregated at his one-room apartment on the ground level of the base's new Bachelor Officers' Quarters. Kinsman had eyed the piano at the Club; it had been months since he'd last played. But it was already surrounded by a dozen ham-fisted players.

So he trailed along with his fellow squad members to Tenny's quarters. It was well known that their major was seldom without a bottle of bourbon near at hand. And his quarters opened onto the poolside patio.

As the trainees from the other squads saw Tenny's people spilling out of his sliding glass doors and sitting around the pool—armed with plastic cups and a suspicious-looking bottle—they quickly joined the party. Some brought six-packs of beer from the PX. Others brought joints. The leggy redhead that Kinsman had spotted that morning carried a half-gallon of Napa Valley rosé wine in a large ice chest.

It was a time to make new acquaintances.

By the time the sun had gone down and the few skinny palm trees that ringed the pool were swaying in the offshore night breeze, the trainees were comrades in arms.

"So then they turn off the damn Flight Profile Computer, tilt the simulator forty degrees, and tell me I've gotta set it straight in twenty seconds—or else."

"Yeah? You know what they pulled on me? Total electrical failure. I told 'em they oughtta hang rosary beads on the dashboard."

Kinsman was sitting on the newly planted grass. It felt stiff, brittle, despite its daily waterings. Beside him was the cooler with the wine in it. On the other side of the wine was the redhead, wearing shorts and a fatigue shirt. The plastic name tag pinned to her shirt pocket said merely: O'Hara.

"You do have a first name," Kinsman said to her.

"Yes, of course." Her voice was a cool, controlled contralto.

"I have to guess?"

"It's a game I play. You guess my name and I'll guess yours."

Why are all women crazy? Kinsman asked himself. *Why can't they just be straightforward and honest?*

"Well let's see," he said to her, taking a sip of the wine. "With that last name, and your red hair, I'll bet you get kidded a lot about Scarlett O'Hara . . . is that why you're sensitive about your name?"

She smiled at him and nodded. It was a good smile that made her eyes sparkle. "And there was a movie star," she said, "years ago, named Maureen O'Hara. I get that a lot, too."

"But your name isn't that, either. It's something more down to earth."

"Plain as any name can be."

Kinsman laughed. "Well then, it's either George M. Cohan or Mary."

"It's not George M."

"But it was Mary, Ma-ary," Kinsman sang softly. "Pleased to meet you, Mary."

"Pleased to meet you, Lieutenant Kinsman."

Now let's see how long it takes you to figure out that I was named after one of the great political disgraces of the Grand Old Party.

But an angry voice cut across everyone's conversation.

"I don't give a shit who they team me with! I left my paper blank."

Frank Colt. Kinsman looked up and there he was, standing at the pool's edge, silhouetted against the moon-bright sky. Like most of the others, Colt was wearing normal off-duty blues. But on him it looked like a dress uniform. The shirt was perfectly fitted, the slacks creased to a knife-edge.

All other talk stopped. Colt was glaring at one of the trainees from another squad, a stranger to Kinsman. He was a lanky, rawboned kid: light hair, bony face, big fists.

"We already heard about you," the kid was saying to Colt. "Top scores in the simulator. Best record in the group. Think you're pretty hot stuff, dontcha?"

"I do my job, man. I do the best I can. I'm not here to goof around, like some of you dudes. This isn't a game we're playing. It's life and death."

"Aw, don't be such a pain in the ass! You just think you're better'n everybody else."

"Maybe I do. Maybe I *am*."

Kinsman glanced over at Major Tenny, sitting on a beach chair a few meters away. Tenny was watching the argument, like everyone else. He was frowning, but he made no move to break it up.

"Yeah?" the other lieutenant answered. "Know what I

think? I think they're givin' you all the high scores b'cause you're black and nobody wants a bunch of civil rights lawyers down here b'cause we flunked out our token . . ."

Colt's hand flicked out and grabbed the kid by the jaw. "Don't say it, man. Call me black, call me dumb, call me anything you want. But if you say 'nigger' to me I'll break your ass."

Tenny was getting out of his chair now. But too late. Colt released the kid's jaw. The lieutenant took a short step forward and swung at Colt, who simply ducked under the wild haymaker and gave a quick push. The lieutenant spun into the pool with a loud splash.

Kinsman found himself on his feet and heading for Colt. Everybody else went to the aid of the kid in the pool. Colt walked away, back toward his quarters. Kinsman followed him and caught up with him in a few seconds.

"Hey, Frank."

Colt turned his head slightly, but he didn't slow down.

Kinsman pulled up alongside him. "Jeez, what a shithead he was! He got what he deserved."

"At least he said what was on his mind," Colt answered. "Plenty other guys around here feel the same way."

"That's not true."

"No? Suppose I started making time with that redhead the way you were? How many rednecks come outta the woodwork then?"

"I thought you were married."

"I was. Ain't no more."

"Oh. I'm sorry."

"No big deal. Lots of chicks in the world. Why tie yourself down to just one?"

The grapes sound sour.

They had reached the doorway into the section of the BOQ where Colt and Kinsman were quartered. Colt opened the fiberboard doors and they hustled up the stairs to the second floor.

As they started down the corridor toward their rooms,

Kinsman said, "I hope you're not too tough to live with. I picked you for my partner this morning."

"You *what*?" Colt stopped dead.

Kinsman studied his face. It was almost totally devoid of expression, except for the suspicious, wary eyes. They were probing him, looking for the kicker, the payoff, the flick of the whip.

"This morning," Kinsman said. "Colonel Murdock's buddy system . . . I wrote down your name."

"Why the hell you wanna do that?" Colt started down the corridor again, not waiting for an answer.

Kinsman kept stride with him. "Because you're the best pilot in our group and I don't want to wash out because my partner fucked up."

"That's it, huh?"

"Yeah."

Colt had reached his door. He unlocked it and swung it open. "I didn't put anybody down. I left my paper blank."

Kinsman nodded. "We all heard."

"Didn't think anybody'd wanna be stuck with me."

"Because you're black."

"Because they're out to *get* me, man. They want to knock me off. And if they get me, they get my buddy, too."

"Nobody's out to get you, Frank. That's not the Ku Klux Klan out there."

"Sure. Sure. Just wait . . . you want to be my buddy, ol' buddy? Then they'll be out to get you, too."

"Listen," Kinsman said. "They're down on you because you've been behaving like a paranoid sonofabitch."

Colt smiled coldly. "Maybe you're right. Maybe I oughtta act more humble . . . Yassuh, Massa Kinsman, suh. I's shore powerful grateful that y'all took notice of a po' li'l ol' darkey lak me."

Grinning, Kinsman said, "Go to hell, Frank."

Immediately Colt responded, "Why this is hell, nor am I out of it."

With a shake of his head, "All I can say, buddy, is that you sure know how to break up a party. And I was just starting to get someplace with Mary O'Hara."

"That's her name, huh?" Colt gave an enigmatic little shrug, as if he was carrying on another debate with someone invisible, then said, "Guess I owe you for breaking it up. Come on in, I've got a bottle of tequila in my flightbag."

"Say no more!"

By the time Major Tenny knocked on Colt's door, he and Kinsman were sitting on the floor, passing the half-empty bottle back and forth with elaborate care.

Colt climbed slowly to his feet and walked uncertainly to the door. The Major's squat bulk filled the doorway.

"Nice show you put on down there. The poor bastard damn near drowned."

"Too bad," Colt said.

Tenny walked in and spotted Kinsman. "What the hell are you guys up to?"

Kinsman waved the bottle of tequila at him. "Cultural relations, boss. We're studying the effect of tequila on the Gross National Product of Mexico."

"Our good neighbor to the south," Colt added.

"Tequila?" Tenny strode over to Kinsman, bent down and took the bottle. He sniffed at it, then tasted it. "Dammitall, this *is* tequila."

"What'd you expect?" Kinsman asked. "Hydrazine?"

Tenny shook his head, a frown on his swarthy features. "I can't let you men drink a whole bottle of tequila. You'll be in no shape for duty tomorrow morning."

"I have an idea!" Colt said brightly. "Why'n't you help us finish it up? Might save our lives."

"And our immortal souls," Kinsman murmured.

"To say nothing of our immoral careers," added Colt.

"That's immortal, not immoral."

"You have your career, I'll have my career."

Tenny scowled at them both. "If you think you can manage to shut the door, I'll do my best to help you out."

Within minutes Tenny was sitting on the carpeted floor between the two lieutenants, his back propped against the wall.

"Did you know," Kinsman was asking him, "that ol' Frank and I were born and raised within a few miles of each other? Right in little ol' Philadelphia. Both of us."

"Only my neighborhood wasn't as classy as his," Colt said. "Not as many Quakers. He's a Quaker, y'know . . ."

"Used to be. When I was a kid. Not anymore. Now I'm an officer and a gentleman. No more Quaker. No more family ties."

"And we're both named after Presidents," Colt went on. "I shoulda been named Dwight Eisenhower Colt, on account of he was President when I was born. But my Momma was a big Democrat . . . almost named me Harry Truman Colt!"

Tenny let them ramble for a while, but finally he said, "Frank—you're gonna get your ass kicked outta here if you can't get along with the others."

"If *I* can't . . ."

"Murdock was puking into a wastebasket when he heard what happened at the pool tonight. He's got a very weak stomach and his first instinct was to transfer you to Greenland, or farther."

"Sonofabitch."

Turning to Kinsman, Major Tenny asked, "You really want to be his partner?"

Kinsman nodded. Gently. His head was already hurting.

"Okay. Frank, you've got a buddy. You're not alone. And you've got me. I think you're the best damned flyer I've ever laid eyes on. Now keep your temper under control and keep your mouth zipped and you'll be okay. Got it?"

"Sure," Colt said, suddenly dead sober. "The Jackie Robinson bit. Anything else you want me to do, boss? Walk on water? Shine shoes?"

Tenny grabbed him by the shirt. "You stupid bastard! You wanna be an astronaut or not?"

"I want to."

"Then don't fuck yourself over. There's only one man can ruin things for you, and that's *you*. Learn some self-control."

Colt said nothing as long as Tenny held his shirt. They merely glared at each other. But when the Major slowly released him, Colt said quietly, "I'll try."

"And stop going around with that goddamned chip on your shoulder."

"I'll try," Colt repeated.

Tenny turned to Kinsman. "And you . . . you help him all you can. He's too good a man to lose."

"How come you got the window seat?" Colt whispered.

He was lying beside Kinsman in the cramped metal womb of the Space Shuttle's mid-deck passenger compartment. Zipped into a snug-fitting pressure suit, complete with plastic helmet and visor, Kinsman lay on his back in the foam-padded contour chair next to the compartment's side hatch—with the only window in the compartment.

"Lucky, I guess," he croaked back at Colt. His voice nearly cracked. His throat was dry and scratchy. Inside the gloves his palms were wet.

Six astronaut-trainees sat in nervous silence inside the Shuttle as it stood on its tail during the final few minutes of countdown before being blasted straight up from its launch pad. The earphones in their helmets were not patched in to the launch control center, or even to the Shuttle's flight deck, on the level above them. So the six trainees waited in nerve-stretching silence.

The pressure suits were heavy, smothering, a frightening reminder that they were leaving the safety of air and warmth behind them. *NASA doesn't make you wear these damned monkey suits*, Kinsman grumbled to himself. NASA astronauts rode into orbit in their shirt-sleeves. But the Air Force had to be different. Combat readiness was the watchword, even if the only thing to be combatted was the possibility of a sudden emergency blowing the air out of the spacecraft.

Kinsman mentally counted the rungs on the ladder that disappeared through the open hatch into the ribbed metal overhead. *By the time I've counted the rungs ten times we'll lift off,* he told himself. He counted slowly; at first he had thought that five times would be enough.

Up on the flight deck, at the other end of the ladder, the Shuttle's four-man crew was going through the final stages of countdown. They were watching the instruments glow to life, listening to the commands flickering across the electronic communications net that spanned the entire globe of Earth. They could see the master sequencer computer's numbers clicking down toward zero.

But in the passenger compartment, strapped into their chairs, the trainees could only wait and sweat.

Kinsman gave up counting and turned his head to look out the small circular window set into the hatch. All he could see was the steel spiderwork of the launch tower and, far beyond it, the bare brown rugged hills that ringed Vandenberg.

Helluva way to go, he thought to himself. *Lying on your back with your legs sticking up in the air like a woman in heat.*

"Five seconds!" he heard a voice sing out from the deck above.

The time stretched out to infinity. But then, a vibration, a banging shock—*Christ! Something's gone wrong!*—and finally the roar of six million flaming demons burned into every bone of his body. Kinsman had a brief glimpse of the tower sliding past the corner of his vision, then the hills faded from view as he was pressed down, flattening into the seat beneath him, a giant's hand squeezing his chest, making his eyeballs hurt, and the roar, the bellow, the inescapable, overpowering, shattering fury of the rocket engines that shook every atom of his being.

With an effort he turned his head to look at Colt and saw that his partner's eyes were squeezed shut, his mouth gaping wide. Kinsman tried to see the other four trainees, but their seats were slightly in front of his and he could not see their faces.

The pressure got worse and there was a jolt when the two solid-rocket strapon boosters were jettisoned.

Going through fifty klicks, Kinsman knew. *Maximum pressure's behind us now.*

The weight on his chest began to diminish. The howl of the engines suddenly whined down to nothingness.

And he was falling.

Zero gravity, he told himself. *Free fall.* His arms were floating loosely off the seat arms that they had been plastered to. With a blink of his eyes, Kinsman rearranged his perspective. He was no longer lying on his back, he was sitting upright. They all were.

His stomach was fluttering. He forced himself to relax his tensed muscles. *You're floating,* he told himself. *Just like at the seashore, when you were a kid. Beyond the breakers. Floating on the swells.*

He turned and grinned at Colt. "How do you like it?"

Colt's answering grin was a bit queasy. "I'll get used to it in a couple minutes."

Major Pierce came floating down from the overhead hatch without touching the ladder and landed lightly on his booted feet. Back on Earth he was a nondescript man in his forties, patrician high-bridged nose, darting snake's eyes. *He could damned well be a ballet dancer up here.*

"Very well, my little chickadees," the Major said. "Anyone feel like upchucking?"

The four other trainees had to turn around in their seats to see Pierce, who was standing at the bottom of the ladder, behind their seats. Kinsman stared at the Major's boots, fascinated to see that they were not quite touching the deck.

"Very well," Major Pierce commanded, "unstrap and try to stand up. By the numbers. And move *slowly.* Meyers, you have the honor of being first."

Jill Meyers got up from her seat, her face going from

brow-knitted concentration to wide-eyed surprise as she just kept right on rising, completely off her feet, until her helmet clicked gently against the metal juncture of the bulkhead and the overhead. While the others laughed, Jill thrashed about and finally found an anchoring point by grabbing the handle of one of the electronics racks that covered the forward bulkhead.

"Newton's First Law of Motion," Pierce said in a tone of bored disgust, as the laughing stopped. "A body in motion tends to remain in motion unless acted upon by an outside force."

Redfaced, Jill nodded.

Her partner, the lanky, whipcord-lean Lieutenant Smith, got up from his seat next. Smitty was tall enough to raise a long slender arm up to the metal overhead to prevent himself from soaring off his feet.

"That's cheating, Mr. Smith," said Major Pierce.

"Yessir. But it works."

Kinsman smiled at the Mutt and Jeff look of the Meyers/Smith team. Jill was the smallest member of the trainees; Smitty barely squeezed in under the Air Force's six-three height limit for astronauts.

Mary O'Hara and Art Douglas went next. Then Colt got cautiously to his feet, and finally Kinsman. It was like standing in water up to your neck, with the tides trying to pull you this way and that.

"Well, at least you didn't break any bones," Pierce sniffed as the six trainees bobbed uneasily in their places.

"Very well now," the Major went on. "We're go for a three-day mission. By the time we touch down at Vandenberg again, you will each know every square centimeter of this Shuttle more intimately than your mother's . . ."—he hesitated and smiled a fraction— ". . . face. And each team will get an opportunity to go EVA with Captain Howard, the Payload Specialist, to perform an actual mission task. In the meantime, stay out of the crew's way and don't get into mischief."

"Sir, will we get a chance to fly the bird?" asked

Douglas. He was a little smaller than Kinsman, prematurely balding, moonfaced, but sharp-eyed and sharp-tongued: the squad's lawyer.

Pierce closed his eyes momentarily, as if seeking strength from some inner source. "No, Lieutenant, you will *not* touch the controls. You know the mission profile as well as I do. We are not going to risk this very expensive piece of aerospace hardware on your very first flight into orbit."

"I know the plan, sir," Douglas replied agreeably, "but I thought maybe the Commander would let us sneak in a little maneuver, maybe."

"Majors Podolski and Jakes are the Commander and Pilot, respectively, on this mission. They will do all the maneuvering. If you are a good little lieutenant, Mr. Douglas, perhaps Major Podolski might allow you to come up on the flight deck and watch him for a few moments."

"Peachy keen," sneered Lieutenant Douglas.

It was like living in a submarine. Outside, Kinsman knew, was the limitless expanse of emptiness: planets, moons, comets, stars, galaxies stretching out through space to infinity. But inside the Air Force Shuttle Orbiter, serial number AFASO-002, six young trainees and four middle-aged officers clambered over each other, stuck elbows in each other's food trays, and got in each other's way.

"If it weren't for the zero gee," Kinsman said to Colt, "I'd *really* be ready for a murder."

"Or two," Colt agreed.

They were floating inside the unpressurized payload bay, moving cautiously in their cumbersome spacesuits. It was a hollow, dark, eerie place, as long as a tennis court and half as wide, empty except for the two bulbous packages shrouded by aluminum foil wrappings that were strapped to the deck some ten meters from where Colt and Kinsman were working. The only light inside the cavernous bay came from their helmet lamps.

"Pierce really meant it when he said we were gonna lay our hands on every stringer and weld in this bucket,"

Colt grumbled. He was floating head-down as the two of them opened an access panel in the cargo deck, fumbling with the tools in their heavily gloved hands.

So far that morning, the second of their three-day mission, they had tested the Orbiter's smoke detection sensors and gone over the electronics racks that were built into the rear of the payload bay, back near the rocket engines at the ship's tail.

Now they were checking out the environmental control system: the heat exchangers and radiators that kept the Orbiter's interior at a temperature that was tolerable for the crew and safe for the ship's electronics gear.

Kinsman pried the hatch off at last. "Now we're supposed to trace the coolant lines up through here and into the radiators in the bay doors, right?"

There was no answer from Colt, but Kinsman sensed that he was nodding.

"Uh, yeah, right," Colt said, realizing that facial expressions and head movements couldn't be seen from inside the visored helmets. Even their words had to be carried by their suit radios from throat mikes to earphones.

They worked steadily, fastening one access hatch back in its place before opening the next one, following the pale blue coolant lines up from the deck, through the curving bulkhead, and toward the radiators that were built into the big cargo doors over their heads.

"I don't get it," Kinsman complained as they worked. "Why the hell are we getting all the shit jobs? Jill and Smitty already went EVA, and Mary and Art got to place the first payload in orbit. We're still stuck doing this crap."

He couldn't see Colt's face, but the expression came through the voice in his earphones. "We're the special ones, man. You and I got the highest marks, so they're gonna take us down a peg. Keep our heads from getting big."

"You think that's it?"

Colt chuckled. "Sure. My being black's got nothing to

do with it. Neither does your picking me as a partner. Nothin' at all."

"It's good to see you're not being overly sensitive," Kinsman joked.

"Or bitter."

"Well—they've got to let us go EVA tomorrow. There's no way they can keep us from going outside."

For a long moment Colt didn't respond. Then he said simply, "Wanna bet?"

The passenger quarters in the mid-deck were crowded enough when all six trainees were lumped into the metal shoebox together, but when a couple of officers came down from the flight deck, the tensions became impossible.

The end of the second day, the trainees were milling around the galley, which looked to Kinsman like a glorified Coke machine. They were punching buttons, pulling trays from the storage racks, gliding weightlessly to find an unoccupied corner of the compartment in which to eat their pasty dinners.

Kinsman leaned his back against a folded-up bunk, legs dangling in air, and picked at his food. The tray was already showing signs of heavy use; it was slightly bent and no longer gleamed, new-looking. The food, a combination of precut bite-sized chunks of imitation protein and various moldy-looking pastes, was as appetizing as sawdust.

Jill Meyers drifted by, empty-handed.

"Finished already?" Kinsman asked her.

"This food was finished before it started," she said.

"It's chock-full of nutrition," he quipped.

"So's a cockroach."

Major Jakes slid down the ladder and headed for the galley. Automatically, the lieutenants made room for him. He was an overweight, jowly, crewcut, sullen-looking, graying man when Kinsman had first seen him, back at Vandenberg. His physical looks hadn't changed, but now there was a happy grin on his face.

Jakes brought his tray to the corner where Kinsman was sitting, literally on air. The Major was humming to himself cheerfully.

After setting himself cross-legged beside Kinsman and taking a few bites of the tasteless food, he asked:

"How's it going, Lieutenant?"

Kinsman shrugged, a motion that moved his entire weightless body. Never complain to officers, he knew from his Academy training. Especially when they're trying to buddy up to you.

"I don't see Colt around."

"Frank?" Kinsman realized that Colt was not in sight. "Must be in the pissoir."

Jakes made a small clucking sound. "Your redheaded friend is missing too."

Kinsman took a sip of lukewarm coffee from the squeeze bulb on his tray. "Maybe they're in the airlock. You go nuts down here trying to find some elbow room."

Jakes made an agreeable nod. "Yeah, I guess so. Like the fo'c'sle of an old sailing ship, huh?"

Why me? Kinsman wondered. *Why is he buddying up to me?*

"You're from Pennsylvania, aren't you?"

"Yessir. Philadelphia area . . ."

"Main Line, I know. My people have relatives down there. I'm from the North Shore—Boston, you know. Cradle of Liberty."

"Where the Cabots talk only to the Lodges."

"Yeah." Jakes nibbled at a chunk of thinly disguised soybean meal. "And neither of 'em talk to my folks. We were sort of the black sheep of the clan. My old man could build the yachts, all right, but they'd never let us sail 'em."

"Black sheep," Kinsman muttered. *Welcome to the club, buddy. Try to imagine what a black sheep you become when you leave a Quaker family to join the Air Force.*

"Did you really pick Colt for your partner?"

"Yes," Kinsman said, suddenly wary.

"I hear he's a troublemaker."

"He's a damned fine officer."

"Maybe. I hear you're just as good. Colt's got a reputation, well . . ."

Kinsman could feel his back stiffening. "Sir," he said, "if I were in a tight situation, there's no one I'd rather have beside me than Frank Colt. Present company included."

Jakes grinned at him. "Snotty little shavetail, eh? Yeah, that's what I heard. Well, you and Colt are two of a kind, all right. Full of piss and vinegar. I guess that's good. This isn't a game for marshmallows."

They finished their dinners quickly and stowed the dirty trays in the galley's cleansing unit. Jakes swam back up to the flight deck, and Kinsman was about to join Jill and Art Douglas in an argument about the Air Force's medical insurance plan for astronauts.

But Major Pierce and Captain Howard eased down the ladder and suddenly the compartment was crowded again.

"Meyers and Smith," Pierce said, "you've got fifteen minutes before you launch Payload Number 2. Get rid of those trays and start suiting up for EVA. Captain Howard will brief you, starting now."

Howard was a dour, shriveled little man. Kinsman had never seen a crewcut manage to look messy before, but somehow Howard's did. He was gray-haired, old for a captain. *Hell, he's old for a major or light colonel*, Kinsman thought. *But he must know his stuff.*

Under Howard's direction, the O'Hara/Douglas team had operated the cargo boom that had swung the Shuttle's first payload—a small, laser-bearing navigational beacon satellite—into orbit. And Captain Howard himself had gone EVA twice in the two days of the mission, once to check on a defunct communications satellite that had been orbited years earlier, and once to inspect a newly orbited Russian satellite.

Now Mutt and Jeff are going to have their fun while Colt and I still sit around, twiddling our thumbs, Kinsman grumbled to himself. *Hell, they've already been EVA once!*

Howard took them up to the flight deck for their briefing, pressure suits and all. Pierce followed right behind them. Suddenly the passenger compartment was empty except for Douglas and Kinsman.

"Where the hell did Colt and Mary get to?" Art asked.

Kinsman peered through the thick glass of the airlock window, but they weren't inside.

"Maybe they took a walk outside," he said.

Douglas looked annoyed. "I'll bet the sonofabitch has her out in the payload bay."

"If he does, about the only thing they can do out there is hold hands. With gloves on, at that."

"Oh yeah? I wouldn't put it past Colt to figure out some way to make it even inside pressure suits."

"Maybe they both got into one suit."

The joke went completely past Douglas. He glided over to the suit locker and checked the racks. "No, they both took their suits."

"If they're out in the payload bay without Pierce's permission," Kinsman said, "they could be in trouble."

"Yeah, and he'll be down here to watch Howard take Jill and Smitty outside."

Nodding, Kinsman pushed over to the suit rack. With Douglas' silent help he quickly zipped himself into the bulky suit, sealed the helmet onto the neckpiece, and glided over to the airlock.

"If I'm not back in three days, call the Mounties." But a glance at Douglas' uncomprehending face made Kinsman realize that nothing got beyond his helmet except a muffled jumble of meaningless sound.

It took an agonizingly long minute for the airlock to cycle. As soon as the red light showed that all the air had been pumped out, Kinsman spun the outer door open and stepped into the payload bay.

Sure enough, the two spacesuited figures were floating in the middle of the cavernous section, side by side.

Kinsman launched himself toward them, then grabbed a handgrip in the overhead doors to stop before he crashed into them.

"Hey, you two, Howard's going to be out here in another minute. Scramble!"

"Aw shit, this's the only place where you can relax, man."

Mary was already jackknifing into a position that aimed her at the airlock.

"Listen, buddy," Kinsman said, "she can bend all the regulations in the book and get away with it. You can't. Let's move."

Grousing to himself, Colt followed Mary back to the airlock. Kinsman played tail gunner and went through the lock last.

By the time he stepped back into the passenger compartment, it was crowded again. All six trainees were there, together with Captain Howard and Major Pierce. Howard, Jill, and Smitty were all suited up for working in the payload bay, except for their helmets.

As Kinsman lifted his own helmet off, he heard Pierce demanding:

". . . just what do you people think you're doing?"

"I decided to go out into the payload bay, sir," Kinsman heard himself answering, before Colt or anyone else could speak. "I was getting a touch of claustrophobia in here."

Pierce glared at him.

"Lieutenant O'Hara came out to tell me I should return. Lieutenant Colt came out too . . . in accordance with the regulation that trainees should not enter the unpressurized areas without proper assistance and backup."

Major Pierce looked from Kinsman to Colt to O'Hara and back to Kinsman. He planted his fists on his hips and focused his glittering snake's eyes on Kinsman. "That is the dumbest story I've ever heard a shavetail try to pull, Lieutenant!"

"That's the way it happened, sir."

"Claustrophobia?"

"Only a temporary touch of it, sir. We were warned about it in training. Since there's no medical officer on board . . ."

"That's enough!" Pierce snapped, closing his eyes momentarily. "All right. I'll let it stand. But I'm going to remember this, Kinsman. I'll be watching you . . . you and your claustrophobia. And the rest of you! No one budges out of this compartment without my direct approval. Is that understood?"

"Yessir!"

"You all know that you are not—repeat, *not*—authorized to enter the unpressurized sections of this craft without my approval."

"Unless there's a medical or other type of emergency," Kinsman replied.

Glaring, Pierce said, "I could put the whole squad of you on report for this."

No one said a word.

Pierce looked hard at Colt, who returned his stare evenly. Then he glared at O'Hara, who glanced toward Kinsman.

Shaking his head, the Major mumbled, "You're on thin ice, Kinsman. Very thin ice."

"Yessir," Kinsman answered.

Pierce went back up to the flight deck and the tension cracked. Howard took Meyers and Smitty through the airlock. Kinsman, Colt, and O'Hara slowly took off their pressure suits and began stowing them away.

"Why'd you do that?" Colt asked Kinsman.

Feeling impish, Kinsman grinned at him. "Instinct. I figured you'd catch more hell than I would."

Colt frowned. "What difference does it make? We're both on the same team; he'll kick my ass out the same time he kicks yours out."

Nodding, Kinsman said, "Frank, you've memorized the book of regulations, but you haven't figured out the people yet. He won't kick us out for something *I've* done. Not something this trivial."

Colt's answer was a derisive snort.

"You could say thank you to him," Mary suggested to Colt. "He was trying to save both our necks."

"And his own, too," Colt said. "If I go, he goes."

Kinsman laughed. "You're welcome, buddy."

"Think nothin' of it," Colt answered.

Kinsman looked at Mary O'Hara. Somehow he knew that she would have been in more trouble, too, if Pierce had thought she'd gone off with Colt. *But she doesn't say a word about that end of it.* La belle dame sans merci. *The beautiful lady who never says thank you.*

It took an hour before Jill and Smitty came back in from their launching task. Howard, looking smaller and older even than he had before, pointed a dirty-nailed forefinger at Kinsman.

"You and your buddy better get a good night's sleep. You're going to have a big day tomorrow."

But, lying in his bunk after lights-out, floating softly against the nylon mesh that kept him from drifting away, Kinsman could not sleep.

The bunks were stacked so tightly that he could feel the heat from Colt's body, bulging a few centimeters above his face, and smell the faint trace of perfume that Mary O'Hara wore, in the next bunk down.

Yet it wasn't her scent or Colt's troubled grunting and tossing above him that kept Kinsman awake. Not even the nervous anticipation of going outside tomorrow, for the first time.

"Damn Jakes," he muttered to himself. "And Pierce. All of them . . . all of them . . ."

But he saw in his mind's eye the crystal-blue sky of the Mediterranean as he flew his F-15 on a "peace-keeping" mission. The Turks wanted to slaughter the Greeks. The Greeks wanted to invade Turkey. Lebanon was going through another of its convulsions, this time trying to throw off the Syrians who had effectively annexed the splintered nation. And Israel still held a hundred million Arab neighbors at bay.

Flying out of Cyprus, the handful of Air Force planes was the visible show of American determination to stabilize the area. Flying out of Damascus, a squadron of Russian MiG-28's symbolized the Soviet determination to counter the American efforts.

In his half-sleep, Kinsman remembered all the feints and mock dogfights they went through. It would have taken only the press of a button to destroy one of the Russian fighters. More than once, somebody fired a burst of cannon fire into the empty air. More than once, a missile "happened" to whoosh out of its rack and trace a smokey arrow of death that came close to one of the beautiful swept-wing planes.

Each time Kinsman saw a Soviet aircraft in his gunsights, he heard his father's stern voice: *"Once you put on their uniform, you will do as they order you to do. If they say kill, you will kill."*

"No," Kinsman told himself. "There are limits. I can hold out against them."

But he had been overjoyed when his application for astronaut training finally came through.

Even grimy old Philadelphia looked good to him, on the way back from the Middle East. He had dinner with Neal McGrath and his wife, Mary-Ellen, in an Indian restaurant on Chestnut Street, within sight of Independence Hall and the cracked old Liberty Bell. Neal was a congressman now. Diane Lawrence (née Lorenz) had a one million-selling hit record to her credit and was fast becoming one of the nation's favorite folk singers.

And his father—sick, old, his home a few miles away turned into a private hospital-cum-office—refused to see Kinsman as long as he wore an Air Force uniform.

When he finally slid out of his bunk, Kinsman felt too keyed-up to be tired. Colt seemed tensed like a coiled spring, too, as they pulled on their pressure suits.

"So the Goldust Twins finally get their chance to go EVA," Smitty kidded them as he helped Kinsman with the zippers and seals of his suit.

"I thought they were gonna keep us after school," Colt said, "for being naughty yesterday."

"Pierce'll find a way to take you guys down a notch," Jill said. "He's got that kind of mind."

"Democracy in action," Kinsman said. "Reduce everybody to the same low level."

"Hey!" Art Douglas snapped, from across the compartment, where he was helping Colt into his suit. "Your scores weren't that much higher than ours, you know."

"Tell you what," Colt said. "A couple of you guys black your faces and see how you get treated."

They laughed, but there was a nervous undertone to it.

Kinsman raised his helmet over his head and slid it down into place. "Still fits okay," he said through the open visor. "Guess my head hasn't swollen too much."

Captain Howard slid down the ladder railing, already suited up, but with his helmet visor open. The pouches under his eyes looked darker than usual; his face was a gray prison pallor.

"You both checked out?"

Mr. Personality, thought Kinsman.

Howard wasn't satisfied with the trainees' check of their suits. He went over them personally. Finally, with a sour nod, he waved Colt to the airlock. The lock cycled and then Howard himself went through.

Kinsman slid his visor down and sealed it, turned to wave a halfhearted "so long" to the others, then clumped into the airlock. The heavy hatch swung shut and he could hear, faintly, the clatter of the pump sucking the air out of the phonebooth-sized chamber. The red light went on, signaling vacuum. He opened the other hatch and stepped out into the payload bay.

Colt and Captain Howard seemed to be deep in conversation, back beside the only remaining satellite in the bay. Kinsman shuffled toward them, keeping the lightly magnetized soles of his boots in contact with the steel strips set into the deck plates.

Colt tapped Howard on the shoulder and pointed to Kinsman. *Like scuba divers in an underwater movie,* Kinsman said to himself. Howard turned, tapped the keyboard on his left wrist, and held up four fingers.

Kinsman touched the button marked *four* on his own wrist keyboard.

Howard's voice immediately came through his earphones. "We're using channel four for suit-to-suit chatter. Ship's frequency is three; don't use it unless you have to talk to the flight deck."

"Yessir," said Kinsman.

"Okay. Let's get to work."

Under Howard's direction, Colt and Kinsman peeled away the protective aluminized sheeting from the third and final satellite in the bay. It was a large, fat drum, tall as a man and so wide that Kinsman knew he and Colt could not girdle it with their outstretched arms. The outer surface of the satellite was covered with dead black solar cells.

"Kinsman, you come up top here with me to unfold the antennas," Howard ordered. "Colt, get back to the main bulkhead and open the doors."

Floating up to the top of the satellite with the Captain beside him, Kinsman asked, "What kind of a satellite is this? Communications?"

"In a polar orbit?"

"Oh. No, I guess not. We've changed orbital planes so often that I didn't realize . . ."

"Start with that one." Howard pointed to the largest antenna, in the center of the drumhead.

Kinsman hung head-down over the satellite and read the assembly instruction printed on it by the light of his helmet lamp. The antenna support arms swung up easily and locked into place. Then he opened the parasol-folded parabolic dish that was the antenna itself.

"Now the wave guide," Howard commanded laconically.

"It's not an observation satellite," Kinsman said as he worked. "No ports for cameras or sensors."

"Keep your mind on your work."

"But what the hell's it for?" Kinsman blurted.

With an exasperated sigh, Howard said, "Strategic Command didn't bother to tell me, kid. So I don't know. Except that it's top secret and none of our damned business."

"Oh . . . a ferret."

"A what?"

"Scuttlebutt that we heard back at the Academy," Kinsman explained. "Satellites that gather electronic intelligence from other satellites. This bird's going into a high orbit, right?"

Howard hesitated before answering, "Yes."

Nodding inside his helmet, Kinsman went on, "She'll hang up there and listen on a wide band of frequencies, mostly the freaks the Soviets use. Maybe some Chinese and European bands, too. She just sits in orbit and passively collects all their chatter, recording it. Then when she passes over a command station in the States they send up an order and she spits out everything she's recorded over the course of a day or a week. All data-compressed so they can get the whole wad of poop in a few seconds."

"Really." Howard's voice was as flat and cold as an ice tray.

"Yessir. The Russians have knocked a few of ours down, or so they told us at the Academy."

Howard's response was unintelligible.

"Sir?" Kinsman asked.

"I *said*," he snapped, "that I never went to the Academy. I came up the hard way, so I don't have as much inside information as you bright boys."

Touchy!

"Colt, when the hell are you going to get them doors open?"

"I'm ready anytime, sir," Colt's voice came through the earphones. "Been waiting for your order."

"Well open 'em up, dammit, and get back here."

Soundlessly the big clamshell doors began to swing open. Kinsman started to return his attention to the satellite, but as the doors swung further and further back, he saw more and more stars staring at him: hard, unwinking points of light, not like jewels set in black velvet, as he had expected, not like anything he had ever seen before in his life.

"Glory to God in the highest . . ." Kinsman heard himself whisper the words as he rose, work forgotten, drifting up toward the infinitely beautiful stars.

"Get your ass back here, Kinsman!" Howard shouted. It was like ice picks jabbing at his eardrums.

"But I never thought . . ." Kinsman found himself drifting halfway down the payload bay, high enough so that his head and shoulders were out in the open. He grabbed a hinge of the open door to steady himself.

Colt was beside him. "Fan*tas*tic!"

Kinsman realized his mouth was hanging open. But he didn't care. Inside the helmet, in the utter privacy of his impervious personal suit, he stared at the universe, seeing it for the first time.

"All right, all right." Howard's voice was softer, gentler. "Sometimes I forget how it hits some people the first time. You've got five minutes to see the show, then we've got to get back to work or we'll miss the orbit injection time. Here"—and Kinsman felt a hand on his shoulders—"don't go drifting loose. Use these for tethers."

He felt a line being hooked into one of the loops at the waist of his suit. Looking around, he saw Howard do the same thing for Colt.

"Go out and take a good look," Howard said. "Five minutes. Then we've got to count down the satellite."

Kinsman floated free, outside the confines of the ship, and let the full light of Earth shine on his face. It was dazzling, overpowering, an all-engulfing expanse of curving blue decked with brilliant white clouds. Hardly any land to be seen, just unbelievably blue seas and the pure white of the clouds.

It was *huge*, filling the sky, spreading as far as he could see: serene blue and sparkling white, warm, alive, glowing, a beckoning, beautiful world, the ancient mother of mankind. The Earth looked untroubled from this distance. No divisions marred her face, not the slightest trace of the frantic works of her children soiled the eternal beauty of the planet. It took a wrenching effort of will for Kinsman to turn his face away from her.

By turning his body, Kinsman could see the Sun shining so fiercely that even his heavily tinted photochromic visor wasn't enough protection. He squeezed his tearing eyes shut and spun away, angry yellow splotches flecking his vision.

"Can't see the Moon," he heard Colt say.

"Must be on the other side of the Earth," he answered.

"Look! That red star. I think it's Mars."

"No," Kinsman said, "it's Antares . . . in Scorpio."

"Christ, it's beautiful."

When I consider thy heavens, the work of thy fingers, the moon and the stars, which thou hast ordained . . .

"All right, all right," Howard's voice broke through to them. "Time to get back to work. You'll get plenty chance to see more, soon enough."

Reluctantly, Kinsman turned away from the stars and back to the dark interior of the payload bay. Colt trailed behind him. Working with Captain Howard, they set the satellite on the Shuttle's payload deployment arm, a long metal boom that swung the squat drumlike mechanism up and completely outside the emptied cargo bay.

"Good work," Howard said. He touched his keyboard and reported back to the flight deck.

"Now we wait," he said to Colt and Kinsman. "You guys were so good we finished eight minutes ahead of schedule."

Kinsman felt himself smiling at the Captain. Not that they could see each other's faces through the tinted visors.

But something had softened Howard. *He's just as wiped out about all this grandeur as we are, only he won't let his emotions show.*

They switched their suit radios to the flight deck's frequency and listened to the final orbital maneuvering which placed the Shuttle in the right spot for launching the satellite. Twice the control jets at the rear of the ship, by the root of the big tail fin, flared—such quick puffs of light that they were gone before they had truly registered on Kinsman's eyes. When the moment came to release the satellite, it was utterly unspectacular.

". . . three, two, one," said Major Jakes' heavy voice.

There was no sound, just a brief puff of escaping gas as the tiny thruster built into the bottom end of the satellite pushed the drum away from the boom arm. The satellite quickly dwindled into the distance and disappeared among the stars.

As the boom swung back inside the payload bay and folded itself into place along the deck, Captain Howard said:

"Now for the final chore. It's a big one; we've been saving it for you boys."

Kinsman tried to glance over at Colt, but when he turned his head all he saw was the inside lining of his helmet.

"You were too excited to notice," Howard was explaining, "but we haven't detached the booster fuel tank that we rode up on. It's still strapped to the Orbiter's belly."

"Can't re-enter with that thing hanging onto us," Colt said.

"Right. We have no intention of it. We're heading now for a rendezvous point where the last six missions have separated their booster tanks and left them in orbit. One of these days, when the Air Force gets enough astronauts and enough money, we're going to convert all those empty tanks into a permanent space station."

"I'll be damned," Kinsman said, grinning to himself.

"Your mission," Howard went on, "is to separate our tank and attach it to the assembly that's already there."

"Simple enough," Colt said. "We did something like that at the neutral buoyancy tank in Alabama."

"It sounds easy," Howard said. "But I won't be there to help you. You're going to be on your own with this one."

"Okay," Kinsman said. "We can handle it."

Howard said nothing for a long moment. Kinsman saw him floating before them, his dark visor looking like the dead, empty eye of some deformed cyclops.

"All right," the Captain said at last. "But listen to me. If something happens out there, don't panic. Do you hear me? Don't panic."

"We won't," Colt said.

What's he worried about? Kinsman wondered.

But he put the thought aside as Howard began testing them on their proficiency with their suit maneuvering units. They jetted themselves back and forth along the length of the empty payload bay, did pirouettes, planted their feet at precise spots that the Captain called out to them—all on puffs of cold gas from the pistol-like thruster units.

"There'll be no umbilicals or tethers on this task," Howard warned them. "Too much tankage hanging around to foul up your lines. You'll be operating independently. On your own. Do you understand?"

"Sure."

"No funny stuff and no sightseeing. You won't have time for stargazing. Now fill your propellant and air tanks. I'm going inside to check with the flight deck."

"Yessir."

"He's pretty edgy," Kinsman said on their suit-to-suit frequency after Howard had disappeared through the airlock.

"Just puttin' us on, man."

"I don't know. He said this is the most difficult task of the whole mission."

"That's why they saved it for us, huh?"

"Maybe."

He could sense Colt shaking his head, frowning. "Don't let 'em get to you. He had other jobs . . . like inspecting that Russian satellite. That was tougher than what we're gonna be doing."

"That was a one-man task," Kinsman said. "He didn't need a couple of rookies getting in his way. And the Reds probably have all sorts of alarm and detection systems on their birds."

"Yeah, maybe . . ."

"He's a strange little guy."

Colt said, "You'd think he'd have made major by now."

"Or light colonel. He's as old as Murdock."

"Yeah, but he's got no wings. Flunked out of flight training when he was a kid."

"Really?"

"That's what Art was telling me. He's nothing more than a glorified Tech Specialist. No Academy. Lucky he made captain."

"No wonder he looks pissed off most of the time."

"*Most* of the time?"

Kinsman said, "I got the feeling he enjoyed watching us go bananas over the stars."

"Hey, yeah, I forgot all about that."

Kinsman turned and rose slightly off the deck plates so that he could look out at the sky again. *How quickly the miraculous becomes ordinary.*

"Sure is some sight," Colt said from beside him.

"Makes me want to just drift out of here and never come back," said Kinsman. "Just go on and on forever."

"You'd need a damned big air tank."

"Not a bad way to die, if you've got to go. Drifting alone, silent, going to sleep among the stars . . ."

"That's okay for you, maybe, but I intend to be shot by a jealous husband when I'm in my nineties," Colt said. "That's how I wanna go: bareass and humpin'."

"White or black?"

"The husband or the wife? Both of 'em . . . honkies, man. Screwin' white folks is the best part of life."

Kinsman could hear his partner's happy chuckling.

"Frank," he asked, "have you ever thought that by the time you're ninety there might not be any race problems anymore?"

Colt's laughter deepened. "Sure. Just like we won't have any wars and all God's chillun got shoes."

"All right, there it is," Captain Howard told them.

The three men were hovering just above the open clamshell doors of the payload bay, looking out at what seemed to Kinsman to be a giant stack of beer bottles. *Except that they're aluminum, not glass.*

Six empty propellant tanks, each of them nearly twice the size of the Orbiter itself, were arranged in two neat rows. From this distance they could not see the connecting rods that held the assembly together.

"You've got three hours," Howard told them. "The booster tank linkages that hold it to the Orbiter are built to come apart and reattach to the other tanks . . ."

"Yeah, yeah, we know," Colt said impatiently.

Kinsman was thinking, *This shouldn't take more than an hour. Why give us three?*

"Working in zero gee on a task like this ain't easy," Howard said, as if in answer to Kinsman's unspoken question. "It's different from the water tank. You'll be floating free, no resistance at all. Every move you make will make you *keep on* moving until you make a countermove to cancel the motion."

"We learned all that in training," Colt insisted. "And how we shouldn't overheat ourselves inside the suits."

"Yeah, sure you did. Pardon me. I should've remembered you guys know everything already." Howard's voice was acid again. "All right, you're on your own. Just don't panic if anything goes wrong."

* * *

Almost an hour later, as they were attaching the empty propellant tank to the other six, Colt asked:

"How many times we practice this stunt in training?"

"This particular business?"

"Naw . . . just taking pieces apart and reassembling them."

Kinsman looked up from the bolt-tightening job he was doing. Colt was floating some forty meters away, up at the nose end of the fat propellant tank. He looked tiny next to the huge stack of tanks, gleaming brightly in the strong sunlight. But his voice in Kinsman's earphones sounded as if he were inside the helmet with him.

"Hell," Kinsman answered, "we did so much of this monkeywork I thought they were training us to open a garage."

"Yeah. That's what I was thinking. Then why was Howard so shaky about us doing this? You havin' any troubles?"

Kinsman shrugged inside his suit, and the motion made him drift slightly away from the strut he was working on. He reached out and grabbed it to steady himself.

"I've spun myself around a couple times," he admitted. "It gets a little confusing, with no up or down. Takes some getting used to."

Colt's answer was a soft grunt.

"The suit heats up, too," Kinsman went on. "I've had to stop and let it cool down a couple times."

"Yeah. Me too."

"Maybe Howard's worried about us being so far from the ship without tethers."

"Maybe." But Colt didn't sound convinced.

"How's your end going?" Kinsman asked. "I'm almost finished here."

"I oughtta be done in another ten minutes. Three hours! This damned job's a piece of cake if ever . . . *Holy shit!*"

Kinsman's whole body jerked at the urgency in Colt's voice. "What? What is it?"

"Lookit the Shuttle!"

Turning so rapidly that he bounced his shoulder into the tank, Kinsman peered out toward the spacecraft, some seventy-five meters away from them.

"They've closed the payload bay doors. Why the hell would they do that?"

Colt jetted down the length of the tank, stopping himself as neatly as an ice skater with a countering puff of cold gas from the thruster gun. Kinsman reached out and touched his arm.

"What the hell are they doing?" he wondered.

Colt said, "Whatever it is, I don't like it."

Suddenly a cloud of white gas jetted from the Shuttle's nose. The spacecraft dipped down and away from them. Another soundless gasp from the reaction jets back near the tail and the Shuttle slewed sideways.

"What the hell they doin'?" Colt shouted.

The Shuttle was sliding away from them, scuttling crabwise farther from the propellant tanks where they were stranded.

"They got trouble! Somethin's wrong . . ."

Kinsman punched the stud on his wrist keyboard for the flight deck's radio frequency.

"Kinsman to flight deck. What's wrong? Why are you maneuvering?"

No answer. The Shuttle was dwindling away from them rapidly now.

"Jesus Christ!" Colt yelled. "They're gonna leave us here!"

"Captain Howard!" Kinsman said into his helmet mike, trying to keep the tremble out of his voice. "Major Podalski! Major Pierce . . . come in! This is Kinsman. Colt and I are still outside the spacecraft! Answer, please!"

Nothing but the crackling hum of the radio's carrier wave.

"Those sonsofbitches are stranding us!"

Kinsman watched the Shuttle getting smaller and smaller. It seemed to be hurtling madly away from them, although the rational part of his mind told him that the spacecraft was only drifting; it hadn't fired its main engines at all. But the difference in relative velocities between the tankage assembly and the Shuttle was enough to make the two fly apart from each other.

Colt was moving. Kinsman saw that he was aiming his thruster gun.

Grabbing Colt's arm to stop him, Kinsman snapped, "NO!" Then he realized that his suit radio was still on the flight deck's frequency.

Banging the stud on his wrist, Kinsman said, "Don't panic. Remember? That's what Howard warned us about."

"We gotta get back to the Shuttle, man! We can't hang here!"

"You'll never reach the Shuttle with the maneuvering gun," Kinsman said. "Not enough range."

"But something's gone wrong . . ."

Kinsman looked out toward the dwindling speck that was the Shuttle. It was hard to see now against the glaring white of the Earth. They were passing over the vast cloud-covered expanse of Antarctica. With a shudder, Kinsman felt the cold seeping into him.

"Listen. Maybe nothing's gone wrong. Maybe this is their idea of a joke."

"A joke?"

"Maybe that's what Howard was trying to tell us."

"That's crazy . . ."

"No. They've been sticking it to us all through the mission, haven't they? Pierce is a snotty bastard, and this looks like something he might dream up."

"You don't joke around with lives, man!"

"We're safe enough; got four hours' worth of air. As long as we don't panic we'll be okay. That's what Howard was trying to tell us."

"But why the hell would they do something like this?" Colt's voice sounded calmer, as if he wanted to believe Kinsman.

Your paranoia's deserted you just when you need it most, Kinsman thought. He answered, "How many times have they called us hotshots, the Goldust Twins? We're the two top men on the list. They just want to rub our noses in the dirt a little . . . just like the upper classmen used to do at the Academy."

"You think so?"

It's either that or we're dead. Kinsman glanced at the digital watch set into his wrist keyboard. "They allowed three hours for our task. They'll be back before that time is up. Less than two hours."

"And if they're not?"

"Then we can panic."

"Lotta good it'll do then."

"Won't do much good for us now, either. We're stranded here until they come back for us."

"Bastards," Colt muttered. Now he was convinced.

With a sudden grin, Kinsman said, "Yeah, but maybe we can turn the tables on them."

"How?"

"Follow me, my man."

Without using his thruster gun, Kinsman clambered up the side of "their" propellant tank and then drifted slowly into the nest created by the other six tanks.

Like a pair of skin divers floating in the midst of a pod of whales, Colt and Kinsman hung in emptiness, surrounded by the big, curving, hollow tanks.

"Now when they come back they won't be able to see us on radar," Kinsman explained. "And the tanks ought to block our suit-to-suit chatter, so they won't hear us, either. That should throw a scare into them."

"They'll think we panicked and jetted away."

"Right."

"Maybe that's what they want."

"Maybe. But think of the explaining they'd have to do back at Vandenberg if they lost the two of us. Four officers' careers, down the drain."

Colt giggled. "Almost worth dyin' for."

"We'll let them know we're here," Kinsman said, "after

they've worked up enough of a sweat. I'm not dying for anyone's joke—not even my own."

They waited, while the immense panorama of the Earth flowed beneath them and the stern stars watched silently. They waited and they talked.

"I thought she split because we were down in Houston and Huntsville and she couldn't take it," Colt was saying. "She was white, you know, and the pressure was on her a lot more than me."

"I didn't think Houston was that prejudiced. And Huntsville struck me as being pretty cosmopolitan . . ."

"Yeah? Try it with my color, man. Try buying some flesh-colored Band-Aids, you wanna see how cosmopolitan everybody is."

"Guess I really don't know much about it," Kinsman admitted. "Must've been pretty rough on you."

"Yeah, but now that I think back on it, we were having our troubles in Colorado, too. I'm not an easy man to live with."

"Who the hell is?"

Colt chuckled. "You are, man. You're supercool. Never saw anybody so much in charge of himself. Like a bucket of ice water."

Ice water? Me? "You're mistaking slow reflexes for self-control."

"Yeah, I bet. Is it true you're a Quaker?"

"Used to be," he said automatically, trying to shut out the image of his father. "When I was a kid." *Change the subject!* "I was when that damned Shuttle started moving away from us. A real Quaker."

With a laugh, Colt asked, "How come you're not married? Good-looking, rich . . ."

"Too busy having fun. Flying, training for this . . . I've got no time for marriage. Besides, I like girls too much to marry one of them."

"You wanna get laid but you don't wanna get screwed."

"Something like that. Like you said, there's lots of chicks in the world."

"Yeah. Can't concentrate on a career and a marriage at the same time. Leastways, I can't."

"Not if you want to be really good at either one," Kinsman agreed. *Oh, we are being so wise. And not looking at our watches. Cool, man. Supercool.* But out beyond the curving bulk of the propellant tanks the sky was empty except for the solemn stars.

"I don't just wanna be good," Colt was saying. "I got to be the best. I got to show these honkies that a black man is better than they are."

"You're not going to win many friends that way."

"Don't give a shit. I'm gonna be a general someday. Then you'll see how many friends I get."

Kinsman shook his head, chuckling. "A general. Jeez, you've sure got some long-range plans in your head."

"Damn right! My brother, he's all hot and fired up to be a revolutionary. Goin' around the world looking for wars to fight against colonialists and injustice. Wanted me to join the underground here in the States and fight for justice against The Man."

"Why doesn't he stay in the States?" Kinsman asked.

"The FBI damn near grabbed him a year or so back."

"What for?"

"Hit a bank . . . to raise money for the People's Liberation Army."

"He's one of those?"

"Not anymore. There ain't no PLA anymore. Most of 'em are dead, the rest scattered. I watched my brother playin' cops and robbers . . . didn't look like much fun to me. So I decided I ain't gonna fight The Man. I'm gonna *be* The Man."

"If you can't beat 'em . . ."

"Looks like I'm joinin' 'em, yeah," Colt said, with real passion building in his voice. "But I'm just workin' my way up the ladder to get to the top. Then *I'll* start givin' the orders. And there are others like me, too. We're gonna have a black President one of these days, you know."

"And you'll be his Chief of Staff."

"Could be."

"Where does that leave us . . ."

A small sharp beeping sound shrilled in Kinsman's earphones. *Emergency signal!* Automatically, both he and Colt switched to the Shuttle's flight deck frequency.

"Kinsman! Colt! Can you hear me? This is Major Jakes. Do you read me?"

The Major's voice sounded distant, distorted by ragged static, and very concerned.

Kinsman held up a hand to keep Colt silent. Then, switching to their suit-to-suit frequency, he whispered, "They can't see us in here among the tanks. And they haven't picked up our suit-to-suit talk. The tanks are blocking it."

"We're getting their freak scattered off the tanks?" It was a rhetorical question.

"Kinsman! Colt! Do you read me? This is Major Jakes."

Their two helmeted heads were close enough for Kinsman to see the grin glittering on Colt's dark face.

"Let 'em eat shit for a coupla minutes, huh?"

"Right."

The Shuttle pulled into view and seemed to hover about a hundred meters away from the tanks. Switching back to the flight deck's frequency, the two lieutenants heard:

"Pierce, goddammit, if those two kids have been lost I'll put you up for a murder charge."

"Now you were in on it too, Harry."

Howard's voice cut in. "I'm suited up. Going out the airlock."

"Should we get one of the trainees out to help search for them?" Pierce's voice.

"You've got two of them missing now," Jakes snarled. "Isn't that enough? How about *you* getting your ass outside to help?"

"Me? But I'm . . ."

"I think it would be a good idea," said a new voice, with such weighty authority that Kinsman knew it had to be the Mission Commander, Major Podolski. Among the three majors he was the longest in Air Force service, and therefore as senior as God.

"Eh, yessir," Pierce answered quickly.

"And you too, Jakes. You were all in on this, and it hasn't turned out to be very funny."

Colt and Kinsman, holding on to one of the struts that connected the empty tanks, could barely suppress their laughter as they watched the Shuttle's cargo doors swing slowly open and three spacesuited figures emerge.

"Maybe we oughtta play dead," Colt whispered.

"No. Enough is too much. Let's go out now and greet our rescuers."

They worked their way clear of the tanks and drifted into the open.

"There they are!" The voice sounded so jubilant in Kinsman's earphones that he couldn't tell who said it.

"Are you all right?"

"Is everything . . ."

"We're fine, sir," Kinsman said calmly. "But we were beginning to wonder if the spacecraft malfunctioned."

Dead silence for several moments.

"Uh, no . . ." Jakes said as he jetted up to Colt and Kinsman. "We . . . uh, well, we sort of played a little prank on you two fellas."

"Nothing personal," Pierce added.

Sure, Kinsman thought. *Nothing personal in getting bitten by a snake, either.*

They were great buddies now, as they jetted back to the Shuttle. Kinsman played it straight, keeping himself very formal and correct. Colt fell into line and followed Kinsman's lead.

If we were a couple of hysterical, jibbering, scared tenderfeet, they'd be laughing their heads off at us. But now the shaft has turned.

Once through the airlock and into the passenger compartment, Colt and Kinsman were grabbed by the four other trainees. Chattering, laughing with them, they helped the two lieutenants out of their helmets and suits. Pierce, Jakes, and Howard unsuited without help.

Finally, Kinsman turned to Major Pierce and said, tight-lipped, "Sir, I must make a report to the Commanding Officer."

"Podolski knows all about . . ."

Looking Pierce in the eye, Kinsman said, "I don't mean Major Podolski, sir. I mean Colonel Murdock. Or, if necessary, the Judge Advocate General."

Everything stopped. Jill Meyers, who had somehow wound up with Kinsman's helmet, let it slip from her fingers. It simply hung there in midair as she watched, wide-eyed and open-mouthed. The only sound in the compartment was the faint hum of electrical equipment.

"The . . . Judge Advocate General?" Pierce looked slightly green.

"Yessir. Or I could telephone my uncle, the senior Senator from Pennsylvania." Now even the trainees looked scared.

"Now see here, Kinsman," Jakes started.

Turning to face the Major, close enough to smell the fear on him, Kinsman said, "This may have seemed like a joke to you, sir, but it has the look of racial discrimination about it. And it was a damned dangerous stunt. *And* a waste of the taxpayers' money, too."

"You can't . . ." Pierce somehow lost his voice as Kinsman turned back toward him.

"The first thing I must do is to see Major Podolski," Kinsman said evenly. "He's involved in this, too."

With a resigned shrug, Jakes pointed toward the ladder.

Kinsman glanced at Colt, and the two of them glided over to the ladder and swam up to the flight deck, leaving absolute silence behind them.

Major Podolski was a big, florid-faced man with an old-style RAF moustache. His bulk barely fit into the Commander's left-hand seat. He was half-turned in it, one heavy arm draped across the seat's back, as Kinsman rose through the hatch.

"I've been listening to what you had to say down there, Lieutenant, and if you think . . ."

But Kinsman put a finger to his lips.

Podolski frowned.

Sitting lightly on the Payload Specialist's chair, behind the Commander, Kinsman let himself grin.

"Sir," he whispered, "I thought one good joke deserved another. My uncle was voted out of the Senate years ago."

He could see a struggle of emotions play across Podolski's face. Finally a curious smile won out. "I see . . . you want them to stew in their own juices for a few minutes, eh?"

Glancing up at Colt, Kinsman answered, "Not exactly, sir. I want reparations."

"Repa . . . what're you talking about, Mister?"

"This is the first time Frank and I have been allowed up on the flight deck."

"So?"

"So we want to sit up here while you fly her back through re-entry and landing."

Podolski looked as if he had just swallowed a lemon, whole. "Oh you do? And maybe you want to take over the controls, too."

Colt bobbed his head vigorously. "Yes, *sir!*"

"Don't make me laugh."

"Sir . . . I meant it about the Judge Advocate General. And I have another uncle . . ."

"Never mind!" Podolski snapped. "You can sit up here during re-entry and landing. And that's all! You sit and watch and be quiet and forget this whole stupid incident."

"That's all we want, sir," Kinsman said. He turned toward Colt, who was beaming.

"You guys'll go far in the Air Force," Podolski grumbled. "A pair of smartasses with the guts of burglars. Just what the fuck this outfit needs." But there was a trace of a grin flitting around his moustache.

"Glad you think so, sir," said Kinsman.

"Okay . . . we're due to break orbit in two hours. You

guys might as well sit up here through the whole routine and watch how it's done."

"Thank you, sir."

The Major's expression sobered. "Only . . . who's going to tell Pierce and Howard that they've got to sit downstairs with the trainees?"

"Oh I will," Colt said, with the biggest smile of all. "I'll be glad to!"

AGE 27

Looking like a middle linebacker for the Pittsburgh Steelers, Joe Tenny sat in the cool shadows of the Astro Motel's bar. Swarthy, barrel-shaped, his scowling face clamped on a smoldering cigar, Tenny would never be taken by the other drinkers for that rarest of all birds: a good engineer who is also a good military officer.

"Afternoon, Major."

Tenny turned on his stool to see old Cy Calder, the dean of the press service reporters covering Vandenberg and Edwards Air Force Bases—and the fledgling Air Force astronaut corps.

"Hi!" said Tenny. "Whatcha drinking?"

"I'm working," Calder answered with dignity. But he settled his once-lanky frame onto the next stool.

"Double scotch," Tenny called to the bartender. "And refill mine."

"An officer and a gentleman," murmured Calder. His voice was gravelly, his face seamed with age.

As the bartender slid the drinks down to them, Tenny said, "You wanna know who got the assignment?"

"I told you I'm working."

Tenny grinned. "Keep your mouth shut 'til tomorrow?

Murdock's gonna make the official announcement at his press conference."

"If you can save me the tedium of listening to the good Colonel for two hours merely to get a single name from his pudgy lips, I'll buy the next round, shine your shoes for a month, and arrange to lose an occasional poker pot to you."

"The hell you will!"

Calder shrugged. Tenny took a long pull on his drink. "No leaks ahead of time? Promise?"

Calder sipped at his drink, then said, "On my word as an ex-officer, former gentleman, and fugitive from Social Security."

"Okay. But keep it quiet until Murdock's announcement. It's gonna be Kinsman."

Calder put his glass down on the bar carefully. "Chester A. Kinsman, the pride of the Air Force? That's hard to believe."

"Murdock picked him."

"I know this mission is strictly for publicity," Calder said, "but Kinsman? In orbit for three days with *National Geographic*'s prettiest female? Does Murdock want publicity or a paternity suit?"

"Come on, Chet's okay . . ."

"Really? From the stories I hear about him, he's cut a swath right across the Los Angeles basin and has been working his way toward the Bay area."

Tenny countered, "He's young and good-looking. The girls haven't had many unattached astronauts to play with. NASA's gang is a bunch of old farts compared to these kids. And Chet's one of the best of them, no fooling."

"Wasn't he going around with that folksinger . . . Diane something-or-other, for a while?"

"Never mind. You know what he did over at Edwards? He and Frank Colt have built a biplane, an honest-to-God replica of an old Spad fighter. From the wheels up. He's a solid citizen."

"Yes, and I hear he's been playing Red Baron with it.

Who do you think buzzed that airliner last week? And Colonel Murdock's helicopter . . ."

He was cut off by a burst of talk and laughter. Half a dozen lean, lithe young men in Air Force blues—with captain's shining new double silver bars on their shoulders—trotted down the carpeted stairs that led into the bar.

"There they are," said Tenny. "You can ask Chet about it yourself."

Kinsman was grinning broadly at the moment, as he and the five other astronauts grabbed chairs in one corner of the bar and called their orders to the bartender.

Calder took his drink and headed for their table, followed by Major Tenny.

"Hold it," Frank Colt snapped. "Here comes the press."

"Tight security."

"Why, boys"—Calder tried to make his rasping voice sound hurt—"don't you trust me?"

Tenny pushed a chair toward the newsman and took another one for himself. Straddling it, he told the captains, "It's okay. I spilled it to him."

"How much he pay you, boss?"

"That's between him and me."

As the bartender brought a tray of drinks, Calder said, "Let the Fourth Estate pay for this round, gentlemen. I want to pump some information out of you."

"That might take a lot of rounds."

To Kinsman, Calder said, "Congratulations, my boy. Colonel Murdock must think very highly of you."

They all burst out laughing. "Murdock?" Kinsman said. "You should've seen his face when he told me I was it!"

"Looked like he was sucking on lemons."

Tenny explained. "The choice for this flight was made by computer. Murdock wanted to be absolutely fair, so he put everybody's performance ratings and personality profiles into the computer—and out came Kinsman's name."

"It was a fix," Colt muttered, mainly for effect.

"If he hadn't made so much noise about being so damned

impartial," Tenny went on, "Murdock could've reshuffled the cards and tried again. But I was right there when the machine finished its run, so he couldn't back out of it."

"We was robbed," said Smitty.

Calder grinned. "So the computer thinks highly of you, Captain Kinsman. I suppose that's still some kind of honor."

"More like a privilege. I've been watching that *National Geographic* chick through her training. Ripe."

"She'll look even better up in orbit."

"Once she takes off her pressure suit . . . et cetera."

"Hey, y'know, nobody's ever done it in orbit."

"Yeah . . . free fall, zero gravity."

Kinsman looked thoughtful. "Adds a new dimension to the problem, doesn't it?"

"Three-dimensional." Tenny took the cigar butt from his mouth and laughed.

Calder got up slowly from his chair and silenced the others. Looking down fondly on Kinsman, he said:

"My boy—many years ago, I imagine it was before you were even born, I happened to interview a charter member of the Mile High Club. He was an intrepid aviator who, in 1915, at an altitude of precisely 5,280 feet, while circling St. Paul's cathedral, successfully penetrated an Army nurse. This was in an open cockpit, mind you. He achieved his success despite fogged goggles, cramped working quarters, and a severe case of windburn."

They all laughed.

"Since then," Calder went on, "there's been damned little to look forward to. The skin divers claimed a new frontier, but in fact they are retrogressing. Any silly-ass dolphin can do it in the water.

"But you have something new going for you: weightlessness. Floating around in free-fall, chasing tail in three dimensions. It beggars the imagination!"

Even Tenny looked impressed.

"Captain Kinsman, I pass the torch to you. To the founder of the Zero Gee Club!"

As one man, they rose and silently toasted Kinsman.

When they sat down again, Major Tenny burst their balloon. "You guys haven't given Murdock credit for much brains. You don't think he's gonna let Chet go up with that broad all alone, do you? The Manta ain't as big as a Shuttle, but it still holds three people."

Kinsman's face fell, but the others' lit up.

"It's gonna be a three-man mission!"

"Two men and the blonde!"

Tenny warned, "Now don't start drooling. Murdock wants a chaperone, not a gang bang."

It was Kinsman who understood first. Slouching back in his chair, chin sinking to his chest, he muttered, "Goddammitall . . . he's sending Jill along."

A collective groan.

"Murdock made up his mind an hour ago," Tenny said. "He was stuck with you, Chet, so he hit on the chaperone idea. He's giving you some real chores to do, too. Keep you busy. Like mating the power pod."

"Jill Meyers," said Art Douglas, with real disappointment on his face. "At least he could've sent Mary O'Hara. She's fun."

"Jill's as qualified as you guys are, and she's been taking this gal through her training. I'll bet she knows more about this mission than any of you do."

"She would."

"In fact," Tenny added maliciously, "she *is* the senior captain among you rocket jockeys. So show some respect."

Kinsman had only one comment. "Shit."

The key to the Air Force's role in space was summed up in two words: *quick reaction*. The massive Space Shuttle that NASA developed was fine for missions that could be planned long in advance, but the Air Force wanted and needed a spacecraft that was smaller and more easily put into operation. The smaller, delta-shaped Manta was the answer. Launched by solid rocket boosters, carrying no more than three astronauts, the Manta could put Air Force personnel into orbit within hours of a decision to go.

The bone-rattling roar and vibration of lift-off suddenly died away. Sitting in his contour seat, scanning the banks of dials and gauges a few centimeters before his eyes, Kinsman could feel the pressure and tension slacken. Not back to normal. To zero. He was no longer flattened against his seat, but touching it only lightly, almost floating in it, restrained only by his harness.

He had stopped counting how many times he had felt weightlessness after his tenth orbital mission. Yet he still smiled inside his helmet.

Without thinking about it, he touched a control stud on the chair's armrest. A maneuvering jet fired briefly and the ponderous, overawing bulk of Earth slid into view through the port in front of him. It curved huge and awesome, blue mostly, but wrapped in dazzlingly pure white clouds, beautiful, serene, shining.

Kinsman could have watched it forever, but he heard the sounds of motion through his earphones. The two women were stirring behind him. The Manta's cabin made the Shuttle seem roomy: their three seats were shoehorned in among racks of instruments and equipment.

Jill was officially second pilot and biomedical officer on this mission. The photographer, Linda Symmes, was simply a passenger occupying the third seat, beside Jill.

Kinsman's earphones crackled with a disembodied link from Earth. "AF-9, we have confirmed you in orbit. Trajectory normal. All systems green."

"Check," Kinsman said into his helmet mike.

The voice, already starting to fade, switched to ordinary conversational speech. "Looks like you're right on the money, Chet. We'll get the orbital parameters out of the computer and have 'em for you by the time you pass Woomera. You're set up for the rendezvous maneuver on the second orbit."

"Roger, big V. Everything here on the board's in the green."

"Rog. Vandenberg out." Faintly. "And hey . . . good luck, Founding Father."

Kinsman grinned at that. He slid his faceplate up, loosened his harness, and turned in the seat. "Okay, ladies, you can take off your helmets if you want to."

Jill snapped her visor open and started unlocking the helmet's neck seal.

"I'll go first," she said to Linda, "and then I can help you with yours."

"Sure you don't need any help?" Kinsman offered.

Jill pulled her helmet off. "I've had more time in orbit than you have, Chet. And shouldn't you be paying attention to the controls?"

So this is how it's going to be, Kinsman thought.

Jill's face was round and plain and bright as a new penny. Snub nose, wide mouth, short hair of undistinguished brown. Kinsman knew that under her pressure suit was a figure that could most charitably be described as ordinary.

Linda Symmes was entirely another matter. She had lifted her visor and was staring out at him with wide blue eyes that combined feminine curiosity with a hint of helplessness. She was tall, nearly Kinsman's own height, with thick, honey-colored hair and a body that he had already memorized down to the last curve.

In her sweet, high voice she said, "I think I'm going to be sick."

"Oh for . . ."

Jill reached into the compartment between their two seats. "I'll take care of this. You stick to the controls."

And she whipped a white plastic bag open and stuck it over Linda's face.

Shuddering at the thought of what could happen in zero gravity, Kinsman turned back to the control panel. He pulled his faceplate shut and turned up the air blower in his suit, trying to cut off the obscene sounds of Linda's struggles.

"For Chrissake," he yelled to Jill, "unplug her suit radio! You want me chucking up all over, too?"

"AF-9, this is Woomera."

Trying to blank his mind to what was going on behind him, Kinsman thumbed the switch on his communications panel. "Go ahead, Woomera."

For the next hour Kinsman thanked the gods that he had plenty of work to do. He matched the orbit of the Manta with that of the Air Force orbiting laboratory, which had been up for nearly a year, intermittently occupied by two- or three-astronaut teams.

The lab was a fat cylinder, silhouetted against the brilliant white of the cloud-decked Earth. As he pulled the Manta close, Kinsman could see the antennas and airlock and other odd pieces of gear that had accumulated in the lab. *Looking more like a junk heap every trip.* Riding behind it, unconnected in any way, was the squat cone of the new power pod.

Kinsman circled the lab once, using judicious squeezes of the maneuvering jets. He touched a command signal switch and the lab's rendezvous radar beacon came to life, announced by a green light on his control panel.

"All systems green," he said to ground control. "Everything looks okay."

"Roger, Niner. You are cleared for docking."

This was a bit more delicate. *Be helpful if Jill could read off the computer . . .*

"Distance, eighty-eight meters," Jill's voice pronounced firmly in his earphones. "Approach angle . . ."

Kinsman instinctively turned his head, but his helmet cut off any possible sight of her. "Hey, how's your patient?"

"Empty. I gave her a sedative. She's out."

"Okay," Kinsman said. "Let's get docked."

He inched the spacecraft into the docking collar on one

end of the lab, locked on and saw the panel lights confirm that the docking was secure.

"Better get Sleeping Beauty zippered up," he told Jill as he touched the buttons that extended the flexible access tube from the hatch over their heads to the main hatch of the lab. The lights on the panel turned from amber to green when the tube locked its fittings around the lab's hatch.

Jill said, "I'm supposed to check the tube."

"Stay put. I'll do it." Sealing his faceplate shut, Kinsman unbuckled and rose effortlessly out of the seat to bump his helmet lightly against the overhead hatch.

"You two both buttoned tight?"

"Yes."

"Keep an eye on the air gauge." He cracked the hatch open a few millimeters.

"Pressure's okay. No red lights."

Nodding, Kinsman pushed the hatch open all the way. He pulled himself up and into the shoulder-wide tube, propelling himself down its curving length by a few flicks of his gloved fingers against the ribbed walls.

Light and easy, he reminded himself. *No big motions. No sudden moves.*

When he reached the laboratory hatch he slowly rotated, like an underwater swimmer doing a lazy rollover, and inspected every inch of the tube seal in the light of his helmet lamp. Satisfied that it was locked in place and airtight, he opened the lab hatch and pulled himself inside. Carefully, he touched his slightly-adhesive boots to the plastic flooring and stood upright. His arms tended to float out, but they touched the equipment racks on either side of the narrow central passageway. Kinsman turned on the lab's interior lights, checked the air supply, pressure, and temperature gauges, then shuffled back to the hatch and pushed himself through the tube again.

He re-entered the Manta upside-down and had to contort himself in slow motion around the pilot's seat to regain a "normal" attitude.

"Lab's okay," he said finally. "Now how the hell do we get her through the tube?"

Jill had already unbuckled the harness over Linda's shoulders. "You pull, I'll push. She'll bend around the corners all right."

And she did.

The laboratory was about the size and shape of the interior of a small transport plane. On one side, nearly its entire length was taken up by instrument racks, control equipment, and the computer, humming almost inaudibly behind lightweight plastic panels. Across the narrow separating aisle were the crew stations: control desk, two observation ports, biology and astrophysics benches. At the far end, behind a discreet curtain, was the head and a single hammock.

Kinsman sat at the control desk, in his fatigues now, one leg hooked around the webbed chair's single supporting column to keep him from floating off. He was running a formal checkout of the lab's life support systems: air, water, heat, electrical power. All green lights on the main panel. Communications gear? Green. The radar screen to his left showed a single large blip close by—the power pod.

He looked up as Jill came through the curtain from the bunkroom. She was still in her pressure suit, with only the helmet removed.

"How is she?"

Looking tired, Jill answered, "Okay. Still sleeping. I think she'll be all right when she wakes up."

"She'd better be. I'm not going to have a wilting flower around here. I'll abort the mission."

"Give her a chance, Chet. She just lost her cookies when free-fall hit her. All the training in the world can't prepare you for those first few minutes."

Kinsman shook his head. *But it's fun!* he thought. *Like skiing. Like skydiving. Only better.*

Jill shuffled toward him, keeping a firm grip on the chairs in front of the work benches and the handholds set into the equipment racks.

Kinsman got up and pushed toward her. "Here, lemme help you out of that suit."

"I can do it myself."

"Shut up."

After several minutes, Jill was free of the bulky suit and sitting in one of the webbed chairs in her coverall fatigues. Ducking slightly because of the curving overhead, Kinsman glided into the galley. It was about half as wide as a phonebooth, but not as deep nor as tall.

"Coffee, tea, or milk?"

Jill grinned at him. "Orange juice."

He reached for a concentrate bag. "You're a tough girl to satisfy."

"No, I'm not. I'm easy to get along with. Just one of the fellas."

That's a dig, Kinsman recognized. *But who's it aimed at? And why?*

For the next couple of hours they checked out the lab's equipment in detail. Kinsman was reassembling one of the high-resolution cameras after cleaning it, parts hanging in midair all around him as he sat intently working, while Jill was nursing a straggly-looking philodendron that had been smuggled aboard months earlier and was now inching from the biology bench toward the ceiling light panels.

Linda pushed back the curtain from the sleeping area and stepped uncertainly into the main compartment.

Jill noticed her first. "Hi. How're you feeling?"

Kinsman looked up. She was in tight-fitting coveralls. He bounced out of his webchair, scattering camera parts in every direction.

"Are you all right?" he asked.

Smiling sheepishly, "I think so. I'm rather embarrassed . . ." Her voice was high and soft.

"Oh, that's all right," Kinsman said eagerly. "It happens to practically everybody. I got sick myself my first time in orbit."

"That," said Jill as she dodged a slowly-tumbling lens

that ricocheted gently off the ceiling, "is a little white lie, meant to make you feel at home."

Kinsman forced himself not to frown.

Jill added, "Chet, you'd better pick up those camera parts before they get so scattered you won't be able to find them all."

He wanted to snap an answer, thought better of it, and replied merely, "Right."

As he finished the job on the camera, he took a good look at Linda. The color was back in her face. She seemed steady, clear-eyed, not frightened or upset. *Maybe she'll be okay after all.* Jill made her a cup of tea, which she sipped from the lid's plastic spout.

Kinsman went to the control desk and scanned the mission schedule sheet.

"Hey, Jill, it's past your bedtime."

"I'm not sleepy," she said.

"Yeah, I know. But you've had a busy day, little girl. And tomorrow will be even busier. Now get your four hours and then I'll get mine. Got to be fresh for the mating."

"Mating?" Linda asked from her seat at the far end of the aisle, a good five strides from Kinsman. Then she remembered. "Oh . . . you mean linking the power package to the laboratory."

Suppressing half a dozen possible jokes, Kinsman nodded. "Extra-vehicular activity."

Jill reluctantly drifted off her webchair. "Okay, I'll sack in. I am tired, but I never seem to get really sleepy up here."

Wonder what kind of a briefing Murdock gave her? She's sure acting like a goddamned chaperone.

Jill shuffled into the sleeping area and pulled the curtain firmly shut. After a few minutes of silence, Kinsman turned to Linda.

"Alone at last."

She smiled back at him.

"Um, you just happen to be sitting where I've got to

install this camera." He nudged the finished hardware so that it floated gently toward her.

She got up slowly, carefully, and stood behind the chair, holding its back with both hands as if she were afraid of falling. Kinsman slid into the webchair and stopped the camera's slow-motion flight with one hand. Working on the fixture in the viewing port that it fit into, he asked:

"You really feel okay?"

"Yes, honestly."

"Think you'll be up to EVA tomorrow?"

"I hope so," she said. "I want to go outside with you."

I'd rather go inside with you. Kinsman grinned as he worked.

An hour later they were sitting side by side in front of the observation port, looking out at the curving bulk of Earth, the blue and white splendor of the cloud-covered Pacific. Kinsman had just reported to the Hawaii ground station. The mission flight plan was floating on a clipboard between the two of them. He was trying to study it, comparing the times when Jill would be sleeping against the long stretches between ground stations, when there could be no possibility of interruption.

"Is that land?" Linda asked, pointing to a thick band of clouds wrapping the horizon.

Looking up from the clipboard, Kinsman said, "South American coast. Chile."

"There's another tracking station there, isn't there?"

"NASA station, not part of our network. We only use Air Force stations."

"Why is that?"

Kinsman shrugged. "We're playing soldier. This is supposed to be strictly a military operation. Not that we do anything warlike. But we run as though there weren't any civilians around to help us. The usual hup-two-three crap."

She laughed. "You don't like the Air Force?"

"There's only one thing the Air Force has done lately that I'm in complete agreement with."

"What's that?"

"Bringing you up here."

The smile stayed on her face but her eyes moved away from him. "Now you sound like a soldier."

"Not an officer and a gentleman?"

She looked straight at him again. "Let's change the subject."

"Sure. Okay. You're here to get a story. Murdock wants us to get as much publicity as NASA gets. And the Pentagon wants to show the world that we don't have any weapons aboard. We're military, but *nice* military."

"And you?" Linda asked, serious now. "What do you want? How does an Air Force captain get into the space cadets?"

"By dint of personal valor. I thought it would be fun . . . until my first orbital flight. Now it's a way of life."

"Really? You like it that much? Why?"

Grinning, he answered, "Wait until we go outside. Then you'll see."

Jill came back into the main cabin precisely on schedule, and it was Kinsman's turn to sleep. He seldom had difficulty sleeping on Earth, never in orbit. But he wondered about Linda's reaction to being outside as he strapped on the pressure cuffs to his arms and legs. The medics insisted on them, claimed they exercised the cardiovascular system while you slept.

Damned stupid nuisance, Kinsman grumbled to himself. *Some ground-based MD's idea of how to make a name for himself.*

Finally he zippered himself into the nylon webbing of the cocoon-like hammock and shut his eyes. He could feel the cuffs pumping gently. His last conscious thought was a nagging worry that Linda would be terrified of EVA.

When he awoke and Linda took her turn in the hammock, he talked it over with Jill.

"I think she'll be all right, Chet. Don't hold those first few minutes against her."

"I don't know. There's only two kinds of people up here: you either love it or you're scared shitless. And you can't fake it. If she goes ape outside . . ."

"She won't," Jill said firmly. "Anyway, you'll be there to help her. She won't be going outside until you're finished with the mating job. She wanted to get pictures of you actually at work, but I told her she'll have to settle for a few posed shots."

Kinsman nodded. But the worry persisted. *I wonder if Calder's army nurse was scared of flying?*

He was pulling on his boots, wedging his free foot against an equipment rack to keep from floating off, when Linda returned from her sleep.

"Ready for a walk around the block?" he asked her.

She smiled and nodded without the slightest hesitation. "I'm looking forward to it. Can I get a few shots of you while you zipper up your suit?"

Maybe she'll be okay.

At last he was sealed into the pressure suit. Linda and Jill stood back as Kinsman clumped to the airlock hatch. It was set into the floor at the end of the cabin where the Manta was docked. With Jill helping him, Kinsman eased down into the airlock and shut the hatch. The metal chamber was coffin-sized. He had to half bend to move around in it. He checked out his suit once again, then pumped the air out of the chamber. Now he was ready to open the outer hatch.

It was beneath his feet, but as it slid open to reveal the stars, Kinsman's weightless orientation flip-flopped, like an optical illusion, and he suddenly felt that he was standing on his head.

"Going out now," he said into the helmet mike.

"Okay," Jill's voice responded.

Carefully he eased himself through the open hatch, holding onto its edge with one gloved hand as he slid fully outside, the way a swimmer holds the rail for a

moment before kicking free into the deep water. *Outside.*
Swinging his body around slowly, he took in the immense
beauty of Earth, overpoweringly bright even through his
tinted visor. Beyond its curving limb was the darkness of
infinity, with the beckoning stars watching gravely.

Alone now. His own tight, self-contained universe.
Independent of everything and everybody. He could cut
the lifegiving umbilical line that linked him with the
laboratory and float off by himself forever. And be dead in
two minutes. *Ay, there's the rub.*

Instead, he unhooked the tiny gas gun from his waist
and, trailing the umbilical, squirted himself over toward
the power pod. It was riding smoothly behind the lab, a
squat, truncated cone, shorter but fatter than the lab
itself, one edge brilliantly lit by the Sun, the rest of it
bathed in the softer light reflected from the dayside of
Earth below.

Kinsman's job was to inspect the power pod, check its
equipment, and then mate it to the electrical system of
the laboratory. There was no need to connect the two
bodies physically, except to link a pair of power lines
between them. Everything necessary for the task—tools,
power lines, checkout instruments—had been built into the
pod, waiting for an astronaut to use them.

It would have been simple work on Earth. In zero gee
it was complicated. The slightest motion of any part of
your body started you drifting. You had to fight against
all the built-in mannerisms of a lifetime; had to work
constantly to stay in place. It was easy to become exhausted in zero gee.

But Kinsman accepted all this with hardly a conscious
thought. He worked slowly, methodically, using as little
motion as possible, letting himself drift slightly until a
more-or-less natural body motion counteracted and pulled
him back in the opposite direction. *Ride the waves, slow
and easy.* There was a rhythm to his work, the natural
dreamlike rhythm of weightlessness.

His earphones were silent; he said nothing. All he heard was the purring of the suit's air blowers and his own steady breathing. All he saw was his work.

Finally he jetted back to the laboratory, towing the pair of thick cables. He found the connectors waiting for them on the sidewall of the lab and inserted the cable plugs. *I pronounce you lab and power source.* He inspected the checkout lights alongside the connectors. All green. *May you produce many kilowatts.*

Swinging from handhold to handhold along the length of the lab, he made his way back to the airlock.

"Okay, it's finished. How's Linda doing?"

Jill answered, "She's all set."

"Send her out."

She came out slowly, uncertain, wavering feet sliding out first from the bulbous airlock. It reminded Kinsman of a film he had seen of a whale giving birth.

"Welcome to the real world," he said once her head cleared the airlock hatch.

She turned to answer him and he heard her gasp and he knew that now he liked her.

"It's . . . it's . . ."

"Staggering," Kinsman suggested. "And look at you—no hands!"

She was floating freely, pressure suit laden with camera gear, umbilical flexing easily behind her. Kinsman couldn't see her face through the tinted visor, but he could hear the awe in her voice, even in her breathing.

"I've never seen anything so absolutely overwhelming . . ."

And then suddenly she was all business, reaching for a camera, snapping away at the Earth and stars and distant Moon, rapid fire. She moved too fast and started to tumble. Kinsman jetted over and steadied her, holding her by the shoulders.

"Hey, take it easy. They're not going away. You've got lots of time."

"I want to get some shots of you, and the lab. Can you

go over by the pod and go through some of the motions of your work on it?"

Kinsman posed for her, answered her questions, rescued a camera when she fumbled it out of her hands and couldn't reach it as it drifted away.

"Judging distances is a little wacky out here," he said as he handed the camera back to her.

Jill called them twice and ordered them back inside. "Chet, you're already fifteen minutes over the schedule limit!"

"There's plenty slop in the schedule; we can stay out a while longer."

"You're going to get her exhausted."

"I really feel fine," Linda said, her voice lyrical.

"How much more film do you have?" Kinsman asked her.

Without needing to look at the camera, she answered, "Six more shots."

"Okay. We'll come in when the film runs out, Jill."

"You're going to be in darkness in another five minutes."

Turning to Linda, who was floating upside-down with the cloud-decked Earth behind her, he said, "Save your film for the sunset, then shoot like hell when it comes."

"The sunset? What'll I focus on?"

"You'll know when it happens. Just watch."

It came fast, but she was equal to it. As the lab swung in its orbit toward Earth's night shadow, the Sun dropped to the horizon and shot off a spectacular few moments of the purest reds and oranges and finally a heart-catching blue. Kinsman watched in silence, hearing Linda's breath going faster and faster as she worked the camera.

Then they were in darkness. Kinsman flicked on his helmet lamp. Linda was just hanging there, camera still in hand.

"It's . . . impossible to describe." Her voice sounded empty, drained. "If I hadn't seen it . . . if I didn't get it on film, I don't think I'd be able to convince myself that I wasn't dreaming."

Jill's voice rasped in his earphones. "Chet, get inside! This is against every safety reg, being outside in the dark."

He looked toward the lab. Lights were visible along its length and the ports were lighted from within. Otherwise he could barely make out its shape, even though it was only a few meters away.

"Okay, okay. Turn on the airlock lights so we can see the hatch."

Linda was still bubbling about their view outside long after they had pulled off their pressure suits and eaten sandwiches and cookies.

"Have you ever been out there?" she asked Jill.

Perched on the biology bench's edge, near the mice colony, Jill nodded curtly. "Eight times."

"Isn't it spectacular? I hope the pictures come out; some of my settings . . ."

"They'll be all right," Jill said. "And if they're not, we've got a backlog of photos you can use."

"Oh, but they wouldn't have the shots of Chet working on the power pod."

Jill shrugged. "Aren't you going to take more photos in here? If you want to get some pictures of real space veterans, you ought to snap the mice here. They've been up here for six months now, living and raising families. And they don't make a fuss about it, either."

"Well, some of us do exciting things," Kinsman said, "and some of us tend mice."

Jill glowered at him.

Glancing at his wristwatch, Kinsman said, "Ladies, it's my sack time. I've had a very trying day: mechanic, tourist guide, cover boy. Work, work, work."

He glided past Linda with a smile, kept it for Jill as he went by her. She was still glaring.

When he woke up again and went back into the main cabin, Jill was talking pleasantly with Linda as the two of them stood over the microscope and specimen rack of the biology bench.

Linda saw him first. "Oh, hi. Jill's been showing me the

spores she's studying. And I photographed the mice. Maybe they'll go on the cover instead of you."

Kinsman grinned. "She's been poisoning your mind against me." But to himself he wondered, *What the hell has Jill been telling her about me?*

Jill drifted over to the control desk, picked up the clipboard with the mission log on it, and tossed it lightly toward Kinsman.

"Ground control says the power pod checks out all okay," she said. "You did a good job."

"Thanks." He reached out and gathered in the clipboard. "Whose turn in the sack is it?"

"Mine," Jill answered.

"Okay. Anything special cooking?"

"No. Everything's on schedule. Next data transmission comes up in twelve minutes. Kodiak station."

Kinsman nodded. "Sleep tight."

Once Jill had shut the curtain to the bunkroom, Kinsman carried the mission log to the control desk and sat down. Linda stayed at the biology bench, about three paces away.

He checked the instrument board with a quick glance, then turned to Linda. "Well, now do you know what I meant about this being a way of life?"

"I think so. It's so different . . ."

"It's the real thing. Complete freedom. Brave new world. After ten minutes of EVA, everything else is just toothpaste."

"It certainly was exciting."

"More than that. It's *living*. Being on the ground is a drag. Even flying a plane is dull now. This is where the fun is . . . this is where you can feel alive. It's as close to heaven as anyone's gotten."

"You're really serious?"

"Damned right. I've been thinking of asking Murdock for a transfer to NASA duty. Air Force missions don't include the Moon, and I'd like to walk around on the new world, see the sights."

She smiled at him. "I'm afraid I'm not that enthusiastic."

"Wait. Think about it for a minute. Up here, you're free, really free, for the first time in your life. All the laws and rules and prejudices that they've been dumping on us all our lives—they're all *down there*. Up here it's a new start. You can be yourself and do your own thing . . . and nobody can tell you differently."

"As long as somebody provides you with air and food and water and . . ."

"That's the physical end of it, sure. We're living in a microcosm, courtesy of the aerospace industry and AFSC. But there're no strings on us. The brass can't make us follow their rules. We're writing the rule books ourselves. For the first time since 1776 we're writing new social rules."

Linda looked thoughtful now. Kinsman couldn't tell if she were genuinely impressed by his line, or if she knew what he was trying to lead up to. He turned back to the control desk and studied the mission flight plan again.

He had carefully considered all the possible opportunities, and narrowed them down to two. *Both of them tomorrow, over the Indian Ocean. Forty-five minutes between ground stations, and Jill's asleep both times.*

"AF-9, this is Kodiak."

He reached up for the radio switch. "AF-9, Kodiak. Go ahead."

"We are receiving your automatic data transmission loud and clear."

"Roger, Kodiak. Everything normal here; mission profile unchanged."

"Okay, Niner. We have nothing new for you. Oh wait . . . Chet, Lew Regneson is here and he says he's put twenty bucks on your butt to uphold the Air Force's honor. Keep 'em flying."

Keeping his face as straight as possible, Kinsman answered, "Roger, Kodiak. Mission profile unchanged."

"Good luck!"

Linda's thoughtful expression had deepened. "What was that all about?"

He looked straight into those cool blue eyes and lied, "Damned if I know. Regneson's one of the astronaut corps. Been assigned to Kodiak for the past six weeks. He must be going ice-happy. Thought it'd be best just to humor him."

"Oh. I see." But she looked unconvinced.

"Have you checked any of your pictures through the film processor yet?"

Shaking her head, Linda said, "No, I don't want to risk them on your equipment. I'll process them myself when we get back."

"Damned good equipment," Kinsman said, "even if it was built by the lowest bidder."

"I'm fussy."

He shrugged and let it go. At least the subject of the conversation had been changed.

"Chet?"

"What?"

"That power pod . . . what's it for? Colonel Murdock got awfully coy when I asked him."

"Nobody's supposed to know until the Pentagon releases the news . . . probably when we get back. I can't tell you officially," he grinned, "but generally reliable sources believe that it's going to power a radar system that will be orbited next month. The radar's a new type, experimental. If it works well it'll become part of our ABM early-warning system."

"Anti-Ballistic Missile?"

With a nod, Kinsman explained, "From orbit you can spot missile launches in their first few minutes, give the States a longer warning time."

"So your brave new world is involved in war."

"Sort of." Kinsman frowned. "Radars won't kill anybody, of course. They might save lives."

"But this *is* a military satellite."

"Unarmed. Two things this brave new world doesn't have yet: death and love."

"People have died in space."

"Never in orbit. On re-entry, yes. In ground or air accidents. But no one's ever died up here. And no one's made love, either."

Despite herself, it seemed to Kinsman, she smiled. "Have there been many chances for it?"

"Well, the Russians have women cosmonauts. And Jill and a couple of other women astronauts have been flying orbital missions for a couple of years now."

She thought it over for a moment. "This isn't exactly the bridal suite at the Waldorf. In fact, I've seen better motel rooms along the Jersey Turnpike."

"Pioneers have to rough it."

"I'm a photographer, Chet, not a pioneer."

Kinsman hunched his shoulders and spread his hands helplessly, a motion that made him bob slightly on his chair. "Strike three, I'm out."

"Better luck next time."

"Thanks." He returned his attention to the mission flight plan. *Next time will be in exactly sixteen hours, sweetie.*

When Jill came out of the sack it was Linda's turn to sleep. Kinsman stayed at the control desk, sucking on a container of lukewarm coffee. All the panel lights were green. Jill was taking a blood specimen from one of the white mice.

"How're they doing?"

Without looking up, she answered, "Fine. They've adapted to weightlessness beautifully. Calcium levels have evened off, muscle tone is good . . ."

"Then there's hope for us two-legged types?"

Jill returned the mouse to the colony entrance and snapped the lid shut. It scampered through to rejoin its clan in the transparent maze of plastic tunnels.

"I can't see any physical reason why humans can't live in orbit indefinitely," she answered.

Kinsman caught a slight but definite stress on the word *physical.* "You think there might be emotional problems in the long run?"

"Chet, I can see emotional problems on a three-day

mission." Jill forced the blood specimen into a stoppered test tube.

"What do you mean?"

"Come on," she said, her face showing disappointment and distaste. "It's obvious what you're trying to do. Your tail's been wagging like a puppy's whenever she's in sight."

"You haven't been sleeping much, have you?"

"I haven't been eavesdropping, if that's what you mean. I've simply been watching you watching her. And some of those messages from groundside . . . is the whole Air Force in on this? How much money's being bet?"

"I'm not involved in any betting. I'm just . . ."

"You're just taking a risk on fouling up the mission and maybe killing the three of us just to prove that you're Tarzan and she's Jane."

"Goddammitall, Jill, now you sound like Murdock."

The sour look on her face deepened. "Okay. You're a big boy. If you want to play Tarzan while you're on duty, that's your business. I won't get in your way. I'll take a sleeping pill and stay in the sack."

"You will?"

"That's right. You can have your blonde Barbie Doll, and good luck to you. But I'll tell you this . . . she's a phony. I've talked to her long enough to dig that. You're trying to use her, but she's trying to use us, too. She was pumping me about the power pod while you were sleeping. She's here for her own reasons, Chet, and if she plays along with you it won't be for the romance and adventure of it all."

My God Almighty, Jill's jealous!

It was tense and quiet when Linda returned from the bunkroom. The three of them worked separately: Jill fussing over the algae colony on the shelf above the biology bench; Kinsman methodically taking film from the observation cameras for return to Earth and then reloading them; Linda clicking away efficiently at both of them.

Ground control called up to ask how things were going. Both Jill and Linda threw sharp glances at Kinsman. He replied merely:

"Following mission profile. All systems green."

They shared a meal of pastes and squeeze tubes together, still mostly in silence, and then it was Kinsman's turn in the sack. But not before he checked the mission flight plan. *Jill goes in next, and we'll have four hours alone, including a stretch over the Indian Ocean.*

Once Jill retired, Kinsman immediately called Linda over to the control desk on the pretext of showing her the radar image of a Russian satellite.

"We're coming close now." They hunched side by side at the desk to peer at the orange-glowing radar screen; close enough for Kinsman to scent a hint of very feminine perfume. "Only a thousand kilometers away."

"Should we blink our lights at them or something?"

"It's unmanned."

"Oh."

"It *is* a little like flying in World War I up here," Kinsman realized, straightening up. "Just being up here is more important than which nation you came from."

"Do the Russians feel that way, too?"

Kinsman nodded. "I think so."

She stood in front of him, so close that they were almost touching.

"You know," Kinsman said, "when I first saw you on the base, I thought you were the photographer's model, not the photographer."

Gliding slightly away from him, she answered, "I started out as a model . . ." Her voice trailed off.

"Don't stop. What were you going to say?"

Something about her had changed, Kinsman realized. She was still coolly friendly, but alert now, wary, and . . . sad?

Shrugging, she said, "Modeling is a dead end. I finally figured out that there's more of a future on the other side of the camera."

"You had too much brains for modeling."

"Don't flatter me."

"Why on Earth should I flatter you?"

"We're not on Earth."

"Touché."

She drifted over toward the galley. Kinsman followed her.

"How long have you been on the other side of the camera?" he asked.

Turning back toward him, "I'm supposed to be getting your life story, not vice versa."

"Okay . . . ask me some questions."

"How many people know you're supposed to lay me up here?"

Kinsman felt his face make a smile, an automatic delaying tactic. *What the hell*, he thought. Aloud, he replied, "I don't know. It started out as a little joke among a few of the guys . . . apparently the word has spread."

"And how much money do you stand to win or lose?" She wasn't smiling.

"Money?" Kinsman was genuinely surprised. "Money doesn't enter into it."

"Oh no?"

"No. Not with me."

The tenseness in her body seemed to relax a little. "Then why . . . I mean . . . what's it all about?"

Kinsman pulled himself down into the nearest chair. "Why not? You're damned pretty, neither one of us has any strings, nobody's tried it in zero gee before . . . why the hell not?"

"But why should I?"

"That's the big question. That's what makes an adventure out of it."

She looked at him thoughtfully, leaning her tall frame against the galley paneling. "An adventure. There's nothing more to it in your mind than that?"

"Depends," Kinsman answered. "Hard to tell ahead of time."

"You live in a very simple world, Chet."

"I try to. Don't you?"

She shook her head. "No, my world's very complicated."

"But it includes sex."

Now she smiled, but there was no pleasure in it. "Does it?"

"You mean never?" Kinsman's voice sounded incredulous, even to himself.

She didn't answer.

"Never at all? I can't believe that . . ."

"No," she said, "not never at all. But never for . . . for an adventure. For job security, yes. For getting the good assignments; for teaching me how to use a camera in the first place. But never for fun . . . at least, not for a long, long time has it been for fun."

Kinsman looked into those frigid blue eyes and saw that they were completely dry and aimed straight back at him. His insides felt odd. He put a hand out toward her but she didn't move a muscle.

"That's . . . that's a damned lonely way to live," he said.

"Yes, it is." Her voice was a steel ice pick, without a trace of self-pity in it.

"But . . . how did it happen? Why . . . ?"

She leaned her head back against the galley paneling, her eyes looking away, into the past. "I had a baby. He didn't want it. I had to give her up for adoption—or have it aborted. The kid should be five years old now. I don't know where she is. Or him." She straightened up, looked back toward Kinsman. "But I found out that sex is for making babies or making careers. Not for fun."

Kinsman sat there feeling as if he had just taken a low blow. The only sound in the cabin was the faint hum of electrical machinery, the whisper of the air fans.

Linda broke into a grin. "I wish you could see your face . . . Tarzan the Ape Man, trying to figure out a nuclear reactor."

"The only trouble with zero gee," he muttered, "is that you can't hang yourself."

* * *

Jill sensed something was wrong, it seemed to Kinsman. From the moment she came out of the sack, she sniffed around, giving quizzical looks. Finally, when Linda retired for her final rest period before re-entry, Jill asked him:

"How're you two getting along?"

"Okay."

"Really?"

"Really. We're going to open a Playboy Club in here. Wanna be a bunny?"

Her nose wrinkled. "You've got enough of those."

For more than an hour they worked their separate tasks in silence. Kinsman was concentrating on recalibrating the radar mapper when Jill handed him a container of hot coffee.

He turned in his chair. She was standing beside him, not much taller than his own seated height.

"Thanks."

Her face was very serious. "Something's bothering you, Chet. What did she do to you?"

"Nothing."

"Really?"

"For Chrissake, don't start that again! Nothing, absolutely nothing happened. Maybe that's what's bothering me."

Shaking her head, "No, you're worried about something and it's not yourself."

"Don't be so damned dramatic, Jill."

She put a hand on his shoulder. "Chet . . . I know this is all a game to you, but people can get hurt at this kind of game, and . . . well . . . nothing in life is ever as good as you expect it will be."

Looking up at her intent brown eyes, Kinsman felt his irritation vanish. "Okay, kid. Thanks for the philosophy. I'm a big boy, though, and I know what it's all about."

"You just think you know."

Shrugging, "Okay, I think I do. Maybe nothing is as good as it ought to be, but a man's innocent until proven guilty, and everything new is as good as gold until you find some tarnish on it. That's *my* philosophy."

"All right, slugger." Jill smiled ruefully. "Be the ape man. Fight it out for yourself. I just don't want to see her hurt you."

"I won't get hurt."

"You hope. Okay, if there's anything I can do . . ."

"Yeah, there is something."

"What?"

"When you sack in again, make sure Linda sees you take a sleeping pill. Will you do that?"

Jill's face went expressionless. "Sure," she answered flatly. "Anything for a fellow officer. And gentleman."

She made a great show, several hours later, of taking a sleeping pill so that she could rest well on her final nap before re-entry. It seemed to Kinsman that Jill deliberately layed it on with a trowel.

"Do you always take sleeping pills on the final time around?" Linda asked Kinsman after Jill had gone into the bunkroom and closed the curtain.

"Got to be fully alert and rested for the return flight," Kinsman said. "Re-entry's the trickiest part of the mission."

"I see."

"Nothing to worry about, though."

He went to the control desk and busied himself with the tasks that the mission plan called for. Linda sat lightly in the next chair, within arm's reach. Kinsman chatted briefly with Kodiak station, on schedule, and made an entry in the log.

Three more ground stations and we're over the Indian Ocean, with world enough and time.

But he didn't look up from the control panel; he tested each system aboard the lab, fingers flicking over the console buttons, eyes focused on the red, amber, and green lights that told him how the laboratory's machinery was functioning.

"Chet?"

"Yes?"

"Are you . . . sore at me?"

Still not looking at her, "No, I'm busy. Why should I be sore at you?"

"Well, not sore maybe, but . . ."

"Feeling put down?"

"Yes. Hurt. Something like that."

He punched an entry on the computer's keyboard at his side, then turned to face her. "Linda, I haven't had the time to figure out what I feel. You're a complicated woman; maybe too complicated for me. Life's got enough twists in it."

Her mouth drooped a little.

"On the other hand," he grinned, "we WASPs ought to stick together. Not many of us left."

That brought a faint smile. "I'm not a WASP. My real name's Szymanski . . . I changed it when I started modeling."

"Another complication."

She was about to reply when the radio speaker crackled, "AF-9, this is Cheyenne. Cheyenne to AF-9."

Kinsman leaned over and thumbed the transmitter switch. "AF-9 to Cheyenne. You're coming through faint but clear."

"Roger Nine. We're receiving your telemetry. All systems look good from here."

"Manual check of systems also green," Kinsman said. "Mission profile nominal. No deviations. Tasks about ninety percent complete."

"Roger. Ground control suggests you begin checking out your spacecraft on the next orbit. You are scheduled for re-entry in ten hours."

"Right. Will do."

"Okay, Chet. Everything looks cool from here. Anything else to report, ol' Founding Father?"

"Mind your own business." He snapped the transmitter off.

Linda was smiling at him.

"What's so funny?"

"You are. You're getting very touchy about this whole thing."

"It's going to stay touchy for a long time to come. Those guys'll hound me about this for years."

"You could always tell lies."

"About you? No, I don't think I could do that. If the girl were anonymous, that's one thing. But they all know you, know where you work . . ."

"You're a gallant officer. I suppose that kind of rumor would get back to New York."

Kinsman grinned. "You could even make the front page of the *National Enquirer*."

She laughed at that. "They'd pull out some of my old bikini pictures."

"Careful now." Kinsman put up a warning hand. "Don't stir up my imagination any more than it already is. I'm having a tough enough time being gallant right now."

They remained apart, silent, Kinsman sitting at the control desk, Linda drifting back toward the galley, nearly touching the curtain that screened off the bunkroom.

Patrick AFB called in and Kinsman gave a terse report. When he looked at Linda again, she was sitting at the observation port across the aisle from the galley. Looking back at Kinsman, her face was troubled, her eyes . . . he wasn't sure what he saw in her eyes. They looked different: no longer ice-cool, no longer calculating. They looked aware, concerned, almost frightened.

Still Kinsman stayed silent. He checked and double-checked the control board, making absolutely certain that every valve and transistor aboard the lab was functioning perfectly. Glancing at his watch: *Five more minutes before Ascension calls*. He checked the board lights again.

Ascension called exactly on schedule. Feeling his innards tightening, Kinsman gave his standard report in a deliberately calm and detached way. Ascension signed off.

With a last long look at the controls, Kinsman pushed himself out of the seat and drifted, hands faintly touching the grips along the aisles, toward Linda.

"You've been awfully quiet," he said, standing over her.

"I've been thinking about what you said a while ago." What was it in her eyes? Anticipation? Fear? "It . . . it *has* been a damned lonely life, Chet."

He took her arm and lifted her gently from the chair and kissed her.

"But . . ."

"It's all right," he whispered. "No one will bother us. No one will know."

She shook her head. "It's not that easy, Chet. It's not that simple."

"Why not? We're here together . . . what's so complicated?"

"But life *is* complicated, Chet. And love . . . there's more to it than just having fun."

"Sure. But it's meant to be enjoyed, too. What's wrong with taking a chance when you have it? What's so damned complicated or important? We're above the cares and worries of Earth. Maybe it's only for a few more hours, but it's here and it's now. It's us. They can't touch us, they can't force us to do anything or stop us from doing what we want to do. We're on our own. Understand? Completely on our own."

She nodded, her eyes still wide with the look of a frightened doe. But her hands slid around him and together they drifted back toward the control desk. Wordlessly, Kinsman turned off all the overhead lights so that all they saw was the glow of the control board and the flickering of the computer as it murmured to itself.

They were in their own world now, their private universe, floating freely and softly in the darkness. Touching, drifting, caressing, searching the new seas and continents, they explored their world.

Jill stayed in the hammock until Linda entered the bunkroom, quietly, to see if she had awakened yet. Kinsman sat at the control desk feeling not tired, but strangely numb.

The rest of the flight was strictly routine. Jill and Kinsman did their jobs, spoke to each other when they had to. Linda took a brief nap, then returned to snap a few last pictures. Finally they crawled back into the Manta, disengaged from the laboratory, and started the long curving flight back to Earth.

Kinsman took a last look at the majestic beauty of the planet, serene and unique among the stars. Then they felt the surge of rocket thrust, dipped into the atmosphere, watched as air heated beyond endurance glowed around them in a fiery grip and made their tiny craft into a flaming, falling star. Pressed into his seat by the acceleration, Kinsman let the automatic controls bring them through re-entry, through the heat and buffeting turbulence, down to an altitude where their bat-winged craft could fly like an airplane.

He took control and steered the Manta back toward Edwards Air Force Base, back to the world of men, of weather, of cities and hierarchies and official regulations. He did this alone, silently. He didn't need Jill's help or anyone else's. He flew the craft from inside his buttoned-tight pressure suit, frowning at the panel displays through his helmet's faceplate.

Automatically he checked with ground control as he caught sight of the long black scar of a runway gouged out across the Mohave's rocky waste. His earphones were alive with other men's voices now: wind conditions, altitude checks, speed estimates. He knew, but could not see, that a pair of jet fighters were trailing behind him, armed with cameras in place of guns. *To provide evidence if I crash.*

They dipped through a thin layer of ice-crystal cirrus clouds. Kinsman's eyes flicked to the radar screen slightly to his right. The craft shuddered briefly as he lined it up with the long black arrow of the runway. He pulled back slightly on the controls, hands and feet working instinctively, flashed over scrubby brush and bare rocks, flared the Manta onto the runway. The landing wheels touched down once, bounced them up momentarily, then touched again with a shrill squeak. They rolled for more than a mile before stopping.

He leaned back in the seat and let out a deep breath. No matter how many flights, he still ended up oozing sweat after the landing.

"Good work," Jill said.

"Thanks." He turned off all the craft's systems, hands moving automatically in response to long training. Then he slid his faceplate up, reached overhead, and popped the hatch open.

"End of the line," he said tiredly. "Everybody out."

He clambered up through the hatch, feeling his own weight with a sullen resentment, then helped Linda and finally Jill out of the Manta's cramped cockpit. They hopped down onto the blacktop runway. Two vans, an ambulance, and two fire trucks were rolling from their parking stations at the end of the runway, nearly a mile ahead.

Kinsman slowly took his helmet off as he sat on the lip of the hatch. The baking desert heat annoyed him now. Jill walked a few paces away from the Manta, toward the approaching trucks.

Kinsman clambered down to stand beside Linda. Her helmet was off, her sun-drenched hair shaking free. She carried a plastic bag of film rolls.

"I've been thinking," Kinsman said to her. "That business about having a lonely life . . . you're not the only one. And it doesn't have to be that way. I can get to the East Coast, or . . ."

"Hey, who's taking things seriously now?" Her face looked calm again, cool despite the glaring heat.

"But I mean . . ."

"Chet, come on. We had our kicks. Now you can tell your pals about it, and I can tell mine. We'll both get a lot of mileage out of it. It'll help our careers."

"I never intended to tell anybody . . ."

But she was already moving away from him, striding

toward the men who were running up from the vans. One of them, a civilian, had a camera. He dropped to one knee and snapped a picture of Linda holding out her plastic bag of film and smiling broadly.

Kinsman stood there with his mouth open.

Jill came back to him. "Well? Did you get what you were after?"

"No," he said slowly. "I guess I didn't."

She started to put her hand out to him. "We never do, do we?"

AGE 30

Kinsman snapped awake when the phone went off. Before it could start a second ring he had the receiver off the cradle.

"Captain Kinsman?" The motel's night clerk.

"Yes," he whispered back, squinting at the luminous digits of his wristwatch: *two twenty-three.*

"I'm awfully sorry to disturb you, Captain, but Colonel Murdock himself called . . ."

"How the hell did he know I was here?"

"He doesn't. He said he was phoning all the motels around the base. I didn't admit you were here. He said when he found you he needed you to report to him in person at once. Those were his words, Captain: in person, at once."

Kinsman frowned in the darkness. "Okay. Thanks for playing dumb."

"Not at all, sir. Hope it isn't trouble."

"Yeah." Kinsman hung up. For a half-minute he sat on the edge of the king-sized bed. *Murdock's making the*

*rounds of the motels at two in the morning and he hopes
it isn't trouble. Funny.*

He stood up, stretched his lanky frame, and glanced at
the blonde sleeping obliviously on the other side of the bed.
With a wistful shake of his head he padded out to the
bathroom.

Wincing, he flipped the light switch and then turned
on the coffee machine on the wall next to the bathroom
door. *It's synthetic but it's coffee. Almost.* As the machine
started gurgling he softly closed the bathroom door and
rummaged in his travel kit for his electric razor. The face
that met him in the mirror was lean and longjawed and
just the slightest bit bloodshot. He kept his hair at a
length that made Murdock uncomfortable: slightly longer
than regulations allowed, not long enough to call for a
reprimand.

Within a few minutes he was shaved, showered, and
back in Air Force uniform. He left a scribbled note on
motel stationery against the dresser mirror, took a final
long look at the blonde, wishing he could remember her
name, then went out to his car.

The new fuel regulations had put an end to fast driving.
Kinsman's own hand-built convertible was ready to burn
hydrogen, if and when the government ever made it
available. For now, he had to go with a captain's monthly
allotment of precious gasoline, which kept him moving—
cautiously—through the predawn darkness.

Some instinct made him turn on the car radio. Diane's
haunting voice filled the starry night:

> . . . and in her right hand
> There's a silver dagger,
> That says I can never be your bride.

Kinsman listened in dark solitude as the night wind blew
warmly over him. Diane Lawrence was a major entertainment star now. *How many years since I've seen her?* he
asked himself, and answered, *Too many.*

A pair of official cars zoomed past him, doing eighty, heading for the base. Their turbines screeched and faded into the distance like wailing ghosts. There was no other traffic on the once-bustling highway. Kinsman held to the legal limit all the way to the base's main gate. But he could feel the excitement building up inside him.

There were half a dozen Air Policemen at the gate, looking brisk and polished, instead of the usual sleepy pair.

"What's the stew, Sergeant?" Kinsman asked as he pulled his car up to the gate.

The guard flashed his pocketlight on the badge Kinsman held in his outstretched hand.

"Dunno, sir. We got the word to look sharp."

The light flashed full in Kinsman's face. *Painfully sharp.*

The guard waved him on.

There was that special crackle in the air as Kinsman drove toward the Administration Building. The kind that comes only when a launch is imminent. As if in answer to his unspoken hunch, the floodlights on Complex 204 bloomed into life, etching the tall silver rocket booster standing there, embraced by the dark spiderwork of the gantry tower.

Pad 204. Manned shot.

People were scurrying in and out of the Administration Building: sleepy-eyed, disheveled, but their feet were doing double time. Colonel Murdock's secretary was coming down the hallway as Kinsman signed in at the security desk.

"What's up, Annie?"

"I just got here myself," she said. There were hairclips still in her sandy-colored curls. "The boss told me to flag you down the instant you arrived."

Even from completely across the Colonel's spacious office, Kinsman could see that Murdock was a round little kettle of nerves. He was standing by the window behind his desk, watching the activity centered on Pad 204, clenching and unclenching his fists behind his back. His bald head was glistening with perspiration, despite the frigid air conditioning. Kinsman stood at the door with the secretary.

"Colonel?" she said softly.

Murdock spun around. "Kinsman. So here you are."

"What's going on? I thought the next manned shot wasn't until . . ."

The Colonel waved a pudgy hand. "The next manned shot is as fast as we can damned well make it." He walked around the desk and eyed Kinsman. "You look a mess."

"Hell, it's three in the morning!"

"No excuses. Get over to the medical section for preflight checkout. They're waiting for you."

"I'd still like to know . . ."

"Tell them to check your blood for alcohol content," Murdock grumbled.

"I've been celebrating my liberation. I'm not supposed to be on duty. My leave starts at 0900 hours, remember?"

"Cut the clowning. General Hatch is flying in from Norton and he wants you."

"Hatch?"

"That's right. He wants the most experienced man available."

"Twenty astronauts on the base and you have to make me available."

Murdock fumed. "Listen, dammit. This is a military operation. I may not insist on much discipline from you glamor boys, but you're still in the Air Force and you will follow orders. Hatch says he wants the best man we've got. I'd rather have Colt, but he's back East attending a family funeral or something. That means you're *it*. Like it or not."

Kinsman shrugged. "If you saw what I had to leave behind me to report for duty here you'd put me up for the Medal of Honor."

Murdock frowned in exasperation. Anne tried unsuccessfully to suppress a smile.

"All right, lover-boy. Get down to the medical section

on the double. Anne, you stick with him and bring him to the briefing room the instant he's finished. General Hatch will be here in twenty minutes; I don't want him kept waiting."

Kinsman stood at the doorway, not moving. "Will you just tell me what this is all about?"

"Ask the General," Murdock said, walking back toward his desk. "All I know is that Hatch wants the best man we have ready for a shot immediately."

"Emergency shots are volunteer missions," Kinsman pointed out.

"So?"

"I'm practically on leave. There are eighteen other astronauts here who . . ."

"Dammit, Kinsman, if you . . ."

"Relax, Colonel, relax. I won't let you down. Not when there's a chance to put a few hundred klicks between me and all the brass on Earth."

Murdock stood there glowering as Kinsman left with Anne. They paced hurriedly out to his car and sped off toward the medical building.

"You shouldn't bait him like that," Anne said over the rush of the dark wind. "He feels the pressure a lot more than you do."

"He's insecure," Kinsman said, grinning. "There're only twenty people on the base who're qualified for orbital missions and he's not one of them."

"And you are."

"Damned right, sugar. It's the only thing in the world worth doing. You ought to try it."

She put a hand up to her wind-whipped hair. "Me? Fly in orbit? I don't even like airplanes!"

"It's a clean world, Annie. Brand new every time. Just you in your own little cosmos. Your life is completely your own. Once you've done it, there's nothing left on Earth but to wait for the next time."

"My God, you sound as if you really mean it."

"I'm serious," he insisted. "Why don't you wangle a

ride on one of the Shuttle missions? They usually have room for an extra person."

"And get locked into a spacecraft with you?"

Kinsman's grin returned. "It's an intriguing idea."

"Some other time, Captain. I've heard all about you and your Zero Gee Club. Right now we have to get you through preflight and then off to meet the General."

General Lesmore D. ("Hatchet") Hatch sat in dour silence in the small briefing room. The oblong conference table was packed with colonels and a single civilian. *They all look so damned serious,* Kinsman thought as he took the only empty chair, at the foot of the table. The General, naturally, sat at the head.

"Captain Kinsman." It was a flat statement of fact.

"Good morning, sir."

Hatch turned to a moonfaced aide. "Borgeson, let's not waste time."

Kinsman only half-listened to the hurried introductions around the table. He felt uncomfortable already, and it was only partly due to the stickiness of the crowded little room. Through the only window he could see the first faint glow of dawn.

"Now then," Borgeson said, introductions finished. "Very briefly, your mission will involve orbiting and making rendezvous with an unidentified satellite."

"Unidentified?"

Borgeson went on, "It was launched from the Soviet Union without the usual prior announcement . . . without a word about its nature or mission."

"And it is big," Hatch rumbled.

"Intelligence"—Colonel Borgeson nodded at the colonel sitting on Kinsman's left—"had no prior word about the launch. We must assume that the satellite is potentially hostile in intent. Colonel McKeever will give you the SPADATS tracking data."

They went around the table, each colonel adding his

bit of information. Kinsman began to build up the picture in his mind.

The satellite had been launched nine hours earlier. It was now in a low polar orbit that allowed it to cover every square kilometer on Earth each twelve hours. Since it first went up, not a single radio transmission had been detected going to it or from it. And it was big, even heavier than the ten-ton *Salyut* space stations the Russians had been using for years.

"A satellite of that size," said the colonel from the Special Weapons Center, "could easily contain a beam weapon . . . the, er"—he almost smiled—"the 'death ray' kind of device that Intelligence has been warning us about for so many years."

The weapon could be a very energetic laser or a compact proton accelerator, the colonel explained. In either case, the beam it fired could be used to destroy rockets as they boosted up from the ground.

"A network of such weapons in orbit could provide a very effective ABM system," the colonel said. "They could shoot down our missile strike force before the boosters ever cleared the ionosphere."

"And in a little more than two hours," Borgeson added, "this satellite will pass over Nebraska—where several squadrons of SAC missiles are sitting in their silos."

"This could be the first of many such satellites that they put up," General Hatch said, his face deeply etched with worry. *Or is it hate?* "They could be getting ready to totally negate our strategic strike forces."

"Why not just knock it down?" Kinsman asked. "We can hit it, can't we?"

"We could try," the General answered. "But suppose the damned thing zaps our missiles? Then what? Can you imagine the panic in Washington? It'd make Sputnik look like a schoolyard scuffle." He puffed out a deep sigh, shaking his head at his inner vision. "Besides, we've been ordered by the Chief of Staff himself to inspect the satellite and determine whether or not its intent is hostile."

"In two hours?"

"Perhaps I can explain," said the civilian. He had been introduced as a State Department man; Kinsman had already forgotten his name. He had a soft, sheltered look to him.

"We are officially in a position of cooperation, *vis-à-vis* the Soviets, in outer space programs. Our NASA people and the Russian space people are working out joint programs—the lunar exploration work, the new Mars and Venus probes . . ."

The State Department man went on in his low Ivy League voice, unmindful of the hostility he was generating around the table. "So if we simply try to destroy this new satellite, it could set back our cooperative programs. On the other hand, if we do nothing, it might encourage the Soviets to make additional secret launches. So the Department believes that this very massive Russian satellite is a test . . . a test of our ability to react, to detect, inspect, and verify the satellite's nature."

"We ought to blow it out of the sky," snapped one of the colonels.

"Perhaps," the civilian replied softly. "But suppose it is only a peaceful research station? An astronomical telescope? Suppose there are cosmonauts aboard? What if we shoot it down and kill Russian nationals?"

"Serve 'em right," somebody muttered.

"No," the State Department man said. "I cannot agree. This is a test. We must prove to the Soviets—and to ourselves—that we can inspect their satellites and see for ourselves whether or not they contain weaponry."

The General shook his head. "If they've gone to the trouble of launching a multiton vehicle in complete secrecy, then military logic dictates that it's a weapon carrier. By damn, that's what I'd do, in their place."

"No matter whether it's a weapon or not, the satellite could be rigged with booby traps to prevent us from inspecting it," one of the colonels pointed out.

Thanks a lot, said Kinsman to himself.

"They know we've been inspecting their satellites for years," said Borgeson. "But I'm afraid we're going to have to get inside this one to find out what it's all about."

Hatch focused his gunmetal eyes on Kinsman. "Captain, I want to impress one thought on you. The Air Force has been working for more than twenty years to achieve the capability of placing a military man in orbit on an instant's notice, despite the opposition of NASA and other parts of the government."

He never so much as flicked a glance in the civilian's direction as he continued, "This incident proves the absolute necessity for such a capability. Your flight will be the first practical demonstration of all that we've battled to achieve over these years. You can see, then, the importance of this mission."

"Yessir."

"This is strictly a volunteer mission. Exactly because it is so important to us, I don't want you to try it unless you're absolutely certain about it."

"I understand, sir. I'm your man."

Hatch's weathered face unfolded into a smile. "Well spoken, Captain. Good luck."

The General rose and everyone snapped to attention, even the civilian. As the others filed out of the briefing room, Murdock drew Kinsman aside.

"You had your chance to beg off."

"And miss this? A chance to play cops and robbers in orbit?"

The Colonel flushed angrily. "We're not in this for laughs! This is damned important. If it really is a weapon up there . . ."

"I'll be the first to know," Kinsman snapped. *I've listened to you enough for one morning.*

The countdown of the solid rocket booster went smoothly, swiftly, as Kinsman sat alone in the Manta spacecraft perched on the rocket's nose. But there was always the chance that a man or machine would fail at a crucial point and turn the intricate, delicately poised booster into a flaming pyre of twisted wreckage.

Kinsman sat tautly in the contoured couch, listening to them tick off the seconds. He hated countdowns, hated being helpless, completely dependent on a hundred faceless voices that flickered through his earphones, waiting child-like in a mechanical womb, not truly alive, doubled up and crowded by the unfeeling, impersonal machinery that automatically gave him warmth and breath and life. Waiting.

He could feel the tiny vibrations along his spine that told him the ship was awakening. Green lights began to blossom across the control panels, telling him that every-thing was functioning and ready. Still the voices droned through his earphones in carefully measured cadence:

". . . three . . . two . . . one . . ."

And she bellowed to life. Acceleration flattened Kinsman into the couch. Vibration rattled his eyes in their sockets. Time became a meaningless roar. The surging, engulfing, overpowering bellow of the rocket engines made his head ring even after they had burned out into silence.

Within minutes he was in orbit, the long slender rocket stages falling away behind, together with all sensations of weight. Kinsman was alone now in the squat, delta-shaped spacecraft: weightless, free of Earth.

Still he was the helpless unstirring one. Computers sent guidance corrections from the ground to the Manta's controls. Tiny vectoring jets squirted on and off, micro-scopic puffs of thrust that maneuvered the craft into the precise orbit needed for catching the Russian satellite.

What if she zaps me as I approach her? Kinsman thought.

Completely around the world he spun, southward over the Pacific, past the gleaming whiteness of Antarctica, and then north over the wrinkled, cloud-shrouded mass of Asia. As he crossed the night-darkened Arctic, nearly an hour after being launched, the voices from the ground began talking to him again. He answered them as automatically as the machines did, reading numbers off the control panels, proving to them that he was alive and functioning properly.

Then Murdock's voice cut in. "There's been another launch, fifteen minutes ago, from the cosmonaut base at Tyuratam. High-energy boost. Looks like you're going to have company."

Kinsman acknowledged the information, but still sat unmoving.

Finally he saw it, seemingly hurtling toward him. He came to life. To meet and board the satellite he had to match its orbit and velocity exactly. He was approaching it too fast. Radar and computer data flashed in green flickers across the screens in Kinsman's control panels. His eyes and fingers moved constantly, a well-trained artist performing a new and tricky sonata. He maneuvered the retrojet controls that finally eased his Manta into a rendezvous orbit with the massive Russian satellite.

The big satellite seemed to be stopped dead in space, just ahead of him, a huge inert hunk of metal, dazzlingly brilliant where the sun lit its curving flank, totally invisible where it was in shadow. It looked ridiculously like a crescent moon made out of flush-welded aluminum. A smaller crescent puzzled Kinsman until he realized it was a rocket nozzle hanging from the satellite's tailcan.

"I'm parked off her stern about two hundred meters," he reported into his helmet microphone. "She looks like the complete upper-stage of an Alpha-class booster. I'm going outside."

"Better make it fast." Murdock's voice was high-pitched. "That second spacecraft is closing in fast."

"E.T.A.?"

A pause while voices mumbled in the background, then, "About fifteen minutes . . . maybe less."

"Great."

"You can abort if you need to."

Same to you, pal. "I'm going to take a close look at her. Get inside, if I can. Call you back in fifteen minutes."

Murdock didn't argue. Kinsman smiled grimly at the realization that the Colonel had not reminded him about the possibility of booby traps. Old Mother Murdock hardly forgot such items. He simply had decided not to make the choice of aborting the mission too attractive.

Gimmicked or not, the satellite was too near and too enticing to turn back now. Kinsman quickly checked out his pressure suit, pumped the air from his cockpit into the storage tanks, and then opened the hatch over his head.

Out of the womb and into the world.

He climbed out and teetered on the lip of the hatch, coiling the umbilical cord attached to his suit. Regulations required that astronauts use umbilicals, rather than the pistol-like, independent maneuvering units, on solo EVAs. Kinsman hardly thought about it, except to be grateful that he didn't need to carry a bulky life-support pack on his back. He glanced down at the nightside of Earth. City lights blinked through the clouds, and he could even make out the long stretches of highways, lit by ever-moving trucks.

And the stars were there, sprinkled in countless glory across the black, unending depths of space. They looked back at him steadily, solemnly, the unblinking eyes of infinity.

I'll bet that this is all there is to heaven, he said to himself. *You don't need any more.*

Then he turned, with the careful, deliberate motions of a deepsea diver, and looked at the fat crescent of the nearby satellite. Only ten minutes now. Even less.

He pushed off from his spacecraft and sailed effortlessly, arms outstretched. Behind him trailed the umbilical cord that carried his air and electrical power. As he approached the satellite, the Sun rose over the humped curve of its hull and nearly blinded him despite the automatic darkening of his visor. He kicked downward and ducked behind the satellite's protective shadow.

Still half-blinded by the sudden glare, he bumped into the satellite's massive body and rebounded gently. With an effort, he twisted about, pushed back to the satellite, and planted his magnetized boots on the metal hull.

I claim this island for Isabella of Spain. Now where the hell's the hatch?

It was over on the sunlit side, he found at last. It wasn't difficult to figure out how to open the hatch, even though the instructions beside it were in Cyrillic letters. Kinsman knelt down and turned the locking mechanism. He felt it click open.

For a moment he hesitated. *It might be booby-trapped,* he heard the Colonel warn.

The hell with it.

Kinsman yanked the hatch open. No explosion, no sound at all. A dim light came from within the satellite. Carefully he slid down inside. A trio of faint emergency lights glowed weakly.

"Saving the juice," he muttered to himself.

It took a moment for his eyes to accustom themselves to the dimness. Then he began to appreciate what he saw. The satellite was packed with equipment. He couldn't make out most of it, but it was clearly not weaponry. Scientific gear. Cameras, recording instruments, small telescopes. Three contoured couches lay side by side beneath the hatch; he was standing on one of them. Up forward of the couches was a gallery of compact cabinets.

"Very cozy."

He stepped off the couch and onto the main deck, crouching to avoid bumping his helmet on the instrument rack overhead. He opened a few of the cabinets. *Take home some souvenirs.* He found a small set of hand wrenches, unfastened them from their setting.

With the wrenches in one hand, Kinsman tried the center couch. By lying all the way back on it, he could see the satellite's only observation port. He scanned the instrument panel: Cyrillic letters and Arabic numerals.

Made in CCCP. Kinsman put the wrenches down on the armrest of the couch. They stuck magnetically. Then he reached for the miniature camera at his belt. He took four snaps of the instrument panel.

Something flashed in the corner of his eye.

Tucking the camera back into its belt holster, he looked out the observation port. Nothing but stars: beautiful, cold. Then another flash; this time his eye caught and held the slim crescent of another spacecraft gliding toward him. Most of the ship was in deep shadow. He would never have found it without the telltale burst from its retrojets.

She's damned close!

Kinsman grabbed his tiny horde of stolen wrenches and got up from the couch. In his haste, he stumbled over his trailing umbilical cord and nearly went sprawling. A weightless fall would hardly hurt him, he knew, but it would waste precious seconds while he regained his equilibrium.

Hoisting himself out of the satellite's hatch, he saw the approaching spacecraft make its final rendezvous maneuver. A flare of its retrojets and it seemed to come to a stop alongside the satellite.

Kinsman ducked across the satellite's hull and crouched in the shadows of the dark side. Waiting there in utter blackness, he coiled the umbilical so that it would also become invisible in the shadows.

The other spacecraft was considerably smaller than the satellite, built along the lines of Kinsman's own bat-winged Manta. Abruptly a hatch popped open. A spacesuited figure emerged and hovered dreamlike for a long moment.

Kinsman saw that the cosmonaut had no umbilical. Instead, bulging packs of equipment on his back made him more like a free-roving lunar explorer than a tethered ship-jockey.

Or maybe there are more cosmonauts inside.

A wispy plume of gas jetted from the cosmonaut's backpack and he sailed purposefully over to the satellite's hatch.

Got his own maneuvering unit, too.

Unconsciously, Kinsman hunched deeper in the shadows as the Russian approached. Only one of them; no one else appeared from the spacecraft. The newcomer touched down easily beside the still-open hatch of the satellite. For several moments he did not move. Then he edged away from the satellite and, hovering, turned toward Kinsman's craft, still hanging only a couple of hundred meters away.

Kinsman felt himself start to sweat, even in the cold darkness.

The cosmonaut jetted away from the satellite, straight toward the Manta.

Dammitall! Kinsman raged at himself. *First rule of warfare, you stupid ass; keep your line of retreat open!*

He leaped off the satellite and started floating back toward the spacecraft. It was nightmarish, drifting through space with agonizing slowness while the cosmonaut sped on ahead. The cosmonaut spotted Kinsman as he cleared the shadow of the satellite and emerged into the sunlight.

For a moment they simply stared at each other, separated by a hundred meters of nothingness.

"Get away from that spacecraft!" Kinsman shouted, knowing that their radios were not on the same frequency.

As if to prove the point, the cosmonaut put a hand on the lip of the Manta's hatch and peered inside. Kinsman flailed his arms and legs, trying to raise some speed. But still he moved with hellish slowness. Then he remembered the wrenches he was carrying.

Almost without thinking he tossed the entire handful of them at the cosmonaut. The effort swung him wildly off balance. The Earth slid across his field of vision, then the stars swam by dizzyingly. He caught a glimpse of the cosmonaut as the wrenches rained around him. Most of them missed and bounced noiselessly off the spacecraft. But one banged into the intruder's helmet hard enough to jar him, then rebounded crazily out of sight.

Kinsman lost sight of the Manta as he spun around. Grimly he fought to straighten himself, using his arms and legs as counterbalances. Finally the stars stopped whirling. He turned and faced the Manta again, but it was upside-down. It didn't matter.

The intruder still had one hand on the spacecraft hatch. His free hand was rubbing the spot where the wrench had hit his helmet. He looked ludicrously like a little boy rubbing a bump on his head.

"That means get off, stranger," Kinsman muttered. "No trespassing. U.S. property. Beware of the eagle. Next time I'll crack your helmet in half."

The newcomer turned slightly and reached for one of the equipment packs attached to his belt. A weird-looking tool appeared in his hand. Kinsman drifted helplessly and watched the cosmonaut take up a section of his umbilical line. Then he applied the hand tool to it. Sparks flashed.

Electron torch! He's trying to cut my line. He'll kill me!

Frantically, Kinsman began clambering along the long umbilical line, hand over hand. All he could see, all he could think of, was that flashing torch eating into his lifeline.

Desperately he grabbed the line in both hands and snapped it hard. Again he tumbled wildly, but he saw the wave created by his snap race down the line. The intruder found the section of line he was holding suddenly buck violently out of his hand. The torch spun away from him and winked off.

Both men moved at once.

The cosmonaut jetted away from the Manta, looking for the torch. Kinsman hurled himself directly toward the hatch. He planted his boots on the spacecraft's hull and grasped the open hatch in both hands.

Duck inside, slam shut, and get the hell out of here.

But he did not move. Instead he watched the cosmonaut, a strange, sun-etched outline figure now, drifting some twenty meters away, quietly sizing up the situation.

That sonofabitch tried to kill me.

Kinsman coiled catlike on the edge of the hatch and sprang at his enemy. The cosmonaut reached for the jet controls at his belt but Kinsman slammed into him and they both went hurtling through space, tumbling and clawing at each other. It was an unearthly struggle, human fury in the infinite calm of star-studded blackness. No sound except your own harsh breath and the bone-carried shock of colliding arms and legs.

They wheeled out of the spacecraft's shadow and into the painful glare of the Sun. In a cold rage, Kinsman grabbed the airhose that connected the cosmonaut's oxygen tank with his helmet. He hesitated a moment and glanced into the bulbous plastic helmet. All he could see was the back of the cosmonaut's head, covered with a dark, skin-tight, flying hood. With a vicious yank, Kinsman yanked out the airhose. The cosmonaut jerked twice, spasmodically, then went inert.

With a conscious effort Kinsman unclenched his teeth. His jaw ached. He was trembling and covered with a cold sweat.

He saw his father's face. *They'll make a killer out of you! The military exists to kill.*

He released his death grip on his enemy. The two human forms drifted slightly apart. The dead cosmonaut turned gently as Kinsman floated beside him. The Sun glinted brightly on the white spacesuit and shone full into the enemy's lifeless, terror-stricken face.

Kinsman looked into that face for an eternally long moment and felt the life drain out of him. He dragged himself back to the Manta, sealed the hatches, and cracked open the air tanks with automatic, unthinking motions. He flicked on the radio and ignored the flood of interrogating voices that streamed up from the ground.

"Bring me in. Program the AGS to bring me in, full automatic. Just bring me in."

It was six weeks before Kinsman saw Colonel Murdock again. He sat tensely before the wide mahogany desk while Murdock beamed at him, almost as brightly as the sunshine outside.

"You look thinner in civvies," the Colonel said.

"I've lost weight."

Murdock made a meaningless gesture. "I'm sorry I haven't had a chance to see you sooner. What with the Intelligence and State Department people crawling around here the past few weeks, and all the paperwork on your citation and your medical disability leave . . . I haven't had a chance to, eh, congratulate you on your mission. It was a fine piece of work."

Kinsman said nothing.

"General Hatch was very pleased. He recommended you for the medal himself."

"I know."

"You're a hero, Kinsman." There was wonder in the Colonel's voice. "A real honest-to-God hero."

"Shove it."

Murdock suppressed a frown. "The Reds haven't made a peep about it. They're keeping the whole thing hushed up. Guess they're too embarrassed to admit that we can board one of their satellites any time we want to, within a few hours of its being launched. State Department expected the sky to fall in on them, but nothing's happened. The Russians have taken their beating without a word. And you've proved that the Air Force has an important mission to perform in space, by God! Bet the Congress will change our name to Aerospace Force now."

"I committed a murder."

"Now listen, son. I know how you feel. But it had to be done."

"No it didn't," Kinsman insisted quietly. "I could have gotten back inside the Manta and de-orbited."

"You killed an enemy soldier. You protected your nation's frontier. Sure, you feel like hell now but you'll get over it."

"You didn't see the face I saw inside the helmet."

Murdock shuffled some papers on his desk. "Well . . . okay, it was rough. You're getting a medical furlough out of it, when there's nothing physically wrong with you. For Chrissakes, what more do you want?"

"I don't know. I've got to take some time to think it over."

"What?" Murdock stared at him. "What're you talking about?"

"Read the debriefing report," Kinsman said tiredly.

"It . . . eh, hasn't come down to my level. Too sensitive. But I don't understand what's got you so spooked. You killed an enemy soldier. You ought to be proud . . ."

"Enemy," Kinsman echoed bleakly. "She couldn't have been more than twenty years old."

Murdock's face went slack. "She?"

Kinsman nodded. "Your honest-to-God hero murdered a terrified girl. That's something to be proud of, isn't it?"

AGE 31

Lieutenant Colonel Marian Campbell drummed her fingers lightly on her desktop. The psychological record of Captain Kinsman lay open before her. Across the desk sat the Captain himself.

She appraised him with a professional eye. Kinsman was lean, dark, rather good-looking in a masculine way. His gray-blue eyes were steady. His hands rested calmly in his lap; long, slim pianist's fingers. No fidgets, no twitches. He looked almost indifferent to his surroundings. *Withdrawn*, Colonel Campbell thought.

"Do you know why you're here?" she asked him.

"I think so," he replied with no hesitation.

Marian leaned back in her chair. She was a big-boned woman who had to remind herself constantly to keep her voice down. She had a natural tendency to talk at people in a parade-ground shout. Not a good attribute for a psychiatrist.

"Tell me," she said, "what you think you're here for."

When she tried to keep her voice soft it came out gravelly, rough. The voice was meant for an opera stage, despite the drawback that its owner was tone-deaf.

Kinsman took a deep breath, like an athlete about to exert himself to the utmost. Or like a man who's bored.

"I've been under psychiatric observation for five months now. Suspended from active duty. Your people have been trying to figure out what the effect on me has been of killing that Russian girl."

Colonel Campbell nodded. "Go on," she murmured.

"You're the chief of the psychiatric section. I guess my case is in your hands for a final decision."

"That's very true," she said. "It's up to me to decide whether you return to active duty or not."

Kinsman regarded her steadily for a moment, then shifted his attention to the window. The blinds were half closed against the burning afternoon sun. For a moment he seemed like a little boy in a stuffy classroom, yearning for the bell that will free him to go outside and play.

"Colonel Murdock wants you permanently removed from duty. He more or less told me that I should find you psychologically unfit."

"I'm not surprised," Kinsman said, looking back at her. "Why not?"

He made a small motion with his shoulders that might have been a shrug. "Murdock would be happy to get rid of me. We're too different from each other." He thought a moment, then added, "That's not paranoia; you can check it out with any of the other astronauts."

Marian chuckled. "We already have. You're not paranoid."

"I didn't think so."

"But you do seem to have some problems. I've got to determine if your problems are too big to allow you to fly again."

"That's what I thought."

She did not respond and he didn't add anything. They sat looking at each other across the cluttered desk for several moments. Colonel Campbell's office bore the privilege of her rank and station. It was just another one of the starkly functional offices at the Air Force hospital, but a lieutenant colonel who is chief psychiatrist has more latitude in decorating her office than most others. The square little room was festooned with hanging plants. A young rubber tree sprouted in the corner near the window. Instead of a couch, there was a long metal stand bearing exotic tropical flowers.

He's outstaring me, Marian Campbell thought.

"Well," she said at last, "how do you feel about all this? What do you want to do?"

This time his answer was slow in coming. "I don't honestly know," he said. "Sometimes I think I want out of the Air Force. But that would take me out of the space program, and that's all I really want."

"To be out of the space program."

"No!" he snapped. "To be *in* it. NASA's starting up manned lunar missions again. I want to be part of that."

"You want to go to the Moon?"

"Yes."

"To get away from here?"

"As far away as I can," he said fervently.

She shook her head. "You can't run away from your problems."

Kinsman gave her a look of unconcealed disgust. "You've never been in orbit, have you?"

"No," she admitted.

"Then you don't know. That business about not running away from your problems . . . it's a slogan. Pure crap. You get your feet off the ground, get out of this office and up into a plane where you can be on your own—you'll get away from your problems easily enough."

"But you have to come down sometime. You have to return and face things."

"I suppose so." He looked out the window at the hot Texas afternoon for a long moment. Then, "You know, I sometimes wonder if some aircraft crashes . . . some of the unexplained ones, aren't caused by the pilot's unconscious desire to stay away from his problems."

"Suicide?" She suppressed an impulse to make a note on his file. *Do it after he leaves, don't do anything to break his train of thought.*

"Not suicide, exactly. Not a desire to die. But . . . well, every now and then a really good pilot wracks up his plane for no apparent reason. Maybe he just didn't want to put his feet back on the ground."

"How do you think you'd feel if you were allowed to fly again?"

His grin was immediate. "Terrific!"

"You wouldn't try to . . . avoid your problems?"

"No," he said, the grin turning into a knowing smile. "I've got a better way to get away from my problems. That's what the Moon is for."

Colonel Campbell thought, *Never-never land.*

"That's the one thing I want," Kinsman said. "The one thing I need. To return to active astronaut status. To get in on the lunar program."

"But it's not an Air Force program," Colonel Campbell said. "The civilians are doing it—NASA and the Russians, isn't it? It's a cooperative program."

Nodding, he answered, "But they're looking for experienced astronauts. The Air Force is letting some of our people work for NASA on detached duty. Friends of mine have already been to the Moon . . ."

He was set up for the tough questions now.

"What do you think your real problem is?" Colonel Campbell asked, letting her voice grow to its natural volume.

Kinsman looked startled for a moment. "I killed that Russian girl . . ." His facial expression went from surprise to pain.

"She tried to kill you, didn't she?"

"Yes."

"You're a military officer. You were on a military mission."

"Yes."

"Then why did you become . . ." She reached for the glasses on her desk and perched them on the tip of her nose. Reading from the file, ". . . despondent, withdrawn, hostile to your fellow officers." She looked up at him. "It also says you lost weight and complained of insomnia."

Kinsman hunched forward in his chair, clasped his long-fingered hands together.

Looking up at her, he asked, "Have you ever killed someone?"

Marian Campbell moved her head the barest centimeter to indicate *no*.

"Lots of Air Force officers have," Kinsman went on, "but at remote distances. You press a button and a machine falls out of the air or a building on the ground explodes. I killed her in hand-to-hand combat. I saw her face."

"But you were doing your duty . . ."

"I could have done my duty without killing her!"

"In hindsight."

He shook his head. "Ever heard of Richard Bong?"

"Who?" she asked.

"I've had a chance to read up on Air Force history quite a bit over the past few months," Kinsman said. "Bong was a fighter pilot in World War Two. In the Pacific. He shot down so many Japanese planes that some general came over to the island where he was stationed to pin a medal on him."

Colonel Campbell regretted that she hadn't turned on the tape recorder in the bottom drawer of her desk. *Too late now*, she chided herself.

"The Japanese pulled an air raid on Bong's base while the general was there," Kinsman was saying, "and he and the general dove into the same slit trench. One of the Jap planes was hit by anti-aircraft fire and started to burn. The Japanese pilot didn't have a parachute. Or maybe it just didn't open. Anyway, he jumped out of his burning plane and fell to the airstrip like a rock. He hit the ground just a few feet in front of Bong and the general."

"I don't see . . ."

"Bong never shot down another plane, for the rest of the war. He flew combat missions, but he couldn't hit anything with his guns."

"Oh," said Colonel Campbell. "Now I understand."

"It makes a difference," Kinsman said. "It's one thing to kill by remote control. It's something else when you see who you've killed face-to-face."

"And you think that's what was bothering you?"

"It's still bothering me."

"But you can handle it now," she lead him.

"As long as I'm not put into combat missions," Kinsman answered.

"And the fact that the cosmonaut was a woman has nothing to do with it?"

Kinsman's jaw dropped open and suddenly he was glaring at her. "How the hell should I know?" he snapped. "How high is up?"

"I don't know, Captain. You tell me."

Kinsman shrugged and shook his head.

"Very well. That's enough for today. You can go."

She watched him stand up slowly, looking slightly puzzled. He went to the door, hesitated, then opened it and left the office without looking back.

Colonel Campbell opened the bottom drawer of her desk and pulled out the book-sized tape recorder. She turned it on and began speaking into the built-in microphone.

After more than fifteen minutes, she concluded:

"He's definitely looking for help. That's good. But we're nowhere near his problem yet. We've only scratched the surface. He's built a shell around himself and now not only can no one break through it to get to him, he can't crack it himself to get out of it. It could be something from childhood; we'll have to check out his family."

She clicked the recorder's STOP button and turned to look out the window. The hot Texas sky was turning to molten copper as the sun went down. A helicopter droned overhead somewhere. The screeching whine of a jet fighter roared past.

"One thing's certain," Marian Campbell said to her tape recorder. "Killing that cosmonaut was only the triggering trauma. There's more, buried underneath. And if it's buried too far down, if we can't get to it fairly quickly, he's finished as an Air Force officer. And as an astronaut."

The breeze that whipped across the flight line did little to alleviate the heat. The sun beat down like a palpable force, pressing the life juices out of you.

Marian Campbell walked slowly around the plane, checking the control surfaces, the propeller, sweating in her zippered coveralls and waiting for Kinsman to show up.

It was a single-engined plane with broad, stubby wings and a high, bulbous glass canopy that made it look like a one-eyed insect. It was painted red and yellow, except for the engine cowling, where permanent black streaks of oil stains marred the decor.

She saw a tall, lithe figure approaching through the shimmering heat haze along the flight line. The sun baked the concrete ramp so that it felt like standing on a griddle. *Come on*, she groused to herself, *before I melt into a puddle*. Then she grinned sheepishly. *It would be a damned big puddle*, she knew.

Kinsman was wearing a civilian's open-necked, short-sleeved shirt and light blue slacks. He looked wary as he came up to the plane.

"No need to salute," Marian called to him. "Let's keep it informal, shall we?"

He nodded and put a hand out to touch the plane's wing. The metal must have been scorchingly hot, but Kinsman ran his fingers along it lightly and almost smiled.

"A Piper Cherokee. She's an old bird, but she still looks good," he said.

"Are you speaking about the plane or about me?" Marian asked.

He looked more startled than amused. "The plane, of course, Colonel."

"My name's Marian . . . as in Robin Hood. And yes, I know the joke: 'Who's Maid Marian? Everybody!'"

Kinsman still didn't smile.

With an inner sigh, Marian asked, "Do I call you Chet, Chester, or what?"

"Chet."

"Okay, Chet. Let's get upstairs where the air is cooler."

She clambered heavily up onto the wing and squeezed through the cabin hatch. Kinsman followed her and sat in the co-pilot's seat, on the right. He stuck his foot out to keep the door open as she gunned the engine to life.

He was silent, watching, as she taxied to the far end of the two-mile-long runway. It had been built to accommodate heavy bombers. This puddle-jumper could take off and land along the runway seven times in a row and still have concrete to spare ahead of it.

They got the tower's clearance, Kinsman dogged the hatch shut, and the little engine buzzed its hardest as they rolled down the runway and lifted up into the air.

Marian banked the plane and made a right turn as ordered by the tower controller, and they headed away from the Air Force Base and into the Texas scrubland.

"Want to see the Alamo?" she asked.

"Sure," Kinsman said.

She asked the controllers for a route to San Antonio.

"Whose plane is this?" Kinsman asked as they climbed to cruising altitude.

"Mine," Marian said.

"Yours? You own it?"

"Sure. You think you jet jockeys are the only guys who like to fly? Why do you think I joined the Air Force in the first place?"

He grinned at her. "You like to fly."

"Doesn't everybody?"

She could see him visibly relaxing. They were barely

five thousand feet above the ground, but he already felt safe and removed from the pressures below.

"Want to take over for a while?" she asked.

"Sure."

She let go of the controls and Kinsman took the wheel in his hands.

"No aerobatics unless you warn me first," she invited.

"I'm not a stunt flier," he said.

"It's a good thing you're slim," Marian said. "It's usually a pretty tight squeeze in here with most men. I take up more than my fair share of the space."

He didn't take his eyes off the horizon, but he asked, "Is this supposed to be some form of therapy? I mean, why'd you invite me for this?"

"Because I know you like to fly, and I thought you needed some relaxation. We're not just brain-pickers, you know. We're doctors. We're concerned about your overall health."

Kinsman made a small sound that might have been a grunt. "One of your doctors liked to talk to me when I was trying to play the piano in the rec hall. Every time I'd sit down to play, he'd pop up and start asking me questions. Then he said I was hostile and suspicious."

Marian laughed. "That was Jeffers. He's the idiot on my staff."

They flew for a while and chatted easily enough, but he never got close to anything about his emotional problems. Finally, Marian had to dredge the subject up to the surface.

"We had to check back into your family history," she said.

"I know. I got a phone call from a friend."

"Senator McGrath?"

"Yes. He wanted to know if it was okay to talk to you. I told him it was."

"We had a good chat on the telephone."

"What did you find out about me?"

Marian pursed her lips for a moment and considered

what she could do if he suddenly decided to dive the plane into the ground.

"He told me about your parents. The conflict with your father. He died while you were stationed in California, didn't he?"

Kinsman nodded. "While I was in orbit, as a matter of fact. I had gone to see him while he was sick, like a dutiful son. He didn't recognize me."

"That's a pity," Marian said.

Very coolly, Kinsman replied, "We didn't see each other very clearly when he was alive and well, you know."

He talked easily enough, seemingly holding nothing back. But it was like a blank wall. All he wanted was to be reassigned to astronaut duty for the lunar missions. Nothing else mattered to him. And yet there was something choking him. Something inside his brain that had put a wall around him, an invisible barrier that cut him off from any real human contact.

"I've been waiting for the zinger," he said, after nearly an hour of talk.

Marian's hands were still resting in her lap. "The zinger? What's that?"

He glanced at her. "Aren't you going to ask me if I'm impotent? Jeffers and all your other shrinks did."

Is he asking for help? "I've read your file," Marian answered. "You told them you're not."

"I told them I don't think I am."

"Explain?"

"I've been more-or-less restricted to quarters for the past five months. Not much of a chance to find out."

"Go on . . ."

"I can get an erection easily enough," Kinsman went on, as clinically cool as if he were reading from a textbook. "I've even awoken from my nightmares with a hard-on."

"Nocturnal emissions?" Marian asked.

"Wet dreams? Yeah, a few times."

"Then you're functional."

"The equipment works," he said, still as distant as the

horizon. "What bothers me is I haven't felt much like trying. I mean, it's been five *months* and I haven't even felt horny. I haven't tried to date a girl, haven't even made a pass at one."

We know, Colonel Campbell said to herself.

"You're closer to me right now than any woman's been since . . . since . . ."

And suddenly his hands were shaking. He pulled them away from the control wheel. The plane, built for amateur pilots, flew onward as steadily as a plow horse.

Marian took the controls. "Since when?" she asked.

"You know."

"I want to hear you say it."

"Since I murdered that girl in orbit. Since I killed her. I ripped the air lines out of her helmet and killed her. Deliberately! I could've backed off. I could've gotten back to my own craft and de-orbited. But I killed her. I murdered her."

"Good," Marian said.

"Good?" He glared at her with pain-filled eyes.

"It's good that you're showing some emotion about it. You've kept it frozen beneath the surface for too long. You've been acting more like a robot than a human being, these past five months."

Kinsman looked down at his hands. They were still trembling.

"It's all right, Chet. It's over and done with. There's nothing you can do to bring her back. What you have to decide now is . . . where do you go from here?"

He put his hands palms-down on his thighs. "What'd Richard III say? 'Let's to it, pell-mell. If not to heaven, then hand-in-hand to hell.' "

Marian gave a ladylike snort. "Neither one," she said, pointing off to her left. "It's only San Antonio."

The Alamo is in the heart of San Antonio, but the four corners of the city are marked by four military bases. Colonel Campbell landed her plane at Kelly AFB, and they commandeered a hydride-burning gray sedan from the motor pool to go to town.

GENTLEMEN WILL TAKE OFF THEIR HATS, read the sign above the Alamo's front entrance. That, and the muggy crowds that shuffled through the old shrine, were the two main impressions Marian got from their half-hour at the Alamo.

Outside, in the shade cast by the graceful trees beyond the old mission's battered stone walls, Kinsman suddenly asked:

"May I take you to dinner?"

Marian felt pleased. "It's been some time since a young man has invited me to dinner."

He grinned at her. "Maybe you can help me with my problem."

Her cheeks went hot and she cursed herself for an idiot. *He's joking with you!* she told herself sternly. *You're old enough to be his . . . well, his big sister, anyway.*

"You are qualified for I.F.R., aren't you?" Kinsman asked, seriously. "No problem if we stay out after dark."

Marian nodded. "I think I'd feel safer, though, if you made the instrument landing. I don't like landing at night."

"Okay," he said. "So let's get some dinner. My treat."

They found a dinner theater only a few blocks from the Alamo, close enough so that they didn't have to move their car from the parking garage. The theater was in an old hotel; a small stage had been set up at one end of the high-ceilinged ornate old dining room. Marian imagined heroes from the Old West dining here in regal splendor. Now the red-clothed tables were small and jammed together. The hotel called it intimate; what they meant was that they could squeeze more dollars out of a show this way.

Even the show was a cheap production. Four singers in ordinary street clothes, reviving a set of songs by an old Parisian café entertainer named Jacques Brel. The two men and two women were good, though; the songs were all highly-charged, emotional, theatrical, pointed.

Marian started watching Kinsman as the lights went down after dinner and the singers pranced on stage. He sat impassively, laughed at the right places, applauded along with everyone else. Until a song called "Next."

He sat straight up in his chair as the theme of the song became clear to him—a young European soldier being marched with his comrades into a mobile army whorehouse, "gift of the army, free of course." Marian felt her eyes burning brighter than the stage lights as she watched Kinsman's face freeze in something very close to horror.

He reached his hand out to her and she grasped it tightly in hers. He hung on to her as the lead male sang:

> All the naked and the dead
> Should hold each other's hands
> As they watch me scream at night
> In a dream no one understands.

Kinsman released her hand when the song ended. When the show finally ended and the ornate chandeliers and wall sconces lit the big room full of dinner tables once again, he turned to Marian with a faintly embarrassed expression on his face.

They drove back to Kelly Air Force Base through the warm, muggy night in silence. Marian was content to wait until they were airborne again before trying to open him up. They checked the car back at the motor pool and let a sleepy-eyed corporal drive them in a jeep to the flight line.

Kinsman hopped up on the Cherokee's wing and pulled the hatch open, ducked inside and took the pilot's seat. Then he helped Marian settle her bulk into the right-hand seat.

He checked the control panel's gauges carefully, got his clearance from the tower controller, and taxied out to the runway. The edge lights stretched like glowing pearls, seemingly going off to the horizon.

As he waited for final takeoff clearance, Kinsman revved the engine. The whole plane shuddered and strained like an excited terrier being held in check by a leash. Somehow the engine noise sounded louder in the darkness, to Marian.

And then they were racing down the runway and up into the air. Kinsman handled the plane smoothly, his hands sure and steady. As they climbed to cruising altitude, Marian saw a sky full of stars above them, and the even more numerous lights of San Antonio below.

"One of the best Mexican restaurants this side of the Rio Grande is down there," she said.

"Really?" Kinsman answered.

She nodded vigorously. "Too bad we missed it."

"Yeah. The food we had wasn't all that good, was it?"

The plane was droning along through the darkness. Marian said, "But I enjoyed the show."

Kinsman might have nodded in the darkness, she couldn't tell.

"How did you like it?" she asked.

"The show?"

"Yes."

And suddenly he was laughing. A soft, happy, satisfied chuckle.

Puzzled, Marian asked, "What's funny?"

"You are."

"I'm *funny*?" She didn't know whether to be glad or angry.

"Not *per se*," Kinsman said. "It's the situation between us that's funny."

He turned onto their homeward-bound course, checked the radio frequency for the mid-route controller, then turned toward her.

"Look," he said, "you know damned well that something clicked in my head during the show, when I grabbed your hand. And I know you know. But you're trying to lead up to the subject subtly, to see if you can get me to talk about it."

"What clicked?" she asked.

"During that song, 'Next,' I finally realized what the hell has been bothering me."

"Yes?"

"They got to me," Kinsman said flatly.

Marian felt her eyebrows rise. "They got to you? Who . . . ?"

Kinsman said, "All these years I thought I was my own man. I joined the Air Force to get into space, to get away from all the ugliness of Earth. But I didn't escape. I couldn't."

"You brought some of the ugliness along with you."

"Sort of. I . . . murdered that cosmonaut. Maybe if she had been a man I wouldn't feel so badly about it. But the thing is—they got to me."

"Who?" she demanded.

"The Air Force," he said. "The training. The military mind-set."

"I don't understand."

Gesturing with one hand in the cramped cabin, Kinsman said, "Look, when I joined the Air Force it was strictly for astronaut status. Sure, they put me through the same training everybody gets, and I even had to fly combat patrol in Cyprus back before I became eligible for astronaut. But I never hit anything with a gun or a missile. Never."

"So?"

"So once I went into the astronaut program I figured I had it made. I had what I wanted. The Air Force hadn't gotten to me. Their training hadn't turned me into a military machine. I was my own man."

Marian began to feel the inner tingle that she always got when a puzzle became clear to her.

"But I was wrong," Kinsman said. His voice was serious now but not somber. "When I got into a combat situation —hand-to-hand fight, yet—all that military training came into play. I wasn't a happy-go-lucky astronaut anymore.

I was a trained killer. A military automaton. I killed her just the way an infantryman becomes conditioned to stick a bayonet in another human being's belly."

"And you think that's what's been bothering you?" Marian asked as softly as she could.

"For the past five months I've been trying to figure it out. How could I have done it? How in the hell could I have deliberately ripped out a human being's air line? How could I willingly kill somebody?"

"And now you have the answer."

"Yes." It was an unshakably firm response. "I'm not as smart as I thought I was. The military training got to me. God knows, put me in the same situation and I might even do the same thing all over again."

"Chet, listen to me very carefully," Marian said slowly. "You *think* you have the answer and you're feeling pretty good about it . . ."

"Damned right!"

"But that's only the beginning of the answer. There's still a lot more, buried down inside you. A lot that you haven't brought up into the light yet."

He shook his head. "I don't think so."

"I *do* think so."

"You want to dig deeper," he said.

"I want you to dig deeper into yourself."

"If you keep me off-duty, under observation, much longer, Murdock's going to drum me out. You know that."

"Yes," she admitted. "That's true."

"What I need is to get back to active duty. I want to get in on that lunar exploration program."

"You want to run off to the Moon?"

"Yes, but I'm not running away. I know better now. I know myself better."

"Well enough to risk your life, and the lives of others?"

He grinned at her. She could see his teeth in the darkness of the cockpit. "You're trusting me with your life right now, aren't you?"

Almost ruefully, she agreed, "I suppose I am."

"Just tell it to Murdock."

The next morning Lieutenant Colonel Marian Campbell was back in uniform, back in her office, sitting behind her desk.

Colonel Murdock's round, bald face looked distinctly unhappy, even in the small screen of the viewphone.

"Just what are you trying to tell me, Colonel Campbell?" he asked testily.

She took a deep breath, then replied, "In my opinion, Colonel, Captain Kinsman is fit to resume his duties."

"Resume . . . ? But I thought he was psychologically, er, well . . . unbalanced."

"He was troubled by what happened to him on his last mission, of course. But in my opinion, he's worked through those troubles and he's ready to go back to active duty."

Murdock looked suspicious. "I don't understand. For five months you shrinks have been working him over, and not a word of progress. Now, all of a sudden you say he's okay?"

Feeling almost as if she should cross her fingers, Marian Campbell said, "It happens that way sometimes. He's gained the insight he needed to understand what happened to him and why. He's adjusted to it. He's fit for duty."

"Not under me," Murdock said fervently. "I'm going to transfer him out of here just as soon as he comes marching through my door."

"You can't do that!"

Murdock looked startled. Her voice had boomed.

"I mean," Marian said, trying to tone it down, "that I would recommend he be allowed to continue in the astronaut program. It's what he's trained for, and what he enjoys doing."

"That doesn't mean . . ."

She overrode him. "I've checked with Washington, and it appears that there is a shortage of trained personnel with his qualifications. It would be against Air Force policy to waste a man of his background in a different assignment."

"If he's psychologically fit for such duty," Murdock quoted from the regulations.

"He is," Marian said.

The Colonel gave her a shrewd stare. It seemed almost ludicrous, his face was so tiny on the phone screen.

"You are guaranteeing that he's mentally sound?"

Marian Campbell stiffened her back. "There are no guarantees in the medical profession, Colonel. But I will personally draft the report on Captain Kinsman, recommending that he be returned to the duties for which he has been trained."

"That ties my hands, if I want to transfer him."

"Unless you transfer him to the NASA program," Marian blurted.

Murdock's face took on a knowing look. "So that's how he worked out his emotional problems. He twisted you around his little finger, didn't he?"

Just to wipe the smirk off his face, Marian made herself smile and say, "It wasn't his *little* finger, Colonel."

Murdock's face flamed red. He cut off the connection.

Marian leaned back in her chair. *Well, old gal, now you've got a reputation for screwing around with your patients.* She almost wished it were true.

She hauled the tape recorder out of its drawer and started to dictate her final report on Kinsman. But in the back of her mind she was thinking:

What else can you do? Keep him here? That will kill him just as surely as cutting off his oxygen. You've got to let him go.

Over the faint hum of the air conditioning she thought she heard distant piano music. From the recreation hall. A light, happy piece of Mozart. She listened for several minutes. No one interrupted the pianist.

So now he can go to the Moon. Maybe he'll find what he needs there. But he won't. He's suicidal. You know that. You know it and you're letting him go. He's going to kill himself, one way or the other. Himself, and maybe others besides. And you're letting him go out and do it because you're too weak to keep him here and watch him die one day at a time.

She turned on the tape recorder and watched the spools slowly turning as she fought back an urge to cry.

AGE 32

"Any word from him yet?"

"Huh? No, nothing."

Kinsman swore to himself as he stood on the open platform of the little lunar rocket jumper. It was his second trip to the Moon, and it wasn't going well.

"Say, where are you now?" Bok's voice sounded gritty with static in Kinsman's helmet earphones.

"Up on the rim. He must've gone inside the damned crater."

"The rim? How'd you get . . ."

"Found a flat spot for the jumper. Don't think I walked this far, do you? I'm not as nutty as the priest."

"But you're supposed to stay down here on the plain! The crater's off limits."

"Tell it to our holy friar. He's the one who marched up here. I'm just following the seismic rigs he's been planting every three, four klicks."

He could sense Bok shaking his head. "Kinsman, if there are twenty officially approved ways to do a job, I swear you'll pick the twenty-second."

"If the first twenty-one are lousy."

"Headquarters is going to be damned upset with you. You won't get off with just a reprimand this time."

"I suppose headquarters would prefer that we just let the priest stay lost."

"You're not going inside the crater, are you?" Bok's voice edged up half an octave. "It's too risky."

Kinsman almost laughed. "You think sitting inside that aluminum casket you're in is *safe?*"

The earphones went silent. With a sigh, Kinsman wished for the tenth time in the past hour that he could scratch his twelve-day-old beard. *Get zipped into the suit and the itches start.* He didn't need a mirror to know that his face was haggard, sleepless, his black beard mean-looking.

He stepped down from the jumper—a rocket motor with a railed platform and some equipment on it, nothing more —and planted his boots on the solid rock of the ringwall's crest. With a twist of his shoulders to settle the weight of the pressure suit's bulky backpack, he shambled over to the packet of seismic instruments and the fluorescent marker that the priest had left there.

"He came right up to the top, and now he's off on the yellow brick road, playing Moon explorer. Stupid bastard."

Did you really think you'd leave human stupidity behind you, back on Earth? a voice in his head asked him. *Or human guilt?*

Reluctantly, he looked into the crater. The brutally short horizon cut across its middle, but the central peak stuck its worn head up among the solemn stars. Beyond it there was nothing but dizzying blackness, an abrupt end to the solid world and the beginning of infinity.

Damn the priest! God's gift to geology . . . and I've got to play guardian angel for him.

Kinsman turned back and looked outward from the crater. He could see the lighted radio mast and squat return rocket, far below on the plain. He even convinced himself that he saw the mound of rubble marking their buried base shelter, where Bok lay curled safely in his bunk. The Russian base was far over the horizon, on the other side of Mare Nubium, and out of radio contact, unless they relayed a message back through headquarters in Houston.

"Any sign of him?" Bok's voice asked.

"Sure," Kinsman retorted. "He left me a big map with an X to mark the treasure."

"Don't get sore at me!"

"Why not? You're sitting inside. I've got to find our fearless geologist."

"Regulations say one man's got to be in the base at all times."

But not the same one man, Kinsman flashed silently.

"Anyway," Bok went on, "he's got a few hours' oxygen left. Let him putter around inside the crater for a while. He'll come back."

"Not before his air runs out. Besides, he's officially missing. Missed his last two check-in calls. That data goes straight back to Houston, just like everything else. My job is to scout his last known position. Another of those sweet regs."

Silence again. Bok didn't like being alone in the base, Kinsman knew.

"Why don't you come on back in," the engineer's voice returned, "until he calls in. Then you can get him with the jumper. You'll be running out of air yourself before you can find him inside the crater."

"I've got to try."

"You can't make up the rules as you go along, Kinsman! This isn't the Air Force, you're not a hotshot fighter pilot anymore. NASA has rules, regulations . . . they'll ground you if you don't follow the game plan."

"Maybe."

"You don't even like the priest!" Bok said. "You've been tripping all over yourself to stay clear of him whenever you're both inside the base here."

Kinsman felt his jaw clench. *So it shows. If you're not careful, you'll tip them both off.*

Aloud, he said, "I'm going to look around. Give me an

hour. Better call Houston and give them a complete report. Put my frequency on automatic record, in case anything happens. And stay in the shelter until I come back." *Or until a relief crew arrives.*

"You're wasting your time. And taking an unnecessary risk. They'll ground you for sure."

"Wish me luck," Kinsman said.

A delay. Then, "Luck. I'll sit tight here."

Despite himself, Kinsman grinned. *I know damned well you'll sit tight there. Some survey team. One goes over the hill and the other stays in his bunk for two weeks straight.*

He gazed out at the bleak landscape surrounded by starry emptiness. Something caught at his memory.

"They can't scare me with their empty spaces," he muttered to himself. There was more to the verse but he couldn't recall it.

"Can't scare me," he repeated softly, shuffling to the inner rim of the crater's ringwall. He walked very deliberately, like a tired old man, and tried to see from inside his bulbous helmet exactly where he was placing his feet.

The barren slopes fell away in gently terraced steps until, many kilometers below, they melted into the crater floor. *Looks easy . . . too easy.* With a shrug that was weighted down by the pressure suit's backpack, Kinsman started to descend into the crater.

He picked his way across the gravelly terraces and crawled feet first down the breaks between them. The bare rocks were slippery and sometimes sharp. Kinsman went slowly, step by step, trying to make certain he didn't puncture the metallic fabric of his suit.

His world was cut off now and circled by the dark rocks. The only sounds he knew were the creakings of the suit's joints, the electrical hum of its pump, the faint wheeze of the helmet's air blower, and his own heavy breathing. Alone, all alone. A solitary microcosm. One living creature in the universe.

They cannot scare me with their empty spaces
Between stars—on stars where no human race is.

There was still more to it: the tag line that he couldn't remember.

Finally he had to stop. The suit was heating up too much from his exertion. He took a marker beacon from the backpack and planted it on the broken ground. The Moon's soil, churned by eons of meteors and whipped into a frozen froth, had an unfinished look about it, as if somebody had been blacktopping the place but stopped before he could apply the final smoothing touches.

From a pouch on his belt Kinsman took a small spool of wire. Plugging one end into the radio outlet on his helmet, he held the spool at arm's length and released its catch. He couldn't see it in the dim light, but he felt the spring fire the wire antenna a hundred meters or so upward and out into the crater.

"Father Lemoyne," he called as the antenna drifted slowly in the Moon's gentle gravity. "Father Lemoyne, can you hear me? This is Kinsman."

No answer.

Down another flight.

After two more stops and nearly an hour of sweaty descent, Kinsman got his answer.

"Here . . . I'm here . . ."

"Where?" Kinsman snapped. "Do something. Make a light."

". . . can't . . ." The voice faded out.

Kinsman reeled in the antenna and fired it out again. "Where in hell are you?"

A cough, with pain behind it. "Shouldn't have done it. Disobeyed. And no water, nothing . . ."

Great! Kinsman raged. *He's either hysterical or delirious. Or both.*

After firing the spool antenna a third time, Kinsman flicked on the lamp atop his helmet and looked at the radio direction-finder dial on his forearm. The priest had his suit radio open and the carrier beam was coming through even though he was not talking. The gauges alongside the radio-finder reminded Kinsman that he was about halfway down on his oxygen, and more than an hour had elapsed since he had spoken to Bok.

"I'm trying to zero in on you," Kinsman called. "Are you hurt? Can . . ."

"Don't, don't, don't. I disobeyed and now I've got to pay for it. Don't trap yourself too . . ." The heavy, reproachful voice lapsed into a mumble that Kinsman could not understand.

Trapped. Kinsman could picture it. The priest was using a cannister-suit, a one-man walking cabin, a big, plexidomed, rigid can with flexible arms and legs sticking out of it. You could live in it for days at a time, but it was too clumsy for climbing. Which is why the crater was off limits.

He must've fallen and now he's stuck.

"The sin of pride," he heard the priest babbling. "God forgive us our pride. I wanted to find water; the greatest discovery a man can make on the Moon. . . . Pride, nothing but pride . . ."

Kinsman walked slowly, shifting his eyes from the direction-finder to the roiled, pocked ground underfoot. He jumped across a two-meter drop between terraces. The finder's needle snapped to zero.

"Your radio still on?"

"No use . . . go back . . ."

The needle stayed fixed. *Either I busted it or I'm right on top of him.*

He turned full circle, scanning the rough ground as far as his light could reach. No sign of the cannister. Kinsman stepped to the terrace edge. Kneeling with deliberate care, so that his backpack wouldn't unbalance him and send him sprawling down the tumbled rocks, he peered over.

In a zigzag fissure a few meters below him was the priest, a giant armored insect gleaming white in the glare of the lamp, feebly waving with one free arm.

"Can you get up?" Kinsman saw that all the weight of the cumbersome suit was on the pinned arm. *Banged up his backpack too.*

"Can you get up?" Kinsman repeated.

"Trying to find the secrets of God's creation . . . storming heaven with rockets. . . . We say we're seeking knowledge, but we're really after our own glory . . ."

Kinsman frowned. He couldn't see the older man's face behind the cannister's heavily-tinted window.

"I'll have to get the jumper down here."

The priest rambled on, coughing spasmodically. Kinsman started back across the terrace.

"Pride leads to death," he heard in his earphones. "You know that, Kinsman. It's pride that makes us murderers."

The shock boggled Kinsman's knees. He turned, shaking. "What . . . did you say?"

"It's hidden. The water is here, hidden . . . frozen in fissures. Strike the rock and bring forth water . . . like Moses. Not even God Himself was going to hide this secret from me . . ."

"What did you say," Kinsman whispered, colder than ice inside, "about murder?"

"I know you, Kinsman . . . anger and pride. . . . Destroy not my soul with men of blood . . . whose right hands are . . . are . . ."

Kinsman ran. He fought back toward the crater rim, storming the terraces blindly, scrabbling up the inclines with four-meter-high jumps. Twice he had to turn up the air blower in his helmet to clear the sweaty fog away from his faceplate. He didn't dare stop. He raced on, breath racking his lungs, heart pounding until he could hear nothing else.

Finally he reached the crest. Collapsing on the deck of the jumper, he forced himself to breathe normally again, forced himself to sound normal as he called Bok.

The engineer listened and then said guardedly, "It sounds as though he's dying."

"I think his regenerator's shot. His air must be pretty foul by now."

"No sense going back for him, I guess."

Kinsman hesitated. "Maybe I can get the jumper close enough to him." *He found out about me!*

"You'll never get him back here in time. And you're not supposed to take the jumper near the crater, let alone inside it. It's too risky."

"You want me to just let him die?" *He's hysterical. If he babbles about me where Bok can hear it . . . Christ, it'll be piped straight back to Houston, automatically!*

"Listen," the engineer said, his voice rising, "you can't leave me stuck here with both of you gone! I know the regulations, Kinsman. You're not allowed to risk yourself or the third man of the team in an effort to help a man in trouble. Those are the rules!"

"I know. I know." *You've already killed one human being. Are you going to let another one die, because of it? Where does it end, Kinsman? Where does it end?*

"You don't have enough oxygen in your suit to get down there and back again," Bok insisted. "I've been calculating . . ."

"I can tap the jumper's propellant tank."

"But that's crazy! You'll get yourself stranded!"

"Maybe." *If NASA finds out about it they'll bounce me back to the Air Force. Back to Murdock.*

"You're going to kill yourself over that priest! And you'll be killing me too!"

"He's probably dead by now," Kinsman said. "I'll just put a marker beacon down there, so another crew can get him out when the time comes. I won't be long."

"But the regulations . . ."

"Were written Earthside," Kinsman snapped. "The brass never planned on anything like this. I've got to go back, just to make sure."

He flew the jumper back down the crater's inner slope,

leaning over the platform railing to see his marker beacons as well as listening to their piping radio beeps. In a few minutes he was easing the spraddle-legged platform down on the last terrace before the helpless priest.

"Father Lemoyne."

Kinsman stepped off the jumper and made it to the edge of the fissure in two lunar strides. The white shell was inert; the lone arm unmoving.

"Father Lemoyne!"

Kinsman held his breath and listened. Nothing . . . wait . . . the faintest, faintest breathing. More like gasping. Quick, shallow, desperate.

"You're dead," Kinsman heard himself mutter. "Give it up, you're finished. Even if I got you out of here, you'd be dead before I could get you back to the base."

The priest's faceplate was opaque to him; he only saw the reflected spot of his own helmet lamp. But his mind filled with the shocked face he had seen in that other visor, the face when she had just realized that she was dead.

Kinsman looked away, out to the too-close horizon and the uncompromising stars beyond. Then he remembered the rest of it:

> They cannot scare me with their empty spaces
> Between stars—on stars where no human race is.
> I have it in me so much nearer home
> To scare myself with my own desert places.

Like an automaton, Kinsman turned back to the jumper. His mind was blank now. Without thought, without even feeling, he rigged a line from the jumper's tiny winch to the metal lugs in the cannister-suit's chest. Then he took apart the platform railing and wedged three rejoined sections into the fissure above the fallen man, to form a hoisting lever. Looping the line over the projecting lever arm, he started the winch.

He climbed down into the fissure and set himself as solidly as he could on the bare, scoured-smooth rock. Grabbing the priest's armored shoulders, he guided the oversized cannister up from the crevice while the winch strained silently.

The railing arm gave way while the priest was only partway up and Kinsman felt the full weight of the monstrous suit crush down on him. He sank to his knees, gritting his teeth to keep from crying out.

Then the winch took up the slack. Grunting, fumbling, pushing, Kinsman scrabbled up the rocky slope with his arms wrapped halfway around the big cannister's middle. He let the winch drag the two of them to the jumper's edge, then reached out and shut the motor.

With only a hard breath's pause, Kinsman snapped down the suit's supporting legs, so the priest could stay upright even though unconscious. Then he clambered onto the jumper's platform and took the oxygen line from the rocket tankage. Kneeling at the bulbous suit's shoulders, he plugged the line into its emergency air tank.

The older man coughed once. That was all.

Kinsman leaned back on his heels. His faceplate was fogging over again, or was it fatigue blurring his vision?

The regenerator was hopelessly smashed, he saw. *The old bird must've been breathing his own juices.* When the emergency tank registered full, he disconnected the oxygen line and plugged it into a special fitting below the regenerator.

"If you're dead, this is probably going to kill me, too," Kinsman said. He purged the entire suit, forcing the contaminating fumes out and replacing them with the oxygen that the jumper's rocket motor needed to get them back to the base.

He was close enough now to see through the cannister's tinted visor. The priest's face was grizzled, eyes closed. His usual smile was gone; his mouth hung open slackly.

Kinsman hauled him up onto the railless platform and strapped him down to the deck. Then he turned to the control podium and inched the throttle forward just enough to give them the barest minimum of lift.

The jumper almost made it to the crest before its rocket

died and bumped them gently onto one of the terraces. There was a small emergency tank of oxygen that could have carried them a little further, but Kinsman knew that he and the priest would need it for breathing.

"Wonder how many Jesuits have been carried home on their shields?" he asked himself as he unbolted the section of decking that the priest was lying on. By threading the winch line through the bolt holes, he made an improvised sled, which he carefully lowered to the ground. Then he took the emergency oxygen tank and strapped it to the deck-section also.

Kinsman wrapped the line around his fists and leaned against the burden. Even in the Moon's light gravity it was like trying to haul a truck.

"Down to less than one horsepower," he grunted, straining forward.

For once he was glad that the scoured rocks had been smoothed by micrometeors. He would climb a few steps, wedge himself as firmly as he could, then drag the sled to him. It took a painful half-hour to reach the ringwall crest.

He could see the base again, tiny and remote as a dream. "All downhill from here," he mumbled.

He thought he heard a groan.

"That's it," he said, pushing the sled over the crest, down the gentle outward slope. "That's it. Stay with it. Don't you die on me. Don't you put me through all this for nothing!"

"Kinsman!" Bok's voice. "Are you all right?"

The sled skidded against a meter-high rock. Scrambling after it, Kinsman answered, "I'm bringing him in. Just shut up and leave us alone. I think he's alive."

"Houston says no," Bok answered, his voice almost frantic. "They've calculated that his air went bad on him. He can't possibly be alive. You're ordered to leave him and return to the base shelter. Ordered, Kinsman."

"Tell Houston they're wrong. Now stop wasting my breath."

Pull the sled free. Push it to get started downhill again. Strain to hold it back . . . don't let it get away from you. Haul it out of the craterlets. Watch your step, don't fall.

"Too damned much uphill . . . in this downhill."

Once he sprawled flat and knocked his helmet against the edge of the sled. He must have blacked out for a moment. Weakly, he dragged himself to the oxygen tank and refilled his suit's supply. Then he checked the priest's suit and topped off its tank.

"Can't do that again," he said to the silent priest. "Don't know if we'll make it. Maybe we can. If neither one of us has sprung a leak. Maybe . . ."

Time slid away from him. The past and future disappeared into an endless now, a forever of pain and struggle, with the heat of his toil welling up to drench him within his suit.

"Why don't you say something?" Kinsman panted at the priest. "You can't die. Understand me? You can't die! I've got to explain it to you . . . I didn't mean to kill her. I didn't even know she was a girl. You can't tell, can't see a face until you're too close. She must've been just as scared as I was. She tried to kill me . . . how'd I know their cosmonaut was just a scared kid? When I saw her face . . . it was too late. But I didn't know, I didn't know . . ."

They reached the foot of the ringwall and Kinsman dropped to his knees. "Couple more klicks now . . . straightaway. . . . Only a couple more . . . kilometers." His vision was blurred and something in his head buzzed angrily.

Staggering to his feet, he lifted the line over his shoulder and slogged ahead. He could just make out the lighted tip of the base's radio mast.

"Leave him, Kinsman," Bok's voice pleaded from somewhere. "You can't make it unless you leave him!"

"Shut . . . up."

One step after another. Don't think, don't count. Blank your mind. Be a mindless plow horse. Plod along. One

step at a time. Steer for the radio mast. Just a few . . .
more . . . klicks.

"Don't die on me. Don't you . . . die on me. You're
my penance, priest. My ticket back. Don't die on me . . .
don't die . . ."

It all went dark. First in spots, then totally. Kinsman
caught a glimpse of the barren landscape tilting weirdly,
then the grave stars slid across his view, then darkness.

"I tried," he heard himself say in a far, far distant voice.
"I tried."

For a moment or two he felt himself falling, dropping
effortlessly into blackness. Then even that sensation died
and he felt nothing at all.

A faint vibration buzzed at him.

The darkness started to shift, turn gray at the edges.
Kinsman opened his eyes and saw the low, curved ceiling
of the underground base. The hum was the electrical
machinery that lit and warmed and brought good air to
their tight little shelter.

"You okay?" Bok leaned over him. His chubby face
was frowning worriedly.

Kinsman nodded weakly.

"Father Lemoyne's going to pull through," Bok said,
stepping out of the cramped space between the two bunks.
The priest was awake but unmoving, his eyes staring
blankly upward. His cannister-suit had been removed and
one arm was covered with a plastic cast.

Bok explained, "I've been getting instruction from the
medics in Houston. They contacted the Russians; a para-
medic's coming over from their base. Should be here in
a few hours. He's in shock and his right arm's broken.
Otherwise he seems pretty good . . . exhausted, but no
permanent damage."

Kinsman pulled himself up to a sitting position on the
bunk and leaned back against the curving wall. His helmet
and boots were off, but he was still wearing the rest of his
pressure suit.

"You went out and got us," he realized.

Bok nodded. "You were only about a kilometer away. I could hear you on the radio, babbling away. Then you stopped talking. I had to go out."

"You saved my life."

"And you saved the priest's."

Kinsman stopped a moment, remembering. "I did a lot of raving out there, didn't I?"

Bok wormed his shoulders uncomfortably. "Sort of. It's, uh . . . well, at least the Russians didn't pick up any of it."

"But Houston did."

"It was relayed automatically. Everything you said. You told me to yourself."

That's it. Now they know.

"They, uh . . ." Bok looked away. "They're sending a relief crew to fly us back."

"They don't trust me to pilot the return rocket."

"I guess not."

That's the end of it, Kinsman said to himself. *NASA doesn't want any neurotic ex-killers on their payroll.*

"You haven't heard the best of it, though," Bok said, eager to change the subject. He went to the shelf at the end of the priest's bunk and took a small plastic bottle. "Look at this."

Kinsman took the stoppered bottle in his hand. Inside it was a tiny sliver of ice, floating on water.

"It was stuck in the cleats of his boots."

"Father Lemoyne's?"

"Right. It's really water! Tests out okay and I even snuck a taste of it. It's real water, all right."

"It must have been down in that fissure after all," Kinsman said. "He found it without knowing it. He'll get into the history books now." *And he'll have to watch his pride even more now.*

Bok sat on the shelter's only chair. "Chet . . . about what you were saying out there . . ."

Kinsman expected tension, but instead he felt only numb. "I know. They heard it in Houston."

"They're going to try to keep it quiet. They made a quick check with the Air Force and . . ."

Kinsman heard himself replying calmly, "They can't keep something that big from leaking. At the very least, it means I'm finished with NASA."

"We'd all heard rumors about an Air Force astronaut killing a Russian during a military mission. But I never thought . . . I mean . . ."

"The priest figured it out. Or at least he guessed it."

"It must've been rough on you," Bok said.

Kinsman shrugged. "Not as rough as what happened to her."

"I'm . . . sorry." Bok's voice trailed off helplessly.

"It doesn't matter."

Surprised, Kinsman realized that he meant it. He sat upright. "It doesn't matter anymore. They can do whatever they want to. I can handle it. Even if they ground me and throw me to the news people . . . I think I can take it. I did it, and it's over with, and I can take what I have to take."

Father Lemoyne's free arm moved slightly. "It's all right," he whispered hoarsely. "It's all right."

The priest turned his face toward Kinsman. His gaze moved from the astronaut's eyes to the plastic bottle in Kinsman's hands. "It's all right," he repeated, smiling. "It's not hell we're in; it's purgatory. We'll get through. We'll make it all right."

Then he closed his eyes and his face relaxed into sleep. But the smile remained, strangely gentle in that bearded, haggard face; ready to meet the world or eternity.

AGE 33

It looked like a perfectly reasonable bar to Kinsman. *No*, he corrected himself. *A perfectly reasonable pub.*

The booths along the back wall were all empty. A couple of middle-aged men in business suits were conversing quietly as they stood at the bar itself with mugs of light Australian lager in their hands. The bartender was a beefy, redfaced Aussie.

Only the ceiling of raw rock broke the illusion that they were up on the surface in an Australian city.

Kinsman ordered a scotch and walked slowly with it to the last booth, where his back would be to the rock wall and he could see the entire pub. Tiredly, he wondered when the British Commonwealth was going to discover the joys of ice cubes. Half a tumbler of good whiskey and just two thumbnail-sized dollops of ice that immediately melted away and left the scotch lukewarm.

Like the Wicked Witch of the West, he thought. *Melting, melting. Like me.*

Kinsman glanced at his wristwatch. The dedication ceremonies should soon be over. The pub would start to fill up then. *Better finish your drink and find someplace to hide before they start pouring in here.*

He gulped at the whiskey, and as he put the glass down on the bare wood of the booth's table, Fred Durban walked into the pub.

He looked damned good for a man pushing seventy. Tall and spare as one of the old rocket boosters he had engineered, back in the days when you pressed the firing button and ducked behind sandbags because you had no idea of what the rocket might do.

Kinsman felt trapped. He couldn't get up and leave because he'd have to walk right past Durban and the old man would recognize him. If he stayed, Durban would spot him.

The old man walked slowly toward the bar, looking almost British in his tweed jacket and the pipe that he always had clamped between his teeth. He looked down the bar, then toward the booths. His face lit up as he spotted Kinsman. Briskly, he strode to the booth and slid into the bench on the other side of the narrow table.

"You couldn't take all the speechifying either, eh?"

Wishing he were somewhere else, Kinsman nodded.

"Can't blame you. I've been in this game for a thousand years now, and the *only* part of it that I don't like is when those stuffed shirts start congratulating themselves over the things we did."

"Uh, sir, I was just leaving . . ."

"Hey, come on! You wouldn't leave me here to drink all alone, would you?"

Before Kinsman could answer or maneuver himself out of the booth, Durban turned toward the barkeep and called, "Can I have a mug of beer, please, and another of whatever my friend here is drinking?"

The bartender nodded. "Ryte awhy, mate."

"Now then, the logistics are taken care of." Durban carefully placed his pipe in the ashtray, then fished in his jacket pockets to produce a pouch of tobacco, lighter, and all the surgical instruments that pipesmokers carry with them.

"I really should be going," Kinsman said, starting to feel desperate.

"Where to?"

"Well . . ."

"There's nothing going on except that damned dedication ceremony. Everybody else is there except thee and me. Except for the miners." He started reaming out the pipe and dumping the black soot into the ashtray. The barkeep brought their drinks and put them down on the table.

"How much?" Durban asked.

"I'll keep a tab runnin'. Got a bloody computer t' keep track of you blokes. Prints up your bill neat an' clean when you're ready t' go. Even keeps track o' the ice!" He laughed his way back to the bar.

"I haven't seen much of the mines yet," Kinsman said, still trying to get away.

"Nothing much to see," Durban muttered, putting the pipe back together. "Take the tour tomorrow morning. Just some tunnels with automated machinery chipping away at the rock. The real work's done by a half-dozen engineers in the control center. Looks just like the Kennedy Space Center."

"Or the surface . . ."

"Desert. They won't let you up there by yourself. It's fifty degrees Celsius up there. That's why the miners live down here."

"I know." *The sun will broil you in minutes. And it's empty up there. Clean and empty. No one to see you. No one to watch you. They wouldn't find your body for days.*

Durban took a long swallow of beer. "Fifty degrees," he murmured. "Sounds hotter if you say 120 Fahrenheit."

"Like the Moon."

Durban nodded. "That's why we opened this training center here. People will have to live underground on the Moon, so we'll train them here at Coober Pedy."

"It was your idea, wasn't it?"

Another nod. "Not mine exclusively. Several other people thought of it too. Years ago. But when you get to be an old fart like me in this game, they give you credit for enormous wisdom." He laughed and reached for his beer again.

Kinsman sat quietly, wondering how he could break away, while Durban alternately sipped his beer and packed his pipe. The old man still had a tinge of red in his silvery hair. His face was thin, ascetic, with skin like ancient parchment. But the cobalt-blue eyes were alive, alert, inquisitive, framed by bushy reddish brows. Durban had seen it all, from the struggling beginnings of rocketry when people scoffed at the idea of exploring space, to the multinational industry that was now on the verge of colonizing the Moon.

"You look damned uncomfortable, son. What's wrong?"

Kinsman felt himself wince. "Nothing," he lied.

Those bushy eyebrows went up. "Am I bothering you? Did I say something I shouldn't? Am I keeping you from a date or something?"

"No sir. None of the above. I'm just . . . well, I guess I feel out of place here."

Durban studied him. "You were on the plane with me, the LA to Sydney flight, weren't you?"

"Yessir."

"I thought I recognized you. Saw your picture in the papers or something, a few years back. But you were in uniform then."

He can't know, Kinsman told himself. *There's no way he could possibly know.*

"I'm still in the Air Force," he said to Durban. "I'm on . . . medical disability."

"Astronaut?"

"I was."

Durban said, "Do I have to buy you another drink to get you to tell me your name?"

"Kinsman," he blurted. "Chet Kinsman." He grasped the whiskey in front of him and took a long pull from it.

"Chester A. Kinsman," Durban murmured. "Now where did I . . . oh, of course!" He grinned broadly. "The Zero Gee Club! Now I remember. Old Cy Calder told me about you."

Kinsman put his drink down with a shaking hand. "The Zero Gee Club. I had forgotten about that."

"Forgotten about it?" Durban looked impressed. "You mean you've gone on to even greater things?"

"No." Kinsman shook his head. "Different. But not greater."

"Calder died a couple of years ago," Durban said.

"I didn't know."

His voice lower, "Just about all my old friends are dead. That's the curse of a long life . . . you get to feel you're the last of the Mohicans."

"You think dying young is better?"

Instead of answering, Durban picked up his lighter and started puffing his pipe to life. Clouds of bluish smoke rose slowly, swirled around his head, and then were pulled ceilingward toward the vents set into the solid rock.

"You said," he asked between puffs, "you were on . . . medical disability. . . . What happened?"

"Accident," Kinsman said automatically, feeling his insides congealing.

"Where? In orbit?"

"Yes."

"You got hurt? Funny, I didn't hear anything about . . ."

"It happened a long time ago," Kinsman said, seeing the face of the cosmonaut screaming as she died. "It just . . . it's been hard for me to shake it off. Emotionally, you know."

Durban blew out another cloud of smoke. "Still, I've got a pretty good network of spies in all parts of this game. Odd I never heard about it."

Stop pumping me, Kinsman snarled silently. "Maybe it wasn't important enough to make the gossip rounds," he lied. "To anybody except me, that is."

Durban looked skeptical. "So you've been on disability for how long now?"

"A while." *Let him think the time is classified.*

"H'm. And what are you doing here?"

Kinsman shrugged. "Looking for a job, I guess."

"A job?"

"I can get an honorable discharge from the Air Force. I thought I might get a civilian job."

Durban's bushy eyebrows knit together. "The Air Force

is willing to let a trained astronaut go? Who's your boss out there at Vandenberg?"

"Colonel Murdock."

"Bob Murdock?" Durban broke into a grin. "I've known Bobby since we used to fill out requisition forms over his forged signature. Don't tell me he's still a light colonel!"

"No, he's got his eagles."

"And he's willing to let you quit the Air Force? Why?"

Kinsman shook his head. *Because I'm a nervous wreck and a murderer. Or is it the other way around?*

"Personal, eh?"

"Very."

"I can introduce you to some NASA people who . . ."

"I've done a tour of duty with NASA. They shipped me back to the Air Force. The big aerospace corporations are where the jobs are now. Or so they tell me."

"And that's why you're here. To talk to the corporation people. Any luck?"

"All negative. They won't touch me without seeing my Air Force records, and my record shows a big blank space where it counts."

Durban stared at him. "What the hell happened?"

Kinsman did not reply.

"Okay, okay . . . it's very personal. I'm just plain curious, though. Not much happens in this game without me hearing about it, you know."

You won't hear about this one, Kinsman told himself. He finished his drink, put the heavy-walled glass back on the bare table.

"I hope you won't go probing into this, Mr. Durban. It's very sensitive . . . to me personally, as well as to the Air Force."

"I can see that," Durban said.

"I wouldn't have mentioned anything at all about it," Kinsman went on, "except that you . . . well, you seem like someone I can trust."

"But only so far."

"Believe me, I've told you more than anyone else. But please don't push it any father . . . I mean, farther."

"All right."

"I'd like your word on that."

The eyebrows shot up again. "My word? You mean there's a gentleman left in this world who'd take a man's word and a handshake on something bigger than a five-dollar bet?"

Smiling despite himself, Kinsman answered, "I don't even need the handshake. Your word is good enough for me."

"Well I'll be . . ." Durban's gaze shifted from Kinsman to the front of the pub. "Looks like a couple more fugitives from the ceremonies just slinked in."

Kinsman glanced toward the pub's front entrance and saw Frank Colt looking uncomfortably out of place next to a lanky, sandy-haired Russian in the tan and red uniform of the Soviet Cosmonaut Corps. Colt was in his Air Force dress blues.

Durban stuck his head out from the booth and called, "Piotr . . . over here."

"Ahah! An underground meeting!" the Russian boomed out in a voice three times his size.

The two men came over and slid into the booth: the Russian next to Durban and Colt beside Kinsman.

"Chet, may I introduce Major Piotr Leonov, Cosmonaut First Class. And a fine *basso*, if you ever want to get up an operatic quartet."

"We have already met," the Russian said, taking Kinsman's extended hand in a friendly but not overly strong grip.

"We have?"

"At your base near Aristarchus. I piloted the craft that brought medical aid for your renegade Jesuit."

Comprehension began to light in Kinsman's mind.

"You were quite asleep at the time," Leonov went on. "Apparently you had had a strenuous time, rescuing the priest."

Kinsman nodded. "Well, it's good to meet you when my eyes are open."

Leonov laughed.

"This is Captain Frank Colt," Kinsman said to Durban. "Top flier in the Vandenberg crew. I don't know how well he sings but he's a damned good man to work with in orbit."

"I've got a natural sense of rhythm," Colt said, straight-faced, testing Durban.

"I've heard about you," Durban said. "Aren't you the one who saved that Comcon satellite when its upper stage misfired and it looked like the whole damned thing was going to splash into the Pacific?"

With a nod, "I got the replacement stage mated to the satellite, yeah."

"And damned near fried his ass off," Kinsman added.

"You should have asked us for assistance," Leonov said, grinning. "We would have been glad to help save your military communications satellite."

"You sure would," Colt snapped. "You'd tote it back to Moscow with you."

Leonov shrugged elaborately. "Wouldn't you, with one of ours?"

A waitress appeared at their table: very young, miniskirt showing smooth strong thighs, low-cut blouse showing plenty of bosom, long blond hair, and a pretty face with placid cow eyes.

"Service is improving," Durban said.

"The ceremonies are breaking up," Colt told him. "This place'll be jammed in a few minutes."

The waitress took their order and flounced off to the bar.

"Nothing like that in Cosmograd, eh Piotr?" Durban nudged the Russian.

"My dear Frederick," Leonov countered, a quizzical smile on his bony face, "just because you did not see any of the beautiful women of our city does not mean that they do not exist. Being good Soviet women, they tend to hide from capitalists."

"Hide? Or are hidden?"

Leonov shrugged. "What difference? The important fact is that I know where they are, and you do not."

As the girl came back with their drinks, Colt asked Kinsman quietly, "How's it going?"

Kinsman jabbed his thumb toward the floor. "Lousy."

"I still wish you'd let me help. We can go over Murdock's head. The other astronauts will . . ."

"You don't want to get involved in it, Frank. It won't do you any good."

Colt made a disgusted face.

"A toast!" Leonov called, raising his glass. It looked like a tumbler of water. Kinsman guessed that it was at least four ounces of straight vodka. "To international cooperation in space. An end to all military secrets. Peace and total disarmament. Brotherhood throughout the cosmos. Friendship among all . . ."

"Is this a toast or a speech?" Colt grumbled.

"*Nazdrovia!*" Leonov snapped back and tossed down half his drink in one gulp.

"I've got a toast," Durban said. "May the work that is done here, underground, end up with the four of us meeting underground again . . . on the Moon."

They drank again. And again. The waitress brought fresh drinks. Through it all, Kinsman kept wishing he could get away, escape. The whiskey was not making him drunk. It couldn't. He wouldn't let it.

"Frank, my friend," Leonov said over their glasses, "why are you scowling? It is no crime to be drinking with a Russian."

Colt hunched his shoulders and leaned forward over the table. "Pete, I'm just drunk enough to tell you to go to hell. You know I don't believe a word of this peace and friendship bullshit."

"And I am drunk enough to know capitalist brainwashing when I hear it."

"Come on now," Durban said, relighting his pipe for the *n*th time. "Let's not get into a political squabble."

"Easy enough for you," Colt grumbled. "Mr. International Astronautical Federation. You can go around the world being friendly and setting up programs where we gotta cooperate with the Reds. But we"—Colt's gesture included Kinsman—"we gotta figure out how to cooperate with 'em without letting 'em steal the fuckin' store! We gotta defend the nation against 'em and cooperate with 'em at the same time. How d'you do that?"

Kinsman sat back in the booth, utterly sober, staring at his glass and trying to disappear from the face of the Earth.

Colt's superpatriotism always surprised and embarrassed Kinsman. *Childhood prejudice*, he knew. *Blacks were anti-Establishment when you were a kid and you expect them to be anti-Establishment forever.*

But America was truly multiracial now. There were black generals, black bank presidents and board chairmen. The talk was that there would be a black President before much longer.

What will they call the White House then? Will they repaint it? More likely they'll repaint the new President.

Leonov was chuckling. "Frank, my friend, I refuse to get angry with you. We are both alike! You want to fly in space; so do I. Your government has ordered you to be an intelligence officer for the duration of this international conference and ferret out as many of our secrets as you can. My government has ordered me to be an intelligence officer for the duration of this meeting and ferret out as many of your secrets as I can. How do you think I can roam around this underground rabbit's nest without a KGB 'guide' at my elbow?"

Intelligence officer? Kinsman snapped his attention to Leonov's eyes. The Russian met his gaze, smiling pleasantly, a bit drunkenly. There was no hatred there, not even suspicion. *He doesn't know about me.* Still, Kinsman's knees felt too weak to stand on.

"You already know all our goddamned secrets," Colt growled.

"Just as you know ours," countered Leonov.

"Then let's get off the subject," Durban suggested, his voice a bit edgy, "and talk about something more congenial."

"Such as what?"

Durban sucked on his pipe for a moment. It was out again. He took it from his mouth and jabbed the stem in Kinsman's direction.

"Chet here is looking for a job. What can we do for him?"

Jesus Christ! He's going to spill it all over the place!

"No, really," Kinsman said. "I'd rather . . ."

"Defect!" Leonov suggested jovially. "We will treat you handsomely in the Soviet Union."

Colt glowered. "Sure. In the basement of some psychiatric prison."

The Russian pretended to be hurt.

"I'm serious," Durban insisted. "There are too few experienced astronauts—and cosmonauts—to let one walk away from the game."

For God's sake leave me alone! Kinsman screamed silently. But he could say nothing to them. He was frozen there, pinned into the booth. Trapped.

"They don't want experience anymore," Colt muttered. "They want youth. Murdock's even got *me* slated to train the little bastards instead of doing the flying myself."

"The private corporations . . ." Durban began.

"Are all talk, and not much else," Colt said. "Chet and I are executive timber as far as they're concerned. But they're not hiring fliers. They'd rather let Uncle Sam take the risks while they sit back and wait till everything's set up for them at the taxpayer's expense. *Then* they'll move in and make their profits."

Durban puffed his pipe in silence.

Suddenly serious, Leonov said, "I know how you must feel. If I thought that I would have to spend the rest of my life in an office, or training others to do what I most want for myself, I would go mad."

"We need a new program," Durban said. "A priority program that's got to get going *now*, before they have time to train the next generation of kids."

"Such as what?" Colt asked.

"Not a military program," Leonov said. "Let us not make cosmic space more militarily useful than it is already."

"No," Durban said slowly. "But it should be an international program . . . something we can all participate in."

"Something that needs a corps of experienced astronauts," Kinsman heard himself saying. "Something that will get us out there to stay. Away from here permanently."

"I've been mulling over an idea for a while now," Durban said. "Maybe the time is ripe for it: a hospital."

"What?"

"On the Moon. A lunar hospital, for old gaffers like me, with bad hearts. For people with muscular diseases who are cripples here in this one-gravity field, but could lead normal lives on the Moon, in one-sixth gee."

Leonov smiled approvingly.

"Nobody's gonna put up funding for an old soldiers' home on the Moon," Colt was saying.

"Want to bet?" Kinsman was suddenly surging with hope. "What's the average age of the Congress? Or the Presidium of the USSR?"

"My father . . ." Leonov said. "He is confined to bed because of his heart's weakness. But in zero gravity . . . or even on the Moon . . ."

"And Jill Meyers," Kinsman added, "with all those damned allergies of hers." *I can stay in the Air Force! If they go into a medical base on the Moon I can stay in and work on that and never get into a combat situation. I can stay on the Moon, away from it all!*

They drank and made plans. Kinsman's head started to spin. The pub filled up with dignitaries from the conference that had officially inaugurated the underground training facility. The four men stayed in their booth, drinking and talking, ignoring everyone else. The international businessmen and government officials drifted away after a while and the pub began to fill up with its regular customers—the hard-drinking, hard-handed miners who dug for opal and copper, who lived underground to escape the searing heat of the desert above, the miners who were being crowded out of half their living area to make room for the space training facility.

The noise level went up in quantum jumps. Laughing, rowdy men. Blaring music from the stereo. Higher pitched laughter from the extra barmaids and waitresses who came on duty when the regulars came off shift.

Durban was yelling over the noise of the crowd, "Why don't we adjourn to my room? It's quieter there, and I've got a couple of bottles of liquor in my bags."

"Gotta make a pit stop first," Colt said, pointing to the door marked *Gents* near their booth.

"Me too," said Kinsman.

Inside the washroom the noise level was much lower. Colt and Kinsman stood side-by-side at the only two urinals.

"Y'know, I think the old guy's really got a workable idea," Colt said happily. "We can lay this hospital project on top of everything else that the Air Force and NASA and the private companies are doing . . . and with Durban pushing it, with his connections . . ."

"I still won't get off the ground," Kinsman suddenly realized.

"Huh? Sure you will, Chet. Murdock can't . . ."

Kinsman shook his head. "It doesn't matter, Frank. My psychological profile will shoot me down. They won't let me back into space again."

Zipping up and heading for the only sink, Colt said, "You can't let it beat you, man. You can't let it take the life outta you."

Wonderful play on words.

Gesturing Kinsman to the sink ahead of himself, Colt

said, "It's over and done with. You gotta stop acting . . . well, you know."

Kinsman looked into the mirror above the sink, into the haunted eyes that always stared back at him. "I act sick? Mentally unwell? Disturbed?"

"You act like a goddamned dope," Colt grumbled.

Wiping his hands on the cloth toweling that hung from a wall-mounted fixture, Kinsman said, "Frank, for a minute back there I got excited. I thought maybe Durban was right and this hospital project would make enough new slots for astronauts that I'd get another chance. But we both know better. They won't let me fly again. You, sure. But not me. I'm grounded."

Colt went to the sink as a couple of miners banged through the door and headed for the urinals. A gust of noise and raucous music bounced off the tile walls as the door swung shut.

"Listen, man, one thing I've learned about the Air Force—and everything else," Colt said over the splashing water of the sink. "If you take just what they want to give you, you'll get shit all the time. You gotta fight for what's yours."

Kinsman shook his head. "My family were Quakers, remember?" *And that's the best joke of all.*

Colt was moving toward the towel machine when one of the miners jostled into him.

"D'ya mind, mate?"

Wordlessly, Colt stepped away from him, turned and started wiping his hands on the toweling.

"Bloody foreigners all over the plyce, ain't they?" said the miner's companion.

Kinsman looked at them for the first time. They were no taller than he or Colt, but they were heavy-boned, big-knuckled, and half drunk.

Colt was wiping his hands very deliberately now, looking at Kinsman with his back to the two miners.

"Bad enough they're tykin' up half th' bloody pits to

put their bloody spyce cadets into," said the one at the sink, "but now they're goin' t' stink up the bloody pub."

"An' myke goo-goo eyes at th' girls."

"We oughtta bring in a few bloody chimpanzees t' serve 'em their drinks."

"Foreigners," said the second miner, loudly, even though the washroom was small enough to hear a whisper in. "You remember what we did t' those Eye-Tyes back in Melbourne, Bert?"

"They weren't Eye-Tyes; they were bloody Hungarians."

"Wops, Hunkies, whatever. Treated 'em ryte, din't we?"

"Gave 'em what they deserved."

Kinsman was between Colt and the door. He wanted to tell his friend to leave, to ignore the drunken Aussies and walk out. But he couldn't.

Colt was slowly, methodically, wiping his black hands on the white toweling. The first miner stepped from the sink to stand a few inches away from him.

"Least we never had t' deal with bloody Fiji Islanders before."

Colt said nothing. He surrendered the towel, and the miner grinned at him with crooked teeth.

"Or Yank niggers," he added.

Colt grinned back. His right fist traveled six inches and buried itself in the man's solar plexus. The miner gave a silent gasp and collapsed, legs folding as he sank to the tiled floor.

The other miner stared but said nothing.

Kinsman opened the door and Colt followed him out into the noisy, crowded pub. They saw Durban and Leonov already standing at the end of the bar, near the door that led to the corridor.

"See what I mean," Colt said as they elbowed their way through the press of bodies. "Gotta fight for respect, every time."

Out in the corridor, Leonov said, "I was about to call your embassy to send a searching party for you."

"We got into a small discussion with a couple of the friendly natives," Colt answered.

"Say, if you youngsters will slow down a little," Durban pleaded, "I'll show you where my room is."

"And the liquor," Leonov beamed, immediately slowing his pace to walk beside the elderly man.

They labored up the rising slope of the corridor. It had originally been a tunnel, hewn out of solid rock. Only the floor was smoothed and covered with spongy plastic tiles. The walls and ceiling were still bare—grayish brown, unfinished rock. Fluorescent lights hung every ten meters or so, connected by dangling wires.

The others were busily chatting among themselves about the new hospital project. Kinsman stayed silent. *Could I talk Murdock into it? Would they let me fly again? I'd have to work it out so that I was assigned to the hospital project and nothing else. They'd never let me get away with that. They could reassign me whenever they wanted . . .*

"HEY, YOU THERE! TH' YANKS!"

Turning, Kinsman saw a dozen or so miners advancing up the tunnel corridor toward them. In the lead were the two from the washroom. They all looked drunk. And violently angry.

"That's the black barstard that beat me up," the miner yelled. "Him an' his friend there."

Colt moved to stand beside Kinsman. And suddenly Leonov was on his other side.

The miners halted a few feet in front of them. They wanted to fight. They were spoiling for blood. Kinsman stood rooted there, his mind blazing with the memory of the moment when he had felt blood-lust. He was sweating again, panting with exertion, reaching for the cosmonaut's fragile airhose . . .

Not again, he told himself, trying to control his trembling so that the others could not see it. *Not again!*

"What is this?" Leonov snapped. "Why are we accosted by a mob?"

"Back off Russkie," said one of the miners. "This is none of your fight."

"These are my friends," Leonov said. "What concerns them concerns me."

"He beat me up," said the miner that Colt had hit.

"An' him," his companion pointed at Kinsman. "He helped th' black bugger."

"Beat you up?" Leonov asked mildly. "Where are your scars? Where is the blood? I see no bruises. Are you certain you did not merely faint?"

The miner turned red as the men around him grinned.

"I was there with 'im," the other miner said. "They jumped Bert and pummelled 'im 'til he dropped. In th' midsection."

"While you watched?" Leonov asked.

"We ain't takin' that from no foreigners!" The mob surged forward.

"Now that's enough!"

Frederick Durban stepped between Kinsman and Leonov to face the angry miners.

"We are the guests of the Australian government," he said firmly, "and if any harm comes to us, you'll all go to jail."

"What about 'im?" one of the miners yelled. "They can't go beating up our blokes an' get awhy with it!"

"Nobody beat anybody up," Colt shouted back. "The guy called me a nigger and I punched him in the gut. He folded like a pretzel. One punch."

"That's a bloody lie! The other one held me an' the black barstard kicked me too!"

Very calmly, Durban took the pipe from his mouth and said, "All right, let's settle this here and now. But not with a riot."

"How then?"

"There's an old custom where I come from . . . mining country, back in Colorado." He turned slightly back toward Kinsman and winked. "When two men have a difference of opinion, they settle it fairly between them-

selves. Do you two want to fight it out right here . . .
Marquess of Queensberry rules?"

Colt shrugged, then nodded.

"Oh no you don't!" snapped the miner. "He's a bloody
tryned killer. A soldier. Probably a karate expert . . .
chops bricks with 'is bare hands an' all that."

Durban scowled from under his shaggy eyebrows. "Very
well then. Suppose *I* represent the American side of this
argument. Would you be afraid to fight me?"

"You? You're an old man?"

"I may be almost seventy," Durban said, stuffing his
pipe into a jacket pocket, "but I can still take on the
likes of you."

The miner looked bewildered. "I . . . you can't . . ."

"Come on," Durban said, very seriously. He raised his
bony fists.

One of the other miners put a hand on the first one's
shoulder. "Forget it, Bert. He's cryzy."

Bert stood there, uncertain. Durban was ramrod straight,
looking like a gnarled old tree next to a snorting red-eyed
bull.

Kinsman watched, unable to move. *The guy'll kill him
with one punch. Then what can we do? What can I do?
Can I fight? Can I raise my fists in anger again? Or in
self-defense?*

The miner finally stepped back, muttering and shaking
his head. They all turned and began to walk slowly back
down the tunnel corridor, back toward the pub.

Durban let his hands drop to his sides.

Colt puffed out a breath of relief. "Thanks, man."

"Very courageous of you," Leonov said thoughtfully.

But Kinsman said nothing. *What would I have done if
it had come to blows? What would I have done?*

The four men walked slowly back to Durban's room,
two levels up closer to the surface.

"The whiskey's in that brown carry-all," Durban said
as they entered the windowless room. "Help yourselves."
He went straight to the bed and stretched out on it.

Colt and Leonov went to the whiskey. Kinsman took a close look at the old man. His face was ashen, his thin chest heaving.

"Are you all right?"

"I've got some pills here . . ." He fished in his jacket pockets. The pipe fell out and dropped to the floor, spilling black ashes across the thin carpeting.

"I'll get you a glass of water."

Kinsman went to the sink across from the bed and took a plastic cup from the dispenser above it.

Durban propped himself up on one elbow to drink down the pill.

Leonov had taken the small room's only chair. Colt was sitting on the dresser top, next to the open whiskey bottle. They both had plastic cups in their hands.

"Hey, you need a doctor?" Colt asked.

"No . . ." Durban closed his eyes and took a deep breath. "Just a little too much excitement for my heart. That, and the climb upstairs."

Leonov said, "We have a cardiac specialist with the Soviet delegation."

Sitting up on the bed, Durban waved a hand at the Russian. "No, it's all right. I'll be okay in a minute."

Kinsman sat on the edge of the bed and helped the old man out of his jacket, then pulled off his shoes.

"You see," Durban said, sinking back against the pillows, "I really do need a low-gravity home. Damned heart's not fit to live on Earth anymore. It wants to be on the Moon."

"We'll get you there," Colt said.

"Yes," Leonov agreed, raising his cup to the proposition.

Kinsman shook his head. "If that miner had punched you, it would probably have killed you."

Durban smiled at him. "Oh, I knew he wouldn't hit me. He couldn't."

"He came damned close."

"Not a bit of it. I'm obviously an old and frail man. It would ruin his self-image if he hit me. His *machismo*. He knew that if he hit me I'd go down with one punch.

I could see it in his eyes. He was afraid of beating up an old man."

"Then why . . ."

"I got in front of you fellows so that he would be forced to hit me before anybody else started fighting. That was the best way to prevent the fight from starting."

"You still could've gotten hurt. Killed."

Durban's shaggy eyebrows rose a bit. "Well, sometimes you have to put yourself on the line."

"We could've taken the bunch of them," Colt said. "They were brawlers, not trained fighters."

Leonov took a swallow of whiskey and said, "I, for one, am glad that the fight did not come about. My training is not in hand-to-hand combat."

You have to put yourself on the line, Kinsman was repeating to himself.

"Maybe you could have taken them all singlehandedly, Frank," Durban said, "but I doubt it. Besides, there are better ways of winning what you want than punching people. Much better ways."

"The tongue is mightier than the fist?" Colt asked.

"The brain is mightier than the biceps," Durban replied.

Kinsman got to his feet. "I've got to phone Murdock."

"Bobby? Why?"

"To tell him that I'm not quitting the Air Force. I'm not going to take an honorable discharge, or any kind of discharge. I'm not quitting."

Colt broke into a wide grin. "Great! And tell him for me what I think about being assigned to training."

Leonov said, "You realize, of course, that if you start a high-priority program to build a hospital complex on the Moon, my superiors will become very suspicious of you."

"That's fine, Piotr," Durban said from his reclining position. "I'll put the idea before the International Federation and get them to make this an international cooperative project. Then you can come in on it too."

"We shall all meet on the Moon," said Leonov.

"The sooner the better," Durban agreed.

"To the Moon." Colt raised his cup.

"I'll be there," said Kinsman.

AGE 35

As soon as he stepped through the acoustical screen at the apartment's doorway, the noise hit Kinsman like a physical blow. He stood there a moment and watched the tribal rites of a Washington cocktail party.

My battlefield.

The room was jammed with guests, and they all seemed to be talking at once. It was an old Georgetown parlor, big, with a high, ornately panelled ceiling. The streets outside had been quiet and deserted except for the police monitors in their armored suits standing at each intersection. They looked like a bitter parody of astronauts in pressure suits, Kinsman had thought.

But here there was life, chatter, laughter. The people who made Washington go, the people who ran the nation, were here drinking and talking and ignoring the enforced peace of the streets outside.

Kinsman recognized fewer than one in ten of the partygoers. Then he saw his host, Neal McGrath, over at the far end of the room by the empty fireplace, tall drink in hand, head slightly bent to catch what some wrinkled matron was saying to him. *The target for tonight.* McGrath was the swing vote on the Senate's Armed Services Committee.

"Chet, you did come after all!"

He turned to see Mary-Ellen McGrath approaching him, hands extended in greeting.

"I hardly recognized you without your uniform," she said.

He smiled back at her. "I thought Aerospace Force blues might be a little conspicuous around here."

"Nonsense. And I wanted to see your new oak leaves. A major now."

A captain on the Moon and a major in the Pentagon. Hazardous duty pay.

"Come on, Chet. I'll show you where the bar is." She took his arm and led him through the jabbering crowd.

Mary-Ellen was Kinsman's own height. She had the strong, honest face of a woman who could stand beside her husband in the face of anything from Washington cocktail parties to the tight infighting of rural Pennsylvania politics.

The bar dispenser hummed impersonally to itself as it produced a heavy scotch and water. Kinsman took a stinging sip of it.

"I was worried you wouldn't come," Mary-Ellen said over the noise of the crowd. "You've been a hermit ever since you arrived in Washington."

"Pentagon keeps me pretty busy."

"And no date? No woman on your arm? That isn't the Chet Kinsman I used to know back when."

"I'm preparing for the priesthood."

"I'd almost believe it," she said, straight-faced. "There's something different about you since the old days. You're quieter . . . more subdued."

I've been grounded. Aloud, he said, "Creeping maturity. I'm a late achiever."

But she was serious, and as stubborn as her husband. "Don't try to kid around it. You've changed. You're not playing the dashing young astronaut anymore."

"Who the hell is?"

A burly, balding man jarred into Kinsman from behind, sloshing half the drink out of his glass.

"Whoops, didn't get it on ya, did . . . oh, hi, Mrs. McGrath. Looks like I'm waterin' your rug."

"That won't hurt it," Mary-Ellen said. "Do you two know each other? Tug Wynne . . ."

"I've seen the Major on the Hill."

Kinsman said, "You're with ABC News, aren't you?"

Nodding, Wynne replied, "Surprised to see you here, Major, after this morning's committee session."

Kinsman forced a grin. "I'm an old family friend. I've known the Senator since we were kids."

"You think he's gonna vote against the Moonbase program?"

"I hope not," Kinsman said.

Mary-Ellen kept silent.

"He sure gave your Colonel Murdock a hard time this morning." Wynne chuckled wheezily. "Mrs. McGrath, you shoulda seen your husband in action."

Kinsman changed the subject. "Say, did you know old Cy Calder, used to work for Allied News Syndicate out on the West coast."

"Only by legend," Wynne answered. "He died four, five years ago, I heard."

"Yes. I know."

"Musta been past eighty. Friend of yours?"

"Sort of. I knew him . . . Lord, it was almost ten years ago. Back when we were starting the first Air Force space missions. Helluva guy."

Mary-Ellen said, "I'd better tend to some of the other guests. There are several old friends of yours here tonight, Chet. Mix around, you'll find them."

With another rasping chuckle, Wynne said, "Guess we *could* give somebody else a chance to get to the bar."

Kinsman started to drift away, but Wynne followed behind him.

"Murdock send you over here to soften up McGrath?"

Pushing past a pair of arguing, arm-waving cigar smokers, Kinsman frowned. "I was invited to this party weeks ago. I told you, the Senator and I are old friends."

"And how friendly are you with Mrs. McGrath?"

"What's that supposed to mean?"

Wynne let his teeth show. "Handsome astronaut, good-looking wife, busy senator . . ."

"That's pretty foul-minded, even for a newsman."

"Just doin' my job," Wynne said, still smiling. "Nothing personal. Besides, you've got nothing to complain about, as far as newspeople are concerned. We know which astronaut killed that Russian girl, even if the Air Force won't officially give out the story."

It was the hundredth time since he'd arrived in Washington that a news reporter had faced him with the accusation. The Pentagon public relations people had worked assiduously to keep the story "unofficial," citing the growing cooperation between the Soviet and American space efforts as the reason. The media had responded by downplaying the story, treating it as history rather than news—spurred into compliance, perhaps, by the government's tough new laws regarding licensing for broadcasting stations and mailing permits for newspapers and magazines.

Freezing his emotions within himself, Kinsman answered merely, "Aerospace Force. The name's been changed to Aerospace Force."

Wynne shrugged and raised his glass in a mock salute. "I stand corrected, Major."

Kinsman turned and started working his way toward the other end of the room. A grandfather clock chimed off in a corner, barely audible over the human noises and clacking of ice in glassware. *Eighteen hundred. Royce and Smitty ought to be halfway to Copernicus by now.*

And then he heard her. He didn't have to see her, he knew it was Diane. The same pure, haunting soprano, a voice straight out of a fairytale:

Once I had a sweetheart, and now I have none.
Once I had a sweetheart, and now I have none.
He's gone and leave me, he's gone and leave me,
He's gone and leave me to sorrow and mourn.

Her voice stroked his memory and he felt all the old joy, all the old pain, as he pushed his way through the crowd.

Finally he saw her, sitting cross-legged on a sofa, guitar hiding her slim figure. The same ancient guitar; no amplifiers, no boosters. Her hair was still straight and long and black as space. Her eyes were even darker and deeper. The people were ringed about her, standing, sitting on the floor. They gave her the entire sofa to herself, an altar that only the anointed could use. They watched her and listened, entranced by her voice. But she was somewhere else, living the song, seeing what it told of, until she strummed the final chord.

Then she looked up and looked straight at Kinsman. Not surprised. Not even smiling. Just a look that linked them as if all the years since their brief time together had dissolved into a single yesterday. Before either of them could say or do anything, the others broke into applause. Diane smiled and mouthed, "Thank you."

"More, more!"

"Come on, another one."

" 'Greensleeves.' "

Diane put the guitar down carefully beside her, uncoiled her slim legs, and stood up. "Later, okay?"

Kinsman grinned to himself. He knew it would be later or nothing.

The crowd muttered reluctant acquiescence and broke the circle around her. Kinsman stepped the final few paces and stood before Diane.

"Good to see you again." He suddenly felt awkward, not knowing what to do. He held his drink with both hands.

"Hello, Chet." She wasn't quite smiling.

"I'm surprised you remember. It's been so long . . ."

Now she did smile. "How could I ever forget you? And I've seen your name in the news every once in a while."

"I've listened to your records everywhere I've gone," he said.

"Even on the Moon?" she asked, with a look that was almost shy, almost mocking.

"Sure," he lied. "Even on the Moon."

"Here, Diane, I brought you some punch." Kinsman turned to see a fleshy-faced young man with a droopy moustache and tousled brown hair, carrying two plastic cups of punch. He wore a sharply tailored white business suit complete with vest and florid wide scarf.

"Thank you, Larry. This is Chet Kinsman. Chet, meet Larry Davis."

"Kinsman?"

Diane explained, "I met Chet in San Francisco, a thousand years ago, when I was just getting started. Chet's an astronaut."

"Oh really?"

Somehow, the man antagonized Kinsman. "Affirmative," he snapped in his best military manner.

"He's been on the Moon," Diane went on.

"That's where I heard the name," Davis said. "You're one of those Air Force people who wants to build a base up there. Weren't you involved in some sort of rescue a couple of years back? One of your people got stranded or something . . ."

"Yes." Kinsman cut him short. "It was all blown up out of proportion by the news media."

They stood there for a moment, silent and unmoving, while the party pulsated around them.

Diane said, "Mary-Ellen told me you might be here tonight. You and Neal are both working on something about the space program?"

"Something like that," Kinsman said. "Organized any more protest demonstrations?"

She forced a laugh. "There's nothing left to protest about. Everything's so well organized around the country that nobody can raise a crowd anymore. Public safety laws and all that."

"It does seem quieter. Nobody's complaining."

"They can't," Diane said. "You ought to see what we have to go through before every concert. They want to check the lyrics of every song I do. Even the encores. Nothing's allowed to be spontaneous."

"You manage to get in some damned tough lyrics," Kinsman said. "I've listened to you."

"The censors aren't always very bright."

"Or incorruptible," Davis added, smirking.

"So everybody's happy," Kinsman said. "You get to sing your songs about freedom and love. The crowd gets its little feel of excitement. And the government people get paid off. Everybody gets what they want."

Diane looked at him quizzically. "Do you have what you want, Chet?"

"Me?" Surprised. "Hell, no."

"Then not everybody's satisfied."

"Are you?"

"Hell, no," she mimicked.

"But everything *looks* so rosy," Davis said, with acid in his voice. "The government keeps telling us that unemployment is down and the stock market is up. And our President promised he won't send troops into Brazil. Not until after the elections, I bet."

Diane nodded. Then, brightening, "Larry, did I ever tell you about the time we tried to get Chet to come out and join one of our demonstrations? In his uniform?"

"I'm agog."

She turned to Kinsman. "Do you remember what you told me, Chet?"

"No . . ."

It was a perfect day for flying, for getting away from funerals and families and all the ties of Earth. Flying so high above the clouds that even the rugged Sierras looked like nothing more than wrinkles. Then out over the desert at Mach 2, the only sounds in your earphones from your own breathing and the faint, distant crackle of earthbound men giving orders to other earthbound men.

"You told me," Diane was laughing now, "that you'd rather be flying and defending us so that nobody bombed us while we were demonstrating for peace!"

It was funny now; it hadn't been then.

"Yeah, that sounds like something I might have said."

"How amusing," Davis said. "And what are you protecting us from now? The Brazilians? Or the Lithuanians?"

You overstuffed fruit, you wouldn't even fit into a cockpit. "From politicians. I'm on a Pentagon assignment. My job is Congressional liaison."

"Twisting senators' arms is what he means," came Neal McGrath's husky voice from behind him.

Kinsman turned.

"Hello, Chet, Diane . . . em, Larry Davis, isn't it?"

"You have a good memory for names."

"Goes with the job."

Kinsman studied McGrath. It was the first time they had been this physically close in many years. Neal's hair was still reddish and the rugged, outdoors look hadn't yet been completely erased from his features. He looked like a down-home farmer; Kinsman knew he had been a Rhodes scholar, once. McGrath's voice was even softer, throatier than it had been years ago. The natural expression of his face, in repose, was still an introspective scowl. But he was smiling now.

His cocktail party smile, thought Kinsman. Then he realized, *Neal's starting to get gray. Guess I am, too.*

"Tug Wynne tells me I was pretty rough on your boss this morning, Chet." The smile on McGrath's face turned just a shade self-satisfied.

"Colonel Murdock lost a few pounds, and it wasn't all from the TV lights," Kinsman said.

"I was only trying to get him to give me a good reason for funneling money into a permanent lunar base."

Kinsman answered, "The House Appropriations Committee approved the funding. Isn't that a good enough reason?"

"No," McGrath said firmly. "Not when we've got to

find money to reclaim every major city in the nation, plus new energy exploration, *and* crime control, *and* . . ."

"And holding down the Pentagon before they go jumping into Brazil," Diane added.

"Thanks, pal," Kinsman said to her. Turning back to McGrath, "Look, Neal, I'm not going to argue with you. The facts are damned clear. There's energy in space, lots of it. And raw materials. To utilize them, we need a permanent base on the Moon."

"Then let the corporations build it. They're the ones who want to put up Solar Power Satellites. They want to mine the Moon. Why should the taxpayers foot the bill for a big, expensive base on the Moon?"

"Because the heart of that base will be a low-gravity hospital that will . . ."

"Come on, Chet! You know it'll be easier and cheaper to build your hospital in orbit. Why go all the way to the Moon when you can build it a hundred miles overhead? And why should the Air Force do it? It's NASA's job."

Kinsman could see that McGrath looked faintly amused: he enjoyed arguing. *He's not fighting for his life.*

Glancing at Diane, then back to McGrath, Kinsman answered, "NASA's fully committed to building the space stations and helping the corporations to start industrial operations in orbit. Besides, we've got an Air Force team of trained astronauts with practically nothing to do."

"So build your hospital in orbit. Or cooperate with NASA, for a change, and put your hospital into one of their space stations."

"And it'll cost twenty times more than a lunar base will," Kinsman said. "Every time you want a Band-Aid you'll have to boost it up from Earth. That takes energy, Neal. And money. A permanent base on the Moon can be entirely self-sufficient."

"In a hundred years," McGrath said.

"Ten!"

"Come on, Chet. You guys are already spending billions on military satellites. You can't have the Moon, too. Let it go and stop pushing this pipe dream of Fred Durban's."

"A lunar base makes sense, dammitall, on a straight cost-effectiveness basis. You've seen the numbers, Neal. The base will pay for itself in ten years. It'll *save* the taxpayers billions of dollars in the long run."

A crowd was gathering around them. McGrath automatically raised his voice a notch. "That's just like Mary-Ellen saves me money at department store sales. I can't afford to save that kind of money. Not this year. Or next. The capital outlay is too high. To say nothing of the overruns."

"Now wait . . ."

"There's never been a military program that's lived within its budget. No, Moonbase is going to have to wait."

"We've already waited twenty years."

The rest of the party had stopped. Everyone was watching the debate.

"Our first priority," McGrath said, more to the crowd than to Kinsman, "has got to be for the cities. They've become jungles, unfit for human life. We've got to reclaim them and save the people who're trapped in them before they all turn into savages."

"But what about energy?" Kinsman insisted. "What about jobs? What about natural resources? Space operations can give us all those things."

"Then let the corporations develop those programs. Let them take the risks and make the profits. We're putting enough money into the Pentagon . . . including some damned expensive satellites that your brass-hat bosses won't even tell us lowly senators about."

The laser satellites, Kinsman realized. *It's griping him that he hasn't been briefed personally about them.*

"The corporations aren't going to develop anything, Neal, unless the government takes the initiative. You know how they work—let Uncle Sam take the risks and then when it's safe they'll come in and take the profits."

McGrath nodded. "Sure. Fine. But NASA's the agency that's running with that particular ball. The Aerospace

Force has no business extending its gold-plated tentacles all the way to the Moon."

It's like he's running for re-election, Kinsman said to himself. Then he realized, *Of course he is! They always are.*

"Sure, Neal, play kick the Pentagon," he said. "That's an awfully convenient excuse for ducking the issue."

With the confident grin of a hunter who had finally cornered his quarry, McGrath asked, "So you want to build a military base on the Moon, despite the fact that we've signed treaties with the Russians to keep the Moon demilitarized . . ."

"This base isn't going to be a fortress, for God's sake. You know that. It's a hospital. We're just using military astronauts to get the work done, because we have a trained corps of people who aren't being utilized. The Russians *want* to work with us on this."

"All right, all right." McGrath waved his hand, still grinning. "Even so. You put up this hospital of Durban's, this super geriatrics ward on the Moon, at a cost of billions. How's that going to help the welfare class in the cities? How's that going to rebuild New York or Detroit?"

"Or Washington," somebody muttered.

Kinsman said, "It will create jobs . . ."

"For white engineers who live in the suburbs."

"It will save lives, for Chrissake!"

"For rich people who can afford to go to the Moon to live."

"It'll give people hope for the future."

"Ghetto people? Don't be silly."

"Neal," Kinsman said, exasperation in his voice, "maybe space operations won't solve any of those problems. But neither will anything else you do! Without a strong space effort you won't have the energy, the raw materials, the new wealth that you need to rebuild the cities. Space gives us a chance, a hope—space factories and space power satellites will create new jobs, increase the Gross National Product, bring new wealth into the economy. Nothing that you're promising to do can accomplish that, and nothing short of that can solve the problems you're so damned worked up about."

His smile a bit tighter, McGrath said, "Perhaps so. But your Moonbase won't do that. Industrial operations in orbit will do it. The corporations will do it."

"But the corporations aren't moving fast enough. They're waiting for us to pave the way for them."

"That's why NASA's building the space stations," McGrath said, "to encourage the corporations to start testing out industrial operations in orbit."

"But that's not enough! We need the Moon. The most economical way to supply those space stations and the orbital factories that the corporations will eventually build is with raw materials from the Moon."

Diane touched his arm, a curious look in her dark eyes. "Chet, why do you want a Moonbase so much?"

"Why? Because . . . I was just telling you . . ."

She shook her head. "No, I don't mean the official reasons. Why do *you* dig the idea? Why does it turn you on?"

"We need it. The whole human race needs it."

"No," she repeated patiently. "*You.* Why are you for it? What's in it for you?"

"What do you mean?"

"What makes you tick, man? What turns you on? Is it a Moonbase? Power? Glory? What moves you, Chet?"

They were all watching him, the whole crowd, their faces eager or smirking or inquisitive. *Floating weightless, standing on nothing, alone, free, away from all of them. Staring back at the overpowering beauty of Earth—rich, brilliant, full, and shining against the black emptiness. Knowing that people down there are killing themselves, killing each other, killing their world and teaching their children how to kill. Knowing that you're part of it, too. Your eyes filling with tears at the beauty and the horror. To get away from it, far away, where they can't reach you, where you can start over, new, fresh, clean. How could they see it? How could they understand?*

"What moves you, Chet?" Diane asked again.

He made himself grin. "Well, for one thing, the synthetic coffee at the Pentagon . . ."

A few people laughed, a nervous titter. But Diane wouldn't let him off the hook. "No—get serious. This is important. What turns you on?"

Stall! They don't really want to know. And they wouldn't understand anyway. "You mean aside from the obvious things, like women?"

She nodded gravely.

"I never thought about it. Kind of hard to say. Flying, I guess. Getting out on your own responsibility, away from committees and chains of command."

"There's got to be more to it than that," Diane insisted.

"Well . . . have you ever been out in the desert, at an Israeli outpost, dancing all night by firelight because you know that at dawn there's going to be an attack and you don't want to waste a minute of living?"

There was a heartbeat's span of dead silence. Then one of the women asked in a near-whisper, "When . . . were you . . ."

Kinsman said, "Oh, I've never been there. But isn't it a romantic picture?"

They all broke into laughter. *That burst the bubble.* The crowd began to dissolve, breaking into smaller groups. Dozens of private conversations began to fill the silence that had briefly held them.

"You cheated," Diane said, frowning.

"Maybe I did."

"Don't you have anything except ice water in your veins?"

He shrugged. "If you prick us, do we not bleed?"

"Don't talk dirty."

He took her by the arm and headed for the big glass doors at the far end of the room. "Come on, we've got a lot of catching up to do."

He pushed the door open and they stepped out onto the balcony. Shatterproof plastic enclosed it and shielded them from the humid, hazy Washington air—and from anything that might be thrown or shot from the street below.

"Being a senator hath its privileges," Kinsman said. "My apartment over in Alexandria is about the size of this balcony. And no air conditioning is allowed."

Diane wasn't listening. She stretched catlike and pressed herself against the plastic shielding. To Kinsman she looked like a black leopard: supple, fascinating, dangerous.

"Sunset," she said, looking out toward the slice of red sky visible down the street. "Loveliest time of the day."

"Loneliest time, too."

She turned to him, her eyes showing genuine surprise. "Lonely? You? I never thought of you as being lonely. I always pictured you surrounded by friends."

"Or enemies," Kinsman heard himself say.

"You never did marry, did you?"

"You did."

"That was a long time ago. It's even been over for a long time."

"I orbited right over your wedding," he said. "I waved, but you didn't wave back."

Her eyebrows went up. "You walked out on me, remember? It wasn't my idea for you to go. You chose a mother-loving airplane over me."

"I was young and foolish."

"You'd still make the same choice today, and we both know it."

"Maybe." Kinsman looked into her deep, dark eyes. She wasn't angry with him. Curious, perhaps. Puzzled. Hurt? "But that doesn't mean that I like making the choice that way, Diane. We all have our problems, you know."

"You? You have problems? Weaknesses?"

"I've got a few, tucked away here and there."

"Why do you hide them?"

"Because nobody else gives a damn about them." Before

Diane could reply, he said, "I sound sorry for myself, don't I?"

"Well . . ."

"Who's this Larry character?"

"He's a very nice guy," she said firmly. "A good agent and a good business manager. He doesn't go whizzing off into the wild blue yonder . . . or, space is black, isn't it?"

"As black as the devil's heart," Kinsman answered. "I don't go whizzing off anymore, either. I've been grounded."

She blinked at him. "Grounded? What does that mean?"

"Clipped my wings," he said. "Deballed me. No longer qualified for flight duty. No orbital missions. No lunar missions. They won't even let me fly a plane anymore. Got some shavetail to jockey me around. I work at a desk."

"But . . . why?"

"It's a long, dirty story. Officially, I'm too valuable to risk. Something like that."

"Chet, I'm so sorry. Flying means so much to you, I know." She took a step toward him.

"Let's get out of here, Diane. Let's go someplace safe and watch the Moon come up and I'll tell you all the legends about your namesake."

He could see her breath catch. "That's . . . that's some line."

He wanted to reach out and hold her. Instead he said lamely, "Yeah, I suppose it is."

She came no closer. "I can't leave the party, Chet. They're expecting me to sing."

"Screw them."

"All of them?"

"Don't talk dirty."

She laughed, but shook her head. "Really, Chet, I can't leave."

"Then let me take you home afterward."

"I'm staying here tonight."

There were things he wanted to tell her, but he checked himself.

"Chet, please . . . it's been a long time."

"Yeah. Hasn't it, though."

The party ended at midnight, when the sirens sounded the curfew warning. Within fifteen minutes Kinsman and everyone else had left the stately redbrick Georgetown house and taken taxis or buses homeward. Precisely at twelve-thirty electrical power along every street in the District of Columbia was cut off.

Kinsman fumbled his way in darkness up the narrow stairs to his one-room apartment. It was still unfamiliar enough for him to bark his shins on the leg of the table alongside the sofabed. The long, elaborately detailed string of profanity he muttered to himself started and ended with his own stupidity.

In less than an hour of staring into the darkness he drifted to sleep. And if he had any dreams, he didn't remember them the next morning. For which he was grateful.

The Pentagon looked gray and shabby in the rain. It bulked like an ancient fortress over the greenery of Virginia. The old parking lots, converted into athletic fields for the Defense Department personnel, were bare and empty except for the growing puddles pockmarked by the fast-falling raindrops. Off in the mists, like enchanted castles in the clouds, the glasswalled office buildings of Crystal City lent a touch of contrast to the brooding old stone face of the Pentagon.

Feeling as cold and gray within himself as the weather outside, Kinsman watched the Pentagon approach through the rain-streaked windows of the morning bus. As always, the bus was jammed with office workers, many of them in uniform. They were silent, morose, wrapped in their private miseries at 7:48 in the morning.

The Pentagon corridors had once been painted in cheerful pastels, but now they were faded and glum.

Kinsman checked into his own lime-green cubbyhole office, noted the single appointment glowing on his desktop computer screen, and immediately headed for Colonel Murdock's office.

Frank Colt was already there, slouched in a fake leather chair in the Colonel's outer office. Otherwise, the area was unpopulated. Even the secretaries' desks were empty. *Frank always arrives on the scene ahead of everybody else. Wonder how he does it?*

"Morning," said Colt, barely glancing up at Kinsman.

"I'm glad you didn't say *good* morning," Kinsman replied.

"Sure as shit ain't that."

Kinsman nodded. "Murdock in yet?"

Colt gave him a surly look. "Hey, man, it's only eight o'clock. He told us to be here at eight sharp, right? That means he won't waltz in for another half-hour. You know that."

The Colonel's got his own car, he doesn't have to hit the bus on schedule.

"How'd the party go last night?" Colt asked.

"Lousy. Neal's just as stubborn as he ever was."

"We're gonna hafta lower the boom on him."

"That might not be so easy."

"I know, but what else is there, man?"

"Maybe if we briefed him about the laser satellites . . . I think he's pissed about not being in on that."

"Murdock doesn't have the guts to suggest that upstairs."

"I know."

The secretaries began drifting in, chatting over their plastic cups of synthetic coffee. The Colonel's private secretary, an iron-gray woman with a hawklike, unsmiling face, arrived last—befitting her rank.

"The Colonel will be a few minutes," she informed Kinsman and Colt. "He's briefing the General on yesterday's testimony."

Yesterday's fiasco, thought Kinsman.

The two majors sat in front of the chief secretary's desk.

Kinsman felt like a schoolboy who had been sent down to see the principal and was forced to wait in torment before the man would allow him into his office.

"You catch the late news last night?" Colt asked.

Kinsman shook his head.

"Shoulda seen our beloved leader," Colt said solemnly.

The secretary glanced at him, but quickly turned her attention back to the morning mail on her desk.

"Murdock was on the news last night?"

"Sure was. Big floppy handkerchief and all."

"Terrific."

"They showed the part where he got mixed up between miles and kilometers and wound up saying the Moon's bigger'n the Earth."

They both laughed. The secretary glowered at them.

Colonel Murdock burst into the room, his usual worried frown etched into near panic. His uniform jacket was unbuttoned, his tie pulled loose.

The secretary rose with a handful of papers.

"Not now!" Murdock's voice was high and shrill.

Christ, he's already four-o'clock nervous and it's not even eight-thirty yet!

"Get in here, both of you!" the Colonel said as he opened the door to his private office.

By Pentagon standards, Murdock's office was almost sumptuous: a big mahogany desk, several comfortable chairs, and even a leatherlike sofa at the far wall; a computer terminal, desktop viewscreen, and more video screens along the wall opposite the desk. Most impressive of all, it was an outside office, with a real window that overlooked the gray river and fog-shrouded National Airport.

That's the one thing he's good at, Kinsman thought. *Feathering his own nest.*

"We've got troubles," the Colonel said. He sat at his desk hard enough to make his jowls quiver.

Colt and Kinsman took the chairs closest to the desk.

"What kind of troubles, sir?" Colt always addressed the

Colonel in the formally correct manner. But he always looked to Kinsman as if he were on the edge of laughing at the man. Something about Murdock amused Colt; probably the same flustered incompetence that usually infuriated Kinsman.

"The General is apeshit over the way the Armed Services Committee hearings are going. He's getting pressure from the Deputy Director, and the Deputy Director's getting it from the Secretary. Which means the White House itself is putting on the squeeze!"

Kinsman smiled inwardly. *Newton was right. For every force there's a reaction. If the Senate wasn't putting up resistance to Moonbase, the White House wouldn't even know it was in the plans.*

Colt was saying, "Sir, if the White House is interested, why don't they put the squeeze on the Committee directly? If they leaned on Senator McGrath, for example . . ."

"Can't, can't, can't!" Murdock panted. "McGrath is aiming at Minority Leader next time around. He'd use pressure from the White House to show his people how good he is—fighting against the Pentagon and even the President to save the taxpayers' precious dollars."

"Politics," Colt said, making it sound disgusting.

"We've got to come up with something, and fast," Murdock said, his pudgy little hands fluttering on the desktop. "The General wants us to go with him to the Deputy Director's office at three this afternoon."

No wonder he's terrified, Kinsman realized. *It's guillotine time.*

Colt seemed completely unawed. "It seems to me, sir, that there's only one thing we can do."

Murdock's hands clenched into childlike little fists. "What? What is it?"

"Well, sir, of course I'm not in on all the details of the upper echelon's big picture . . ."

He's deliberately drawing it out. Kinsman suppressed a

grin as he watched Murdock's wide-eyed, open-mouthed anticipation.

". . . but it seems to me, sir, that Senator McGrath would be much more sympathetic to the entire Aerospace Force program plan if he were fully briefed on the ABM satellite program and . . ."

"No!" Murdock shrieked. "Can't do that! One leak about that and the whole ABM program will be splashed all over the news media! That's Cosmic Top Secret! We can't tell it to just any senator!"

"The Senate Armed Services Committee already knows about it," Colt said. "Sir."

"Only the Chairman," Murdock snapped. "Nobody else has been briefed."

"But they all know about the program," Kinsman pointed out. "McGrath knows about it, and he's sore because he hasn't been formally briefed. He *is* the ranking minority member of the committee."

Murdock shook his head. "There's no connection between our Moonbase program and the anti-missile satellites."

"There could be," Colt answered. "There *will* be, sooner or later."

"The Moon is not a military area," Kinsman said.

"Then why the fuck are we tryin' to set up a base there?" Colt's anger, like his cool, was carefully planned and judiciously used, Kinsman knew. But Murdock's reaction was a startled gasp.

"We're *military*, man," Colt went on. "We can talk about hospitals and peaceful applications of space technology and even cooperate with the Russians, but we're in this for military reasons. Anything else is just gravy . . . icing on the cake."

"We are bound by international treaty," Kinsman said, keeping his voice low, calm. "Military weaponry cannot be put on the Moon."

"You think the Russians won't put weapons there?"

"The Russians have always lived up to the letter of their treaty obligations," Kinsman said.

"So have we," Murdock added.

Colt shrugged. "Yeah. Sure they have. But they always find a lotta room in between the letters for themselves. What's to stop them from knocking down our ABM satellites as fast as we put 'em up? How much you wanna bet we're gonna be knocking off *their* ABM satellites when they try to orbit them? There's gonna be a war in orbit, man. Maybe it'll only be machines and nobody'll get hurt, but it'll be a war, just the same."

"We can't tell people like McGrath that we'll be fighting in space!" Murdock said, his voice trembling. "He'd have the whole thing in front of the news cameras in a hot second. We'd all go down in flames."

Kinsman glanced at his wristwatch. "Sir . . . I've got to get over to the Capitol. The Committee hearings resume at ten."

He left the Colonel's office like a suburban businessman fleeing a downtown pornography shop, hoping that nobody noticed he was there. Once in his own office, he squeezed behind his compact metal desk and punched out a phone number on his communicator keyboard.

Mary-Ellen's face filled the tiny viewscreen on his desk. "Hello, Chet. How are you feeling this morning?"

"Okay, I guess. Aspirin helps."

She smiled ruefully. "And I've got to get this place into some semblance of order for a dinner party tonight."

"Um, Mary, I've got to bug out of here and get to the hearings. Is Diane there?"

Her face clouded briefly. "I don't think she's awake yet."

Dammitall! "Look . . . when she gets up, would you ask her to meet me at the hearings at noon? I've got to talk with her. It's important."

Mary-Ellen nodded as if she understood. "Certainly, Chet. I don't know if she'll be free, but I'll tell her."

"Thanks."

The District's Metro connected the Pentagon with the

Capitol by a direct tube, so Kinsman didn't have to go out into the bleak morning again. The subway train was bleak enough: crowded, noisy, dirty with graffiti and shreds of refuse. It was hot and rancid in the jam-packed train. Smells of human sweat, a hundred different breakfasts, cigarettes, and the special steamy reek of rainsoaked clothing.

The morning's hearings were given over to an anti-military lobby consisting of, it seemed to Kinsman, housewives, clergymen, and public relations flaks. The old rococo hearing chamber was buzzing with witnesses and their friends, photographers, reporters, senators and their scurrying aides. TV cameras were jammed into one side of the chamber, their dazzling lights bathing the long green-topped table where the Committee members sat, and the witness desk that faced them.

Who signs their energy permits? Kinsman wondered idly as a middle-aged woman with too much makeup on her face read from a prepared text in a penetrating voice with a jangling New York accent:

"We are not against the development of useful programs that will benefit the American taxpayer. We support and endorse the efforts of American industry to develop Solar Power Satellites and thereby provide new energy for our nation. But we cannot support, nor do we endorse, spending additional billions of tax dollars on military programs in space. Outer space should be a peaceful domain, not a place in which to escalate the arms race."

Kinsman slouched on a bench in the rear of the crowded hearing chamber, watching the lady testify on one of the TV monitors, wishing that he didn't agree with her.

The woman looked up from her prepared text and said from memory, "Let us never forget the words that we left on the Moon, engraved on the *Apollo 11* spacecraft: 'We came in peace for all humankind.' "

The crowd she had brought with her applauded, as did several of the senators. Kinsman snorted at the mis-quotation. *Feminist revisionism.* He saw that McGrath was smiling at the woman as she got up from the witness desk, but not applauding her.

An aide came to McGrath's side, appearing magically from behind the Senator's highbacked chair and whispering into McGrath's ear. He looked up, shaded his eyes from the TV lights, and scanned the room. Then he spoke to the aide, who disappeared as mystically as he had arrived.

The next witness was a minister and former Army chaplain who now headed his own church in Louisiana. As he was being sworn in, McGrath's aide suddenly popped up beside Kinsman.

"Major Kinsman?"

Kinsman jumped as if he were abruptly being arrested.

"Yes," he whispered.

Wordlessly, the young man handed him a note which read:

See you in the corridor when the session ends.—Diane

It was neatly typed, even the signature. *She must have phoned Neal's office.* By the time he looked up from the yellow paper, the aide was gone.

Kinsman sat through two more witnesses, both university professors. The first one, when he wasn't busy playing with his moustache, was an economist who showed charts which he claimed proved that *private* development of space industries by corporations would help the national economy, but government development of space would only increase the inflation rate. The other, an aging, grossly overweight biophysicist, insisted that space development of any kind was unsound ecologically.

"It will cost more in energy and environmental degradation," he intoned in a deep, shaking, doomsday voice, "to get large numbers of workers into space than those workers will ever be able to return to the people of this Earth in the form of energy or usable goods. Space is only for the rich; it will be the poor peoples of the Earth who pay the price for the privileged few."

As soon as Kinsman saw that the Committee Chairman was going to gavel the session into adjournment, he ducked out the big polished wooden double doors and into the corridor. Diane was walking up the hall toward him.

"Perfect timing," he said, taking her by the arm.

Her smile was good to see. "I can't make it a long lunch, Chet," she warned. "I've got to meet Larry and fly up to New York for a contract signing."

"Oh."

"I'll only be gone overnight. I've got a concert here Friday night, then the whole weekend's taken up with briefings and medical checkups . . ."

"With what?"

The click of their footsteps on the marble floor was lost as the rest of the crowd from the hearing chamber poured out into the corridor.

Raising her voice, Diane said, "I've been invited to fly up to the opening of Space Station Alpha. Didn't Neal tell you?"

"No, he didn't."

"I thought he had. We're going up on the special VIP flight Monday. Just for the day."

Kinsman felt stunned.

Diane was grinning at him. "I thought it'd be fun to see what it's like up there. Maybe I'll find out what fascinates you about it so much."

Nodding absently, Kinsman led Diane to the elevators that went down to the basement cafeteria.

"You've been invited to Alpha," he muttered. "That's more than anybody's done for me."

Diane said nothing.

An elevator opened and he ushered her into it, then slapped the DOOR CLOSE button before any of the crowd coming down the corridor could reach them.

"You'll be tied up all weekend?" Kinsman asked.

"That's what they told me."

"I thought maybe we could get together for dinner or something."

Diane gave a little shake of her head. "I don't think so, Chet. I'm sorry."

The elevator door slid open and they were faced with another crowd, this time the clerks and secretaries who were lined up for their cafeteria lunch. Silently, numbly, Kinsman got into line behind Diane. They picked up their trays and selected their food: Diane a fruit salad, Kinsman a bowl of bean soup. Both passed the steam tables with their pathetic-looking "specials." Both took iced fruit drinks.

Kinsman led Diane through the crowd to the farthest corner of the busy, clattering cafeteria and found a table that was big enough only for the two of them.

"It's not the fanciest restaurant in town," Kinsman said as they sat down. "But it's the toughest to bug."

"What did you say?" Diane's eyes went wide.

He gestured at the crowded cafeteria. "Nobody knows who's going to sit where. And the background noise is high enough to defeat mikes set in the ceiling."

"You're serious?"

Kinsman nodded. "You remember last night, you were asking me why I want Moonbase so much?"

She nodded.

"It's not just a lunar base, Diane." He hesitated, wondering how much he could tell her, how far he could trust her. "It's a new world. I want to build a new world."

"On the Moon."

"That's the best place for it."

"You *are* serious, aren't you?"

"I sure as hell am."

She tried to laugh; it came out as a nervous giggle. "But the Moon . . . it's so desolate . . . so forsaken . . ."

"Have you been there?" he countered. "Have you watched the Earth rise? Or planted footprints where no human being has ever walked before? Have you been anywhere in your whole life where you really were on your own? Where you had the time and the room and the peace to think?"

"That's what you want?"

"Being here is like being in jail. It's a madhouse. I'm locked into Pentagon level three, ring D, corridor F, room number . . ."

"But we're all in that same jail, Chet. One way or another, we're all locked up in the same madhouse."

"It doesn't have to be that way!" He reached out to grasp her hand. "We can build a new world, a new society, all those things you sing about in your songs— love, freedom, hope—we can have them."

"You can have them," Diane said. "What about all the billions of others who can't go to your new world, no matter what?"

"We've got to start someplace. And we've got to start now, right *now*, before we sink so far back into the mud that we won't have the energy or the materials or the people to do the job. Civilization's cracking apart, Diane!"

"And you want to run away from the catastrophe."

"No! I want to prevent it." Realizing the truth of it as he spoke the words, Kinsman listened to himself, as surprised as Diane at his revelation. "We can build a new society on the Moon. We can set the example, just the way the new colonies of America set an example for the old world of Europe. We can send energy back to the Earth, raw materials—but most of all, we can send hope."

"That's not your real reason," she said. "That's not what's really driving you."

"It's part of it. A big part."

Diane studied his face. "But only part. What's the rest of it, Chet? Why is this so important to you?"

"It's the freedom, Diane. There are no rulebooks up there. No chains of command. You can work with people on the basis of their abilities, not their rank or their connections. It's—it's so completely different that I don't know if I can describe it to you. There's nothing like it on Earth."

"Freedom," Diane echoed.

"In space. On the Moon. A new society. A new world. A world that you could be part of, Diane."

She shook her head. "Not me. I can see how important it is to you, Chet, but it's not for me." Her hand slid away from his. "If I'm going to help build a new world, it'll be right here on *terra firma*. That's where we need it."

He leaned back in his chair. "By singing folk songs."

"They give people hope too, you know."

Kinsman clenched his empty hand. "You'll never make a new society on Earth, kid. Too many self-interests. Too much history to undo. Society's locked in place here. The only way to unlock it is to build a showplace . . ."

"A Utopia?" She grinned at the thought.

"It won't be Utopia. But it'll be better than anything here on Earth."

She started to shake her head again, but Kinsman leaned forward intently.

"Listen to me," he said urgently. "Whether you agree with me or not doesn't matter. But you've got to tell Neal that the longer he fights against the Moonbase appropriation, the closer he's pushing us into a big military buildup in space. A full-scale weapons race that can only end in all-out nuclear war."

Diane stared at him. "I should tell Neal . . . why do you think that I . . ."

"You've got to!" Kinsman insisted. "I can't talk to him directly. Not even through Mary-Ellen. They'll know what I'm doing. But you can warn him. He'd listen to you."

Her face was a frantic mixture of fear and disbelief. "But I won't see him until . . ."

"See him. Tell him. It's important. Vital."

"But why can't you . . ."

"He'll want specifics from me that I can't give him. And any conversations I have with him are probably monitored."

"How did you . . ."

"You can talk to him," he went on, ignoring her

objections. "Tell him it's either a peaceful Moonbase or a full-scale military buildup in orbit. He'll understand."

Kinsman walked Diane to the front entrance of the Capitol and down the long granite steps that gave the building its impressive facade. Larry Davis was waiting for her in a real limousine, complete with liveried driver.

"Come on," he yelled out the car's window. "We'll miss the flight and there's not another one 'til six!"

Kinsman deliberately held Diane for a moment and kissed her. She seemed surprised.

"Call me when you get back to town," he said.

"Okay," she answered shakily.

"And talk to Neal."

"Yes . . . yes." She ran down the last few steps and into the waiting limousine.

The car pulled away with a screech of tires on the wet paving, a rare sound in conservation-conscious Washington. Kinsman watched the limousine thread its way through the sparse traffic. *Not a bad way to travel*, he mused, *for somebody who's concerned about the hungry poor.*

The weather had cleared enough for Kinsman to take the bus back to the Pentagon. The sky was still gray as he waited for the bus in the three-sided enclosure at the curb, but the rain had ended. The steamer finally chugged into sight. Just as the doors opened for Kinsman, another man came running down the Capitol steps hollering for the driver to wait for him.

Kinsman saw that it was Tug Wynne puffing toward the bus, and silently wished the driver would close the doors and move on. But the black driver was in no hurry. He waited patiently for the burly newsman.

Kinsman took a back seat in the nearly empty bus and, sure enough, Wynne came over to him.

"Mind if I sit with ya?"

"No," Kinsman lied. "Go right ahead."

Wynne slid into the seat, wedging Kinsman solidly

between the window and his own bulk. From the smell of it, Wynne's lunch had been mostly bourbon.

"Not much fireworks in this morning's hearings, eh?"

"Not much," Kinsman agreed. The bus lurched around a corner and headed down Delaware Avenue, chuffing.

"You see the look on the Chairman's face when that perfessor started talking about the dangers of beaming microwaves through the air?"

"That's when he closed the session, wasn't it?"

"Sure was. He's not gonna give any eco-nut a chance to scare people about the power satellites. Not with GE back in his home district!" Wynne chuckled to himself.

"It was time to break for lunch anyway," Kinsman said.

"Yeah. Say, wasn't that Diane Lawrence in the cafeteria with you?"

"Yes. She was at the party last night. Didn't you hear her singing?"

Wynne looked impressed. "And now she's breaking bread with you. Fast work. Or is she an old family friend, too?"

"I've known Diane for years," Kinsman said, staring out of the window at the passing buildings. This part of Washington was drab and rundown. Not much money between the Capitol and the Navy Yard. Just people's homes. Kids playing on the sidewalks. *They'll grow up to stand in unemployment lines.*

Wynne jarred him out of it. "Haven't seen you with any women since you came to Washington."

"My private life," Kinsman said, still looking out the window, "is my private life."

"Sure. I know. And I guess it must make some kinda mental block . . . killing that girl and all."

Kinsman whirled on him. "Stop fishing, dammit. I've got nothing to say to you on that subject."

"Sure. I understand. But you know, reporters hear things . . . rumors float around. Like, I heard you got hurt pretty bad yourself, up there." He waggled a forefinger skyward.

"Bullshit," Kinsman snapped.

"I know you gotta deny it, and all. But what I heard was that you got hurt . . . radiation damage, they say. And now you're impotent. Or sterile."

Thinking of the thousands of nights he had spent alone since returning from that mission and the agonies of the few times he had tried to make love to a woman, Kinsman laughed bitterly.

"That's what they say, do they?" he asked Wynne.

The older man nodded, his expression blank.

"Well, you can tell them for me that they're all crazy."

Wynne nodded gravely. "Glad to hear it. But how come nobody's ever seen you out with a woman? In all the time since you've been in the District . . ."

The sonofabitch thinks I'm a homosexual! "Listen. I'm heterosexual and I'm not sterile. I've never been involved in any accidents in space that would impair my abilities in any way. Is that clear?"

"Major, you have a way of making your points."

"Good."

And it's not a lie, either. Not completely. I'm not impotent . . . except when I'm with a woman.

The office of the Deputy Director made Colonel Murdock's carefully acquired luxuries seem petty and vain. This office was huge, and in a corner of the Pentagon so that it had *two* windows. Rich, dark wood panelling covered the walls. Deep carpeting. Plush chairs. Flags flanking the broad, polished, curved desk.

General Sherwood was a picturebook Aerospace Force officer: handsome chiseled profile, silver-gray hair, sparkling blue eyes. He sat before the Deputy Director's desk looking perfectly at ease, yet so alert and intelligent that he gave the impression he could instantly take command of an airplane, a spacecraft, or a whole war.

He carries those two stars on his shoulders, thought Kinsman, *with plenty of room to add more*.

Ellery Marcot, the Deputy Director, was a sloppy

civilian. Tall, high-domed, flabby in the middle, he peered at the world suspiciously through thick, old-fashioned bifocals. His suit was gray, his thinning hair and moustache grayer, his skin as sallow as an old manila file folder. Kinsman had never seen him without a cigarette. His desk was a chaotic sea of papers, marked by islands of ashtrays brimming with cigarette butts.

"Gentlemen," he said, after the polite handshakes were finished and the General, Colonel Murdock, Colt, and Kinsman were seated according to rank before his desk, "we have reached a critical decision point."

General Sherwood nodded crisply, but said nothing. It would have been easy to assume that his Academy-perfect exterior was nothing more than an empty shell. His eyes were *too* sky-blue, his hair just the right shade of experienced, yet virile, silver. But Kinsman knew better. *He'll get those other two stars. And soon.*

Marcot blinked myopically at them. "For the past four years, the Aerospace Force has struggled to maintain some semblance of an effective program for manned spaceflight. We have had to battle against NASA, against the Congress, and even against the White House."

"And the State Department, sir," Colt added.

Murdock turned sharply toward Colt. But then he saw General Sherwood smiling and nodding.

"Yes, the State Department too," Marcot agreed, "and their ideas of *détente* in space."

"But we have made significant progress," the General said.

"Along the wrong road," Marcot snapped.

"It was the only road available at the time," General Sherwood replied, his voice just a trifle harder than it had been a moment earlier.

Kinsman spoke up. "Sir, if it hadn't been for this Moonbase program, and the cooperative Russian program that's linked with it, the Aerospace Force would have been required to surrender all manned operations to NASA."

"I understand that, Major," said Marcot. "But the Armed Services Committee is not impressed."

"Their attitude is disastrous," General Sherwood agreed. "If they have their way, they'll give space entirely to the corporations and leave them defenseless up there."

"The corporations don't seem all that anxious to get into space," Marcot said, grinding his cigarette into an already-choked ashtray.

"We *must* have a military presence in space," the General said. "It is undeniable."

Marcot lit another cigarette, then rummaged through his messy papers. "State Department doesn't agree. Sent me a memo . . . it's here someplace . . ."

"It's the same as our military presence in Antarctica," Colt said. "We've got to show the Russians that we're ready and able to defend our interests, wherever they are."

"The Russians are going ahead with their share of the lunar base," Colonel Murdock said, his voice sounding almost hopeful.

"All the more reason for us to be there alongside them," Sherwood said. "We can't let them have the Moon all to themselves."

Feeling like a tightrope walker, Kinsman said, "With all due respect, sir, the Armed Services Committee won't be impressed with that argument. Senators like McGrath are against anything that looks like the old Space Race."

Marcot peered at him through a haze of smoke. "McGrath," he muttered.

"That's why we initiated the hospital program," Kinsman went on. "The Air Force has always pioneered in flight medicine, and it would be in keeping with Air Force traditions and missions to build a hospital on the Moon. That would give us a presence on the Moon *plus* a role there that has real meaning."

"And whose idea was it," Marcot asked, "to make the base a joint Russian-American project? Durban's, wasn't it? Him and his international pipe dreams."

"That was done for funding purposes," Kinsman said. "It was easier to get the program started by showing that the Russians were going to share the costs."

"Well, the funding is about to run out," Marcot grumbled. "Our munificent Congress is backing out of the program now that the preliminary explorations are finished and it's time to put up the big money for a permanent base."

"And we can't divert funds from our laser satellite program," General Sherwood said. "That's going to take every nickel we can squeeze out of the politicians."

"Maybe the Aerospace Force should forget about the Moon and concentrate on the laser satellites. If we can actually develop an anti-missile network in orbit . . ." Marcot let his voice trail off.

"Leave the Moon to the Russians?" General Sherwood asked.

"What good is the Moon?" Marcot demanded. "It has no real military value."

"It will when it starts supplying those orbital factories that the corporations are talking about," Colt pointed out.

"That's ten years away," Marcot said. "Twenty."

Kinsman said nothing, but thought to himself, *So the Russians will win control of the Moon after all, despite all we've done over all these years.* He shrugged inwardly. *Maybe they deserve it. Maybe men like Leonov will do better with it than we would.*

"I still don't want the Reds on the Moon alone," General Sherwood insisted. "Ten years, twenty years, fifty years from now—if the Moon will ever have any military importance, then we must not give it to the Russians by default!"

Marcot sank back in his chair, cowed momentarily by the General's fire. "Well then," he said at last, sucking hard on his cigarette, "how do we get around this guy McGrath—without compromising the ABM satellite program?"

"We could brief him on the laser satellites," Kinsman

heard himself saying. "I think a large part of his resistance to the Moonbase idea is that he's out in the cold on the ABM program."

Shaking his head, Marcot answered, "The White House has forbidden us to tell McGrath anything about it. He's a rabble-rouser—as soon as we tell him we're planning to put a hundred laser-armed satellites into orbit he'll blab it to the press."

"Neal has a sense of responsibility, sir."

"And a nose that's sniffing for the Minority Leader's job. And from there to the White House. He'll have us plastered all over the media as warmongers who want to extend the arms race to outer space."

"I can see the headlines," General Sherwood agreed.

Colonel Murdock nodded.

Marcot tapped the ash from his latest cigarette. "No . . . I don't see any way around it. Either you convince McGrath that Moonbase is necessary"—he looked straight at Kinsman—"or we have to forget about the Moon and concentrate on the laser satellite program."

General Sherwood turned to Kinsman. "It's up to you, then, Major. Do you think you can handle it?"

"If he can't, sir, no one can," Colt said before Kinsman could open his mouth.

Colonel Murdock's expression could have turned sweet cream into yogurt, but he remained silent.

"The first thing I'll need," Kinsman heard himself say, "is a seat on that VIP flight Monday to Alpha. McGrath's going up for the dedication ceremonies. It might be a good chance to work on him."

"Or flush him out of an airlock," Marcot muttered.

Sherwood gestured to Colonel Murdock. "See to it, will you?"

"Yessir. But we'll have to bump . . ."

"Then bump," the General snapped. "Whoever."

Marcot blew a big, relieved cloud of smoke toward the ceiling. "That's it, then. We push ahead with the ABM satellites and handle the Moonbase situation separately."

"And let McGrath determine whether we build Moon-base or not," General Sherwood muttered. He was not pleased.

"He's going to make that determination anyway," Marcot said. "We're just admitting the obvious."

Kinsman said nothing.

Returning to his office, Kinsman slumped behind his metal desk, staring at the old photograph of a lunar landscape that was taped on the wall next to his chair. The picture showed an astronaut—himself—kneeling in his pressure suit, working over a gadgety-looking piece of scientific gear. Kinsman had forgotten what the equipment was, what it was supposed to do. The photograph was faded, its edges browning and curling.

Getting old, he said to himself. *And useless.*

Beyond the machine and the man, in the picture, the broad plain of a lunar *mare* stretched out to the abrupt horizon, where a rounded, worn mountain showed its tired-looking peak. Above it all, riding in the black sky, was the half-sphere of Earth. Years earlier, when the photo had been new, the Earth had been brilliant blue and white. Now it looked faded and gray, along with everything else in the office.

Suddenly Kinsman got up from his desk and went out into the corridor, toward Colonel Murdock's office.

What are you going to tell him? he asked himself.

The answer was a mental shrug. *Damned if I know. But I've got to tell him something.*

You can quit, you know. Walk away from it. Murdock would be happy to let you go.

The voice in his head became sardonic. *And do what? Wait 'til I'm Durban's age, so they can carry me to the Moon on a stretcher?*

There's more to life than getting to the Moon.

He answered immediately, *No there's not. Not for me. That's where I've got to be, away from all this crap.*

They're going to bring all this crap with them! You know that.

He shook his head doggedly. *Not if I can help it.*

The Colonel's outer office was empty again. Not even Colt was there now. But Kinsman went to Murdock's door and rapped sharply on it.

"What? Who is it?"

Kinsman smiled at the thought of how the Colonel must have jumped at the sound. He tried the door but it was locked.

"It's Kinsman," he called. Then, thinking there might be a superior officer locked inside with Murdock, he added, "Sir."

"Ah . . . just a minute . . ."

Footsteps. Muffled voices. Then the door opened. Murdock looked flustered.

"What is it?" the Colonel demanded, holding the door open just a few centimeters.

Kinsman heard the other door, the one that opened directly onto the corridor outside, snap shut softly. Whoever had been in the office with Murdock had left.

"I've got to talk with you," Kinsman said, "about this McGrath business."

Colonel Murdock was one of the few men Kinsman knew who could look furious and worried at the same time. Now he also looked sheepish, with a little boy's caught-in-the-act expression on his chubby face.

He yanked the door open all the way. "All right, come on in."

"If I'm interrupting anything . . ."

Murdock glared at him. "Just a White House liaison man, a representative from the Defense Intelligence Agency who briefs the President every morning. That's all!"

"I spooked him?" Kinsman punned.

Murdock ignored it. He plopped himself down in his desk chair. "Make it fast, Kinsman. I've got a golf date that I can't afford to miss."

Taking the chair directly in front of the Colonel's desk, Kinsman realized he didn't quite know where to begin.

"I . . . it's this whole McGrath thing," he said. "I've

been put squarely on the spot. If I can't turn Neal around, Moonbase goes down the tubes."

Murdock shrugged. "That's right."

"I don't like it."

"You don't like it? You don't like what?"

"The whole setup," Kinsman explained. "Making the whole Moonbase program hinge on one man. Pressuring McGrath the way we're going to have to."

"You can put all the pressure on him that you can lay your hands on. We'll back you up."

Kinsman shook his head. "That's what I don't like."

"So what?" Murdock snapped. "You still have to follow orders, just like the rest of us."

"But Neal McGrath has been a friend of mine since we were both kids . . ."

"Which is why you got picked for this job. You ought to be able to find a few things in his background that could help to persuade him. Everybody's got bones in their closets."

"Yeah," Kinsman murmured. "Everybody."

"It's either a success with McGrath," the Colonel pointed out, "or the whole Moonbase program goes into mothballs."

"And the Russians get the Moon to themselves."

"While we—all of us, including you, Kinsman—go to work on the ABM satellites. You'll be here in the Pentagon for the rest of your life on that one." Murdock smiled slyly.

"It's wrong . . ."

"It's *decided*. You heard the Deputy Director. Your job is to convince McGrath. Otherwise, forget about Moonbase."

"We shouldn't be throwing the Moon away," Kinsman insisted.

"Then get McGrath to vote in favor of the base. Get him to swing the minority votes on the committee. Put Durban to work on him. Do whatever you like."

"Durban's in the hospital."

Murdock shrugged.

"Dammitall!" Kinsman exploded. "I don't want this! I don't want any part of it. I want to be flying, not crawling around these goddamned corridors like some roach!"

"Listen to me, hotshot," Murdock snapped back, his face reddening. "You're grounded. Understand? You'll never fly another Air Force plane or spacecraft again. Never! We should never have let you back on flying duty after you killed that Russian."

Kinsman couldn't answer. His voice choked in his throat.

"You want the Moon so goddamned much," Murdock was yelling now, "you better get your friend McGrath to vote the right way. Because the only way you're going to get off this planet, mister, is as a passenger."

His pulse was thundering in Kinsman's ears, the way it had so long ago, when he had let his temper run away and lead him to murder.

But Murdock was smiling triumphantly at him. "I know you, Kinsman. I know what makes you tick. You want to get to the Moon and leave us all behind you. Fine! I'm all for it. But you'd better make sure there's a base up there for you to go to; otherwise you'll be flying a desk for the rest of your life."

"McGrath," Kinsman croaked, "will never go for it. Never."

"I've sweated blood over you," Murdock went on, ignoring Kinsman's words. "You always thought you were so goddamned superior. Hotshot flier. You and Colt, a couple of smartasses. Well, you just goddamn better do the job you're assigned to do, or you'll be shuffling papers at a desk until you drop dead!"

For a moment Kinsman said nothing. It took every effort he could muster not to get up from the chair and punch the fat leering face that gloated at him.

Finally he said, "I could resign my commission. I could quit the Aerospace Force."

"And do what?" Murdock asked smugly. "Get a job with NASA? Or one of the big corporations?"

"You don't think so."

The Colonel's stubby-fingered hands were rubbing together, as if by their own volition. "I don't know if anybody else would hire a man with as disturbed a mental background as yours, Kinsman. After all, if they ask us for your background, we'd have to tell them how— unbalanced—you can be."

Kinsman was on his feet and grabbing the Colonel's shirt before he realized what he was doing. Murdock was white-faced, half out of his chair, hanging by Kinsman's fists.

Closing his eyes, Kinsman released the Colonel.

"Okay," he said, forcing his breath back to normal. "You win. I'll work on McGrath."

Murdock dropped back into his chair. He smoothed his shirt and looked up at Kinsman furiously. But there was still fear in his eyes.

"You'd better work on McGrath," the Colonel said, his voice trembling. "And the next time . . ."

"No!" Kinsman leveled a pointed finger at him. "The next time you try holding that over my head, the next time you say anything about it to me or anyone else, there'll be another murder."

"You . . . you just get to McGrath."

"Sure. I'll get to him." Kinsman headed for the door. *I'll take him just like Lee took Washington.*

He was staring at the ceiling, waiting for the sleep that was taking longer and longer to come to him, when the buzzer sounded.

In the darkness, Kinsman groped for the switch on the wall over his sofabed. "Yes?"

"Chet, it's me. Diane."

Wordlessly he pushed the button that opened the front door of the building. Only after he let go of it did he think to ask if she were alone.

He rolled out of the sofabed and turned on the battery-powered lamp on the end table. The main electrical service was shut down for the night, of course. Only the battery-operated devices, like the building's security locks, could be used after midnight. Kinsman often wondered if the refrigerator were really insulated well enough to keep everything fresh overnight. He never kept enough food in it to worry about.

By the time she knocked on his apartment door, he was in a shapeless gray robe and had lit a couple of candles. His wristwatch said 1:23 A.M.

He opened the door. Diane stood there alone, wearing a sleeveless light blouse and dark form-fitting slacks.

"I thought you went to New York," Kinsman said.

"I took the bus back after dinner," Diane answered, stepping into the room.

Even in candlelight, the apartment looked shabby. The open sofabed was a tangled mess of sweaty sheets. The desk was littered with paperwork. The room's only chair looked stiff and uninviting.

"Would you like a drink?" Kinsman asked. "I've got some scotch and there's a bottle of vodka around here someplace . . ."

"Any beer?"

"Might not be very cold."

Diane unslung the heavy leather bag from her shoulder and let it clunk to the floor. She sat on the edge of the bed, kicked her boots off, and leaned back tiredly.

"Beer's fine . . . even warm beer."

"Why the hell did you come back tonight? And how'd you get from the bus terminal to here at this time of the night?"

"Phoned for a cab and waited at the bus terminal until they scared one up for me."

Kinsman took the four steps to his kitchenette and opened the refrigerator. The beer bottles seemed fairly cold to his touch.

"That terminal's not a good place to hang around," he said, peering into the shadowy shelves above his sink for a clean glass.

"There were a couple of cops. I talked with them while I waited. They even encouraged the taxi company to find something for me."

Handing her the bottle and the glass, Kinsman said, "It pays to be beautiful."

"And famous," she added immediately.

"But . . . why?" he asked, sitting on the floor beside the bed. "What was so important about getting back here?"

She took a swallow of beer from the bottle. "That was a pretty heavy message you laid on me this afternoon."

"Yeah. Have you had a chance to see Neal?"

"Not yet."

"When?"

"Tomorrow. I mean, later today—right after his committee hearing."

"Good."

"But I've got to know something, Chet. That's why I'm here."

"I can't go into details, Diane. They're classified. But it's damned important that Neal realizes what's at stake."

"What the hell is at stake?" she asked.

"I can't tell you all of it . . ."

"Is this room bugged?"

He shook his head in the shadows. "No, I go over the place pretty thoroughly every few days. And I've got a couple of friends in the Pentagon who keep track of who's listening to whom. My conversations with Neal are monitored, but I'm not important enough to have my apartment wired."

He couldn't see her face too well in the flickering candlelight, but Diane's voice was suddenly high with concern. "Is Neal always watched? Is his office wired, or . . ."

"His office must be. And his home was during the party. They spot-check his phones, I'm sure. That's pretty standard procedure for a senator. He knows about it; they all do. And they know how to protect themselves from it. But it means that I can't tell him everything that he needs to know."

"Just what is it that he needs to know?"

Instead of answering, Kinsman got up and padded to the kitchenette for the scotch.

Almost an hour later, after two more beers for Diane and several long pulls of scotch for himself, he was saying:

". . . and that's the politics of it. I can't tell you what the satellite program is all about, but Marcot and General Sherwood will clobber Neal if they get the chance. Unless, of course, he votes for the Moonbase program."

Diane said, "But what about you, Chet? Where do you stand in all this?"

"Right in the middle. I want Moonbase because I want to be there. I want to live on the Moon. I want to set up that new world I was telling you about."

"But if it's a military base . . ."

"Yeah, I know. Even if we start out as a hospital, even if we work jointly with the Russians, there's always the chance that the brass will start turning it into a supply center for a *real* military effort."

"They could do that?"

"Sure. Mine the lunar ores and build military satellites out of them, then place them in orbit around the Earth. Just like the corporations want to do with the solar power satellites."

"But the Russians will be there too, won't they?"

Kinsman nodded. "And they'll do the same thing, once they see us doing it."

"And you're caught in the middle of all this."

"Yeah, they've got me surrounded." He leaned his head back against the wall and heard himself go on, "But that doesn't matter. It's where I've got to be if I'm ever going to make it there."

"There?"

"To the Moon."

"It's like an obsession with you," Diane said.

He grinned. "Leonardo da Vinci."

"What?"

"He built gliders and tried them out himself. They never worked too well, but it was enough to get him to say, 'Once you have tasted flight, you will walk the Earth with your eyes turned skyward. For there you have been, and there you long to return.'"

Diane smiled at him. "I see . . ."

"Do you?" Kinsman asked. "Do you know what it's like to have everybody around you call you a nut? You were nice about it, you called it an obsession. At the Pentagon they call us *Luniks*."

"Us?"

"Yeah, there's a few of us, here and there. A couple in NASA, too. Guys like me. Guys willing to fight with everything we've got to get the hell off this lousy dungheap and out into the new world. Hell, I'll bet I could build a mountain just from the paperwork in the Pentagon that'd reach the Moon. We could *walk* there!"

Diane laughed.

"Murdock and Sherwood and Marcot think we're crazy. Maybe we are. But they use us. They use us to get what they want."

"And you?"

"Sure, I'm using them to get what I want, too. But now the game's getting rough, and I don't think we can all stay happy. The big boys are starting to use their muscle on us, and we *Luniks* don't have much to muscle back with."

"So what are you going to do?" she asked.

"You know, once I said I'd sell my soul for the chance to get back to the Moon. Now I might have to make that choice."

"You need Neal's help, don't you?"

"He's got to vote for the Moonbase program. If he doesn't there'll be nobody left in space but the warbirds."

"Chet . . . do they know about us? Can they use our relationship to hurt Neal? To threaten him?"

Suddenly confused, Kinsman asked, "Us? What relationship?"

"Neal and me . . ."

Kinsman felt as if he were in free-fall, everything dropping away.

Diane sat straight up on the bed. "You didn't know about us?"

"Mary-Ellen," Kinsman heard himself mutter.

"She knows," Diane said. "We've tried to keep it as quiet as possible. Nobody in Washington would really care, of course, but they could use it against Neal back in Pennsylvania. A divorce case and an affair with a pop singer—they'd crucify him back home."

"You and Neal," Kinsman said, still numbed by it. "And Mary-Ellen knows."

"Yes. . . . We love each other, Chet. Neither one of us wanted it to happen, but it has."

"Then when you stayed at their place after the party . . . Jesus Christ, I got him to go out and meet you, way back in San Francisco!"

"Yes, I met him then. Years ago. But it wasn't until the Presidential campaign, when I was doing benefits for the New Youth Alliance . . ."

"And Mary-Ellen's just sitting back and letting the two of you have your fun. Or does she have a lover, too?"

"No. She's been awfully good about the whole thing. Says she doesn't want to hurt Neal. It makes me feel like hell."

But you sleep with him anyway. In her home.

"Do you think they'll really get divorced?" he asked.

Diane pushed her hair back away from her face with an automatic gesture. "I don't know. We'll see what happens after the Senate race the year after next."

"So that's why he invited you up to the space station. It wasn't just public relations." Kinsman put a slight emphasis on the word *public.*

"Your Pentagon people don't know about this, do they?"

Diane asked. "I mean, if they did they could use it to pressure Neal to vote their way . . ."

He looked up at her. "Diane . . . I'm one of those Pentagon people."

"But you're his friend. You wouldn't . . ."

"I'm Mary-Ellen's friend, too."

"She doesn't want him hurt."

"Yeah."

Diane swung off the bed and sat on her heels beside Kinsman, on the floor. "Chet . . . you're *my* friend, too. You wouldn't hurt the three of us, would you?"

"And what about me? What do *I* get?"

Diane reached out and put a hand on Kinsman's shoulder.

He wanted to laugh. "When you first came tapping at my chamber door, I had the crazy idea that you had come all the way down from New York to see me, to be with me."

"That was part of it," she said.

"I wanted you, Diane. I really did. I needed you."

"I'm here."

Shaking his head, "No. Not as a bribe. Not because Neal's home with his wife and you're lonely. Not to make me think there's a chance you might leave him for me."

"Chet . . . what can I do? What can I say?"

"Nothing. Not a damned thing."

She pulled away from him. "I'd better go, then."

"Where to? There are no taxis at this time of the morning. You can't walk the streets alone."

"But there's no room here."

Kinsman got to his feet. "Stretch out on the bed. Get some sleep. Just don't take your clothes off."

He padded around to the other side of the bed, blew out the candles, and lay down in the darkness. He could feel the warmth of her body next to his, hear her breathing slowly relax into sleep.

For a moment he thought of his interrogation by Tug Wynne. *If he could see me now.* Kinsman grinned at the irony of it. He didn't have to reach down to his crotch to know what was happening. *I'm not impotent, really. Stupid maybe. But not really impotent.*

Several times his eyes closed and he drifted toward sleep. But each time he saw the cosmonaut drifting in silent space, her dead arms reaching out toward him.

McGrath took Mary-Ellen and their two children back to Pennsylvania for the weekend. They were to remain there while he flew to Florida and the new Space Shuttle that would take the VIPs to the dedication ceremonies aboard Space Station Alpha.

Kinsman spent the weekend doing Murdock's work for the Colonel. He pulled a handful of Pentagon strings and became a VIP, much to the disappointment of a lieutenant colonel at Wright-Patterson AFB, who suddenly received a phone call advising him that he'd been bumped from the Alpha dedication junket.

Before flying down to Cape Canaveral, Kinsman visited Walter Reed Hospital, where Fred Durban was.

The old man was a permanent invalid now, in the cardiac ward. Kinsman sat beside his bed, the smell of antiseptics and quiet death everywhere; the clean, efficient, coldly impersonal feel of the hospital setting his nerves on edge. Durban's room was bright with flowers. The window looked out on leafy trees and a bright lovely blue sky. But the other bed in the room held a retired general, now engulfed by life-support equipment that snaked wires and tubes into every part of his body. He was more machine than man.

It didn't bother Durban, though. "I know it looks awful, but that's just what I want them to do for me when I start sinking below the red line."

The old man was painfully emaciated. His once-reddish hair was now nothing more than a wisp of white. His arms were bone-thin, the skin translucent. *He belongs in a china shop, not a hospital.* But those shaggy eyebrows were still formidable, and Durban's voice was cheerful.

"I'm just trying to hang on long enough so that you

youngsters can build my lunar hospital. Up there I'll be a whole lot better. I've warned the staff here that they'd better keep me alive until they can transfer me to Moonbase."

Kinsman nodded and tried to smile at him. "We're working on it. Working hard."

"Damned right. Wish they had room to set up a hospital section aboard the new space station, though. I'd settle for that, right now."

"I'm going up there tomorrow."

"To Alpha? Good! Tell me about it when you get back."

"I will."

"But how's our Moonbase program working out?"

Kinsman shrugged. "The usual snags with Congress. Committees . . . you know."

Durban closed his eyes. "I've spent my whole damned life arguing with those shortsighted bastards. Anything further downstream than the next election—forget it, as far as they're concerned."

"They don't have much foresight, that's true."

Durban lay quietly for a moment. The conversation stalled. Then he asked, "But the survey work . . . the site selection and all the preliminary planning . . . that's all been done, hasn't it?"

"Yessir. Once we get past the Senate we can start actual construction."

"Good." Durban smiled. "In a couple of years I'll be on the Moon, getting my second wind."

Kinsman said nothing.

Still smiling, the old man lifted his frail hand. "I know what you're thinking. In a couple of years I'll be six feet under."

"No . . ."

"Don't try to kid me, son. I can read your face like a blueprint. Von Braun never made it into space at all, you know. Neither did Clarke or Sagan. At least I've been in orbit."

"We'll get you to the Moon, don't worry."

"I don't have a worry in the world. I know they'll never let me ride the Shuttle in the shape I'm in. If I can build my strength back up, then fine. If not, I'll die here . . . probably right in this room."

Kinsman had nothing to say.

But Durban went on, "But I'll *still* be with you on the Moon. I've left instructions in my will that I want to be buried there. At Moonbase. And I've got enough money stashed away to pay for it, too, by damn!"

Kinsman smiled at him. "You're a stubborn *Lunik*."

"Damned right, sonny. One thing I learned early in the game. It takes more than talent, more than brains, more than connections, even. Takes stubbornness. Look at von Braun. Not the world's most brilliant engineer, but a hard-driving man who found what he wanted and went after it, hell or high water. By God, World War Two was an *opportunity* for him! The Cold War, the Space Race, he turned them all to his advantage. Other people sneered at him, called him a Nazi, an opportunist, an amoral monster. But he never wavered from his goal. He wanted the Moon and he went out and got it. We *all* got it, thanks to him."

Not all of us, Kinsman answered silently.

"You go get Moonbase started," Durban said. "Don't let them sidetrack you."

"We're trying."

"Going to the new space station, eh? Rubbing shoulders with the politicians and their sycophants. Good. But don't let 'em stop there. Keep driving for the Moon."

"Yessir."

Durban lifted his head slightly from the pillow. "I'll watch the ceremonies on TV . . . at least I can turn 'em off when they get too boring."

Kinsman wanted to laugh.

"All right, you run along now. No fun watching an old man trying to stay alive." Durban winked at him. "Besides, I'm due for a bath . . . got a cute young nurse who thinks I'm too old to do her any harm."

Getting up from the chair, Kinsman said, "I'll come back when I return from the station."

"Fine. I'll be waiting right here. I'm not going anyplace."

Even in the earliest morning, the Florida sun was blindingly hot. Cape Canaveral was flat and scrubby, not at all like the hilly California coast.

Kinsman had flown to the Cape the previous night, and slept in the Bachelor Officers' Quarters at nearby Patrick Air Force Base. Now, just after dawn, he had driven a motor pool car to Kennedy Space Flight Center, to see the place before the newshounds and tourists cluttered it up.

Most of the old buildings were still there, including the mammoth Vehicle Assembly Building, which was still used by the NASA people. The ancient gantries, tall stately spiderworks of steel standing against the brazen sky, were strictly tourist attractions now. History had been made there, blasting out flame and mountainous billows of steam as the Saturns and Deltas and Titans had launched men and automated probes to the farthest reaches of the solar system. Now they stood quietly, gawked at by visitors from all over the world, lectured over by National Park Service guards surrounded by eager, curious youngsters and their sweating, sunburned, bored parents.

The real action was now out at the airstrip, where the Shuttle took off and landed. Unlike the old Shuttles that Kinsman had flown, the new designs were truly reusable aerospace craft. There were two of them, one atop the other, joined together like an unlikely pair of technological Siamese twins.

The bottom one was the jet-powered Lifter. It was all fuel and engines, with a tiny cockpit perched high up on its massive blunt nose. It flew to the topmost reaches of the atmosphere, nearly a hundred kilometers above the ground, and then released its piggyback partner. The Orbiter, smaller of the two mates, carried the passengers and payload. It went the rest of the way into orbit.

Both planes landed separately at the airstrip, ready to be reunited for another flight.

Standing at the airstrip's edge, Kinsman stared at the ungainly-looking pair, one atop the other. *She'll never fly, Orville. Gimme a good old rocket booster and a ballistic re-entry vehicle, the way God meant men to fly into space.*

But he knew that this new Shuttle was making space operations practical. Military men could rocket into orbit atop flaming boosters, but businessmen—and their hirelings—rode the Shuttle. It was much cheaper, more efficient, and the gee loads on the passengers were negligible.

Fred Durban could ride into orbit on that bird, he knew, *if he was healthy enough to get out of bed.*

The Shuttle would carry twenty passengers on this trip. NASA was making three Shuttle flights to the newly completed space station, all on this one day. The whole world would watch the station's official dedication ceremonies via satellite-relayed TV.

"Hey you! What the hell are you . . ."

Kinsman turned to see an Air Policeman yelling at him from a jeep parked a dozen meters away. The AP was in crisp uniform, with gleaming white helmet and dead-black sidearm buckled to his hip. Kinsman was in his khakis. He walked toward the jeep slowly.

"Oh, sorry, Major. I couldn't see your rank with your back turned." The kid sprang out of the jeep and saluted. He dwarfed Kinsman.

Returning the salute, Kinsman explained, "I just wanted to look at this bird before everybody else got here. Can you give me a lift back to the Administration Building parking lot?"

"Yessir, sure." He waited for Kinsman to seat himself in the jeep, then sprinted around and slid under the steering wheel. As he switched on the nearly silent electric motor, the AP asked, "You *walked* out here from the Admin Building, sir?"

Kinsman nodded as the breeze blew into his face.

* * *

The rest of the morning was a hateful blur to Kinsman. *Now I know what it's like to be invaded and conquered.*

Crowds of strangers. Solicitous young Air Police—men and women—pointing you in the right direction. Smiling, unctuous public relations people from NASA and the big corporations taking you by the elbow and telling you how proud and happy you should be that you're here to help make this day a success.

And not one of them knew Kinsman. No one recognized his name or the astronaut's emblem on his shirt. He was a six-foot chunk of meat to them, a statistic. *I was working in space when you were in high school,* he fumed at them silently. But they just smiled and pointed and moved him along: an anonymous visitor, a VIP, a nonperson.

Kinsman was locked into a group of nineteen strangers and walked through all the preflight ceremonies. A brief physical exam, little more than blood pressure, heartbeat, and breathing rate. A safety lecture that was designed to soothe the nerves of jittery civilians who had never gone into orbit before. A five-minute motion picture about what to do during the brief spell of weightlessness when the Shuttle docked with the space station—mainly how to vomit into the bag under zero-gee conditions. And every minute of it under the staring eyes of the news cameras.

Kinsman resented it all: these newcomers, these strangers, these moneygrubbers who had fought against *any* programs in space until their boards of directors became convinced that there was profit to be made Up There.

His nineteen "shipmates" included six news reporters (two female), three freelance writers (one a scenarist from Hollywood), five board members of thirteen interlocked corporations (none of them under fifty years old), two NASA executives who had never been south of downtown Washington before, and three women who had been chosen by national lottery to represent "average taxpayers."

They all looked excited, and chattered nervously as they were marched from the briefing room, past a double column of news cameras, and out into the muggy sunlight. A couple of the business executives seemed a bit dubious about actually taking off, Kinsman thought. And one of the NASA desk-jockeys looked a bit green. *Maybe the movie got to him.*

"I thought there were going to be entertainment stars, too," said one of the women writers.

"They're on the other flight," someone answered.

One of the PR guides hovering near them heard the exchange and recited, "Eight stars from various fields of the entertainment world will be aboard the second Shuttle flight, together with an equal number of senators and congresspersons, and four religious leaders from the major denominations across the nation."

Feeling thoroughly out of place and resentful, like a roustabout who's been forced to work with the clowns, Kinsman climbed aboard a big glass-topped, air-conditioned bus and took the seat that a young, frozen-smiled PR woman led him to.

"Have a pleasant flight, Colonel," she said.

"Thanks for the promotion," Kinsman answered to her departing back.

The bus chugged into motion and the speakers set into each chairback came alive with the news reports of the momentous day:

"And there goes the first busload of visitors to Space Station Alpha. They're on their way!" gabbled a voice that had spent most of its life selling consumer products. "This marks the beginning of a New Era in Space! Twenty ordinary people, just like you and me, will be riding into Outer Space just as easily and comfortably as we ride the daily bus to our homes and offices and shopping centers. Ordinary people, going into orbit, to a great man-made Island in the Sky . . ."

Ordinary people, Kinsman thought. *Am I ordinary? Is anybody?*

One of the "average taxpayers" was sitting beside him.

She stared at him for several minutes as the bus huffed slowly toward the airstrip and the radio voice prattled on.

"They didn't tell us there'd be any soldiers on this flight," she said at last.

Kinsman looked at her. A youngish housewife: softly curled light brown hair, oval face, light eyes, dressed in a brand-new flowered pantsuit.

"I'm in the Aerospace Force," he said, almost in a whisper.

"Well why are they letting *you* up? This isn't a military satellite." She looked almost resentful.

An educated taxpayer. Glancing around and lowering his voice still more, Kinsman said, "Confidentially, I . . . well, I used to be an astronaut. They're letting me see what the new stuff is all about. Sort of like a homecoming for me."

Her minifrown softened. "Oh, I get it. Like inviting the old graduates to the school reunion."

Nodding, "More or less."

"I was wondering why you looked so cool and relaxed. You've been through all this before."

"Well, not exactly anything like this."

"Gosh . . . I've never met an astronaut before. I'm Jinny Woods. I'm from New Paltz, New York."

"Chet Kinsman . . . And, if you don't mind, I'd just as soon keep myself in the background here. I'm just a guest. You're the stars of today's show."

She wriggled with pleasure at his flattery. "You mean I shouldn't tell anybody you're an astronaut?"

"I'd rather you didn't. I don't want a fuss made about it."

"Okay. . . . It'll be our secret."

Kinsman smiled at her while his mind recalled a line that a friend of his had once uttered:

Hell is, I'm booked into Grossinger's for a week and every girl's mother there knows I'm an unmarried medical student.

The bus ride was mercifully brief, but Kinsman wound up being placed beside the same woman inside the Shuttle.

The interior of the rocket plane was much like the interior of a standard commercial jet airliner, except that the seats were plusher, the decor plainer, and there were no windows. Each seatback had a small TV screen built into it. The chairs themselves were large, roomy, comfortable, and equipped with double safety harnesses that criss-crossed over the shoulders and across the chest.

Jinny Woods fumbled with her harness until Kinsman leaned over and helped her with it. She told him about her two children and her husband, who was a salesman. He nodded and admired the way she breathed.

And then they waited.

"What's wrong? Why aren't we moving?" Jinny whispered to Kinsman. She looked as if she were afraid of making a fuss, yet genuinely troubled at the same time.

"It'll take several minutes," Kinsman answered. And in his mind he pictured what was going on down in the cockpit of the massive Lifter, underneath them.

Range safety?

Clear.

Main engine fuel pressure?

Green.

Life support systems?

All green.

Full internal power.

On.

Shuttle 01, you are cleared for taxi.

Roger, Tower. 01 taxiing.

One-quarter throttle. And let's steer clear of the bumps on the ramp. Don't want to shake up the customers.

The whine of the hydrogen turbine engines vibrated through the cabin's thick acoustical insulation. The Shuttle inched forward. Sitting in the heavily padded contour chair, with nothing to look at but the gray curving walls of the cabin and the dead eye of the TV screen in front of him, Kinsman imagined himself sitting in the Command Pilot's seat, nudging the throttles forward and handling the control yoke. The huge, cumbersome double-plane rolled out along the approach ramp and swung onto the five-kilometer-long runway: a broad black road that reached to the horizon and the sky beyond.

Oh-one, hold for final clearance.

Holding.

Range tracking **Go.**

Range safety **Go.**

Meteorology **Go.**

Ground control **Go.**

All systems green.

Oh-one, you are cleared for takeoff.

Roger.

Give 'em a nice easy ride, Jeff.

Only way to fly!

Full takeoff flaps. Full throttle.

Rolling.

Kinsman felt the acceleration pressing him back slightly in his seat. But it was gentle, gentle, nothing like a rocket boost.

Two-double-oh klicks.

Rotate.

The nose came up. Kinsman's hands clutched on his lap, pulling control yoke back, lifting the giant rocket plane off the ground.

He turned to the woman beside him. "We're up."

She was staring at the TV screen in front of her, still looking scared.

Kinsman glanced at his own screen. It was showing a view from a camera in the nose of the Orbiter, as it rode piggyback on the Lifter. He could see the bulbous nose and cockpit of the Lifter below them, and scudding clouds that they had already climbed past.

"When did they turn the screens on?" he wondered.

"Just when we started down the runway. It was scary! You had your eyes closed."

He wanted to smile at her, but couldn't. He didn't answer at all, but kept watching the screen.

Within half an hour they were high over the Atlantic,

which looked like a cloud-flecked sheet of hammered gray metal, far below them.

The intercom speakers hummed to life. "This is Captain Burke speaking. I'm the Command Pilot of your Orbiter aerospace craft. Our big brother down underneath us will be releasing us in approximately five minutes. They'll fly back to the Cape while we light our rocket engines and head onward into orbit and rendezvous with Space Station Alpha. You will hear some noise and feel a few bumps when we separate and light off. Don't be alarmed."

The separation was barely discernible. Kinsman felt a slight sinking sensation as the TV screens showed the Lifter swing away and out of sight. Then a dull throbbing pulsed through the cabin, felt in the bones more than heard. A different kind of vibration.

The Orbiter nosed up.

"Look! I can see the curve of the Earth!"

I know. I've been there. But Kinsman felt the thrill of it all over again. Gradually their weight diminished until they were in zero gravity, hanging loosely against their restraining harnesses.

Jinny swallowed hard several times but managed to keep herself together. Kinsman watched her closely.

"It feels like falling, at first," he said. "But once you get used to it, it's more like floating."

She smiled weakly at him.

He relaxed and luxuriated in the freedom of zero gee. *How many times has it been? Lost count. Way back there someplace I stopped counting.* He wondered what would happen if he got up from his seat and glided freely along the aisle separating the double rows of seats. Probably the NASA people would get hysterical. He pictured himself drifting up to the cockpit, going inside to join the crew and their smoothly functioning equipment. He laughed to himself at the thought of commandeering the spacecraft and bypassing the space station to go on to the Moon. *The first space piracy*, he mused. *Oh, for ten toes!*

Soon enough the flight ended as the Orbiter lined up

with the loading dock in the center of Alpha's set of concentric rings.

This was a piece of piloting that Kinsman had never done, and he watched the TV screen, fascinated, as the ship matched its roll rate with the lazy spin of the space station. Alpha looked like a set of different-sized bicycle wheels nested within one another. Kinsman knew that the biggest one, the outermost wheel, was turning at a rate that would induce a full Earth gravity for the people who lived and worked inside it. The smaller wheels—most of them still under construction—had lighter gravity pulls. The loading dock, at the center of the assembly, was at zero gee, effectively.

The rendezvous and docking maneuvers were flawless, and soon Kinsman and the other passengers were shuffling, still weightless, along a narrow tube that led from the Orbiter's hatch to the loading dock of the station. The tube was slightly claustrophogenic, tight enough to allow the passengers to push themselves along with their hands. Kinsman kept ducking his head, although the tube was actually high enough to accommodate someone several inches taller than he.

The loading bay was even more tightly organized than the groundside takeoff had been. There was a NASA or corporate representative for each of the twenty visitors, and each one guided an individual visitor to the stairs that led "down" to the main living quarters on the outermost wheel.

Kinsman was relieved to be separated from Jinny Woods, although his guide—a sparkling, bright young industrial engineer—treated him like a fragile grandfather.

"Just this way, sir. Now you don't actually need the stairs up here in the low-gravity area, but I'd recommend that you use them anyway."

"I've been in zero gee before," Kinsman said.

Ignoring him pleasantly, the young man went on, "We'll be going down—that is, out toward Level One—where the gravity is at normal Earth value. Your weight will feel like it's increasing as we go down the stairs."

He led Kinsman to a circular hatch set into the "floor" of the loading bay. A metal stairway spiraled down to the other levels of the station.

"Easy does it now!" he said cheerfully, holding Kinsman by the elbow as they took the first steps down.

Kinsman wanted to break free of his grip and glide down the tube until enough gravity built up for him to walk normally. Instead, grumbling inwardly, he patiently let the engineer walk beside him.

"It's easy to get disoriented, you know," the kid said.

Feeling like an invalid, Kinsman let himself be led down the stairs. The metal tube they were in was one of the "spokes" that connected the hub of the station with its various wheel-shaped levels. The tube was softly lit by patches of fluorescent paints glowing palely along the curving walls. *No power drain*, Kinsman realized.

Once safely down on Level One, the twenty first-comers were organized into a guided tour. Kinsman endured it, together with the sullen weight of a full Earth gee that tugged at him like a prisoner's chains.

The station's first level included some laboratory areas, individual living compartments that made submarines look roomy, a galley, and a mess hall. It all looked depressingly efficient and familiar, except that the floor curved upward no matter where you looked, and the occasional windows showed stars turning over and over in lazy spirals against the blackness of infinity.

The tour started at one end of the mess hall and finished at the opposite end, where a bar had been set up. Kinsman took a plastic cup of punch from the automatic dispenser just as the second batch of arrivals appeared, exactly at the spot where his own tour had started.

Looking across the bolted-down tables and chairs along the sloping floor, Kinsman spotted Neal McGrath's tall, dour form among the newcomers. McGrath stared straight at Kinsman and scowled. Kinsman lifted his cup to the Senator.

Is that his normal scowl, or is he really sore at me?

Diane was in McGrath's group, surrounded by station personnel and public relations flaks. *They all want to be in show biz.* Kinsman didn't recognize any of the other "stars."

Gradually the mess hall filled up with the visitors. Kinsman chatted quietly with several people and tried to avoid being pinned down by several others—including Jinny Woods, who had that "I've got a secret" gleam in her eye whenever she looked at Kinsman.

Suddenly some of the station people were setting Diane up atop one of the bigger tables. As she began tuning her guitar the chattering voices of the crowd diminished into expectant silence.

"I've never been in space before," she said. "At least, not this way." They all laughed. "So I'd like to sing a song that's dedicated to the people who made all this possible —the farsighted people who pioneered the way here. It's called, 'The Green Hills of Earth.'"

Kinsman ignored the words of her song and bathed in the magic of her voice. Everyone was silent, turned toward Diane as flowers face the Sun, listening and watching her sad, serious face as she sang.

He felt Neal McGrath's presence beside him. Looking over his shoulder, Kinsman saw that McGrath was staring at him, not at Diane.

"We've got to talk," McGrath said in a throaty whisper.

Kinsman nodded.

McGrath put a hand on his shoulder. "Come on."

"Shh. Wait a minute."

"Now!"

A surge of anger welled up in him and Kinsman yanked McGrath's hand off his shoulder. But then it ebbed away and he turned and whispered, "All right . . . where to?"

McGrath led him back through the corridor that ran

the length of Level One, to the area where the living cubbyholes were. He found an empty room, no name on the door, and ushered Kinsman inside it.

Their presence filled the tiny compartment. There was nothing much else in it: just a bunk built into the wall, a sliver of a desk with a bolted-down swivel chair next to it, and some cabinets along the other wall.

Kinsman tried the bunk. It was springy, comfortable, but narrow. He knew that if he stretched out on it, it would be barely long enough for him.

"You'd have a hard time sleeping on one of these," he said to McGrath.

"What's that supposed to mean?" McGrath growled.

Neal had taken the chair. It looked pitifully small for him. Kinsman thought of an underfed burro bearing an American professional athlete.

Kinsman shrugged. "Not a damned thing, Neal, except that these are pretty damned small bunks."

McGrath's scowl deepened. "Diane told you about her and me."

"That's right."

"Who've you told about it?"

"Nobody."

"Nobody yet," McGrath said, emphasizing the second word.

"Yeah," Kinsman agreed. "Nobody yet."

"Mary-Ellen knows all about it."

"So Diane said."

Hunching forward in his chair, spreading his hands in a gesture that would have indicated helplessness in a smaller man, McGrath asked, "What are you going to do with the information, Chet?"

"I don't know."

He could see the pain in McGrath's face. It wasn't easy for the man to beg. "Most of the people around me know about it."

"But your voters back on the farm don't."

"We . . . I was planning to get the divorce after I'm reelected."

"After you become Minority Leader."

McGrath nodded.

"Mary-Ellen's going to help you campaign, and you'll troup your kids all over the state, and after the voters have sent you back to Washington for another six years you'll get the divorce. Pretty sweet."

"What else can I do?" he asked, with real misery in his voice. "It's not the divorce so much as the timing."

"Those farmers and coal miners won't like knowing that you're running around with a singer, an entertainment star, a left-wing ex-radical from show business. They'll think you're pretty lousy, cheating on your wife, won't they?"

"Yes," he admitted. "They will."

"They'd be right."

McGrath's eyes flashed. "Don't be too righteous about this, Chet. I would never have met her if it wasn't for you."

"That was a hundred years ago."

His voice barely audible, McGrath said, "I fell in love with her right off the bat, the first time I laid eyes on her. I just didn't do anything about it . . . until . . ."

"Will Diane marry you after the divorce?"

"I don't know. We've talked about it. I want to marry her, but she's not so sure."

"She'd make a lousy senator's wife."

Exploding up from the chair, McGrath raised his hands wildly. They banged into the compartment's plastic-sheeted ceiling. "Christ Almighty! I didn't want any of this! I didn't go out looking for it. I never intended to break up my marriage. It wasn't all that good anymore, between Mary-Ellen and me, but . . . Chet, when I'm with Diane I feel like a kid again! Just being in the same room with her! And then when she told me she felt the same way about me . . ."

Kinsman leaned back on the bunk and watched his old friend pace the tiny compartment. *Middle-age change of life*, he told himself, envying the man who could let go of himself so completely.

McGrath stopped in front of Kinsman. Looming over him, he asked, "So what are you going to do about it?"

"I told you, Neal. I haven't decided what to do. Probably nothing."

"If you're thinking of using this to pressure me on the Moonbase deal, forget it! I won't knuckle under."

Kinsman looked up at him. He was stubborn enough to throw his career into the flames. *Maybe.*

"The trouble is," Kinsman said evenly, "if I've found out about it, it's only a matter of time until guys like Marcot and the rest find out . . ."

"They won't. Congress takes care of its own."

"Neal, some crap artist like Tug Wynne will nudge it out of somebody sooner or later."

"Wynne's bureau chief is a friend of mine. He'll keep it quiet or he'll lose a helluva lot of good inside sources. Think I'm the only senator with something to hide?"

Shaking his head, Kinsman countered, "Look, Neal. I haven't been around Washington as long as you have, but I know this much: the Pentagon—the White House—they're out after you. And they've got their own channels to the media, you know. You're playing with the big boys now."

McGrath slowly sank down on the bunk beside Kinsman.

"Do you think for one second," Kinsman went on, "that Wynne or his bureau chief will sit on your story when it's the Pentagon dealing it out? Or the White House? For God's sake, those guys could break it in the fucking *National Enquirer* or plant rumors in any one of sixty daily columns. They could give it to the Hollywood gossips . . . Diane's a TV personality, you know."

"I know."

"And when the Pentagon finds out about you," Kinsman said, "you're going to think I told them."

"What you're saying is that you might as well tell them

yourself and collect the credit for it, because they're going to find out sooner or later anyway."

Kinsman snapped, "No, that's *not* what I'm saying! Goddammitall, Neal, I'm warning you that you're going to have to face this pressure, one way or the other."

"And if I vote for the Moonbase program, the pressure will be off."

"That's right."

"So you and your Pentagon buddies can build a military base on the Moon."

"It's not a military base, Neal. All military operations are confined to low orbits around the Earth. Moonbase has nothing to do with that."

For a long moment McGrath said nothing. Then, "These operations in orbit. Are they the laser-armed satellites? The ones that are supposed to shoot down Russian ICBMs?"

"I'm not supposed to say anything about that."

"But you don't deny it?"

"No," Kinsman said, "I don't deny it."

"It's not a very well-kept secret. They're spending billions on the program."

"So?"

"I'm still against your Moonbase," McGrath said quietly, but with the implacability of a glacier. "No matter what you say, Chet, they'll turn it into a military camp."

"No . . . they can't."

"Bullshit. They're already escalating the arms race into orbital space. Why should I help them spread it to the Moon?"

With a slow shake of his head, Kinsman got up from the bunk. "Neal, you're right. I don't want to see them turn space into a battlefield, either."

"But you want to go to the Moon," McGrath said.

Turning back to face him, "I sure as hell do."

"At any cost."

"At *almost* any cost," Kinsman said.

"So what can I do about it?" McGrath muttered, more to himself than to Kinsman.

"I wish I knew," Kinsman said, feeling trapped and helpless. "I sure as hell wish I knew."

When they got back to the bar at the galley, Diane was nowhere in sight. McGrath went off to look for her. Kinsman took another cup of punch. It was weak stuff, but his mouth felt dry, his innards arid.

People were drifting through the mess hall, drinks in hand, conversing in small groups. Kinsman wandered over to the hall's lone window, a long expanse of plastiglass that looked out on the slowly revolving stars. Most of the PR flaks had disappeared, leaving the visitors pretty much to themselves, at last.

"Well, Major, what do you think of it?"

Kinsman turned to see a cheerful-looking man of about fifty standing before him, a beer bottle clenched in each hand.

"Very efficient." Kinsman grinned at him.

"Beats going back to the bar every five minutes." He tucked one of the beers under his arm and extended a cold, moist hand. "I'm T.D. Dreyer. My outfit did a lot of the structural work on this flying doughnut."

"Your outfit?"

"General Technologies, Inc."

"General Tech? You're *that* Dreyer!"

T.D. Dreyer grinned boyishly, happy to be recognized. He was slightly shorter than Kinsman, barrel-chested and burly of build. His blue-gray leisure suit was carefully tailored to make him look as slim as possible, but his face betrayed him: a chubby, happy man who constantly battled overweight. It was a deeply tanned face. *He either has a sunlamp at his desk or he spends a lot of time out in the field.*

"And I know who you are," Dreyer said. "You're Major Chester Arthur Kinsman, former astronaut, now part of the Aerospace Force's Moonbase team."

A faint chill of panic rushed through Kinsman. "You've got a good intelligence network."

Dreyer's eyes lit up. "You bumped a Wright-Patterson contracting officer who's been giving one of my divisions a hard time. I was going to try a little friendly persuasion on him while we were both here and away from our desks. I made it my business to find out who bumped my pigeon . . . and at the last minute, too."

"Hell, if I had known . . ."

"Naah, don't worry about it. I'll catch up with him next week." Dreyer moved half a step closer to Kinsman and lowered his voice slightly. "Frankly, I have a feeling the guy's scared to fly. I was kinda looking forward to watching him piss his pants when I dragged him over to this viewport."

They laughed together.

"You've been up here before," Kinsman said.

"Sure. Big job like this, I come up and look as often as I can get away from that damned desk in Dallas. Gives the insurance people fits, but I like it up here. It's fun to be away from all those damned numbers crunchers and ribbon clerks."

"I'll drink to that." Kinsman lifted his cup.

After a long pull of beer, Dreyer said, "Y'know, the trouble with being chairman of the board is that you're supposed to be dignified and conservative. My board members don't believe me when I tell 'em we should be pouring every dollar we can find into space operations."

"They think it's too risky?"

Dreyer made a sour face. "They're money manipulators. Scared shitless of anything new. The kind that backed the nice, safe, conservative Erie Canal instead of them newfangled railroads." He laughed heartily at his own joke.

"Dreyer! I thought that was you." A tall, lithe, hollow-cheeked man in his thirties joined them. He wore a one-piece white jumpsuit. His face was bony, ascetic; his reddish-brown hair was shaved so close to the scalp that he almost looked bald. He was empty-handed.

"Well," the newcomer asked, gesturing out toward the view of space, "what do you think of it?"

"Very nice," Dreyer answered. "I think there's a future in it."

"You're being facetious."

"No, but I'm not being polite. Major Kinsman, allow me to introduce Professor Howard Alexander of Redlands University. Howard, this is Chet Kinsman."

Alexander's hands stayed at his sides. "I didn't know that any Air Force people were on the invitations list. Are you on duty with NASA?"

"No," Kinsman said.

"Chet's a former Air Force astronaut. Now he's on the Moonbase team."

"Oh, *that*." The temperature of the conversation dropped fifty degrees.

Dreyer seemed amused. "Professor Alexander is the apostle of the True Faith. He wants to build colonies in space and make them into heavenly paradises."

"And you want to make a profit out of it," Alexander shot back, testily.

"Sure, why not?"

"Because space should be free for all Humankind, that's why. Because we shouldn't bring our selfish, petty greeds out into this beautiful new world."

"Right on," Kinsman said.

Alexander turned toward him. "Nor should we be trying to build weapons and fortifications in space. This is a domain for peaceful existence, not for war."

"I couldn't agree more."

The professor blinked at him.

Kinsman went on. "It would be wonderful if we could leave all the greed and anger and suspicion of our fellow men back on Earth and come out here fresh and clean and newborn."

"I got news for you, fellas," Dreyer said. "It ain't gonna happen that way."

"I'm afraid not," Kinsman agreed.

Alexander shook his head, as if dismissing such unpleasant thoughts from his mind. "It *will* happen that way, if we make it happen that way."

"How'm I gonna do that?" Dreyer asked, suddenly very serious. "You think my board of directors'll risk the company's capital on dreams? They want profits."

"They'll get their profits, from the Solar Power Satellites."

"Sure. Twenty years downstream. We could be bankrupt by then. Where the hell are we going to get the capital to build those big-assed colonies of yours? Plus the lunar mining facilities, and the processing plants, and the factories."

"It would only take five or six billions . . ."

"A year!"

"Surely the major corporations could invest that much in their own future," Alexander said. "And in the future of the human race."

Dreyer shook his head. "Like I said, we're not in the investment business. We work for profits. Nobody in his right mind is going to risk the kind of money your space colonies require."

"Wait a minute," Kinsman said. "Your corporation built this space station, didn't it?"

"Sure. Under Government contract. Cost plus fee. Uncle Sam takes the risks and makes the investment. We do the work for hire and take a small—but guaranteed—profit."

Alexander said, "Think of the profits you could make from selling energy back to Earth, once you've built a few Solar Power Satellites."

"Yeah," Dreyer said, gesturing with a beer-bottle-laden hand. "But you don't need a supercolossal colony in the sky to build Solar Power Satellites. All you need is a tough crew of workmen on the Moon, where the raw materials are, and another crew in orbit, where the construction'll take place."

"But there's more to it than just building the power satellites," Alexander insisted. "The space colony will also be involved in building more colonies, more self-sufficient islands in space."

"What for?" Kinsman asked.

"So that more people can live in space!" Alexander's exasperated tone reminded Kinsman of a Sunday School session he had attended once, as a child, with Neal.

But how do we know God loves us?

Because the Scriptures tell us so!

But how do we know the Scriptures are right?

Because they were inspired by God!

But how do we know they were inspired by God?

Because it says so, right in the Scriptures!

Repressing a grim smile, Kinsman told himself, *At least the Quakers never fell into that dogmatic tailspin. I'll bet Alexander was schooled by Jesuits.*

"And who's gonna pay for these additional colonies?" Dreyer was asking.

"They'll be paid for out of the profits from the Solar Power Satellites!" Alexander was getting edgy.

"Let's sit down," Kinsman suggested, pointing to the empty tables of the mess hall. Most of the visitors had left the area; a few were still clustered at the bar.

"Lemme get a refill," said Dreyer, hefting his empty beer bottles.

The three of them went to the bar. Dreyer got two more beers, Kinsman another cup of the weak punch. Alexander abstained. Then they sat at the end of one of the long mess hall tables: Dreyer at the head, Alexander and Kinsman flanking him on either side.

Kinsman took a sip of the punch. It felt cold and sticky-sweet.

"Now look," Dreyer said to the professor, "don't get me wrong. I like the colony idea. I think it'd be fun to build. And I agree that Solar Power Satellites could make a lot of profit—in time. *If* the Government doesn't nationalize them, once they're built. But how do you raise the initial capital? You're talking about a hundred billion bucks or more."

"Over a ten-year period," Alexander said.

Dreyer shrugged. "That's still ten billion a year, minimum. Even worse than I thought. With no profits until way downstream, and maybe not even then. Who in hell is gonna buy that? My board of directors would toss me out on my ear if I tried to put that one past them."

"If the corporations would all work together . . ."

"They won't."

Kinsman said, "I thought NASA was in on this."

"Only on the transportation end of it," Dreyer said. "NASA's not going to build the colonies. Congress won't appropriate that kind of money."

"Not for Solar Power Satellites?" Kinsman wondered.

"Not for big fancy colonies that would house 10,000 university professors," Dreyer said, as Alexander frowned.

"Or for lunar hospitals," Kinsman muttered.

They talked around and around the subject, Alexander waxing poetic and pathetic by turns, Dreyer shaking his bulldog head and insisting on the economic facts of life. Kinsman looked over his shoulder at the star-filled window and saw their reflections in the glass: Alexander in profile, earnest and ascetic as a saint; Dreyer's back bulking massively; and his own face, lean, dark, bored with the repetitious arguments but searching, thinking, seeking . . . what?

Finally Kinsman knew. He broke into their argument. "Wait a minute. Even if you build your colony in space . . . you're going to need military protection for it."

Alexander looked aghast. "Military! To protect it from what? Martians?"

"Earthlings," Kinsman said. "Maybe the Chinese . . . they're desperate enough to try almost anything. Or terrorists. Your colony would be wide open to a small nuclear bomb. Look what they did in Cape Town."

"That's ridiculous," Alexander snapped. "The Chinese are starving. What good would a space colony do them? And terrorists would never get up to the colony . . . we wouldn't allow any weapons aboard it."

"You're not afraid of the Russians?" Dreyer asked.

"They're on our side for the time being," Kinsman said. "It's the hungry people that're causing the trouble."

With a sardonic smile, Dreyer countered, "The Russians'll be hungry before long. Everybody will be. Including us."

"Now listen to me," Alexander said, looking at Dreyer. "I want to know how much capital your corporation would be willing to invest in the space colony project."

"None."

The professor's mouth went slack, but only for a moment. "None? Nothing at all?"

"Not in the colony," Dreyer answered, with a good-natured grin. "The lunar mining operation . . . now that's a different story. I think maybe we could go in on that with you. Or building orbital factories; that looks profitable. But find another pigeon for your flying Garden of Eden."

"That's *very* shortsighted."

"Yeah, I know. But if I was as visionary as you are I'd go bankrupt."

Abruptly, Alexander pushed his chair back as far as it would go on the little track welded into the floor. Standing, he looked down on Kinsman and Dreyer.

"Someday we'll have our space colonies, and we'll start a new era for the human race . . . without soldiers and without capitalists!"

"Good luck," Kinsman said. Dreyer grinned.

Alexander stalked off.

Dreyer watched him, then turned back to Kinsman. "When he finds a place that doesn't have soldiers or capitalists he's going to be in heaven."

"Guess he'll snub St. Michael unless Mike puts away his armor and weapons."

"Yeah. And there's a few capitalist saints he probably won't get along with, either."

Kinsman laughed.

"He reminds me," Dreyer went on, "of what a kid in the office said about the head of our Technology Forecasting Department: 'He's no prophet; he's a loss.'"

They laughed together and got up and went to the bar for another drink. As they walked slowly back toward the big window that looked out on the stars, Kinsman said:

"I've been thinking . . . let me ask you a hypothetical question."

"Shoot."

Kinsman put out his free hand and touched the plastiglass. It was cold. Space cold. Death cold. He could feel it drawing the heat of his body out of him, pulling his soul into space.

He yanked his hand away and said to Dreyer, "Suppose the government was willing to sink a few billion dollars per year into building lunar mining facilities and orbital factories. Would your board of directors be interested then?"

"Sure!" Dreyer answered immediately. "If Uncle Sugar's taking the risk, why the hell not?"

"That's what I thought," Kinsman said.

"You're talking about a space colony now, or something else?"

"Not a colony. Just the lunar mining facilities and the factories."

"To build Solar Power Satellites."

"No. Something else."

Dreyer said nothing for a long moment. Then, "What do you have in mind?"

Kinsman shook his head.

With a growing grin, Dreyer said, "I've heard that the Air Force is working on some kind of big project that involves lots of satellites. Very hush-hush."

In his best tight-lipped manner Kinsman answered, "I can't confirm or deny rumors."

Dreyer's grin spread. He nodded happily. "We'd be more than glad to work on that kind of a project. With the government providing the investment money and the Aerospace Force behind it, *that* would be a project we could depend on. We'd put a helluva lot of our own discretionary risk money into it. It'd fly, never worry about it."

"Do you think the other industrial contractors would feel the same way?"

"Why the hell wouldn't they?" Dreyer said. Then he added, "I'd just-like to see the look on Alexander's face when he finds out that his precious idea for factories in space will be turning out military satellites!"

Kinsman nodded and tried to grin back at the man, but he couldn't.

He sat once again next to Jinny Woods during the Shuttle's return flight to Florida. But Kinsman's mind was a quarter-million miles away.

"I didn't see you hardly at all," the woman was saying, "once we got up there. You were always in *deep* dark conversations with somebody or other. Who were all those people anyway? Wasn't one of them Senator McGrath? I saw him on television, one of those late-night talk shows. He's so handsome!"

Kinsman made noncommittal noises at her, while his mind raced:

Is this the way history gets made? Somebody wants to find a retreat, a place to hide, and we get a lunar base out of it? Somebody wants to make a buck, open up a new trade route, get the tax collectors off his back. That's what makes the world go 'round?

". . . and the way she sang! I'll bet you didn't even hear her, did you? I looked for you, but you weren't anywhere in sight. You missed the dancers, too. They took us down to the low-gravity sections of the station . . ."

I'll have to spring it on Murdock first. No, first I'll tell Frank about it. If there're any flaws in the picture he'll spot them. Then Murdock. Then we'll work up a presentation for General Sherwood. Probably for Marcot, too. It all ties together so neatly. Why haven't the others seen it?

"You haven't been listening to a word I've said," Jinny Woods complained.

Kinsman stirred and pulled his attention to her. She was pouting.

"I'm sorry," he said. "I was thinking about some of the problems I've got ahead of me, back in my office."

"You sound just like my husband. I guess I talk too much. That's what he tells me."

"No . . . it's my fault."

She brushed a curl away from her eyes. "I'm just so excited by all this! It's all old stuff for you, I know. But nothing like this has ever happened to me before. It's all so new . . . so thrilling!"

She's really pretty, Kinsman noticed. *Nice eyes. Happy as a kid.*

"It's exciting for me too," he told her. "Don't let this calm exterior fool you. No matter how many times you go into orbit, it's always a ball."

She seemed pleased. "Really? I'm not surprised. I guess I just never learned to control my feelings very well. I get awfully gushy, don't I? Do you think we'll ever get to go up there again?"

Do I think about anything else?

"They said they're going to bring us up to Washington next week for a press conference," she went on. "You live in Washington, don't you? I've never been there before and Ralph says he can't leave his job and come with me. I'll be alone in the city."

"Where will you be staying?"

"Some hotel, I guess. They haven't told us where."

Kinsman nodded. "Well, I'll find out and call you when you're in town."

"Oh, that'd be wonderful! Do you have a card or something . . . so I can call you? That'd be easier . . ."

"I'm afraid I can't give out my phone number," Kinsman said, taking on a man-of-mystery disguise.

She fell for it. "Really? Why?"

He put a finger to his lips. "I'll find out where you're staying and give you a call. Trust me."

She nodded slowly, her eyes filled with something approaching awe.

And that was the last he thought of her.

As soon as he arrived back in his one-room apartment Kinsman called Fred Durban. But the old man had slipped into a coma and the hospital would allow no visitors except family.

Then he called Colt and invited himself to Frank's apartment for a drink.

Colt's pad was lush compared to Kinsman's cell: richly carpeted living room, with a balcony that overlooked Arlington Cemetery; big bedroom with a fake zebra hide cover thrown over the water bed.

Scotch in hand, Kinsman explained his idea to Colt. The black officer listened silently, stretched out on his Naugahyde recliner.

". . . and that's it," Kinsman finished. "We mine the ores on the Moon, process them there, ship them to the orbital factories where they're manufactured into laser-armed ABM satellites, and deploy the satellites in orbit around the Earth."

For a long moment Colt said nothing. Then, "You got everything tied together, don't you? One big program that's got something for everybody. Moonbase becomes an important mining center instead of a charity hospital. The big corporations get Uncle Sam to pay for setting them up in business in orbit. The Air Force gets the ABM satellites on-station at half the cost of building them on Earth and launching 'em from the ground."

"Not really half the cost," Kinsman said. "It won't be that cheap, I don't think. And it'll take slightly longer to put the first ABM satellites on-station."

Colt bounded out of his chair. "Shee-it, man, you've got it made! You've pulled seventeen dozen little separate Air Force projects together into one big bee-yootiful program that makes sense. Nobody could vote against it! It'd be like spittin' on the motherlovin' flag!" Colt laughed and stuck his hand out to Kinsman, palm up. "Man, it's the best piece of strategical thinking since Moses led the Children of Israel out of Egypt!"

Kinsman slapped at his hand, then grabbed it. "You really think so?"

"Hell, yes! The brass'll love it. And you get your goddamned Moonbase out of it too. Shrewd, man. Shrewd."

A sigh of relief eased out of Kinsman. "Okay, great. Now the first thing we've got to do is tell Murdock about it."

"First thing tomorrow, we'll corner him."

"Could you do me a favor, Frank?" Kinsman asked. "You tell him. Leave me out of it. As soon as I try to tell him anything he shuts me off. If I bounce this plan off him, he'll find a million reasons to junk it without bucking it further up the chain of command. It'll die right there in his office."

Colt eyed his friend. "Yeah, maybe. But you're the guy who knows all the shit about this. I don't. I couldn't put it across to Murdock as well as you could."

Glancing at the purpling sky and the dark shadow of the Pentagon on the horizon, Kinsman said slowly, "Well . . . we've got all night to rehearse it. Unless you have something else to do."

Colt frowned. "Lemme make a phone call. This is gonna break the heart of the best lookin' piece of ass the Secretary of Agriculture ever had working for him."

"Aw hell, Frank. I didn't mean . . ."

With a wink, Colt said, "Forget it, buddy. She'll keep. And you're right, I *can* impress Murdock with my military bearing."

Kinsman would have paced his office if it had been big enough. Instead he sat at his desk, the chair tilted back against the faded pastel wall, and had nothing to do but think.

You're selling out, you know that. You're giving them what they want: a military base on the Moon. Neal's right, you're spreading the arms race into space. You're willing to start a war up there.

But another part of his mind answered, *They're going to put the ABM satellites up anyway. This way, at least we get a Moonbase out of it. At least I'll be there, away from all this madness.*

And what are you going to do, he asked himself, *when you're standing on the Moon, watching them blow up all the cities of Earth?*

He had no answer for that.

Colt burst into the cubbyhole office, his grin dazzling. "He bought it! He was on the horn to Sherwood before I even finished! Man, did he go for it! Whammo!" He smacked his hands together.

Suddenly Kinsman felt too weak to get to his feet. "And General Sherwood?"

"He wants to see us this afternoon."

"Us?"

"Yeah. I told Murdock that it was all your idea. While he was on the phone with the General. You shoulda seen his face! Like he crapped in his pants!" Colt roared with laughter.

General Sherwood tried to contain his enthusiasm, but as he sat behind his big, aerodynamically clean desk, listening to Kinsman, he began nodding. At first his head moved only slightly, unconsciously, as Kinsman unfolded the logic of his plan. But by the time Kinsman was summing up, the General's head was bobbing vigorously and he was smiling happily.

Colonel Murdock was sitting on the edge of his chair, watching the General intently, his own bald head going up and down in exact rhythm with the General's. Colt sat farther from the desk, back far enough so that Kinsman could not see him.

Standing in front of the General's desk, too wrapped up in presenting the ideas to feel nervous, Kinsman ignored Murdock, ignored Colt, ignored the self-doubts that gnawed at his innards.

He concentrated on the General, reinforcing each nod of his silver-maned head as if it were a biofeedback loop that made him more eloquent, more intelligent, more convincing.

Finally Kinsman finished. He stood there, arms limp at his sides, sweat trickling down his flanks. *My uniform must be soaked*, he thought.

The General's head stopped nodding. "Fascinating," he said, in a voice so low that he might have been talking to himself. "Here I've had each and every one of these programs at my fingertips for months—years, some of them—and I never saw how they could all be interconnected into a single grand design. Watertight compartments. Short-circuited thinking."

He looked up at Kinsman. "Good work, Major. Very good work. Get the presentations staff and the numbers crunchers onto this immediately. I want to see a detailed presentation of this plan before the end of the week."

All his exhaustion blew away. "Yes *sir*," Kinsman snapped.

The rest of the week was a madhouse of meetings, rehearsals, discussions, arguments. Kinsman raced along the Pentagon corridors, from cost-computing analysts to technical artists drawing the block diagrams, from long scrambled phone conversations with industrial leaders such as Dreyer to longer face-to-face meetings with their local technical representatives and engineers. Days, nights blurred together. Meals were sandwiches gobbled at desks, crumbs spilling onto typed lists of numbers, artists' sketches of lunar installations and orbiting satellites. Sleep was something you grabbed in snatches, on couches, in chairs . . . once Kinsman dozed off in the shower of the officers' gym.

The full-scale presentation took two hours. Deputy Director Marcot showed up and chain-smoked through it. Kinsman stood at the head of the darkened conference room, squinting into the solitary light of the slide projector, half-hypnotized by the clouds of blue smoke gliding through the light beam, as he explained picture after picture, graph after graph, list after list. He couldn't see his audience but he could tell they were interested, eager, from the questions that floated up to him out of the darkness.

"What was the basis for the cost estimates on the lasers?"

"Latest industrial information, sir. I took the noncompetitive figures offered by the three top contractors in the heavy laser industry. I thought that if we asked them for competitive bids, the figures we'd get might be artificially low."

Marcot's sarcastic voice was heavy with mock-surprise. "You mean contractors send in artificially low bids deliberately, just to get a half-billion dollars' worth of business?"

Everyone around the conference table chuckled.

They questioned Kinsman for another hour after the final slide had been shown and the lights turned on again. Colt fielded some of the questions, as did the other men and women who had worked on the presentation. But Kinsman took most of the questions himself.

Finally Marcot got to his feet. Waving his inevitable cigarette in Kinsman's general direction, "Okay. Hone it down to half an hour and be prepared to show it to the Secretary first thing next week."

Back in his own office, Colt grabbed Kinsman by the shoulders. "We're on our way, man! The Secretary of Deefense! The big brass head hisself. Marcot bought it!"

Kinsman was too tired and numb to feel exultant.

"C'mon, I'm gonna buy you a drink."

"I just want to get some sleep, Frank. Thanks anyway."

Colt shrugged. "Yeah. We got a weekend's worth of work figuring out how to squeeze all this gorgeous stuff down to half an hour."

Kinsman answered, "Let me lock up all this gorgeous stuff in the vault." The yellow boxes of slides were scattered across Kinsman's desk, each box stamped in red: ULTRA TOP SECRET.

As Kinsman wearily worked on the combination lock to the file cabinet alongside his desk, Colt beamed happily at him.

"Man, you were a ball of fire in there. You coulda sold General Motors stock in the Kremlin. You've really changed, man. You've really come out of your shell."

Over his shoulder, Kinsman said, "I want to go to the Moon, Frank. Even if I have to bring the whole goddamned Aerospace Force with me."

Colt grinned. "You figured it out, heh? You wear The Man's uniform, you gotta do The Man's work. That's the law of life, my friend. But it's good to see you thinking like an Air Force officer. Always thought you had a good head on your shoulders. No more of this peaceful hospital crap."

Kinsman put the boxes of slides into the file drawer, then shut it slowly and clicked the lock. He took the card atop the cabinet and turned it from the white OPEN side to the red LOCKED side.

"Frank," he said, straightening up, "don't get the wrong idea. The Moon is still legally restricted, as far as military weaponry is concerned. The mining operation, okay. But Moonbase will never be a place for war. Understand that. Never."

Colt's grin faded. "And how are you gonna get the Russians to go along with that? They're building a base up there, too, you know. You start mining operations, they'll start mining operations."

"We'll work it out some way."

"Without fighting."

"That's right."

"Damn! You're just as dumb as you always were."

Late Monday afternoon Kinsman stood at the head of the long polished mahogany table in the private conference room of the Secretary of Defense. No need to turn out the lights here: his slides were presented on a wall-sized television screen.

Kinsman spoke directly to the Secretary himself, despite the fact that the table was filled with Marcot and two other deputy directors, and four generals, including Sherwood. Colt was in another room, feeding the slides into the television camera.

Every man at the table watched Kinsman intently, and he looked back at them. The same thoughts were going through each of their heads, he knew: How does this affect my program, my staff, my position in the chain of command?

"To summarize," Kinsman said to the Secretary, "we can bring down the costs of orbiting the ABM satellite network by a factor of five or more if we build them in orbital factories, using raw materials mined on the Moon. The major industrial contractors are eager to begin space manufacturing operations, but need a program such as this to insure that they can do so without unacceptable investment risks." He pressed the button on his palm-sized signaling transmitter, and the next slide appeared on the screen.

It was a list of cost figures.

"The initial costs will be high, of course; significantly higher over the first five years of the program because of the investment in setting up the lunar mining facility and its associated living quarters. But once we begin processing ores on the Moon and shipping them to the orbital factories, the costs of building the laser satellites drops very sharply. By the late 1990's we should have a complete network of ABM satellites in orbit, at a fraction of our original cost estimates. Thank you, sir."

The men around the table stirred, glanced at one another, and then all settled their gazes on the Secretary. He sat at the far end of the table, looking relaxed and thoughtful. He was the tweedy, gray university type. An unlit pipe was clamped in his teeth.

"We're going ahead with the ABM satellites under any circumstances," General Sherwood said, filling the silence. "They're necessary to protect us from missile attack from anywhere on Earth—they're the only defense against the nth nation problem. But they're expensive. This plan allows us to protect ourselves against every nuclear-armed nation at a much lower cost."

The Defense Secretary nodded and started lighting his pipe.

"And by building the satellites in space," Kinsman added, still standing before the blank screen, "out of raw materials mined on the Moon, we not only get the ABM network . . . we get a powerful industrial capacity in orbit, and a full-scale, permanent base on the Moon."

"A base," General Sherwood pointed out, "that is administratively under the control of the Department of Defense."

The Secretary slowly took the pipe from his mouth. "You mean, the Air Force gets its Moonbase, eh Jim?"

General Sherwood broke into a boyish smile. "Yes, sir, that is exactly what I mean."

Smiling back at him, the Secretary said, "Well, it seems to me that the important thing here is that America's industrial power is brought into the space program. I know when I was back with the Institute we had a lot of discussions about how we could get the corporations into the space business without asking them to risk their shirts. This looks like the way to do it."

He's buying it! Kinsman's heart leaped. *He's bought it!*

"I think you're perfectly right about that," said Ellery Marcot. "Perfectly right."

"What I'd like to know," the Secretary said, with a nod toward one of the other generals, "is why our hired planning consultants never brought this whole ball of wax together the way the Major has, here."

The general flushed. "Well, it's one thing if you're sitting out in left field . . ."

"Relax, George," the Secretary said, making a patting motion with his hand. "I was only tweaking you."

He got up from his leather-backed chair. "A very good presentation, Major. Good thinking. I'll speak to the President about it at tomorrow's briefing."

Kinsman could only say, "Thank you, sir," and it was so weak that he wondered if the Secretary heard him.

Turning to General Sherwood, the Secretary asked, "Jim, see that my people get copies of those slides and all the backup material, will you?"

Sherwood rose, beaming. "Certainly, Mr. Secretary. Certainly."

They all filed out of the conference room, leaving Kinsman standing there, rooted to the spot. *We did it*, he told himself. Then he heard himself whisper, "No, *you* did it. Don't blame anyone else."

Kinsman walked slowly out to the anteroom. The others had gone back to their own offices. All except Marcot, who was by the window talking with Murdock. The Colonel had been waiting in the anteroom all through Kinsman's presentation. *He must've walked off the soles of his shoes, pacing up and down.* Murdock looked rumpled, exhausted; hands clasped behind his back, the expression on his face, as he listened to Marcot, halfway between eager anticipation and utter dread.

Frank Colt jounced into the anteroom, tossing the box of slides in one hand. He gave Kinsman a big grin and a thumbs-up sign.

Marcot came up to Kinsman, with Colonel Murdock trailing behind him. For once, there was no cigarette in the Deputy Director's mouth.

"Major, you've done an impressive job. For the first time since I've been here I feel we have a logical program that not only meets the Nation's needs, but guarantees the

Aerospace Force an important role in carrying out those needs."

"Thank you, sir."

"You pulled it all together into a coherent whole. That's exactly what we needed." Marcot jammed both hands into his jacket pockets.

Feeling awkward and a bit foolish, Kinsman merely repeated, "Thank you, sir."

Marcot pulled out a fresh cigarette and lit it. "But we're not out of the woods yet." He blew a cloud of smoke ceilingward. "Not by a long shot."

"What do you mean?" Colt asked.

"There's still the Congress. They'll have to approve an even bigger Air Force appropriation than we started with, to get this program going. We'll still have to face McGrath and his ilk."

It still boils down to that, Kinsman said to himself. He had almost allowed himself to forget Neal in the past few hectic days.

Murdock patted Kinsman on the shoulder and said, "We're on top of that situation, aren't you, Chet? You're the man who's getting to McGrath."

"I've been trying . . ."

Colt said, "But with this new program, the way it all fits together and establishes a defense line in orbit, not even McGrath and the peaceniks in Congress can vote against it."

"Can't they?" Marcot's long, hound-sad face had years of bitter experience written across it. "I can just see McGrath rising on the floor of the Senate and making a very eloquent speech about the Air Force's paranoid schemes for extending the arms race into outer space. I can see his cohorts telling their constituents back home about the hundreds of billions of dollars the Air Force wants to throw away in space, instead of spending them down here on jobs and welfare and urban rebuilding."

"Bullcrap!" Colt snorted.

"But it works," Marcot answered. "It gets the votes."

"Then we've got to stop McGrath," Colt said. "He's the leader of that faction. Get him to vote our way, pull his fangs, *something* . . ."

Murdock bobbed his head. "It's up to you, Chet. It's your job."

Kinsman looked at the Colonel. *Thanks. Thank you all.* To Marcot, he said, "All right, I'll handle McGrath. But I want something in return."

Murdock looked shocked. Officers don't make deals, they carry out orders. But Marcot grinned wolfishly, the way a politician does when he's trading favors and expects to come out ahead.

"You want something?" he said back to Kinsman.

"Yessir. The original motivation for this program was to make certain that we go ahead with Moonbase. That base will need a commanding officer. I want to be that man."

"But that'd be a colonel's slot!" Murdock blurted.

"Then I'll need a promotion to light colonel to go with it," Kinsman answered evenly.

Marcot glanced at Murdock, then said, "First we've got to get the Congress to approve the funds. Then, when we know there's going to be a Moonbase, naturally we'll want someone who's thoroughly familiar with the program and its implications to command that base."

Colt nodded. Murdock still looked bewildered.

Without a smile, without even daring to admit to himself that this was happening, that *he* was forcing it to happen, Kinsman said, "Thank you. I appreciate it."

Raising a yellow-stained finger, Marcot emphasized, "But first we've got to get Congress to vote the funds."

"I know," said Kinsman.

"Very well. We understand each other." Marcot glanced at his wristwatch. "I'm going to be late for a reception. Japanese embassy. Their military attaché has been pumping me about our ABM satellites."

They walked out into the corridor. Marcot headed off

toward his domain; Colonel Murdock, Colt, and Kinsman took the stairs that led up to their lesser offices.

As they climbed the steps, Colt burst out, "You did it, man! You finally did it! Terrific!"

"We've all been working on the program," Kinsman said.

"Naw, I don't mean that. You stood up to 'em and told 'em what you wanted. Commander of Moonbase. And he took it! Man, you got the power now."

They reached the landing and pushed through the gray metal doors into the corridor as Kinsman said, "I just want him to know that I want to be on the Moon, not down here."

"And you talked yourself into a damned quick promotion, doing it," Murdock snapped.

"But Colonel," Colt said quickly, "don't you see? If they move Chet up to light colonel, they're gonna have to give you a general's star."

Murdock blinked and almost smiled. "There's no guarantee . . ."

"You'll still be in command of the overall lunar program," Colt argued smoothly. "And the program's going to be a lot bigger than anybody had thought. You'll be running the whole operation from Vandenberg, while we're up at Moonbase. They'll have to give you a star."

Breaking into a contented grin, Murdock said, "You know, that's right. It's more responsibility, bigger budget, bigger staff. They couldn't pass me over again."

The two majors left the smiling colonel off at his office, then continued down the corridor to their own cubicles. The hallways were empty; the Pentagon had only a skeleton crew after 4:30 P.M. Their footsteps clicked against the floor tiles and echoed off the shabby walls.

"You finally came around," Colt said. "I never thought you'd make it."

"You're making it sound like a religious conversion," Kinsman grumbled.

"Just the opposite, man. Just the opposite. You finally

got it through your skull that if you want something, you gotta give something. You want to be commander of Moonbase, you gotta let them have what they want. No other way."

"We're not going to put weapons on the Moon."

Colt looked at him. "Yeah, I know. But those mines and ore processors . . . long as we're using them to ship raw materials to orbital factories so's they can build laser satellites—then they're part of a weapons system."

Kinsman didn't break stride, but inside he stiffened.

"You're gonna be commander of a military base, *Colonel* Kinsman. Moonbase is gonna be the key to the biggest military operation the world's ever seen."

And that's the price for my soul.

He left Colt and slipped into his own cramped office. The air conditioning had been turned off at the official quitting time for the daytime staff. The paper-strewn cubicle was already muggy and stuffy.

It may be a military base, Kinsman told himself, *and it may be there to supply raw materials for weapons systems, but there'll be no fighting on the Moon. Not while I'm there.*

Then Marcot's cagey, cynical face appeared in his mind. "First get Congress to vote the funds," the Deputy Director was saying.

"The Hungarian recipe for an omelet," Kinsman muttered. "First, steal some eggs."

With a sigh, he sat at his desk and tapped out Neal McGrath's phone number. An answering service responded. Kinsman didn't bother to leave his name with the automated service. Then, out of pure routine, he tapped his own message key on the communications console. The desktop viewscreen lit up and spelled in green glowing letters: PLS CALL MS WOODS: 291-7000 EXT 7949.

Kinsman stared at the message for a long moment. *Persistent woman*, he thought. As he punched the number she had left, he grinned at her use of the "Ms." *Helps her forget she's married, I guess.*

Jinny's face looked blander, plainer than he remembered it, when she appeared on his tiny viewscreen.

"Oh . . . Major Kinsman! You got my call. I was in the shower. They've been touring us all around Washington all day . . ."

No makeup, he realized. *That's what it is.*

"You said you'd call when we got into town," she was gushing, "but we were out all day and I never trust hotel switchboards to get messages straight so I called the Pentagon. I remembered you said you worked in the Pentagon, and asked them to look you up. All I remembered was that you were in the Air Force and you had been an astronaut. I even forgot your rank, but they found your number for me anyway!"

"I'm glad they did, Jinny," he said. *The old oil. You do it automatically, don't you?*

They met for dinner at a Japanese restaurant on Connecticut Avenue. *Marcot's not the only one who'll nibble on sushi tonight.* They had no trouble getting a private little room for themselves, where they could take off their shoes and sit on the floor. The restaurant was nearly empty. Even in the best parts of the city, business disappeared when the sun went down.

"I'm sorry I wasn't able to call you earlier," Kinsman said as they sipped sake. "It's been a wild week for me."

"Me too," Jinny said, looking up at him over the rim of her tiny porcelain cup. Her hair was carefully done, makeup properly in place. She wore a sleeveless frock with a neckline low enough to be inviting, yet still within the bounds of decorum.

Does she or doesn't she? Kinsman asked himself. *As if it matters.*

When they left the restaurant Jinny wound her arm around Kinsman's and said, "I'm so tired . . . they had us on the go all day long. Do you mind if we just go back to my hotel room and have a drink there?"

Like the cobra and the mongoose. But which is which?

Her hotel was a cut above standard government issue.

The bed was a double, the furnishings fairly new and in reasonably good condition. The room was clean without smelling of disinfectant.

Kinsman put money in the automatic bar machine and ordered their drinks: scotch for himself, vodka and tonic for Jinny. The drinks popped out of the dispenser's slot in frosted plastic cups, sealed at the top. *Space-Age technology at your service*, Kinsman said to himself. *Just like zero-gee squeeze bulbs.*

"I've just got to get out of this dress," Jinny said, picking up her pink travelbag and heading for the bathroom. "I'll only be a minute."

Kinsman took the room's only chair and shook his head. *This game's pretty silly, you know.* And a voice inside him answered, *Don't be scared, you're doing fine.*

On an impulse he went to the phone and tapped out the number for Walter Reed Hospital. The hospital's information computer display glowed on the phone screen:

MAY WE HELP YOU?

"Yes," Kinsman said, speaking as clearly as he could for the computer's circuits. "The condition, please, of Mr. Frederick Durban."

SPELLING OF LAST NAME?

"D-u-r-b-a-n. Frederick."

ARE YOU A FAMILY MEMBER?

"His son," he lied.

DURBAN, FREDERICK: DECEASED, 1623 HRS TODAY. FUNERAL ARRANGEMENTS ARE BEING HANDLED BY . . .

Kinsman slammed a fist into the phone's OFF button. *I know what the funeral arrangements are*, he said to himself. Looking out the window at the darkening city, he thought, *Four twenty-three this afternoon. Right in the middle of my goddamned presentation. Right in the fucking middle of it!*

"What's the matter, Chet? You look awful!"

He turned to see Jinny standing a step inside the

bathroom door, her hair loose and tumbling to her shoulders, an iridescent pink nightgown clinging to her.

"A friend of mine . . . died. I just called the hospital and found out."

She stepped to him and put both hands on his chest. "I'm so sorry."

"He was an old man. I expected it. But still . . ."

"I know. It's a shock." She slipped her arms around his neck and kissed him. He kissed back and felt her mouth open for him.

She disengaged from him, took his hand, and walked four dainty steps to the bed. Sitting on its edge, she patted the covers beside her. "Come on, sit down with me."

He remained standing. "Jinny . . . I can't."

She looked up at him, smiling. "If it's my husband you're worried about, never mind. We have an understanding about this . . ."

But he shook his head. The picture was forming in his mind again. He could see her floating helplessly, arms outstretched, reaching toward him, screaming silently, eyes wide and blank . . .

"No," he said, more to himself than to her.

She was staring at him now, looking uncertain, almost afraid.

"I've got to go," he told her.

Jinny got to her feet. "It's because of the man who died?"

"Yes."

"He was someone close to you? A relative?"

"You really don't want to know about it," he said, feeling clammy sweat on his palms. "Please don't ask me anything more about it, Jinny."

"Are you . . . a spy, or something?"

He focused on her for the first time since shutting off the phone. She was standing in front of him, lips parted, braless, nipples erect, wide-eyed with excitement.

"I've got to go now," he said, trying to make it tight-lipped. "I've got to. I'm sorry."

"Will I ever see you again?"

"Maybe. I'd like to. But probably not. Where I'm going . . . probably not."

He went to the door. She rushed after him and gave him a final kiss, hard and desperate. He left her there, clinging to the door, playing the role of the abandoned *femme fatale*.

He loped past a row of phones in the hotel lobby and grabbed the last remaining taxi standing at the curb. As it chugged and rattled out into the sparse nighttime traffic, he gave the black driver the McGraths' address in Georgetown.

Mary-Ellen let him into the apartment, a puzzled look on her face.

"Chet, you look as if you're ready to take on the entire Sioux nation. What's the matter?"

"Where's Neal?"

She led him back to the parlor where the party had been. No one was there now except the two of them. The big room was filled with sofas and wingback chairs, the empty fireplace, the mirrors, paintings, lamps, rugs, bookshelves, end tables, the big circular Persian etched brass hanging by the French windows, a hundred pieces of bric-a-brac acquired over the years of their marriage.

"Neal's out," Mary-Ellen said. "He won't be back for a few days."

Kinsman looked at her. "The Committee hearings are still running."

"He hasn't left town," she said, weariness in her voice. "He's just . . . not here."

"He's with Diane."

She nodded.

"And you're letting him do it?"

"Do you know any way I can stop him from it?"

"I'd think it would be pretty easy for you, if you wanted him to stop."

She dropped into the sofa nearest the dead, dark fireplace. "Chet, nothing is easy."

"Do you love him?" he asked, sitting down beside her.

"Do I breathe?"

"Hey, I'm the one who's supposed to give flip answers to hide his feelings."

Mary-Ellen's hands made a helpless flutter. "What do you want me to say? Do I love him? What a question! We've been married nearly twenty years. We have three children."

"Do you love him?"

"I did. I think maybe I still do . . . but it's not so easy to tell anymore."

"He said you agreed to a divorce after he's reelected."

"Yes."

"But why?" Kinsman asked. "Why do you let him do this to you? Why are you taking it like this?"

"What else can I do? Wreck his career? Would that bring him back to me? Threaten him? Force him to stay with me? Do you think I want that?"

"What the hell *do* you want?"

"I don't know!"

"You're lying," Kinsman said. "You're lying to yourself."

Tears were brimming in her eyes. "Chet, leave me alone. Just go away and leave me alone. I don't want . . ." She couldn't say anything more; she broke down.

Kinsman took her in his arms and held her tightly. "That's better. That's better. I know what it's like to hold it all inside yourself. It's better to let it come out. Let it all out."

"I can't . . ." Her voice was muffled, but the pain came through. "I shouldn't be bothering you . . ."

"Nonsense. That's what shoulders are for. Hell, we've known each other a long, long time. It's okay. You can cry on my shoulder anytime. Maybe if I'd had the sense to cry on yours when I needed to . . ."

She pulled slightly away, but not so far that Kinsman could no longer hold her.

"We have known each other a long time, haven't we?"

"All the way back to Philadelphia," he said.

"I've known you as long as I've known Neal."

"I was jealous as hell of him," Kinsman remembered.

"He . . . he said I'm . . . he said that I couldn't give love. That I'm incapable of it."

Kinsman grimaced. "I haven't been able to give love to anyone for years."

A new look came into her eyes. "Is that what happened to you? All those rumors . . ."

He pulled her closer and kissed her. *Gray-eyed Athena, goddess of wisdom and of war, I'd take you over the treacherous Aphrodite every time.* Their hands moved across each other's bodies, searching, finding, opening, pulling clothes away.

Still half-dressed, he leaned her back on the couch and was on top of her, into her, before the picture of the dead cosmonaut could form in his mind. He heard her gasp and felt her clutching at him, hard, furiously hard, warm, alive, molten, burning all the old bad images out of his brain.

Everything blurred together for a few moments. He found himself sitting on the edge of the couch beside her, staring into those strong, wise gray eyes. Wordlessly she got to her feet and led him to the bedroom. She shut the door firmly, they finished stripping, and went to bed.

They made love and dozed, alternately, until the sun brightened the curtained windows.

"God," she murmured, and he could feel her breath on his cheek, "you're like a teenager."

"It's been a long time," he said. "I've got a lot of catching up to do."

He showered alone, and when he came back into the bedroom to dress, she had gone. He found her in the kitchen, wrapped in a shapeless beige housecoat, munching a piece of dry toast, sitting at the counter that cut the room in half, an untouched glass of orange drink in front of her.

"Hungry?" she asked, wiping toast crumbs from her lips.

"I'll get something from the cafeteria in the Pentagon," he said.

"Have some juice, at least." She pushed the glass toward his side of the counter.

He took it and downed the synthetic juice in one long pull.

"Thanks," he said.

"Thank you."

Suddenly they were both embarrassed. Kinsman felt like a sheepish kid. Mary-Ellen stared down at the toast on her plate.

He didn't know what to say. "I . . . guess I'd better be going now."

"It's awfully early. I don't think the buses are running this early."

He shrugged. "I'll walk for a while."

"Aren't you tired?"

And they both broke up. Kinsman lifted his head and roared; Mary-Ellen laughed with him.

"Tired? For God's sake, woman, I'm exhausted!"

"I should hope so," she said. "You had me scared for a minute, there."

She came around the counter and put an arm around his waist. He took her by the shoulders and they walked together through the parlor, toward the apartment's front door.

"I do thank you, Chet," Mary-Ellen said. "You've made me see myself—everything—in a new light."

"My pleasure."

"Not entirely yours."

"I . . . feel kind of funny about it, though," he admitted. "Christ, it's almost like incest."

She smiled at him. "I know."

"It was a one-time thing, wasn't it? I mean, I don't think either of us could . . . well, *plan* something like that."

They were at the door now. Gently, she disengaged from him. "No, it was a surprise. A once-in-a-lifetime surprise. If we tried to repeat it . . . it wouldn't work."

Nodding, "I guess it wouldn't."

"But it was good."

"Damned good. Thanks. You've chased away a devil that's been haunting me for a long time."

"Then I'm glad."

They kissed, swiftly, almost shyly, and he left.

The door burst open as if it had been kicked, and Neal McGrath's bulk filled the doorway.

Kinsman looked up from his apartment's only chair. The clock on his desk said ten p.m. He had spent the day in the Pentagon, ignoring McGrath's Committee hearings, working with the Secretary of Defense's personal staff on the briefings they would give in the White House.

"You sonofabitch!" McGrath snapped.

Kinsman got up from his chair. "Come on in, Neal. Shut the door. The landlord doesn't like noisy visitors."

He slammed the door shut and took two strides into the shabby room. His tall, rangy body seemed to radiate hot anger.

"You bastard!" McGrath's fists were doubled, white-knuckled. "You screwed my wife."

"While you were screwing your girlfriend."

McGrath stepped toward him, raising his fists.

Kinsman stopped him with a pointed finger. "Hold on, Neal. You're bigger, but I've trained harder. All you're going to do is get yourself hurt."

"I'll kill you, you sonofabitch." But he stopped and let his hands fall to his sides.

"I don't blame you," Kinsman said softly. "What happened last night . . . it was completely unexpected. Hell, Neal, I came to the apartment looking for you. Neither of us planned it. It just happened. You ought to know about things like that."

"Don't hand me that!"

"I know," Kinsman said, keeping his voice low. "Now we're talking about your wife, and that's different. Okay.

But maybe now you know a little of what she's been feeling."

McGrath said nothing. He just stood in the middle of the small room, panting like a bull in the arena, confused by the noise and the sunlight.

"It's not going to happen again," Kinsman added. "We both agreed on that."

"I thought you were my friend," McGrath said, his voice cracking with misery.

"Yeah, I thought so too." Kinsman turned and pulled his chair away from the desk. "Come on, sit down. I'll get you a beer. We've got a lot to talk about."

Numbly, McGrath took the chair. Kinsman went to the refrigerator and pulled out two cold bottles of Bass ale. Fumbling in the drawer for a bottle opener, he wondered, *Will the English ever come into the twentieth century and put screw-tops on their beer?* He found the opener, pried the tops off, then walked over and handed one bottle to McGrath.

"Hope you don't want a glass. They're both dirty."

McGrath gave a grunt that was almost a laugh. "What are we drinking to?" he asked, not looking at Kinsman.

"To understanding," Kinsman said, stretching out on the open sofabed.

"Understanding what?"

The real world, man. The real world. "Understanding why I came up to your place last night, trying to find you. Understanding what's happening in the Pentagon, and in the big corporations, and what's going to happen in the White House and the Congress over the next few weeks."

McGrath sat up straighter in the chair. "What the hell are you talking about?"

"I'm not authorized to tell you, Neal, but I'm going to tell you anyway, and if anybody's snooping on this conversation they can go rush their tapes to whoever they want to."

Inadvertently, McGrath's eyes scanned the room, looking for microphones.

"The Aerospace Force has been working for some time," Kinsman said, "on an experimental program to develop a satellite weapons system that can shoot down enemy ICBMs."

"I know that. Nobody in the Pentagon has seen fit to brief me about it, but I've got my own sources."

"Okay. But now we're ready to go into production with them."

"So are the Russians," McGrath said.

"Yeah, but we're going to do it with ores mined on the Moon and factories in orbit."

"The hell you are."

"The hell we're not! The whole Department of Defense is behind this one, Neal. It's not just a little Moonbase anymore. It's not just us *Luniks*. The whole military-industrial complex is in it. And the White House."

Understanding dawned in McGrath's eyes. "So that's why Dreyer's people have been putting the pressure on. And the big aerospace primes are starting to throw parties again . . ."

"They're lining up their votes."

But with a stubborn shake of his head, McGrath said, "Once we start placing ABM satellites into orbit, the Russians will do the same thing. We can't have that. It costs too much, and it'll lead to war."

"But you just said the Russians are ready to start orbiting their ABM satellites."

"They're ready, but they haven't started yet. If we can work out an agreement with them in Geneva . . ."

"That's not going to happen, Neal. Neither we nor the Russians can afford to throw away a chance to defend their country against ICBMs. We're going ahead with the ABM program, and it'll include factories in orbit and mining operations on the Moon."

"So you can get your Moonbase."

"That's right. I'm going to be commander of that base."

"You want to spend a hundred billion dollars and bring

us to the brink of the final nuclear war, just so you can play soldier on the Moon."

"You know me better than that, Neal. We'll keep the Moon peaceful. There won't be any armaments on the Moon. Just the mines. And the hospital." *And a graveyard.*

McGrath shifted on the chair, making its wooden legs creak. "I'll do everything I can to stop this nonsense. I'm dead-set against it."

"The Pentagon will roll over you like a steam-driver, Neal. It isn't just a minor Air Force program anymore, the kind you can nibble off the list and then go home and show the voters how much money you've saved them. This is the big time. Corporations like General Tech and the big aerospace outfits are in on this. It'll mean employment for those half-empty electronics shops and factories all across Pennsylvania."

"It'll mean inflation . . . and war."

"No, dammitall!" Kinsman raised his voice. "The ABM satellites will protect us from missile attack. Right now, this minute, somebody in Russia or China or seventeen other nations could push a button and inside of half an hour we'd be a mushroom cloud. There's no way to stop an ICBM attack! Any idiot could launch us into World War Three with a heavy thumb."

"It hasn't happened yet."

"You keep the world's population growing and the world's natural resources dwindling and you'll see it happen. Pretty damned soon, too."

McGrath started to say, "I don't see . . ."

"The ABM satellites," Kinsman interrupted, "will make surprise missile attacks impossible. We'll be able to shoot down the missiles long before they get near us. That makes the world safer, Neal. Safer."

"Unless you provoke the Russians into a war because they're afraid that we'll attack them once we have all our satellites in place."

"But they'll be putting up satellites, too. You said so yourself."

"What happens if you two get to fighting in orbit? You could start a war in space over these satellites."

Kinsman took a swig of ale, then answered, "That's pretty far-fetched, Neal. And besides, look at the other benefits we get out of this program."

"Such as?"

"A solid industrial base in orbit. Shipping lunar ores to space factories, which can then start to build Solar Power Satellites and other things that will help people on Earth. Opening the door to space, to all that raw material and all that energy. New jobs. New technologies. New industries. Space is our escape hatch, Neal. It's going to let us get out of this coffin we've built for ourselves down here."

"We've been through all that before. It'll take twenty, thirty years before space operations even begin to help the poor and disadvantaged here on Earth."

"Even so," Kinsman said, "what other programs do you have going that can help them? Everything you're doing, all those welfare programs, all they do is prolong the misery. Space operations open up a new source of wealth."

"For the rich. For the corporations."

"For everybody! If you do it right."

"I don't believe it, Chet. And I can't vote for it. It's impossible."

"Then you'd better kiss the Minority Leadership good-bye," Kinsman said, "and maybe your seat in the Senate, as well."

He stared at Kinsman for a long, silent moment. "So it all boils down to that, does it?"

"You knew it would."

"All this high-flown talk about the future and the benefits to the human race . . . it all comes down to the fact that you're willing to blackmail me, just to get your ass up to the Moon."

"That's right."

"You *are* a sonofabitch. And a cold-blooded one, too."

Kinsman grinned back at the angry, smoldering senator.

"Neal, a fanatic who's willing to die for his cause is even more willing to sacrifice *your* life for his cause."

"So you can get to the Moon. You'd wreck the whole world just to get what you want."

"The world has a way of taking care of itself. And believe me, the world will be better off with me on the Moon. Me, and a few thousand others."

McGrath drained the last of his ale, then hefted the empty bottle in his big hand. "I can't vote for it. Even if I wanted to, I couldn't switch my position on this. My own party people would crucify me."

"Yes, you can. And I'll bet those big, bad industrialists in Pennsylvania will even contribute to your reelection campaign, if you do."

"No," McGrath said firmly.

"You've never voted against national defense appropriations."

"I've always voted against wasteful spending."

"But this isn't wasteful! It'll create jobs, for Chrissake. Look on it as an employment program."

"That will lead us into war."

"That will put you into the White House someday. Sure, some of your supporters will get disenchanted and turn against you. But you'll gain more support than you'll lose—and a wider base of support."

"By going against everything I believe in."

Suddenly exasperated, Kinsman snapped, "What the hell do you believe in, Neal? Your opinions about space operations are stupid. You're just as blindly stubborn about it as my father. All those programs you like, for helping the poor and the needy—they've squandered more goddamned money on bureaucratic bullshit than anything that's ever gone through Congress. And you've got *more* unemployed, more welfare cases right now in your own state than you did when you first came to Congress. Look it up, I've checked the numbers."

"That's . . . hard to believe . . ."

"Sure it is. But it's true. You want to be Minority Leader, you've got ambitions to head your party, but you're turning down an offer that's guaranteed to bring you more support than you've ever had. Just what the hell do you want?"

"I want to be able to live with myself."

"And with who else? Diane? Mary-Ellen? Both of them? Do you want to be able to live with those unemployed workers back home? To be an unemployed worker yourself? Or do you want to make jobs for them? Take your pick."

McGrath got to his feet. For a moment, Kinsman thought he was going to throw the empty bottle against the wall. But he let it drop from his fingers. It bounced once on the thin carpet and rolled toward the sofabed.

Kinsman stood up too.

"I've heard enough," McGrath said. "I'm leaving. If I ever see you near Mary-Ellen again . . ."

Grinning, "One way to guarantee that we don't see each other is to send me a quarter-million miles away."

McGrath glared at him.

"You can have the Minority Leadership," Kinsman said. "All I want is the Moon."

The Committee hearings were scheduled to go on for another week before the senators voted. Kinsman spent the time briefing White House staffers and other key Congressional leaders, including Neal McGrath. The State Department reared its head and mewed about upsetting the delicate balance of terror between East and West. But the National Security Council slapped State down with its intelligence reports that showed the Russians were already building ABM satellites—on the ground—and developing a new class of rocket booster to launch them.

Then came the critical vote on the Moonbase program by the Armed Services Committee. This was still the small program for the lunar hospital; it was only behind the scenes that this program had been linked to the mammoth ABM satellite project. This was a test of strength, and Kinsman held his breath as he sat in the ornate hearing chamber and watched the polling of the senators.

As the roll call went down the long green-topped table, only three senators voted nay. Two abstained.

McGrath was one of the abstentions.

The Moonbase program passed.

Kinsman leaned back on the wooden bench, far in the rear of the room, and let out a year-long sigh.

All right, you've got what you wanted. Now all you have to do is to worry about whether it was the right thing to want or not.

Immediately he answered himself, *No. All you have to do is to* make it *the right thing.*

"So that's how he's going to do it," Kinsman told Frank Colt that evening, as they celebrated at a bar in Crystal City. "He's not going to vote in favor, but he's not going to stand in the way."

The place was jammed. Half the Pentagon seemed to be there, clamoring for drinks. Music blared from omnispeakers set into the red-plush-covered walls. The lighting was low, except for the bar area, where Colt and Kinsman stood, getting jostled by the crowd.

Colt shrugged and hiked his eyebrows. "Politicians. They got more tricks to 'em than a forty-year-old hooker."

Grabbing his drink from the bar before the guy next to him elbowed it over, Kinsman shouted over the noise, "Who cares? We're going to the Moon, buddy!"

The guy next to him gave Kinsman a queer look.

Colt laughed, then turned to look over the crowded, throbbing room. Kinsman did the same, resting his elbows against the bar. All the tables were filled, people were milling around the bar, hollering into each other's ears, laughing, drinking, smoking. There wasn't a square foot of space empty.

"Hey." Colt nudged Kinsman in the ribs. "Now *that* looks like a scrutable Oriental."

Following his gaze, Kinsman saw a stunning Asian woman sitting with an almost equally good-looking brunette at a table in the corner. The Oriental had the delicate facial bones of a Vietnamese.

"They do look lonely," Kinsman said.

Colt nodded. "And hungry . . . waitin' for some gentlemen to offer them a square meal."

"Or a crooked one."

They started pushing through the crowd, heading for the women's table.

"Seems to me," Colt yelled to Kinsman, "that it's been a helluva long time since we tried this kinda maneuver together."

Kinsman nodded. "A helluva long time."

Colt's smile was pure happiness.

The city lay sweltering in muggy, late August heat. The air was thick and gray; the Sun hung overhead like a sullen bloated enemy, sickly dull orange. *Any other town in the world would be empty and quiet on a Saturday like this*, Kinsman thought. But Washington was filled with tourists. Despite the heat and the soaking humidity they were out in force, cameras around sweaty necks, short-tempered, wet-shirted, dragging tired, crying children along with them. Waiting in line to get into the White House, swarming up the steps of the Lincoln Memorial, clumping together for guided tours of the Capitol, the Smithsonian's museums, the Treasury Department's greenback printing plant.

Kinsman waited in the cool quiet of the National Art Gallery, beside the soothing splashing of the fountain just inside the main entrance. Wing-footed Mercury pranced atop the fountain. *Looks like he's giving us the finger*, Kinsman laughed to himself. *Maybe he is.*

Diane showed up a few minutes late, looking coolly

beautiful in a flowered skirt and peasant blouse. Kinsman went to her and they kissed lightly, like old friends, like siblings.

"How'd you get my phone number?" she asked. "I'm only in town for a few days . . ."

"Neal's office."

"But he's back in Pennsylvania during the recess."

Kinsman nodded. "Yes, but his office is still running."

He had taken her by the arm and was leading her back toward the museum's front entrance.

"Where're we going?" Diane asked. "I thought . . ."

"I want to take you to dinner. It's my last day here. I'm moving out to Vandenberg tomorrow morning."

"I know. Neal told me."

They stepped outside, into the soupy heat. "He's up there in the cool Appalachian breezes, mapping out his campaign for the Minority Leadership. Playing family man for Mary-Ellen and the kids and the down-home voters."

"He's pretty sore at you," Diane said as they walked down the steps toward the jitney stop.

"Yeah, I guess he is."

"He said he's going to fight against your Air Force programs once he's Minority Leader."

Kinsman looked at her. "That's his way of saving his conscience, Diane. Behind all the rhetoric, he's going to let us go ahead and do what needs to be done. He's got the White House on his mind now."

"You took advantage of him. And me."

"That's right. And of Mary-Ellen, and of the Aerospace Force, the Pentagon, and the whole human race."

She didn't answer him.

Their talk through dinner was trivial, impersonal, almost like strangers who had nothing in common. *Avoid arguments during mealtime, Chester,* Kinsman could hear his mother telling him. *If you can't say something nice, then don't say anything.*

It was still hot and bright outside when they left the

restaurant. But the downtown Washington streets were already emptying. The tourists were hurrying for their air conditioned hotels and restaurants, exhausted and sweaty after a day of compulsory tramping around the city. They wanted to cool off and relax before the electrical power was shut off for the night.

"Hey, I've got an idea," Kinsman said. "Come on."

He flagged down a cab and helped the puzzled Diane into it. "Washington Monument," he told the driver.

The line of waiting tourists that usually circled the Monument was gone by the time they arrived there.

"Is it still open?" Diane asked.

"Sure." He was holding her hand, leading her up the grassy slope to the immense obelisk that loomed before them. On either side of the path, the silvery solar panels that provided energy for the Monument's night lighting looked like miniature fairytale castles, stretching all the way around the spire.

As they approached the gigantic column, with the twilight sky flaring purple and the flame behind it, the white marble looked gray and dingy.

"The world's biggest phallic symbol," Kinsman said. "Dedicated to the Father of our Country."

Diane grinned sourly. "You would look at it that way, wouldn't you?"

There were only half a dozen people waiting inside, speaking German and another language that Kinsman could not identify. They milled around for a few minutes and then the elevator came down, opened its doors, and discharged about twenty tourists.

As the elevator groaned and creaked its way up to the top of the Monument, Diane whispered, "Is this thing safe?"

Kinsman shrugged. "I'd feel a lot better if it had wings on it."

Finally the elevator stopped and its doors wheezed open. They stepped out and went to a tiny barred window. The entire city lay sprawled below them, wrapped in muggy, smoggy heat, the Sun touching the horizon now, lights beginning to twinkle in the buildings that stretched as far as the eye could see.

"If I have some good luck," Kinsman said, "this is the last time I'll see Washington."

Diane asked, "Why did you call me, Chet? What do you expect from me?"

Surprised, he said quickly, "Nothing. Not a damned thing. I just wanted to . . . well, sort of apologize. To you, and to Neal. I know he won't even talk to me on the phone, so I figured I'd tell you."

"Apologize?"

"For—using you both, as you put it. I think it would have happened anyway; somebody else would have twisted Neal's arm the way I did. But I was his friend, and now I've made him into an enemy."

"You certainly have," she said.

"And you?"

She looked out at the city, so far below. "His enemies are my enemies. Isn't that the way it's supposed to be?"

"So I've heard."

He stood beside her, gazing out at the buildings and the scurrying cars and buses, all those people down there, all the cities and nations and people of the entire planet, and suddenly, finally, the enormity of it all hit him.

Grasping the iron bars set into the stone window frame, Kinsman could feel himself falling, swirling out into emptiness. *Good God*, he thought. *All of them! I've set myself up against all of them. I've forced them to do what I want, without a thought about their side of it. What if I'm wrong? What if it's not the right thing?*

Almost wildly he searched for the Moon in the darkening sky, but it was nowhere in sight.

"Neal says you're going to start a war in space," Diane said, her voice low but knife-edged. "He says your Moonbase is going to lead to World War Three. You're going to kill us all."

"No." The word was out of his mouth before he knew

he had spoken it. "Neal and the rest of you, you just don't understand. The most important thing we'll ever do is to set up permanent colonies in space. It's time for the human race to expand its ecological niche . . . time we stopped restricting ourselves to just one planet. Our salvation lies out there, maybe the only chance for salvation that we'll ever have."

She turned to him. "Chet, you know that's just a rationalization. You say it's important because it's what you want to do."

"Maybe. But that doesn't change a thing. Maybe history is the result of big, massive forces that push people around like pawns. Maybe it's the result of scared, lone individuals who're driven to pull the whole goddamned human race along with them. I don't know and I don't care. I'm going to the Moon. The rest of you will have to figure things out the best you can."

"And you're leaving all this behind?"

He glanced out at the sprawling city. "What's to leave? This whole planet's becoming an overcrowded slum. If we do get into World War Three, it won't be because of a few thousand people living and working in space. It'll be because seven or eight billion are stuck here on the ground."

"But those people are worth fighting for!" Diane said. "We have to fight for social justice and freedom here, on this world. We can't run away!"

"Good. You go ahead and fight for it. I'll help you . . . by running away and sending you back all the energy and raw materials you'll need for your struggle. And maybe some new ideas about how to live in freedom."

She shook her head. "You're hopeless."

"I know. We both decided that a long time ago."

"You're really going to the Moon, in spite of everything."

"Because of everything. Want to come along?"

"Not me. I'll stay here."

"Then we'll never see each other again." The sadness of it, the finality of it, left him feeling hollow, empty.

With a knowing look, Diane said, "Oh, you'll be back, Chet. Don't get dramatic. You won't stay up there forever. Nobody could. You'll be back."

But his eyes were focused beyond her, on the window at her back. Through its narrow aperture he could see the full Moon topping the hazy horizon, smiling crookedly at him.

"Don't bet your life on it," he said.